"Oh, look," Charlotte whispered in a breathy tone. "You have found the mistletoe. We are standing beneath it."

He gazed skyward for the briefest instant. "So we are." He laughed. The deep, rich baritone of mirth sent a shiver of anticipation down Charlotte's spine.

"That means you must kiss me," she demanded.

"And so I shall."

He spun her behind the large oak tree. Charlotte's back met the rough solid tree trunk the same moment Lord Edward's lips descended upon hers.

Warmth invaded every fiber of her being. At first he kissed her with playful bites and nips. She tried to imitate his actions and then his hands adjusted the angle of her head, holding her in place. The pressure of his mouth increased as the tip of his tongue played with hers.

Charlotte struggled to control her breathing. His lips were hot and restless, a temptation she was powerless to resist. Her knees began to weaken, yet she kissed him back, willingly allowing the wondrous sensations to wash over her.

The next kiss was a passionate caress of lips and tongue that filled Charlotte with unfamiliar pulsing heat and need. Something primal within her stirred and her entire body tingled. . . .

THE
CHRISTMAS
HEIRESS

Adrienne Basso

ZEBRA BOOKS
Kensington Publishing Corp.
www.kensingtonbooks.com

ZEBRA BOOKS are published by

Kensington Publishing Corp.
850 Third Avenue
New York, NY 10022

All Kensington titles, imprints, and distributed lines are available
at special quantity discounts for bulk purchases for sales promo-
tion, premiums, fund-raising, educational, or institutional use.

Special book excerpts or customized printings can also be created to fit specific needs. For details, write or phone the office
of the Kensington Special Sales Manager: Attn. Special Sales
Department. Kensington Publishing Corp., 850 Third Avenue,
New York, NY 10022. Phone: 1-800-221-2647.

First Printing: October 2006
10 9 8 7 6 5 4 3 2 1

Printed in the United States of America

CHAPTER 1

A light knock sounded on the bedchamber door. Lord Reginald Aldridge stepped quietly into the room and closed the door, shutting out the musical sounds from the four-piece string quartet that drifted up from below stairs. "I assumed you would be late, so I thought I would wait and escort you downstairs. Are you ready to make your grand entrance?"

"Almost." Lord Reginald's seventeen-year-old granddaughter, Charlotte, shifted impatiently as her maid fussed over the cascading array of honey-brown curls that trailed down the side of her long, graceful neck. "Jones got it all wrong and had to reset my hair, but I believe it is at last acceptable."

"It looks splendid to me," Lord Reginald said.

Charlotte turned, and managed a slight smile as her grandfather walked toward her. Though nearing sixty, he looked and acted like a much younger man. Tonight he wore a black velvet-collared frockcoat and stylish black trousers. A stark white cravat topped a silver-flecked waistcoat that nicely complemented the blue of his eyes and brought out the streaks of silver in his hair.

As he drew beside her, Charlotte noticed he carried a small tray containing two crystal goblets.

"Champagne!" Eagerly, she reached for a glass and after raising it high in a hasty toast, Charlotte gulped down half the contents. "It's wonderful. I love how the bubbles tickle my nose. I must be sure to commend the earl on the quality of his wine cellar when I see him tonight."

Lord Reginald turned an indulgent smile on his only grandchild. "'Tis probably better if you refrain from mentioning the champagne. Worthington and his countess can occasionally be a bit over-the-top when it comes to propriety."

"Hmmm." Charlotte sipped the remaining cold, bubbly liquid in her goblet and considered her grandfather's words. Though she had known the earl and countess of Worthington for most of her life, she had had very limited interaction with them. Until now.

She briefly wondered what else they might find offensive, besides a young woman drinking champagne, but pushed the notion from her mind. If things got out of hand, she knew she could rely on Grandpapa to protect her from the worst of any scandalous gossip.

In Charlotte's opinion, the rules that governed a young woman of society's life were vastly restrictive, monstrously unfair and highly tedious. While growing up, she had been lucky and allowed far more freedom than most aristocratic girls. Her natural curiosity and daring spirit had rarely been harnessed.

However, now she had reached the age of maturity and everything had changed. The scrutiny was far more intense, the expectations high. Fortunately, she was aware, and very capable, of following the rules. If it suited her purpose.

"I suppose we had best join the party or else we shall arrive unfashionably and *inappropriately* late," Charlotte decided. "I merely need to put on my jewelry."

At the mention of jewelry, Jones, Charlotte's maid, scurried about the room, retrieving both the jewel case and key. With a sly smile, Charlotte unlocked the black lacquer box and rummaged impatiently though the pieces nestled on the blue velvet lining. Pushing the garnet, sapphire and emerald gemstones out of the way, Charlotte finally discovered what she sought and extracted a square, flat box.

She flipped open the lid and could not contain the gasp of delight as she beheld the contents. Crafted of the finest gold, silver and diamonds, the necklace was reputed to be the most expensive and coveted piece of jewelry made in England in the past fifty years. It had been commissioned by her father and given to her mother on their wedding day, yet for Charlotte, it represented a connection to the parents she barely remembered. They had both suddenly and tragically died in a carriage accident when she was five years old.

Charlotte swallowed. Her fingers trembled slightly as she lifted out the magnificent necklace. It felt heavy in her hands. She placed it carefully around her throat and fastened the clasp. Then she stood up and turned to face her grandfather.

"How do I look?"

"Exquisite," Lord Reginald replied automatically, but then his smile broke and he cleared his throat loudly. "But are you sure about the necklace, sweetheart? Matrons are the ones usually draped in diamonds. Girls your age wear pearls. I'm sure you have several lovely strands in your jewel box, along with matching earbobs."

Charlotte stiffened her back, temper flashing in her emerald-green eyes. "The lace on my gown is an exact match to the intrigue gold and silver filigree work on the diamond necklace," she insisted. Reaching up, she fingered the clasp nestled at the side of her throat. "No other jewelry I own would be nearly as flattering with my ensemble."

Her hand lingered as she ran her fingers repeatedly over the smooth facets of the center-set stone. The entire piece was a fretwork of open and airy scrolled silver and gold, punctuated with large, flawless rose-cut diamonds that glittered like fire every time she moved.

Charlotte held a vague memory of her mother wearing the necklace, a fog of remembrance that had faded more and more with each passing year. This tangible link to the woman she had barely known was very important to her, but never more so than tonight.

"What do you want to do, Miss Charlotte?" Her maid's voice cut through the silent tension that had been steadily building.

She glanced over and saw that Jones had extracted three different pearl necklaces from the jewelry case, each stunning in its own way. But none could compare to the diamond necklace.

Charlotte gnawed her bottom lip, then cast a pitiful eye toward Lord Reginald. "If you insist that I wear pearls, I shall, Grandpapa," she declared, with a slight exaggeration to the trembling in her voice. "Above all else, I wish to please you and make you proud of me."

"Oh, my dearest girl, of course I am proud of you. No grandfather in the world is luckier than I." Lord Reginald moved closer and Charlotte flung both arms around his neck, sinking into the comfort and love of an embrace she had grown up depending upon. "You know that all I have ever wanted is for you to be happy," he whispered.

"I know." She heard him sigh and mutter under his breath. Charlotte pulled back and glanced up, then smiled inwardly with triumph as the stern set of his jaw and mouth softened. "May I wear the diamonds?"

Lord Reginald's lip tipped into a grin, and a mischievous twinkle entered his eyes. "I shall tell anyone who dares to comment that you are wearing the necklace at my command."

"Thank you."

After a final adjustment to her coiffeur, Charlotte wove her arm through Lord Reginald's. Her stomach fluttered with excitement. This was the first evening event of the house party and above all, she wanted her entrance to be noteworthy.

They had arrived at Farmington Manor two days ago, part of an elite group of guests invited to attend the holiday celebrations of the earl and countess of Worthington. The Worthingtons were old and dear friends of Lord Reginald's, but Charlotte was very aware there was another reason for this invitation.

Now that she had reached a marriageable age, her grandfather had hinted quite broadly that he was very much in favor of a match between her and the earl's oldest son and heir, Edward. In truth, Charlotte had no particular reaction to her grandfather's scheming. Though she had not seen Edward in several years, she had been in his company often when they were children and remembered him as a polite, well-behaved and usually cautious boy who seemed to know everything.

Lord Reginald insisted that Edward had matured into a fine, handsome, steadfast young man, which Charlotte feared might mean he was stuffy, formal and a bit dull, but she was willing to give him a chance.

She was not, however, about to drop into Edward's clutches like an overripe piece of fruit falling from a tree. Charlotte was shrewd enough to know her worth on the marriage mart. Her grandfather was the brother of the Duke of Shrewsbury, her mother had been the sister of the Earl of Huntingdon.

She was her grandfather's sole heir, and a portion of her mother's dowry was also held in trust, to be given to her upon her marriage. With her lineage, looks and impressive dowry, Charlotte knew she would have her pick of any of the eligible wealthy and titled gentlemen of society. And she had decided long ago that she would marry a man of her own choosing, under her own terms, or she would not marry at all.

Charlotte took in her surroundings as they negotiated the numerous hallways on their way to the party. Farmington Manor, the ancestral home of their hosts, was a sprawling mansion. The original section of the house was built during the reign of

Henry Tudor, but extensive remodeling and additions had been commissioned over the years.

The result was an odd blend of several different architectural styles, and Charlotte marveled at how all the pieces fit together, creating an impressive display of aristocratic heritage and wealth.

Yet even for all of its grandeur, Charlotte decided she preferred the atmosphere of their own home, Quincy Court. It was smaller in size than the manor, but just as luxuriously furnished. Her grandfather had excellent taste and a seemingly unlimited supply of funds with which to indulge his passions. And his greatest passion was creating a stylish, comfortable home for his granddaughter.

Finally Lord Reginald and Charlotte reached the main staircase. Descending arm in arm, they followed the noise and entered the main salon, a cavernous room with gilded columns, gold brocade sofas and urns filled with an unusual mix of bright evergreen branches and blooming red hothouse roses. They were the last to arrive, but the happy chatter and murmur of voices rumbling beneath the strains of music told them the party had clearly begun without them.

Since this was an informal event, there was no receiving line. They paused a moment to get their bearings and Charlotte surveyed the room with what she hoped was a casual air.

Many of the other guests were close to her grandfather in age, but there were a few younger people, enough to make things interesting. Charlotte had been introduced to all the houseguests the previous day, but felt no desire to join the small group of young ladies gathered near the fireplace.

They had all been polite toward her, especially Miranda Chambers and her twin sister, Elizabeth, but Charlotte was not overly comfortable in the company of women. Since entering society this past spring, it had been her experience that females and more often, their mothers, were stiff and judgmental toward her. She was unsure if they envied her looks, her money or her confident air.

Whatever the reason, Charlotte had decided it was unimportant. She would make no major concessions to win the approval of anyone, especially a group of tight-lipped women. Tonight she was going to have fun and Charlotte was determined to ignore any frowning faces sent her way.

"Lord Reginald! Miss Aldridge!" Rosemary Barringer, Countess of Worthington, glided toward them. "I am so glad that you have finally arrived. I was beginning to worry that I would have to send a footman out to search for you. More than one guest has found themselves hopelessly turned around, especially on the upper floors. These hallways can seem like a rabbit warren to those unfamiliar with them."

Was the countess trying to be witty? Or was she scolding them for being tardy? Charlotte was tempted to ask if they had misplaced a great number of houseguests over the years, but the pleading glance from her grandfather made her hold her tongue. He so wanted her to make a good impression. And she truly did strive to please him.

"It seems like a splendid party, my lady," Lord Reginald said. "I greatly look forward to the dancing later this evening and I insist you save not one, but two dances for me."

"I would be honored," the countess replied, blushing slightly. Then she turned her attention toward Charlotte and looked her up and down with thoughtful eyes. "The earl and I have greatly valued your grandfather's friendship over the years. It is my dearest wish that our two families become even closer, hopefully through the younger generation."

Charlotte willed herself not to move a muscle, unsure if she should feel flattered or annoyed. The countess was certainly being presumptuous and hardly subtle. What if Charlotte decided she did not want to marry her son?

"Ah, so there you are at last. I have been despondent for over an hour, pining away in the corner like a lost dog. I was beginning to lose hope that I would ever set eyes upon you again, and now, finally my diligence has been rewarded."

Charlotte recognized the male voice. She turned and gifted her rescuer with her most dazzling smile. "Mr. Barringer. How truly delightful to see you."

Jonathan Barringer was the earl and countess's younger son. At twenty-one, he was a handsome, fun-loving rogue, with a biting sense of humor. As a boy, he had been daring, athletic and surprisingly sensitive. He had matured into a fine-looking man; blond, blue-eyed, with a tall, strapping body. Charlotte had always liked him.

"I do not understand why you persist on referring to me as Mr. Barringer," he grumbled. "We have known each other for ages." He lifted her gloved hand, turned it palm up and kissed the sensitive bare flesh on the inside of her wrist. "I insist you call me Jonathan."

Charlotte's smile widened at his obvious charm and teasing flirtation. He always made her feel special.

The countess sniffed with disdain. "Miss Aldridge is acting like a proper young lady, displaying her good breeding and manners. Unlike you. Everyone knows that first-name familiarity should be reserved for family members."

"Such as a husband and wife?" Jonathan asked with an innocent smile. "Are you suggesting that I marry Miss Aldridge, just so I may hear my Christian name uttered by her luscious lips? Goodness, Mother, that is a bit forward, even for you."

The countess's eyes widened with shock. Two spots of color appeared high on her cheeks, but before she could scold her younger son, he whisked Charlotte away.

"You are a very wicked man, Jonathan Barringer," Charlotte declared with a laugh the moment they were out of earshot.

"She almost makes it too easy for me," Jonathan replied with an answering grin.

Charlotte nodded, but said nothing else. Though he might tease her mercilessly, she knew Jonathan loved his mother and would tolerate no criticism of her from an outsider.

"Come, let's mingle," Jonathan suggested.

After only a slight hesitation, Charlotte rested her hand on the sleeve of his coat. She would rather stand off by herself and wait for people to come to her, but she understood Jonathan's responsibilities as a host. So for his sake she smiled politely and greeted the other guests, and even managed not to squirm when several of the women looked her up and down with the scrutiny of a cat sizing up a mouse.

Their slightly raised eyebrows made her doubly glad she had insisted on wearing the diamond necklace. The jewels felt warm against her skin, bringing her comfort and confidence. They set off the details of her gown to perfection and Charlotte knew she was the prettiest girl at the party.

"Have I told you yet how marvelous you look?" Jonathan asked, almost as if reading her thoughts.

"You have not, sir," Charlotte replied, playfully tapping her closed fan on his forearm.

"Forgive me, fair maiden. You are truly a vision tonight."

"So it was worth the wait?" Charlotte wanted to know.

"More than you will ever know."

Charlotte lowered her eyelids, then gazed up through her long lashes. "I simply had to look my best this evening."

Jonathan drew his face closer to hers. "Why?"

"Because you are here."

They both laughed. It was marvelous, harmless fun to flirt with Jonathan. She had long held a deep affection for him, similar to what she believed she would have felt if she had been lucky enough to have had a brother.

Jonathan snatched two champagne goblets from a passing servant and handed her one. Charlotte smiled, pleased he remembered how much she liked the bubbly nectar. The evening progressed and Charlotte found herself beginning to relax and enjoy herself, thanks to Jonathan's witty companionship.

A sudden rustle of interest from a few of the women sitting near them caught Charlotte's attention. Fans were raised to cover their mouths as whispered conversations began. Charlotte turned in the direction they looked and saw Lord Edward Barringer standing beside his mother. She had heard that he was due to return home from London sometime this evening and was not expected to arrive at the party until much later.

Charlotte had not seen Lord Edward for several years and she could understand why he was now the center of so much female attention. He cut a dashing figure in his black evening attire. He was tall and broad-shouldered, lean yet muscular in stature.

His curling dark hair was neatly trimmed to the edge of his shirt collar. His white cravat made his skin appear tanned and healthy and emphasized his uncompromising jaw, and bold nose. Though she could not clearly see his eyes, Charlotte remembered they were an unusual amber-gold color.

There were other attractive, eligible men in attendance, yet judging by the reaction of the women, both married and single, Lord Edward was the most sought after.

Charlotte wondered if he was still cautious by nature. And sincerely hoped he was not.

The music started again. This time the guests began to pair off for dancing, with the earl and countess in the lead. Playing the part of host, Lord Edward first partnered the older women who desired a turn on the dance floor and next began escorting the younger ones. To Charlotte's great annoyance, he barely glanced in her direction.

"Dance with me, Jonathan," Charlotte insisted, becoming tired of standing on the sidelines and waiting to be noticed by the high-and-mighty Lord Edward.

"But I am supposed to partner—"

"Wonderful. It's a quadrille," Charlotte interrupted, allowing her friend no opportunity to protest. She grasped his hand and led the way, making certain they were the fourth couple within a particular set of dancers.

Initially, her mind was distracted, but fortunately Jonathan was an excellent dancer. He guided her through the movements with skill and confidence. Charlotte's nerves settled and she wove in and out gracefully, humming along to the music. Then she executed a half turn and found herself face-to-face with Lord Edward.

He smiled, displaying a row of straight, white teeth that gleamed like pearls.

Charlotte missed a step.

Her feet felt clumsy, and she was momentarily off balance. Jonathan immediately came to her rescue. He clasped her about the waist and centered her in the correct position. They repeated the pattern of the dance and this time Charlotte thought she was ready. But when Lord Edward grinned at her a second time, her mind spun with possibilities.

Her senses reeled and her mind whirred and her pulse hammered with excitement. She could feel the heat emanating from his skin, could smell the soap with which he had bathed. She had the strangest urge to reach out and rest her palm on his chest, but thankfully there was no opportunity to indulge her whimsy.

This was *not* what she had expected.

The dance ended, but before Jonathan could escort her off the floor, Charlotte moved to place herself directly in front of his brother.

"I believe the next is your dance, Lord Edward."

It was a bold move, but Charlotte decided it was past time to test his lordship's intentions.

"I am honored, Miss Aldridge," Lord Edward Barringer answered in a neutral tone.

He bowed, then looked up. She offered him a smile that would melt the bones of a lesser man, but Edward was not fully taken in by it.

He had known Charlotte Aldridge since they were both children, and he clearly remembered the one thing she had always excelled at was getting her own way. Apparently that had not changed. He had no doubts that the man who succumbed to that smile would dance to *her* merry tune for the rest of his days.

Nevertheless, duty demanded that he be a polite host. This was as good a time as any to engage in the one obligatory dance of the evening he had promised his mother he would make with each female guest. Though he was honest enough to admit that dancing with Charlotte would hardly be a chore.

Edward was surprised to feel a pang of momentary disappointment when the dance was announced. It was another quadrille, not the expected waltz. Though in retrospect, he decided perhaps it was better not to hold this lovely young creature in his arms.

Her green eyes sparkled with lively interest as they took their positions. They began moving the moment the musicians struck the correct chords.

Edward was an intelligent man, a keen observer of people, but it was not necessary to notice every nuance to quickly see Charlotte's game. She flirted openly with him, and though he tried not to be, Edward found himself amused at the enticing way she smiled whenever he touched her hand.

She was a very lovely girl. She had high cheek-bones, an upturned nose, a generous mouth and skin that resembled the finest porcelain. The blond streaks in her honey-brown hair shimmered in the glow of the candlelight and he wondered if its length went to just beyond her shoulders or fell as far down as her waist.

Her gown was a deep shade of green that matched her eyes. Styled in the latest fashion, it accentuated her hourglass figure and was flounced at the bodice and hem with yards of intricate lace. And while he thought it ridiculous for a girl of her age to be wearing such a sophisticated piece of jewelry, he had to admit the necklace looked stunning on her.

The diamonds framed the neckline of her gown perfectly, drawing the eye to the soft swells of her breasts above the top of her emerald silk gown. And what impressive breasts they were. Miss Aldridge had a tall, willowy figure, but there was nothing slender about her chest.

"Your grandfather told me you made your curtsey to the queen this past spring," Edward said, the next time they came close. "Did you enjoy yourself?"

"Sometimes. But eventually the endless parties started to become boring. Everywhere you go, you always see the same faces. I was quite content to return home. As for the queen . . ." Charlotte's voice trailed off.

Edward's brow lifted in surprise. Most young women of his acquaintance were in awe of the monarch. "Were you not impressed with her regal bearing and majesty?"

"Personally, I think she takes herself a bit too seriously," Charlotte confided in a hushed whisper.

Edward had difficulty holding back his laughter, but he feared that would only encourage her to make more outlandish remarks. So he managed to restrain himself.

"I was not in London this Season," Edward said. "I spent most of the past year abroad."

"On the grand tour?"

Edward nearly groaned. Unlike his contemporaries, he had spent his time on the continent studying, learning and working hard, determined to gain the knowledge he needed to make himself a successful businessman.

"I visited various European capitals," he answered evasively. "It was very enlightening."

"I assumed you had not been in Town," Charlotte replied. "I am certain I would have remembered if our paths had crossed."

She gave him another enthralling smile and Edward had the strangest sensation that he was suddenly the only person in the room with her. He blinked and shook his head vigorously to ward off the feeling.

He was not searching for a romantic entanglement. Or a bride. At twenty-three, Edward believed he was still too young, too unsettled, too financially insecure to take a wife. One day he would inherit his father's title and become the next earl, but alas, there would be no great fortune to accompany his new status.

Being a sensible and forward-thinking man, Edward was determined to fix that problem. His plans to achieve financial solvency for himself and his family would require all his concentration, a considerable amount of his time and a bit of good luck. There was no room in the equation for a young bride.

Especially someone like Charlotte Aldridge. She was clever and charming and far too lovely. Her perfume was a delicate fragrance, reminiscent of violets. The scent lingered in the air, charging him with a restless, reckless feeling. The less he had to do with her, the better.

The steps of the dance called for them to momentarily separate, and he watched her make a graceful pirouette, her gown floating softly around her calves and ankles. When her shapely legs came into clear view, he could hear the buzz of gossip starting from the group of stiff-necked matrons who were sitting around the edges of the dance floor, watching their every move.

She seemed unaware of it, but then, for an instant, her thoughtful eyes locked with his and a delicately fine eyebrow arched in amusement. The little minx! She was well aware of the sensation she was causing and clearly it did not bother her a bit. Quite the contrary, she seemed to enjoy causing a stir.

Edward was unsure if he felt relief or disappointment when their dance came to an end. As Charlotte sank into a final curtsey, there was no mistaking the welcoming interest in her eyes. Yet he answered her with a polite, remote gaze.

Everyone shuffled about, regrouping for the next dance. Charlotte was claimed by Lord Haddon, a pleasant-looking young viscount. As Edward watched her take the floor, she turned her head and tilted her chin in a provocative pose toward the viscount.

The gesture merely confirmed Edward's earlier opinion—Miss Charlotte Aldridge would be a bundle of trouble for any man who chose to take her on.

CHAPTER 2

The following day, breakfast was served in the morning room, which overlooked the gardens at the back of the estate. When at home, Charlotte seldom left her bedchamber before noon, but at Farmington Manor she found herself wide awake the moment the sun rose.

Memories of the dance she had shared with Lord Edward last night lingered in her mind. Those recollections had made her dreams restless, exciting, filled with new and intriguing possibilities. Charlotte wished the time she spent with him had been longer, wished there had been an opportunity to speak with him privately. But she contented herself with the notion that this was the beginning of the holiday festivities and there would be many chances to rectify that problem over the coming week.

Who knew, perhaps today would be the day he would begin courting her in earnest?

Buoyed by the thought, Charlotte insisted that Jones take extra care with her morning toilette. She wanted everything to be perfect. Her gown was changed twice, her hair done in three different styles before Charlotte was satisfied with her appearance. Feeling confident, yet slightly nervous, she joined the earl and countess, Lord Edward, Jonathan and several other early-rising guests for breakfast.

It was a clear, crisp morning, with blue skies and few clouds. The grass was lightly browned from the nightly freezing temperature, and though Charlotte thought there was something about the day that felt more like spring than winter, the guests seated at the breakfast table spoke longingly of the possibility of snow before Christmas Day arrived.

"I for one dislike the snow," the countess declared. "It's so dreadfully inconvenient. It can keep one house-bound for days and days."

"Snow is so beautiful!" Jonathan protested. "It sparkles and shimmers, white and pristine, especially when it is newly fallen, making everything look clean and fresh and untouched."

"Looks are often deceiving," the countess retorted, as she crumbled the edge of a piece of toast between her fingers. "My sister, bless her heart, slipped and broke her leg one winter on a fresh patch of snow. Though it eventually mended, she was never the same. To this day, it pains her whenever it rains."

Across the breakfast table, Charlotte's eyes met Lord Edward's. His left eyebrow raised and a slightly mocking smile escaped as his mother launched into another desperate tale about the perils of snow. Charlotte found she could not resist returning his grin even though it then forced her to concentrate on keeping her hands steady on her knife and fork.

"There is no need to be so dire," Lord Edward interjected when the countess paused to take a breath. "Most of us will be happy indeed to see the snow. And if it does arrive, we shall all be building snowmen, sledding over it, clearing the frozen lake so we may skate upon the ice and of course engaging in a massive snowball battle."

The countess began pleating her linen napkin into tight, narrow folds. "Very well. If it does snow, I shall stand on the terrace and watch all of you lose your dignity."

"The terrace? Near the south lawn?" Jonathan returned his china coffee cup to its saucer. "A prime viewing location, yet in close enough range to be struck by a stray snowball. Or two."

The countess puffed out her cheeks. "I cannot even begin to elaborate on the consequences that would befall the individual who dared to strike me with a mass of cold, wet, snow," she warned.

"The culprit would be thrown into the dungeons at once," Lord Edward said. "We still have working dungeons, don't we, sir?" he asked, turning to his father.

The earl grinned. "Certainly. I'm sure Harris even knows where the keys to the largest cell can be found."

"Excellent." Lord Edward got to his feet. "Now that my mother is assured of her safety, I would like to invite everyone on a late-morning outing. The decorating of the house will begin in earnest today, and we need to fetch holly, ivy, pine boughs—"

"And mistletoe," Jonathan interjected.

"Yes, mistletoe," Lord Edward agreed. "I hope many of you will decide to join my brother and me."

There was a chorus of enthusiastic interest.

Charlotte added her voice to the mix and hastily finished her cup of hot chocolate.

"Mistletoe?" The countess tried to look disapproving at her son's suggestion, but could not hold the expression for long. "I fear I shall be overruled if I object to having it brought into the house, though I daresay it would not be Christmas without at least one kissing bough."

"Only one?" Jonathan protested loudly.

The countess glowered at her younger son. "I will instruct the servants to fetch the ribbons and bows and bells from the attic so we may all properly adorn the greenery. However, I shall personally supervise the placement of all the decorations. The year Jonathan took charge of putting up the greenery, the front parlor and drawing room ceilings were covered in kissing boughs and positively dripping with mistletoe."

"Aye, now that was a grand Christmas," Jonathan remarked with a dreamy look in his eyes. "You could not take more than three steps without standing beneath a cluster of greenery that required a kiss."

Everyone laughed, and even the countess smiled. "The placement of mistletoe is very important," she insisted. "Most people make the mistake of putting it over a doorway and eventually everyone gets tired of kissing everyone else."

"Tired of kissing?" Jonathan exclaimed in mock horror. "Impossible!"

Plans were made to meet outside within the hour, so those who wished to partake of the holiday activity of gathering greenery could leave before it became too cold.

Charlotte was momentarily disappointed when she

realized her grandfather was not among the group bundled up for the outdoors, but his cheerful smile and merry wave from the terrace windows softened the blow. And made her feel like a very mature woman, since she was the only unattached female attending the outing without a formal chaperone.

Of course there were several married women in the party, and three dowagers, to lend an air of respectability. The older women rode together in an open carriage, their legs covered in heavy blankets, their heads covered in fur hats. Everyone else traveled on foot.

However, when they reached the edge of the woods, the carriage was unable to follow on the narrow path. Those on foot were organized into four groups and Charlotte found herself in the party comprised of the Chambers sisters, Lord Edward, Jonathan and Lord Haddon, the pleasant viscount she had danced with last evening, who was reputed to be sweet on Miranda Chambers.

With Lord Edward in the lead, they walked in companionable silence as they entered the thickest part of the woods. Sunlight glittered through the canopy of bare interlaced branches, creating a mystical atmosphere. Privately, Charlotte thought it was wonderfully romantic. Luxuriating in her surroundings, she slowed her pace and breathed deeply.

"We should probably find a Yule log first," Lord Edward said. "Though we will of course decorate an evergreen tree, my father prefers the older traditions and it usually takes the gardeners hours to find a Yule log he deems suitable."

Everyone nodded in understanding, then set themselves eagerly to the assigned task.

"There." Miss Elizabeth Chambers pointed to a fallen branch. "How about that one?"

Jonathan went over to inspect her choice. "Much too small," he decided. "The log must be wide enough to fill the hall hearth and solid enough to burn for days."

"Is this a better choice?" Charlotte called out merrily. She had hoisted herself onto the base of a fallen tree trunk and settled comfortably in the center. Her feet dangling, she swung them back and forth, feeling quite pleased with her discovery.

"Clever girl," Lord Edward said with an approving smile. He came up beside her and patted the log to test the soundness of the wood. "I will send out the gardeners with a cart and a team of horses to fetch it. Once they cut it to the proper size it will be perfect."

"It will burn until spring," Miranda Chambers said with a shy grin. "Excellent find, Miss Aldridge."

"Thank you." Charlotte was warmed by the compliment, which was sincerely given.

"Now on to the mistletoe," Jonathan exclaimed, hopping onto the log and walking carefully along its length. "It grows best and fullest in the tops of the older oak trees. I shall retrieve a choice specimen to show all of you what we need."

"No, that honor will be mine," Lord Edward declared in a voice that let them all know he would not be put to shame by his younger brother.

"I'll take a piece of that challenge," Viscount Haddon said, not to be outdone. "Though I have not done so since I was a lad, I still remember how to climb a tree."

The gauntlet thrown, each man turned in different

directions and started off on their quest, leaving the women standing alone. The three women stared at each other for a quick moment and then also scattered. Miss Miranda dogged the viscount's heels, and without hesitation Charlotte took off behind Lord Edward. With a philosophical shrug, Miss Elizabeth trooped behind Jonathan.

The fingers inside Charlotte's gloves tingled from the cold, her cheeks and nose felt tight and nearly numb, yet she could not remember the last time she had had so much fun out of doors. The sun had disappeared and the sky had darkened considerably, making her wonder if it truly would snow, as everyone had hoped.

Lord Edward seemed unaware that she was behind him. Fearing she might get separated, Charlotte kept her eyes pinned to the many capes of his dark green greatcoat and did her best to keep up with his long strides. But it was difficult.

She was very thankful indeed when he suddenly stopped, though she nearly plowed into his broad back.

"Miss Aldridge! How thoughtless of me. You should have yelled at me to slacken my pace."

He put out his arms to steady her and Charlotte grasped them, even though her balance was not threatened.

"Ladies do not yell, Lord Edward," Charlotte said in a steady voice. "Besides, I am unsure you would have heard me if I had been so vulgar as to screech. Your mind is exclusively focused upon the task at hand. Apparently, you are taking this lighthearted competition rather seriously."

He shrugged. "'Tis the way of men."

"And small boys."

He had the grace to smile. Charlotte decided she liked the way his eyes sparkled with amusement and crinkled in the corners. It was very attractive.

"Take my hand," he commanded. "I do not want to lose you."

"I would never allow that to happen, sir," Charlotte replied with a flirty smile as she set her hand in his outstretched one.

He seemed different. Gone was his customary quiet dignity, gone was the cautious attitude she remembered so well when he was a boy. His eyes were bright with animation, his face flushed from the cold and exercise, his manner commanding and determined. He looked virile and handsome and incredibly appealing. Winter, and challenges, suited him.

Charlotte wondered briefly if this change had anything to do with the sips of brandy she had seen him taking from his silver flask, but she quickly discarded the notion. It was the spirit of the competition that brought out the transformation.

They walked past a thicket of holly bushes and came to a cluster of stately oak trees. Charlotte tipped back her head to scan the upper branches, unsure if she would be able to see any mistletoe from this great distance. She turned to ask Lord Edward's opinion and discovered he was not looking up into the tree. He was staring at her.

"You are an extremely lovely woman, Miss Aldridge," he said in a surprised tone, as though he had just realized it.

She snapped her eyes up to his and caught her breath. He took a step closer and her eyes widened. Then he raised the hand he still held in his own up to his mouth and pressed his lips against the tips of her gloved fingers. His amber-gold eyes were sharp beneath the lazy lids. She gazed into them and then reached over and removed her glove so he could repeat the gesture on her bare flesh. He willingly complied.

Charlotte sighed, feeling the delicate press of his lips all the way to her toes. Parts of her body that had been chilled in the cold winter air were now heating with warmth. It was the most romantic moment of her life and she felt herself slowly slipping toward a host of new and wonderful sensations.

Was this how seduction felt? It seemed as if the functions of her mind were now dominated by the feeling coursing through her body. Delightful, exciting, forbidden feelings. And if she leaned forward just a bit . . .

"Oh, look," she whispered in a breathy tone. "You have found the mistletoe. We are standing beneath it."

He gazed skyward for the briefest instant. "So we are." He laughed. The deep, rich baritone of mirth sent a shiver of anticipation down Charlotte's spine.

"That means you must kiss me," she demanded.

"And so I shall."

He spun her behind the large oak tree. Charlotte's back met the rough solid tree trunk the same moment Lord Edward's lips descended upon hers.

Warmth invaded every fiber of her being. At first he kissed her with playful bites and nips. She tried to imitate his actions, and then his hands adjusted the angle of her head, holding her in place. The pressure of his mouth increased as the tip of his tongue played with hers.

Charlotte struggled to control her breathing. His

lips were hot and restless, a temptation she was powerless to resist. Her knees began to weaken, yet she kissed him back, willingly allowing the wondrous sensations to wash over her.

The next kiss was a passionate caress of lips and tongue that filled Charlotte with unfamiliar pulsing heat and need. Something primal within her stirred and her entire body tingled. She slid her arms around Edward's neck to keep herself upright. He was solid and lean and muscular and it felt so good to be pressed tightly against his strength.

They kissed again and this time she felt the force of his response. It thrilled her to realize she was capable of inciting such passion within him. She could not seem to stop herself from touching him, running one hand over the broad contours of his back while the other gripped his upper arm, fingertips digging into the hard muscle of his biceps.

He pushed her bonnet aside and began to nibble on the sensitive flesh below her earlobe. Charlotte squealed with delight. Closing her eyes, she arched her neck in invitation, nearly swooning when she felt Edward's lips feathering a trail of kisses down her throat.

His tongue stroked into the tiny hollow just above the neckline of her gown and a new urgency ignited within her. His warm breath had her squirming against the tree trunk, restless with anticipation. She was trembling, her head was spinning, her heart was racing and she never wanted it to stop.

When she felt him begin to draw away, Charlotte caught the lapels of his coat, pulled him forward and brought his lips back to hers. Edward groaned and kissed her back, sliding his tongue into her mouth.

Charlotte tasted heat and passion and a slight trace of brandy. He moved his lips and tongue boldly and a raw sensation jolted her body. She swayed toward him as another burst of heat slid into her breasts, her womb and down between her thighs.

Each press of his lips, each seeking thrust of his tongue sent a lick of desire coursing through her, heating her flesh, weakening her limbs. His hand moved lower and cupped a breast, stroking the nipple with his thumb. Even through the layers of heavy clothing, Charlotte could feel the tip peak and distend.

She felt her cheeks heat with embarrassment, but then he did it again and her embarrassment disappeared as the sensations overtook her. He made her feel beautiful, desirable, powerful. Charlotte arched toward his touch and then caught her lip in her teeth to bite back a groan of pleasure.

"Edward! Miss Aldridge! Are you there?"

It was Jonathan's voice. The words registered in her brain, but Charlotte was loath to acknowledge the call. If she did, then this magical moment would end. Apparently, Edward felt the same, for he lifted his lips to her ear and whispered, "Shhh, do not utter a sound."

She nodded. They waited in silence for a long minute, hearing no additional calls. Edward's arms slackened their grip and Charlotte eased herself away. She leaned against the tree trunk and closed her eyes, trying to stop the pounding of her heart. She felt him move farther away from her, but could still dimly hear his breath coming as hard and heavy as her own.

Merciful heavens! So that was passion, that was desire.

It was indescribably marvelous and far more magical than I ever imagined.

Charlotte licked her swollen lips, drew a deep breath and opened her eyes. Edward was staring at her, his eyes so fiery with passion she nearly felt singed. The daylight cast a glow on his face, outlining the masculine planes and hollows. Her heart skipped a beat. He looked so unbearably handsome, it brought a flood of emotional tears to her eyes.

"Are you all right?"

Charlotte slowly smiled. "What? Oh, yes, I am fine. Perfectly fine."

"Good." An undefinable emotion shone in his eyes, but Charlotte was too pleased with herself to give it much thought.

"We had best get back before they send out a larger search party," he said.

"What about the mistletoe?"

He groaned. "As long as we are here, I suppose I should retrieve some."

With athletic grace, he swung up into the branches of the tree. He climbed steadily higher and Charlotte's gaze never left his solid frame. Her skin tingled with the memory of his kisses and the savage way he had brought their mouths together so impatiently. It had been heavenly, and even more enticing was the knowledge that kissing was just the beginning.

By the time Edward had returned to the ground with a sizable armful of mistletoe, Charlotte was more than ready for another round of kisses. And anything else he cared to teach her.

"How lovely," she exclaimed. Charlotte reached for a cluster of mistletoe, fully intending to hold it over her head, but Edward held the bunches close to his chest, out of her reach.

"We need to find the others," he said.

Though she wanted to protest, Charlotte knew he was right. She offered her hand and he hesitated only a moment before taking it. At his touch, a surge of profound emotions welled up inside Charlotte.

So this is love.

There was seldom a time when Edward Barringer's conscience bothered him. He was a man of breeding, of honor, of character, and he prided himself on endorsing and upholding the many standards of decency and following the civilized rules of society with ease.

This afternoon he had broken those rules. He had kissed an innocent young woman he had no serious intentions toward, had allowed the passion of his body to overrule the common sense of his mind. With Charlotte Aldridge, no less.

Why her, of all the females available? True, she had been aggressive in her pursuit of him, but that was nothing new. Women often paid undue attention to him. When he walked into a ballroom, many female heads turned to regard him, both the young unmarried misses and their matchmaking mothers.

He was not offended by their frank appraisal, nor was he conceited by this attention. He was a practical, pragmatic man who understood the true source of their interest was not **his** person, but rather his title, his lineage, his place in society. It was the way the upper classes had married for centuries and he found no outward fault with the practice.

It was simply a part of his life, but at this point in time, a part he had no interest in pursuing. Thus he avoided showing any sort of favoritism to any female of marriageable age to avoid speculation or raise expectations. Above all, he strove not to unintentionally hurt anyone's feelings, because he most definitely was not in the market for a wife.

Then what were those kisses all about? Too much brandy on too little breakfast and a far too lovely, willing female. Edward dropped Charlotte's hand and pulled out his handkerchief. He had broken into a sweat remembering his actions, feeling deeply the terrible weight of regret. Fortunately, she seemed oblivious to his change of mood.

Once his brow was dry, he promptly thrust his handkerchief and both hands in his pockets. He tried to assume an air of nonchalance, of outward calm and peace, but inside he felt a rise of panic. He chatted and kidded with his brother and Lord Haddon, joking and arguing over who had collected the most mistletoe and whose specimens were the finest. They also teased each other over their tardiness, since theirs was the last group to return. All the other guests who had joined the outing had long since departed for the manor.

"Oh, look, it has started to snow!" Charlotte's voice rang out with girlish delight.

They all gazed up to the sky. Indeed, the snow had begun to fall in a cloud of swirling flakes, fluttering steadily to the ground on the chilled breeze. The heavy flakes clung to the branches of the trees and bushes and coated the ground, quickly transforming everything into a white fairyland of stark, sparkling beauty.

"Careful. It is starting to get slippery," Jonathan warned, taking hold of Miss Elizabeth Chambers's arm to prevent her from tumbling to the ground.

Lord Haddon showed Miss Miranda the same consideration, a task more difficult, since he carried all the mistletoe. Edward feared he might have to do the same for Charlotte, but she ran ahead, twirling merrily, arms outstretched, her infectious laughter echoing through the trees. She looked startlingly, vividly young and incredibly lovely.

"Oh, I do hope there will be enough snow for sledding," she cried. "I have not had the chance to indulge in that pleasure for ages."

"Well, I hope there is enough snow for a snowball fight," Jonathan said. "It would be worth spending an afternoon in the dungeons just to see Mother's face when I hurl one in her direction."

"I believe you shall both get your wish," Viscount Haddon commented. "'Tis falling so thickly I can see but a few feet in front of me."

"The manor house is just over that rise," Edward said. "Fortunately we should reach it within the hour, as I am certain there are several noses pressed against the window glass, anxious for our return."

But even the threat of heavy snow could not contain Charlotte's excitement. She skipped along, sure-footed in the ever-mounting drifts, laughing and teasing them all to join her. Was it just the cold putting the flush in her cheeks, the glow in her eyes? Or was it something else entirely?

She was so full of wild, uninhibited joy. There was a light in her eyes that had an irresistible magic, a beauty in her face that captivated and seduced. Edward found himself wondering, most inappropriately, what she would look like as he was making love to her.

Making love to her! The notion caused him to lose his footing and he barely managed to prevent himself from falling. Charlotte turned and quickly gained his side, latching on to his waist. "Are you all right?"

"Fine," he muttered.

Though they were standing in the vast open, the space around him suddenly seemed very small. He was pressed close to her body and suffered from a nearly irresistible urge to lean forward and kiss her. She was staring too, as if considering the same.

Edward valiantly resisted the lure and cautioned himself against doing anything foolish. He stepped away and blinked through the swirling snow, feeling a profound sense of relief when the manor house came into view. Every window in the house blazed with light, a welcoming beacon of refuge from the storm.

"We are nearly home," he announced.

Everyone quickened their pace, buoyed by the promise of dry, warm shelter and a hot, cozy beverage. It was not until they had reached the top of the south lawn that Edward realized how far Charlotte lagged behind. Alone.

He signalled for the others to continue. Stomping his freezing feet, he waited for her to finally reach him.

"May we go sledding?" she asked prettily, an alluring smile lighting her face.

"Perhaps later, if the snow lets up," he answered briskly.

She dawdled, clearly yearning to say more, but he

gave her no opportunity. Grasping her elbow firmly, he propelled her the final feet to the manor, up the front steps and into the foyer. Handing her off to the waiting servants, Edward made a formal bow and hurried away, not even stopping to divest himself of his wet outer garments until he had safely reached the privacy of his chambers.

Seated before a roaring fire, he slowly sipped a warm brandy, his thoughts in turmoil. There were eight more days until Christmas. How was he possibly going to survive?

CHAPTER 3

Charlotte expected everything to change over the next few days. She expected the world to be different, to sound different, to feel different.

She certainly knew that *she* was different. Her tangled emotions seemed to always be riding on the very edge, and the constant, fluttering sensation in the pit of her stomach swelled to twice its size whenever she was around Edward.

She was in love.

Yet she was also frustrated. And impatient. Lord Edward was always kind and polite and attentive to her conversation, but he never sought her out for a private moment. She flirted constantly with him and he always responded with a ready smile, but more often than not he was distant, formal and self-contained.

Compounding the difficulties were the various holiday activities, which included all the houseguests. During the singing of carols and the tree trimming and the gift wrapping, they were never alone, though Charlotte believed a man as intelligent and clever as Lord Edward should be able to find a way to steal another kiss or two. Her luck was so bad she had not even been able to position herself beneath the kissing bough when Lord Edward was near.

The weather too had seemed to conspire against her. The snow had melted too quickly for an intimate carriage sleigh ride or the fun of sledding down the hill in pairs or even a snowball battle.

Charlotte had no firsthand knowledge of the courting ritual and no mother or close female friends to explain it all to her. At one point she had become so desperate, she had swallowed her pride and asked Jones for advice, but the older maid revealed she had no experience at all with members of the opposite sex.

The final straw had struck last evening, after dinner. The ladies had retreated to the drawing room to allow the gentlemen to linger over their port and cigars. Once the gentlemen rejoined the ladies, everyone adjourned to the music room, eager to hear the special performance arranged for them by the earl and countess.

As they crossed the vast foyer, the heel of Charlotte's shoe caught on the edge of the carpet and dislodged. She waited for the others to pass, then believing she was alone, she lifted her gown. As she stooped to fix her shoe, she felt a steady hand grip her elbow, offering assistance.

It was Lord Edward. He was close enough for her to catch the subtle scent of soap he used, to feel the heat and strength of his body. The experience sent a great rolling wave of desire rippling through her.

They were alone. Charlotte's heart fluttered wildly. It was the ideal moment to steal a kiss. She was near enough for him to grasp her shoulders and pull her to him, to mold her body to his and clasp her tightly in his arms. To put his mouth over hers and feel the trembling of passion that had overtaken her, to rejoice in the willingness of her heart.

Yet he had done none of those things. The instant her shoe was secured, he had released his hold on her elbow and taken one step back, away from her. Charlotte moved forward, but the Chambers sisters and Lord Haddon entered the hallway and the moment was lost.

Charlotte pretended that it did not matter. She threw herself into the evening's activities, outwardly ignoring Lord Edward, yet all the while she was covertly studying him.

All in all, he had a handsome, arresting face, but there was something else, something indefinable that was drawing her to him. She glanced at the other young women around her, wondering if she was the only one to feel so attracted, or did he have this effect on all females whenever they were near?

After a few minutes she decided that no other females were openly regarding him, or casting coy glances his way. Apparently she was the lone woman who had made no secret of her fascination for him, for all the good it did her.

Charlotte watched Lord Edward broodingly for the remainder of the evening and by the following morning she had devised a plan. It was high time to take matters into her own hands.

Charlotte had observed that her grandfather often spent the afternoon in the earl's library, reading the newspaper and smoking one of those dreadful cigars he so liked. And he was usually alone. The morning seemed interminable long, but Charlotte somehow managed to bide her time, hiding her impatience.

And then finally luck was on her side. Everyone scattered to their afternoon activities and she managed to fool them all, letting each group believe she was going with the other. She scampered down the long corridor in the east wing, counting the doors until she found the one she sought. As she opened the library door, she was elated to find her grandfather alone in the room.

Lord Reginald looked up when she entered, his eyes brightening with pleasure. "I thought you were going off to the village this afternoon with the rest of the ladies."

"Even I eventually tire of shopping, Grandpapa," Charlotte quipped as she leant down and kissed his cheek.

The afternoon sun streamed through the long, rectangular stained-glass windows, casting a warm glow on the rosewood paneling. The room smelled pleasantly of leather and beeswax and carried the faint hint of her grandfather's favorite brand of tobacco. Through the window she could see the frost glistening on the grass that was but a poor substitute for a white blanket of snow.

Lord Reginald patted the cushion on the sofa, indicating that she should take the seat beside him. With a smile, Charlotte complied.

"Christmas is but a few days away," Lord Reginald said. "Are you eagerly awaiting the arrival of the Christ child?"

Charlotte smiled at the fond memory. As a young child, she had been fascinated by the story of the baby born in a manager and had pestered her grandfather repeatedly to tell her the story of the child's birth. She wondered now where he had found the patience to always comply with her request, reciting the story with great drama, no matter how many times she asked.

"Our holidays at Quincy Court were very special," Charlotte replied. "I shall always cherish them."

"Ah, but the festivities the earl and countess have provided for all of us are special too," Lord Reginald said. "I am pleased to see that you are enjoying yourself."

"Everyone has been very kind," Charlotte said graciously.

"Yes, the Chambers girls seem like pleasant company."

"I find that I like them both," Charlotte said with surprised honesty. "Miranda has a more adventurous spirit and therefore we have much in common, yet Elizabeth has a sharp wit and can be very entertaining. 'Tis a lovely treat for me to have found such charming female companions."

They spoke for a few minutes of inconsequential matters and then Lord Reginald leaned forward, turning slightly to face his granddaughter. "What is it you really want to say to me, Charlotte?"

"'Tis about Lord Edward." She slanted her grandfather a gaze, surprised at how nervous she suddenly felt. "I know part of the reason we came here was to see if Lord Edward and I would suit."

"That was one of the considerations," Lord Reginald agreed. He waited patiently, his undemanding silence encouraging a jittery Charlotte to reveal her thoughts.

"I have given it considerable thought and consideration and have decided that I would not be adverse to accepting an offer from him," Charlotte blurted out.

"Not adverse, huh?" Lord Reginald snorted. "That's hardly a ringing endorsement. Do you think Lord Edward feels the same?"

Charlotte felt herself blush. Just thinking about Edward, and the kisses they had shared in the forest, made her heart rate accelerate.

"I believe he has developed feelings for me," she replied, proud that she was able to hold her voice even and steady. "Though he is far too much of a gentleman to speak openly about them."

"If he will not speak of them, then how do you know he has them?"

"Well, he kissed me!"

"Ahhh." Lord Reginald leaned back and considered her for a long moment. Charlotte was unable to read the expression in his eyes and worried briefly that she might have revealed too much.

"And you liked it?" Lord Reginald finally asked.

"Very much." Charlotte felt her blush deepen. This was far too intimate a subject to be discussing with anyone, especially her grandfather. She swallowed hard, trying to elevate the odd tickle at the back of her throat. "But it was not just the kisses. I also like Lord Edward. A great deal."

"So do I." Lord Reginald gave her a bemused look. "Marriage is an important lifetime commitment. Are you certain that he is the one you want, Charlotte?"

"I am." She felt her heart flutter for a moment as she said the words and then it settled back into a normal rhythm. "I know this will make me very happy, Grandpapa. Truly."

Relief filled Lord Reginald's face. "Then I am delighted. This is splendid news. I shall speak with the earl immediately and we will draw up the marriage contracts. I can think of no better way to celebrate the arrival of spring than to have your wedding ceremony at Quincy Court."

Charlotte breathed in a quivering sob of delight. *Edward was going to be her husband!* Excitement swarmed through her, yet she somehow managed to suppress a feral smile. It would be unladylike and crude to gloat so openly, but the sense of accomplishment nearly overwhelmed her.

The flowers at Quincy Court would be in bloom by early June, the formal rose garden just starting to bud. She would have the majority of her wedding clothes made in London, but then purchase additional garments on her honeymoon to Paris. Edward would be dazzled by her beauty, her sophistication, her womanly charms and count himself the luckiest man in England to have won her heart.

The chaos of emotions that had been tormenting Charlotte for days began to fade, replaced by a constant stream of happiness. Dearest Grandpapa. No matter what the circumstances, she could always count on him to give her everything she ever needed, everything she ever wanted.

Why should this be any different?

"I am sorry, Father, but what you are suggesting is impossible. I will not marry Charlotte Aldridge."

The Earl of Worthington sputtered with outrage,

clearly speechless at his son's reaction. He turned to his wife, who sat beside him on the salon sofa, her expression revealing the same shock.

"Is there someone else, Edward?" the countess inquired. "We would never insist that you marry Miss Aldridge if your heart has been already claimed by another. As long as she is an acceptable girl, with an acceptable lineage and brings a substantial dowry, we will welcome her into our family."

For the briefest instant, Edward was tempted to lie and say he was involved with someone else. But then his parents would expect him to produce the young woman in question. And since she did not exist, that would be impossible.

"There is no one else," Edward admitted reluctantly. "And the reason for that is because I am far too young to be married."

The countess smiled broadly, all teeth. "Your father was only two years older than you are now when he married me. Besides, you have always been a steady and serious young man, displaying a maturity far beyond your physical years. It is one of your finest qualities. Your father and I both agree that you are more than ready to settle down. And we have decided that Miss Aldridge would be an outstanding choice."

Edward felt the hair on his nape stand up in warning. His mother was always at her most formidable when she engaged in flattery. From what he had observed, she barely tolerated Miss Aldridge, yet she was eagerly overlooking that fact. She must want this match very badly.

"Charlotte Aldridge is a pleasant looking, high-spirited young girl," the earl added. "She is Lord

Reginald's sole heir. And her great-uncle is a duke. What more can you possibly require in a wife?"

"Miss Aldridge's suitability is not in question," Edward replied. "The simple fact of the matter is that I have no plans to marry anyone, anytime soon."

"But you kissed her!" the countess exclaimed. "Most passionately, I was told."

Good God. Edward felt his face infuse with indignant color. He had tried, unsuccessfully, to push all memories of those kisses from his mind, still unsure what had possessed him to throw caution to the wind and react so physically to Charlotte.

One touch of his lips to hers and his famous self-control had vanished. He had devoured her mouth with smoldering sensuality, kissing her as if his life depended on it. Agitation had filled him, igniting a passionate fire of desire in his blood. He could not think clearly, he could only feel.

It had been so difficult to stop. If not for the interruption by his brother, Jonathan. . . Edward shuddered to think how inappropriate his behavior might have become.

But he *had* stopped and well before Charlotte had been compromised. There would be no need to marry for propriety's sake, even if others knew he had stolen a few kisses.

Yet the only way his parents could possibly know about those kisses was from Charlotte. She must have told her grandfather and Lord Reginald had informed his parents. Were they all in this together, conspiring to trick him into marriage?

"I kissed Miss Aldridge because she was standing beneath the mistletoe," Edward maintained, fighting to keep a straight face. "It would have been impolite and downright insulting to refuse. It meant nothing."

His father's face turned angry, but Edward would not relent.

"Miss Aldridge is attractive, but I have no desire to complicate my life with a wife. Especially one so young and spoiled," Edward continued, wanting to make his position perfectly clear.

"This is quite a blow," the countess remarked, with a stiffening upper lip. "I fear you have ruined everything with this unreasonable attitude, Edward."

"I am merely being truthful, Mother."

"And irresponsible," the earl said curtly. "You have obligations, my boy, responsibilities and duties to this family that you cannot ignore."

Adopting a neutral, pleasant facade, Edward held on to his temper. He was very aware of his responsibilities to his family. He took them seriously, far more seriously than many other young men of his class, and it hurt to be so wrongfully accused.

Though it was a bit sooner than he had originally planned, it seemed as though he had no choice but to tell his parents what he intended.

"I would like to assure you both that I take my responsibility as the future earl very seriously," Edward said. "And it has not escaped my notice that our finances are in dire straits."

"Just a run of bad luck," the earl grumbled. "Nothing that can't be fixed with an infusion of funds. In fact, a bride's dowry would set us to rights in no time."

"Even a sizable dowry would only allow us to pay off the most pressing of creditors and stave off ruin for a few years," Edward said softly. "What I propose is that we find a more sensible solution to this problem."

"We have found a solution," the countess insisted with a stony expression. "Charlotte Aldridge is an heiress. She will inherit a considerable amount of property, along with a great fortune one day. As her husband, you would have control of that fortune."

"I do not wish to control someone else's fortune," Edward said calmly. "I am going to make my own."

Neither of his parents could hide their astonishment at his announcement.

"Your own what?" the earl ventured.

"Fortune." Edward was not a man prone to emotional extremes, but this was too important not to speak from the heart. He had thought and planned and considered this all very carefully. He was convinced he could be successful, if only given the chance.

"That is simply ridiculous," the countess snapped. "Men of your class and breeding do not soil their hands by making money."

Ignoring the scowling looks cast his way by both his parents, Edward maintained a calm facade and tried to explain. "Years of indiscriminate spending and foolish investments have depleted our family coffers. We derive a large portion of our annual income from several estates, however agriculture is a chancy business even under the best of circumstances.

"Unfortunately generations of our ancestors have failed to invest the necessary funds back into the land and the profits have steadily dwindled over the years. We need diverse investments in progressive industries to achieve financial solvency and independence, not only for ourselves but for future generations."

The earl's brow raised in puzzlement. "What a bunch of garbled nonsense. Speak plainly, Edward."

"I am going to build a business empire that, God willing, shall eventually bring us financial independence," he proclaimed proudly.

"Work in trade? Have you taken leave of your senses?" An icy edge of panic layered his mother's outcry. "'Tis an unthinkable idea. We shall be shunned by anyone of consequence."

The earl's earlier puzzlement vanished, replaced with thunderous fury. "I will not allow a son of mine to bring such utter disgrace to our family name."

Edward remained expressionless, though he felt the color drain from his face. He had not expected it to be easy, yet this extreme disapproval was far more than he anticipated. True, few men of class took such an active role in business, but he felt the circumstances warranted such action, especially because he believed he had the talent and the dedication to make it a reality.

All he needed was a chance to prove himself.

"I am trying to save our family," Edward said calmly, trying to make that point very clear.

The countess let out a loud gasp of distress and clutched her hand over her heart. "You are going to destroy it."

"Mother, please, there is no need for you to react—"

"Stop it! Stop it, I say!" the earl exploded. "I will listen to no more of this preposterous rubbish. You are upsetting your mother beyond reason."

The earl drew a shuddering breath, seemingly to gather his thoughts. "It is true that we are going through a bit of a rough patch regarding our family finances. Which is precisely why we have decided that it would be best for all concerned if you marry the Aldridge girl. It must be done no later than this coming spring. We expect you to make an announcement at this evening's Christmas Eve ball.

"Lord Reginald and I have already worked out the details with our solicitors. The terms of the marriage contracts are most generous. I have taken the liberty of retrieving the bride's ring from the vault, so you may present it to Miss Aldridge when you formally propose. This afternoon."

The earl fumbled in his pocket and removed a jewel box. He flipped the lid and revealed the contents. Even the old-fashioned, heavy gold setting could not diminish the brilliance of the large sapphire center stone as it sparkled mockingly up at Edward.

"'Tis very large," he commented dryly.

"The ring was given to the first earl by King Henry VIII," the earl replied, ignoring his son's remark. "I am certain Miss Aldridge will find it satisfactory."

The pomposity of the statement brought an ironic smile to Edward's lips. His parents were so blinded by their own archaic rules and traditions they could not even consider the notion of something different. His heart hung heavy with a great sense of failure, for he knew in that moment their opinion would never be swayed.

Nor would his. A business empire was the right course of action, the only way to ensure stability for future generations. Though it troubled him, Edward was determined to achieve this dream despite his parents' vehement objections.

"I will not marry Charlotte Aldridge and I can see that I am obviously wasting my breath trying to make you understand my reasons. You refuse to look beyond your own narrow, biased views of the world." Edward rose to his feet and squarely faced his parents. "Forgive me for upsetting you, Mother, Father. It was never my intention. However, since my presence clearly distresses you both, I shall take my leave and return to London."

The countess began dabbing at the corners of her eyes with her ever-present handkerchief, but one tear escaped and trailed from the corner of her eye down her cheek, then to her chin. She did not bother to brush it away. The earl refused to look directly at Edward, his expression dry and desolate.

There was nothing more to be said.

Heart heavy, Edward took his leave with a shallow bow, vaguely wondering how long it would be until he next set eyes upon his parents.

Charlotte stood in the shadows, staring at the empty doorway that Edward had just strode through on his way out of the house. She had come to the drawing room in search of Jonathan, wanting his opinion on her choice of a Christmas gift for Edward. But when she passed the drawing room doors and heard voices raised in anger, and then her name, she had pressed herself against the heavy wood and stayed to listen.

If only she had walked on!

Charlotte licked her dry lips. She still could not believe what she had just overheard. Edward had not only refused to even consider marriage to her, but he had defied and angered his parents in the process. Was she really so horrible?

She let out a nervous, painful grunt of anger. Of all the irony! She had come to Farmington Manor determined not to be forced into a marriage she did not want and instead found herself wanting a man who had no interest in her at all.

He did not want her. Charlotte's hands gripped into white-knuckled balls and her heart began thumping in a sharp rhythm inside her chest. The pain was worse than anything she had ever known. She stood completely still as a wave of nausea pulsed through her. This could not be happening!

Charlotte felt the tears burning, felt the thick lump build in her throat and could not stifle the sob that escaped. She backed away from the doorway, and scurried down the hall, running wildly until she found an empty room.

Breathing hard, she closed the door and locked it, then flopped onto the nearest chair, her legs suddenly too weak to support her. Her stomach roiled and she clenched her fist against her abdomen. She huddled into herself, surrounded by misery. Though she tried valiantly not to cry, she felt the cold, wet tears escape.

It could not end this way. The thought made her shaky, filled her with restless anger, made her want to scream. He had kissed her, he had held her, he had desired her. How could he not want her?

But apparently the intimacy between them meant nothing to him. How utterly humiliating. She would have made him a good wife. He needed a woman like her in his life. Someone who would challenge and interest him and make him laugh. Someone who would search beneath the proper stiffness he often assumed and bring out the boyish delight.

But it was not meant to be. Edward had rejected her, thoroughly and completely. How foolish she was to desperately want something that would never happen. Oh, Lord, Charlotte groaned inwardly, how would she ever find the courage to tell her grandfather what had happened?

And how could she possibly face the earl and countess? The pressure on her chest increased and she shivered. She wanted to run from the room, run from the house, run back to the safety and comfort of Quincy Court, yet Charlotte felt so frazzled she could barely put two thoughts together.

She took a steadying breath and tried to force herself to stay calm. Running away was not the answer. She had to stay and brazen it out, to act as if nothing was wrong, as if nothing was upsetting her.

She had her pride. It would somehow sustain her. She would face this calamity with courage and grace. No one must ever know how devastated she felt at this moment, no one must ever know how she had yearned for the affections of the one man who would not grant them.

Clearly, Edward was gone from the manor. Perhaps that was for the best. At least she would be spared the humiliation of facing him. How strange that she could love someone so deeply and hate him at the same time. Charlotte shivered, and a feeling like ice traveled up the back of her spine and settled in the pit of her stomach. She stared stonily ahead, unseeing, as a plan began to formulate in her mind.

"Tomorrow is Christmas Day," she whispered miserably, but Charlotte remembered that the Chambers sisters had said they would be departing the day after Christmas. She and grandfather could easily do the same without arousing any undue suspicion.

Two days. She could manage for two days. She fought to draw in air and promised herself she would not think about what she had shared with Edward. She would merely exist, hour by hour.

It was settled. Charlotte sighed heavily and the weariness of her emotions forced her eyes to close. As the darkness swirled around her, a painful feeling of desperate yearning invaded her soul and the need to release her grief was overwhelming. With a quivering cry, Charlotte pressed her face to the sleeve of her gown and wept openly.

She cried for a long time, cried until she had no more tears. When she was done, Charlotte rose to her feet. Standing tall, she squared her shoulders, stiffened her spine, shook out the creases of her gown and stuffed her damp handkerchief in her pocket.

Deliberately ignoring the way her heart was squeezing inside her chest, Charlotte left the room with her head held high, determined to never again allow thoughts of Edward Barringer to bring her to self-pity.

CHAPTER 4

Six Years Later,
London
December

"The newspapers have arrived, my lord."

Though Edward heard his secretary's voice clearly, he did not move a muscle to acknowledge the man's announcement. Instead, he continued to stand before the fireplace in his posh London business office, staring at the dancing flames as if mesmerized. Yet he did not really see the fire. His mind, and his vision, were far away, focused on the incredible turn of events that had suddenly turned his life upside down.

Several minutes passed. Someone cleared his throat sharply. Edward finally turned and saw his secretary, Mr. Crenshaw, standing in the doorway, his gaze down, his arms filled with newspapers. His normally pale complexion was suffused with color.

"Put them on my desk, Crenshaw," Edward instructed. "And make certain to tell anyone who calls that I am busy. I want no one admitted to my office. No one."

"As you wish, my lord."

The clerk bustled out, leaving Edward to wonder how truly bad the newspaper stories were to put his normally reliable assistant in such a state of agitation. Why the man had even reverted to bowing several times in a nervous fit before quitting the room.

Exasperation flared, but swiftly died. It was hardly fair to blame Crenshaw for this current mess, especially because it was a disaster of a personal nature. Though Edward realized when all was said and done, it might affect his business empire too.

Giving the desk, and the newspapers atop it, a wide berth, Edward crossed to the opposite side of the room. He lifted a crystal decanter, positioned on a small mahogany table, and poured himself a full glass of whiskey. Never in his life had he gotten drunk before noon, but today might be an exception.

Lips set in a grim line, he took a long swallow. The intense burn engulfed his throat and stomach, then spread throughout the rest of his limbs. He finished the drink, then refilled the glass.

Unwittingly, his gaze traveled to his desk. The newspapers lay neatly stacked in the center of the polished wood, awaiting his review. Swirling the contents of his glass with a circular motion of the wrist, Edward contemplated those papers for several long minutes, wondering what they had written about him.

Well, there was only one way to find the answer to that pressing question. Edward set his whiskey glass aside and purposefully crossed the room. He reached for the top paper, snapping it to attention between his hands. His eyes quickly scanned the front page, though he knew in his heart he was dallying.

The news concerning Edward Barringer, ninth Earl of Worthington, would not appear on the front page. It would be on the sixth page, among the announcements of engagements and marriages. And the more lurid, juicy details of the scandal would be reported in the gossip column. More than likely as the lead story.

The scent of fresh ink and paper filled his nostrils as he turned the pages. It did not take long to find what he sought:

Mr. George Menton regrets to announce that the marriage of his daughter, Miss Henrietta Menton, to Edward Barringer, Earl of Worthington, will not take place as scheduled this coming Friday morning.

This announcement was only the first part of the blow. The real dirt was on the following page, where the sudden elopement of Miss Henrietta Menton to Mr. Harold Strider was reported. In amazing detail, considering the pair had just run off together in the middle of the night.

Edward refolded the paper and tossed it on his desk. No need to read about the speculation as to why Miss Menton preferred marrying a penniless poet instead of a wealthy, successful aristocrat.

However, Edward could not hold back his smile when he recalled the lines that said, according to a reliable household staff member, the bride had managed to take along her entire trousseau—the very same one that had been created for her marriage to the earl.

He had not realized that Henrietta could be so practical. Though he supposed in her new circumstances she could hardly afford not to be, for it was widely known that her new husband was something of a spendthrift who possessed little wealth. Perhaps this notoriety would aid in the selling of his poetry, but it certainly would not be enough to sustain the couple for very long.

Edward made a mental note to himself to make certain his household staff was always adequately compensated, ensuring that they would never be tempted to become the "reliable" source for any of these stories. Though he supposed the lack of pertinent, truthful information never really stopped the paper from printing a story. Especially one that featured the misfortunes of the members of the wealthy and privileged.

Lord what a mess! He had approached the arrangement of his marriage with the same thoughtful, precise attitude he used to run his business. Before he made a decision, he analyzed it thoroughly, with detached, tempered emotions so as not to be unduly influenced by sentiment or greed. It was a process that had brought him incredible success and few failures.

George Menton had garnered a massive fortune in mining. His family background was humble, yet genteel. Edward admired his business acumen and his dedication to both his work and his family. They had met, ironically enough, after both pulled their financial support from a mining operation that had showed signs of failure.

In hindsight, it had been Menton who first suggested the union with his eldest daughter, but he had been uncharacteristically subtle in his matchmaking attempts. After all, Edward was an earl and men of his class seldom married outside of it, especially when there was no financial need for such an arrangement.

Yet Menton had shrewdly realized that Edward was not an ordinary member of the aristocracy. With him, anything was possible. And thus the mutual respect and close business relationship the two men shared gradually shifted into a social relationship as well and Henrietta Menton entered Edward's life.

Henrietta was a pretty, slender girl devoid of an abundance of womanly curves, which was Edward's preferred style. Though she lacked an impressive family lineage, he thought she was the embodiment of female English refinement. She had been raised with every financial advantage, educated in the finest boarding schools in Europe to be a lady, traveled extensively to complete and polish her manners, and it showed.

Whenever Edward was with her, Henrietta was fashionably and flatteringly dressed, friendly, yet restrained in her conversation, and modest and demure in her actions. A dainty English flower, with pale blond hair, deep blue eyes and a steady temperament.

The ideal wife for an earl.

Yet as he reminisced, Edward recalled several times after their engagement was announced when Henrietta's face was shuttered and unreadable, her manner distracted and withdrawn. He had not been able to spend a great deal of time with her before the wedding and he attributed this occasional behavior to her natural shyness. He thought it would pass once they were married.

Oh, hell, the truth was he had barely thought

about her at all. Certainly not as a woman. She was merely a means to an end, the reward of an excellently negotiated business deal. As he searched within himself, taking responsibility for his part in this fiasco, Edward admitted his biggest mistake was not bothering to take into account Henrietta's feelings and desires.

Edward was looking for contentment and friendship in a marriage. Apparently Henrietta had been searching for something entirely different: love. And she had been smart enough to realize that he would never love her, at least not the way that some men loved their wives.

Perhaps she had done them both a favor by finding a way out of the marriage. But did she have to do so in such a public, humiliating manner?

The sound of thunder growling and clapping, and the bursts of intermittent rain drew Edward's attention away from his melancholy thoughts. He returned to the small mahogany table and picked up his whiskey glass, then went to the windows, opening the center window a few inches, hoping the clean smell of the winter rain would help clear his head.

Alas, it did not, but the cold felt invigorating.

The hesitant knock on his office door was followed by a timid murmur.

"My lord, I do beg your pardon—"

"I said no visitors, Mr. Crenshaw," Edward barked out in a forceful tone. "And I meant it."

"Don't bite the poor man's head off," a familiar masculine voice exclaimed. "He tried valiantly to stop me, but I was having none of it. I told him repeatedly I am not a visitor. I am family."

Despite his mood, which could be described as a miserable mix of despair, anger and misgivings, Edward found himself smiling.

"Hello, Jonathan." He went forward to grasp his brother's outstretched hand and let himself be pulled into a fierce hug.

"I came the moment I heard," Jonathan whispered. Edward pulled back and gave his brother another muted smile. "So, it's all over Town?"

"More or less." Jonathan removed his coat and a shower of cold droplets spattered on the floor. Though it was a task far beneath his duties, Mr. Crenshaw took the sopping wet garment and hung it on a nearby brass coat rack. Then he wisely disappeared.

"I imagine my enemies are celebrating and toasting with glee over my recent misfortune?" Edward asked, though he was uncertain if he really wanted to hear a truthful answer.

Jonathan drew back a pace. "You have far fewer enemies than you may think," he replied. "Those who truly know you are genuinely concerned about your well-being, and as for the rest . . ." Jonathan's voice trailed off, then he shrugged. "They can all rot."

Edward gave his brother a wry smile. The gossip must indeed be scathing if Jonathan was making light of it. Still, it was a relief to hear the truth from someone he could trust. It was also a relief not to have to pretend to be stoic and uncaring over the matter.

"I have learned these past few years that men in business as well as men who enjoy the life of an idle aristocrat share many traits, among them the ability to find great pleasure at a colleague's misfortune," Edward said with a trace of bitterness.

"You are hardly the first man in the world to have misjudged a woman," Jonathan insisted. "Nor will you be the last."

"I might not be the first, but I am surely among the most foolish to be so publicly humiliated," Edward said with a sneer. "Bloody hell, I was nearly left standing at the altar, thrown over for a man who has neither a title or a fortune, nor the means to ever acquire either." He lifted the pile of the newspapers off his desk and then threw them down in disgust. "The *Times* even felt it was enough of a noteworthy event to mention. Lord only knows what fun the scandal rags have made of it. I fear I do not possess a strong enough stomach to read them all and find out."

Jonathan shrugged again. "Do not flatter yourself, brother," he said. "Not everyone in England is all that interested in your affairs. Truth be told, you are known to be a rather boring fellow, with an unenviable reputation for being stodgy *and* straightlaced."

"Which is precisely what makes the scandal even more entertaining," Edward countered, his mouth twisting into a grimace.

Jonathan watched him speculatively. "Did she break your heart?"

"No. Merely wounded my pride." Edward was quiet for a moment, focusing his gaze on the rain that pelted one of the nearby windows. "I'll admit I did not know her very well, but I liked her. She was never silly or giddy, like so many young debutantes one meets these days. Whenever we were together, we were always able to converse on a wide variety of topics, anything from art and music to architecture and history.

"Her observations were thoughtful and perceptive and I believed we were slowly building a rapport. But what assured me most about our future life together was my belief that Henrietta was a sensible young woman."

Jonathan moved closer and set a comforting hand on Edward's shoulder. "Well, she was sensible enough not to marry you, especially when she was in love with someone else."

Edward was momentarily taken aback to hear the words spoken aloud. Henrietta had been in love with another man while engaged to him. And even worse, Edward had been blissfully unaware of it. She was the woman he had chosen to spend the rest of his life with, believing they were a well-suited pair, yet he had gotten it all terribly wrong. How could he have been so blind?

"If you tell me 'tis all for the best, I shall punch you in the nose," Edward told his brother, attempting to lighten the mood.

"It is for the best. And if it makes you feel any better, go ahead and punch me." Jonathan slowly lowered himself to the chair on the other side of Edward's desk. "I think living the rest of your life without love is a very sad business. You deserve better, Edward."

Edward was humbled by his brother's support. Leave it to Jonathan to get to the heart of the matter with such lethal efficiency.

"I feel like such a fool," Edward admitted. "As I look back upon it now, I realize there were clues suggesting that Henrietta might have been coerced by her family into accepting my offer. I imagine she must have felt manipulated and helpless. But I never bothered to pursue the matter with her."

"I suppose you could have asked her," Jonathan said. "Based on what you have said about her, I have a feeling she might have confessed the truth."

"Maybe I did not want to hear the truth," Edward muttered.

He paced the floor, back and forth between the windows, and tried not to think too hard upon the matter. It was simply too distressing.

"You need to come home, Edward," Jonathan suggested. "It will do you good to get away from London, away from the gossip."

"Home? To Farmington Manor?" Edward ceased pacing. He blinked his eyes and tried to focus. "Why go back? So Mother may gloat at my misfortune? I imagine that will lift her spirits enormously."

"Edward, that is unkind and untrue."

Edward sighed. Jonathan was wrong. His mother would delight in hearing that his fiancée had jilted him days before the intended nuptials. It was exactly the type of perverse revenge that would bring her pleasure, a just punishment for all the supposed wrongs he had heaped upon her head, for all the humiliation she was reported to be suffering by his "defection."

For years Edward had been relieved that Jonathan knew none of the ugly details concerning the rift between himself and their parents. But at times such as this, his brother's lack of knowledge was a real hindrance. For if Jonathan knew all, he would know what he was suggesting was ludicrous.

"Returning home will serve no useful purpose," Edward stated flatly. "Besides, I do not want to appear so wounded by this incident that I am forced to flee Town rather than face my business associates or partake of any of the social events of the *ton*. It smacks of cowardice."

Jonathan's snort was loud, yet elegant. "Then why did you tell Crenshaw to admit no one to your office?"

That drew a reluctant, embarrassed grin from Edward. "I am not hiding."

His brother kindly did not challenge the remark they both knew was a lie.

"Come home with me, Edward. It has been years since you visited the estate," Jonathan said, his voice quiet but unmistakably reproachful. "Now that Father is gone, you are the earl and everyone depends upon you. You support us all financially, but 'tis important for the tenants and servants to know that you care enough about the estate to take a personal interest. And I truly believe Mother would be quite pleased to see you."

"And I know the opposite to be true." Edward looked at the ceiling so his brother would not see the exasperation in his eyes. "After years of silence, Mother and I have finally managed to form an uneasy truce. Now is certainly not the time to upset it. The very last thing I need in my life is more female drama."

"She misses you," Jonathan insisted.

She wishes me in hell. Fortunately, Edward caught himself before he spoke his thoughts aloud. "I send her a letter every month, telling her the same inane things in the same formal, distant and proper tone. She replies in kind." A bitter half smile touched his lips. "It has become so routine that the paragraphs practically write themselves. 'Tis only the order of them that varies each month. And of course, our reporting of the current weather changes with the seasons."

He could tell by Jonathan's puzzled expression that his brother was having a hard time grasping all the implications of that statement.

"I knew Mother and Father were hardly enamored with your decision to work, but we all know it saved the family. Father's death occurred so soon after your business was established. We would have been in dire straits without the infusion of funds you were able to supply to the family coffers and stave off the creditors." Jonathan stared across the desk at him. "Forgive me for not realizing that things were still so strained between you and Mother."

Edward heaved a weary sigh. Ever since he had stormed from the house in defiance of his parents six years ago, he knew exactly what he wanted: to be rich and successful beyond anyone's expectation, to own more profitable businesses than any other man, more property than the queen, to create an empire that exceeded all others and prove, without any question, his worth to the parents who had doubted his choice. He had spent every day in single-minded determination toward successfully accomplishing that goal.

It hurt deeply that his mother refused to acknowledge his success. But that was not the entire reason for the chasm between them. She had no difficulty spending the generous allowance he deposited in the bank for her each quarter.

She apparently had come to terms with his highly unfashionable business career by telling the extended family and her friends that his interest in finance was merely a hobby. Amazingly, this seemed perfectly credible to them. Clearly, they never read the financial section of the newspapers.

"It is more than my chosen profession that distresses our mother," Edward admitted.

Jonathan opened his mouth, then closed it. "I know you quarreled after Father's funeral."

Edward's chin shot up in surprise. "Did she tell you about it?"

"No, I heard your voices that day, raised in anger, but could not distinguish the words that were spoken."

"Thank God for that small mercy." Edward closed his eyes, remembering the bitter hurt and anger in his mother's voice, the malice of her words. It was so difficult, so painful reliving those moments. "Trust me, our mother is far happier if I stay away from her."

Jonathan's mouth twitched at one corner. "She was distraught, overcome with grief and fear. We had just buried Father. Of course she was emotional. 'Tis to be expected."

Edward swallowed hard. "She accused me of killing him."

"What? Father died of a heart condition. The doctors insisted there was nothing that could have been done to save him."

"She said I brought him to the brink of ruin, that I knowingly drove him to despair," Edward choked. "That I had abandoned my responsibilities, disgraced the family, had in essence broken his heart. She blamed me for his death and stated most emphatically that she would never forgive me."

Saying the words out loud brought on a rush of feelings. The deep sadness. The horrendous guilt. A part of him had known it was grief that had driven his mother to lash out, yet another part had also given credence to her words.

Ten months. Within ten months of his refusing to follow his parents' dictates and marry Charlotte Aldridge, his father had died. Who knew, perhaps his actions *had* contributed to the heart condition that took the earl's life?

Edward remembered vividly how he felt when he heard the news. Grief-stricken and in shock, he had returned home to bury his father and assume the title. He had just completed his first major real estate deal, and was poised to acquire a very profitable cotton mill, but the elation of his financial triumph was overshadowed by his personal loss and pain.

When his mother had asked for a private word with him after the funeral, he had ironically expected her to pressure him to abandon his business interests and become a proper nobleman. Instead, she had accused him of causing his father's sudden attack.

The guilt, though deeply buried, was still present after all these years, tearing at his gut and ripping at his mind. Was it finally time to try to put these demons to rest?

"You should have told me about Mother's outrageous accusations," Jonathan admonished.

Edward shook his head. "It would have been unfair to pull you into the middle of it. Though we never spoke of it, I think Mother felt the same way. If you knew, you would be forced to take sides, and we each needed you too much."

"Well, now that I know I am determined to mend the rift." Jonathan's face was solemn, his gaze piercing.

Edward nearly winced at the idea. The very last thing he wanted was to drag his brother into this mess. "'Tis best to leave it alone. Your involvement might cause Mother's enmity toward me to increase rather than dissipate."

A deep frown furrowed Jonathan's brow. "That's a valid point. I can be of little help to you unless Mother continues to believe I am a neutral party."

"Jonathan—"

"Don't argue." Jonathan rose to his feet. A determined light filled his eyes. "It will be Christmas in a few weeks. 'Tis the perfect time for you to be at home, celebrating the holiday with your family and friends. I shall write to Mother today and tell her to expect us both at the end of the week. Promise me you will at least consider it?"

Edward answered with a noncommittal inclination of his head, but apparently the gesture was enough to appease his brother. Jonathan sat back down in his chair, then reached for one of the newspapers on Edward's desk.

His brother seemed instantly engrossed in the front-page article, but Edward suspected Jonathan was in fact giving him time to carefully consider this suggestion. And also preparing a rebuttal when Edward voiced his strong objections.

The truth was, Edward knew he needed a change. He certainly couldn't concentrate on work. He was restless, annoyed, on edge and for the first time in many, many years, uncertain of himself. He had always had the ability to focus intently on a task until it was successfully accomplished. But his goal of becoming a married man was most definitely unattainable, thanks to his disappearing fiancée.

Whenever he made a business decision he analyzed it thoroughly, considered every angle, every possible outcome. He did so with fact, and reason and experience. Sometimes with gut instinct. But never with emotion, because it was such an unpredictable factor, such an unreliable measure of a situation.

This approach had made him rich, had built him an empire of money and power, had given him the freedom to make choices in his life that few people had ever dreamed they could. *But has it made you happy?*

The thought came out of nowhere, shocking him back to reality. He walked to the window again and stared out at the rain. Perhaps what he needed was to finally settle the past, to come to terms with all the obligations of his heritage and somehow reconcile them with the man he had now become, the man who some considered an enormous success, based on his impressive bank balance.

Farmington Manor. The memory of his boyhood home whispered softly through his head. The beautiful Tudor-style mansion that stood on hundreds of acres of rolling hills, dense woods and tumbling streams. The place he had always loved, where he had always felt safe and happy. The reason he had sacrificed so much and worked so hard, ensuring that this glorious piece of his family history would be preserved for future generations.

Perhaps Jonathan was right. Maybe it finally was time to go home.

CHAPTER 5

The day was sunny and cold. The trees were bare of leaves, the grass a straw-colored brown. The air smelled clean, crisp and unspoiled. The peaceful quiet of the countryside was broken only by the sounds of nature: the chirping of a winter sparrow, the trickle of an icy stream, the rustling of the wind through the stiff brush.

Edward reined in his mount on the high ridge above the valley and gazed down at the structure below. Sunlight glistened off the stone facade and reflected off the many faceted glass windows. It gave the place an eerie, otherworldly appearance, as though it were somehow frozen in time.

Farmington Manor. Edward's heart skipped a beat. The growing sense of unease he had felt since leaving Town early that morning intensified. What had initially seemed like a plausible idea at the beginning of the week was not nearly as appealing in reality at the end of the week.

Though not superstitious by nature, Edward could not totally dismiss the strong premonition that assaulted him. Trouble lay ahead. Why even the air felt charged with tension, much like the swirling winds announcing the coming of a violent storm.

If not for the man by his side, he might very well have turned his horse in the opposite direction and ridden directly back to the railroad station. Yet having come this far, Edward knew Jonathan would not allow him to retreat until he had set foot inside the front doors of the manor and spoken with their mother.

The uneventful and surprisingly swift train ride from London had lulled Edward into a false sense of ease, had pushed aside the possibility that true difficulties might await him. Jonathan had taken care of all the trip details, easing the burden further, making certain that a fine pair of horses and a luggage coach were waiting for them at the station.

The brothers had elected to finish the journey on horseback, taking advantage of the opportunity for some fresh air. Alas, the ride also gave Edward an opportunity to think upon his upcoming reunion with his mother, and those thoughts were far from pleasant.

"It won't be long now," Jonathan announced, as if sensing his brother's reluctance. "Try to cease looking like a fox run to ground."

Edward regarded his sibling with a jaundiced eye before twitching the reins of his mount and moving his horse down the long hill. Jonathan imitated his actions and fell in step behind him.

They took a well-used path along the edge of the forest, avoiding the bustle of the local village that was clearly visible through the trees. Edward was pleased to note that the rambling village of his boyhood was no longer a sleepy backwater but a thriving town, thanks in part to his investments in the area. He saw several new shops, a tavern and an inn. These new business, as well as the older ones, looked well maintained and prosperous.

"Hampstead seems busy," Edward commented. "The main thoroughfare is crowded with carts and carriages and it isn't even market day."

"Ah, yes, some of the locals even complain about traffic on the roads and a stifling feeling that overshadows the refreshing country climate now that we have new shops, as well as a third tavern," Jonathan replied. "Makes one wonder how they would react if they ever set foot in London."

They moved beyond the village and through the forest. Edward could almost feel his blood leap with recognition as they came into the clearing. Lifting his head, he scanned the horizon. His breath caught. Edward had forgotten the sheer grandeur of the estate. Acres and acres of finely landscaped parkland lay stretched before him, as far as the eye could see. Even in their dormant winter state they were beautiful.

He was struck with an unexpected bolt of melancholy when that special feeling of homecoming hit hard. Bloody hell, he had missed it all much more than he had realized, and yet in order to endure the loss, he had over the years suppressed a deepseated longing to return.

When they finally reached the long front drive, Edward deliberately slowed the pace of his horse. He ambled along, allowing his senses to absorb the achingly familiar sights and sounds that seemed to soothe his weary soul.

They passed beneath arched gates and Edward caught sight of the family crest emblazoned on the wrought iron. Thoughts of his father swarmed his mind and he turned, meeting his brother's eyes.

Jonathan smiled encouragingly. "'Tis the same as it has always been," he said quietly. "Lying almost dormant, waiting for you to return."

Edward had convinced himself that he was prepared for this, but he suddenly realized he was not prepared at all. Aware that he had been leaning forward on his horse, he sat back in his saddle, trying not to let his irritation get the better of him.

It was then that he noticed the figure of a woman walking along the side of the house. She followed the stone path that ran beneath the first-floor windows, her stride long and purposeful as she rounded the corner and headed for the front door. However, she must have heard their approach because she stopped suddenly, pivoted and turned toward them.

With relief, Edward realized it was not his mother, but a considerably younger woman. Still, there was something that struck him as oddly familiar about her. She was tall and slender, yet the fine red wool cloak she wore could not conceal her well-endowed bosom. Her features were distinctly aristocratic. Delicately arched brows and lush lashes framed a pair of large eyes. Edward was not close enough to verify their color, but a flash of memory told him they were green.

"Charlotte Aldridge," he muttered in an astonished voice.

Jonathan, riding beside him, apparently heard the remark. "Ahh, yes, 'tis Charlotte. I was uncertain if she and Lord Reginald would be joining us this year. They visit often, but not usually during Christmas. Apparently they will be staying for the holidays, along with many of the usual family and friends. Isn't that splendid?"

It had been a long, stuffy carriage ride, unusually bumpy and uncomfortable, even though the coach had been one of her grandfather's finest, a plush conveyance made for long journeys. Somehow her grandfather had slept through most of the trip, forcing Charlotte to admit her discomfort was probably not due to the coach or the condition of the road, but rather her unease over the destination at the end of it.

Farmington Manor. Miraculously, she had visited the estate numerous times after that first disastrous Christmas holiday, but never again in December. The countess had been generous with her invitations, and after realizing that Edward was never in residence, Charlotte had agreed to accompany her grandfather whenever he asked her to join him.

Somehow, visiting during the middle of a budding spring or spending a delightful summer month as a houseguest had a healing effect on Charlotte. Farmington Manor was a beautiful estate, with an almost magical charm. When the atmosphere was thick with the perfume of flowers, the fountains spouting an unending stream of water and every blade of grass meticulously groomed, the memories of the winter cold and those stolen kisses beneath the mistletoe were forgotten.

Yet the usual peace and delight she experienced when first arriving at the manor was absent today.

Instead, a headache had plagued her since lunch. Craving exercise and hoping the fresh air and sunshine would ease the pain of her pounding head, Charlotte set off on a walk.

"Shall I accompany you?" her maid asked. "Or would you like me to see if any of the other ladies are interested in taking some fresh air?"

"I prefer to be alone," Charlotte admitted. "If I stay on the grounds within sight of the house, it should be acceptable for me to venture off on my own."

Realizing it was never a good idea to offend the countess on the first day of her visit, Charlotte skirted the edge of the terraced gardens. She followed the graveled path that led to the stables, keeping herself in clear view of the manor, but avoiding the windows so others would not readily see her. She waved cheerily to the stable lads, but did not stop to admire the horses, since she carried no treats with which to spoil them.

By the time she had walked the full length of the rear courtyard, her headache was much improved. Feeling infinitely better, Charlotte followed the stone path around the side of the house and headed for the front door.

The crunching sounds of horse's hooves on the main drive caught her attention. She turned to investigate and beheld two finely dressed gentlemen on horseback coming up the drive. One of them waved. She immediately concluded they were either afternoon visitors coming to pay a call or additional houseguests.

It was hardly her role to greet them, yet it would be rude to disappear inside the house, since they had obviously seen her. Charlotte smoothed the front of her red wool cloak and patiently waited for them to arrive at the front portico.

The sun was positioned at a low angle, almost directly behind the men's heads. The small brim of her fashionable bonnet offered no protection, forcing Charlotte to squint into the bright glare. It made little difference; she still could not see their faces. With a small sigh of annoyance, Charlotte lifted her arm and positioned it over her head, shielding her eyes from the harsh light.

The riders came into clear focus. Tensing, Charlotte squinted harder, adjusted her arm and told herself the light was playing tricks with her vision. She easily recognized the rider on the left as Jonathan Barringer, and for an instant she thought the other man was his older brother, Edward.

That, of course, was ridiculous.

Though he was now the earl, he never came to Farmington Manor. If he did, Charlotte would not.

She moved forward a few paces, out of the harsh glare, then froze. *It was impossible!* Unable to contain the gasp of surprise that escaped her lips, or ignore the bolt of chilling dismay that ran through her body, Charlotte closed her eyes and shook her head sharply, willing the unpleasant vision to go away.

But when she opened her eyes, he was still there, regally perched upon his horse, coming ever closer. *Edward Barringer, Earl of Worthington!*

"What in the name of all that is holy is he doing here?" Charlotte asked herself in alarm.

There was a moment of sheer panic when Charlotte thought her grandfather might have planned this, but she quickly realized that she had been the one, not her grandfather, to insist on accepting the countess's holiday invitation this year.

Charlotte knew the countess and her son were estranged. She had been told, by several very reliable sources, that the earl never visited the manor.

And yet here he was.

For an instant she was paralyzed by something that felt like fear. It seemed to take all of her strength just to keep breathing. The sight of the earl reminded Charlotte vividly of the pain she had felt at his rejection of her, but even more distressing, it reminded her that long ago she had possessed the capacity to love unconditionally, uninhibitedly and recklessly.

And now she no longer did.

Charlotte told herself it did not matter. Six years ago she had been a foolish young girl, unaware of the disappointments and heartaches of life. Now she knew better.

Yet try as she might, Charlotte had never been able to forget how it had felt to be in his arms. The gentle erotic pressure of his mouth on hers, the compelling pleasure of his kisses, the knee-weakening promise of utter fulfillment. With sheer force of will and strong determination, she had consigned the memory to her past, burying it deep, but it had haunted and shaped her future.

For six years she secretly feared he was the reason she had never been able to accept any of the several worthy men who had courted her and begged for her hand in marriage. If only she understood why it had been so different kissing him. Then perhaps she could at last move forward with her life.

The riders were coming closer. In a matter of

moments they would be at the front portico. Pulling herself together, Charlotte straightened her spine and thrust back her shoulders. Then she lifted her chin and met the earl's gaze, staring at him with cool disregard.

At first his face was blank, as if he was having difficulty remembering exactly who she was or why she might seem familiar to him. Boldly, Charlotte took a step forward, noting his color heightened.

Apparently, he did remember her. Yet judging by the astonished expression on his face, it was clear he had not expected to see her.

The years had been kind to him. He was still an attractive man, sleek and elegant in his finely tailored riding clothes. The dark hair peeking out from beneath his beaver hat was thick, yet highlighted by a few streaks of silver at the temples.

Age and maturity had added character to his face along with a potent masculine virility. Charlotte was angry with herself for noticing.

"Good afternoon, Charlotte." Jonathan's greeting was warm and friendly, a reflection of his good humor and innate kindness.

"Hello, Jonathan. How wonderful to see you again," she replied truthfully.

"Miss Aldridge." The earl lifted his hand to his hat and tipped the brim. His face was impassive, save for the frown indentations between his brows.

The contrast between the two brothers could not have been more striking. Jonathan was all relaxed smiles and joviality while the earl's manner was unbending, lacking even the merest hint of a smile on his lips or in his eyes.

"My lord," Charlotte replied. Good manners

dictated that she should curtsey, but Charlotte discovered she could not bend her knee to him.

The earl seemed on the verge of saying something more, then checked himself and mumbled softly beneath his breath. His horse stomped and snorted impatiently, but he controlled the animal effortlessly with his strong thighs.

Where were the footmen? Or the stable hands? The normally efficient servants were nowhere to be seen. Charlotte wished she was close enough to the front door to pull the bell, but she was not and it was too presumptuous even for her to bellow for another man's servants in front of him.

"I'll go and see what's happened to the staff," Jonathan said with an easy grin. "These horses deserve a fine meal and a long rest. As do the riders."

Before Charlotte could protest, Jonathan turned his horse and trotted from the forecourt.

Drat! She was just beginning to get her nerves under control. The last thing she needed was to be left alone with the earl. She briefly considered declaring herself chilled and rushing for the front door, but acting the coward went against her nature.

Endurance and patience, two of the great assets of life. She had always possessed the former in abundance and was learning to court the latter. She certainly had need of both emotions at this moment.

In one fluid motion, the earl dismounted from his horse, standing a mere hairsbreadth away from Charlotte. She glanced discreetly at him and found herself looking up. It made her feel slight, almost delicate, an unusual occurrence for a woman of her height.

He was taller than she remembered, his shoulders broader. He bore himself very straight, like a soldier, even when he made a rigid half bow in her direction. Fortunately, he seemed not to notice the way she stiffened at his proximity.

"Did you have a pleasant journey?" Charlotte asked, thankful the words came without effort, without real thought. She was acutely aware of him standing but a few yards away, large, lean and vital, his gaze on her.

"Yes, thank you." He shifted the reins methodically from one gloved hand to the other, then back again. "The weather seems pleasant enough, though there is a definite chill in the air."

The conversation continued along the same vein for several moments. Charlotte was amazed that they were able to indulge in small talk, yet by some unspoken agreement they had each decided it was preferable to waiting in awkward silence for Jonathan and the stable hands to appear.

After what seemed like hours, when in reality had only been a few minutes, Jonathan returned with two eager young lads on his heels. They apologized for not coming sooner, bowed respectfully, then led the horses away.

Charlotte unintentionally found herself standing beside the earl when they reached the front door. It opened a mere second after his loud knock. As they stepped into the marble foyer, a ripple of something passed through him, but his expression was a mystery to her. She could read nothing in his handsome face.

"My lord! Welcome home!" The usually stuffy, proper family butler, Harris, was grinning from ear to ear. In all the years she had been to the manor, Charlotte had never seen him so animated.

"Thank you, Harris. 'Tis good to be here." The earl's mouth was faintly smiling, his expression one of self-directed mockery. "'Tis good also to see you."

"Thank you, my lord." Harris grinned and bobbed his head enthusiastically, then signalled for the footman to come forward and lend assistance. Charlotte tried not to be impressed as she observed the earl interacting with the staff, calling each by name, asking after their health and their families.

"My lord, you've come back!" Mrs. Hobbins, the plump, white-haired housekeeper, came rustling across the polished marbled floors, the large ring of keys signifying her station in the household jingling loudly with each step. She skidded to a halt in front of the earl, barely stopping short of hugging him. "'Twill be a fine Christmas indeed, with you home to celebrate."

"I can hardly wait to feast on the Christmas goose, Mrs. Hobbins," the earl replied with a more relaxed smile. "Do you think you can persuade Cook to bake a few extra mince pies? They are my favorites, and as I recall the recipe is one passed down from your own family."

The housekeeper's face lit up with pride. "Aye, we will have mince pies on Christmas Eve *and* Christmas Day this year!"

The sudden sound of clattering footsteps drew all eyes to the top of the stairs. Charlotte half expected to see a bevy of servants pushing forward to catch a glimpse of the earl, but instead it was the countess who came into view.

Short, slender, with iron-gray hair and a pale complexion, the countess carried herself with the regal bearing of a queen. Her mouth was thin, set with grooves close to the edges of her lips, and a web of lines radiated from the corner of her eyes, none of which were caused by an overabundance of humor.

Despite the large number of people crowding into the foyer, there was barely a sound to be heard. Head high, the countess glided down the curved steps, halting when she reached mid-staircase. She lifted the quizzing glass she wore on a gold chain 'round her neck up to her left eye and peered through it.

"Is that you, Jonathan? I had not expected you to arrive until late tomorrow." She spoke in a bracing, faintly exasperated tone, pointedly addressing her younger son, yet all the while staring at the earl.

Charlotte saw the earl lean close to his brother and heard him whisper, "You *did* warn her I was coming?"

Jonathan's lips twisted. "She knows."

The earl made a faint nod of his head, but said nothing. They all waited for the older woman to complete her decent. Her back stiffened perceptibly when she reached the final step.

Jonathan moved forward, hesitated, then moved back, remaining at his brother's side. The countess let the quizzing glass she held drop down to her bosom, the gold chain it dangled from glittering in the sunlight.

"You are looking lovely this afternoon, Mother," Jonathan said. "That shade of blue becomes you."

She grinned briefly at her younger son, then glanced at the earl. No smile crossed her lips as she beheld her older son.

"Good afternoon, Madame." The earl bowed slightly, then met his mother's gaze without blinking.

"I must agree with my brother. You are indeed looking well."

She did not reply and her expression grew even more stony. Charlotte had never realized what a proud, humorless, almost morose woman the countess could be. For one absurd instant she was seized with the need to reach out and take the earl's hand. He seemed much in need of some comfort and support.

"If you care to rest before supper, I am certain Mrs. Hobbins has prepared your rooms," the countess said.

"Yes, my lady, all is ready." Mrs. Hobbins bit her lip. "Shall I have His Lordship's luggage brought to the earl's suite?"

The countess's jaw went slack. She looked from the housekeeper to her son, acute discomfort on her face.

"I prefer my usual rooms, Mrs. Hobbins," the earl said. "It will feel like even more of a homecoming for me if I reside in those chambers."

"Very good, my lord." The housekeeper sighed audibly with relief.

"Perhaps it would be best to adjourn to the parlor," Jonathan suggested.

"Would you care for tea?" Harris asked.

"Yes." Jonathan turned toward the countess. "Mother?"

"If you insist I shall come," the countess replied, tightening the shawl around her shoulders. "Will you join us, Miss Aldridge?"

For one wicked moment Charlotte was tempted. She suspected the high drama of watching the earl and countess interact was going to be much better than many theater productions she had attended.

"Thank you, no," she finally answered, good manners winning out over curiosity. This was a family matter and none of her concern. "I will see you all later this evening."

The countess turned. Back ramrod straight, she marched from the foyer. The earl did not immediately follow, but instead spoke to his butler. As she walked slowly toward the staircase, Charlotte clearly heard his orders.

"Bring a large decanter of whiskey with the tea, Harris. I have a feeling I'm going to be needing something stronger to make it through this afternoon."

CHAPTER 6

As he entered the parlor, Edward noted that it had been refurbished, and judging by the quality and opulence of the furnishings it had been a significant expense. How bloody ironic! His mother might vehemently object to the way he made his fortune, but she clearly had no reservations when it came to spending it.

They took their seats on the pair of tapestry sofas that faced each other in front of the hearth. A roaring fire blazed there, keeping out the wintery chill. But, alas, it offered no protection from the coldness of his mother's glare.

Edward sat opposite the countess, leaving Jonathan to make a choice. His brother barely hesitated as he settled himself beside him. A sardonic grin touched Edward's mouth. Jonathan had pledged his support and he meant to keep his word.

Edward appreciated the gesture, especially with his mother looking at him like she wanted to rend him limb from limb. No small task for so slight a woman.

"There is no need to act as if I am here to steal the silver, Madame," Edward said, summoning a smile. "Or that you wish to set the hounds on me."

"I do not believe we keep hounds anymore," Jonathan said with a nervous laugh. "We haven't been fox hunting in years and years. I'm afraid most of the dogs on the estate are spoiled pets, eager to lick your hand in exchange for a tasty morsel or a good scratch behind the ears. Even Father's wolfhounds, those enormous beasts, wiggle frantically for attention whenever anyone is near."

The countess scowled, not at all amused by her younger son. "You are the earl, Edward, now that your father is gone. The silver belongs to you. As do the dogs." She offered him a smile that held more than a hint of bitterness.

Edward forced himself not to retort. He had learned over the years that treading lightly was the best way to deal with a woman's resentment.

Harris arrived, with several liveried footman in tow. They carried in tea and scones, crumpets with butter and jam, pastries and finger sandwiches, plus the requested whiskey decanter and two crystal goblets.

The countess's brows raised at the last item, but she made no comment. At her command, the servants withdrew. She busied herself pouring tea and arranging the light repast on individual plates. Edward saw that even at such short notice Cook had tried to include as many of his favorite treats as possible, yet somehow his mother managed to place only the ones he did not care for on his dish.

He supposed he should feel flattered his mother could recall what he liked, even if she remembered only to deny it to him. Edward ignored the cup of tea she had poured, placing it untouched in front of him, and eyed the whiskey decanter.

"I thought today was to have been your wedding day," the countess said in a quelling tone. "And instead you have come to Farmington Manor."

Edward's shoulder's went rigid. Despite his resolve not to, he felt himself flushing. "As a courtesy, I sent you a message explaining that the ceremony had been called off, even though you were not planning on attending the wedding."

"'Tis difficult for me to travel at this time of the year." The countess sniffed with disdain. "Besides, I had no desire to meet the young woman you had chosen, who in my opinion was nothing more than a title hunter. She was no doubt an ambitious miss, ill-bred, graceless and unsuitable, without consequence or connections. I would never have approved or accepted such a creature into my family, one who would allow her father to try to buy her way into the upper classes by purchasing an earl for his daughter."

Edward hooded his gaze. "I cannot understand why you would object, Mother. Henrietta was gifted with an impressive dowry. You yourself suggested that marriage was the only way for us to pay off all the considerable family debts and regain solvency after generations of financial mismanagement and extravagant living."

The countess gave him a furious glare. "How dare you compare the two?" Fiercely, she set her teacup in its saucer. "Your father and I only wanted the best for you in marriage. We chose an aristocratic young woman with a flawless background, possessing a substantial fortune, who had been raised to take her proper place in society. We would never have done what you were so eager to do, allow your title to be purchased like a trophy by an ill-suited, inferior family."

"My wealth exceeded George Menton's," Edward returned mildly. "Money was hardly the major factor when contracting the union between myself and his daughter."

The countess recoiled as if he had struck her. She stared at him in astonishment, obviously trying to absorb the truth of his blunt pronouncement. "And you are proud and boastful of that fact? You choose to defy your father and me by refusing to marry Charlotte Aldridge and yet you would willingly enter into marriage with a—"

"They wanted you to marry Charlotte?" Jonathan interrupted. "Is that what started the quarrel in the first place?"

"Yes!" the countess exclaimed in a hoarse voice. "Six years ago he refused to marry Miss Aldridge. Everyone agreed it would be an excellent match, but your brother would not even consider the union. What a wretched Christmas that became! It was mortifying for us to have to explain to Lord Reginald that an offer would not be forthcoming.

"Fortunately, Lord Reginald is a gracious man of good breeding, and he forgave us. He has never again spoken of the incident, not even after Edward announced he would wed a woman who would never be able to ease the smell of commerce from her person."

A muscle in Edward's jaw worked visibly. "Though she might not have been born with blood that was blue enough to satisfy you, Miss Menton was every inch a lady," he declared forcefully, his tone taking on a lethal softness. "She dressed as a lady, spoke as a lady and acted as a lady. And since you never had the good fortune to meet her, I must insist that you refrain from assassinating her character."

"Her character? There is no need for me to comment upon it," the countess said scorchingly. "Miss Menton demonstrated her true breeding to one and all with her actions, running off and eloping with a nobody days before your wedding. She might have fooled you by dressing in expensive, fashionable clothes and speaking in sweet, dulcet tones, but blood will tell in the end."

Edward rose from his seat and gave a disgruntled sigh. He reached for the whiskey decanter, splashing the amber liquid into two glasses. His mother's words had bitten into him, striking at the core of his insecurity and hurt.

Silently, he handed Jonathan one of the goblets. Raising his arm in a salute, he said bitterly, "To Miss Menton and her new husband. May they live a long and happy life and be content in each other's company for the rest of their days."

Edward tilted his head and drained his glass. Jonathan, his brows drawing together in a puzzled frown, imitated his brother's actions.

The countess averted her gaze, apparently trying to hide her shock. She lifted her teacup and took a fortifying sip. Edward wished he possessed the nerve to ask her if she wanted a splash of whiskey mixed in with her tea, to settle her nerves.

The countess pressed her lips together and gave a stubborn sniff. "There is still hope for you to make a suitable marriage, Edward, if you decide to be sensible."

"Even with the smell of commerce on my person," he mocked, echoing her words.

"As I said, blood will tell in the end. This peculiar inclination you have to work is not widely known in our circles." In obvious irritation, the countess narrowed her penetrating gaze. "Though you may choose to deny it, you were raised with the expectation of nobility. I believe it would be best if we think upon this unfortunate matter with Miss Menton as a blessing."

"A blessing?" Astonishment shone in Jonathan's eyes. "That is a rather heartless remark, Mother."

"Nonsense." The countess's lips pursed into a sour expression. "Edward has been given yet another chance to make a proper marriage. I can only pray that he will not squander this opportunity."

Edward frowned. Part of him could not help feeling angry at his mother's cold attitude and expectation that he simply substitute a new bride, a *better* bride to replace the woman who had so recently duped him.

"The choice of a wife will remain solely my decision. I do not seek nor do I require your permission or approval, Madame," Edward replied without apology. It was essential that his mother realize he would not be manipulated in this matter.

"Forgive the interruption, my lady, but there is a crisis in the kitchen that requires your immediate attention."

They all turned to face the female who had entered the room. Edward was expecting to see one of the maids, but instead beheld a tiny, slender, shapely, strikingly pretty young woman with lively dark eyes and raven hair that was worn in an elegantly plaited and coiled chignon.

Her gown was subdued in color and style, slightly out-of-fashion, but made of quality fabric. She was not a common house servant, yet she was not a lady. Still, she bore herself with aristocratic grace that seemed to be bred into her very bones. Was she a poor relation of one of the houseguests?

"Thank you, Evelyn," the countess replied. "Tell Cook to wait for me in the dining room. I shall attend to this problem in a moment."

The younger woman curtsied and turned to leave, but Jonathan rushed forward.

"I am delighted to see you again, Miss Montgomery," he exclaimed. "And might I add, you are looking very fetching this afternoon."

"'Tis very kind of you to notice, Mr. Barringer," she replied with a shy smile. "It seems that whenever we chance to meet you remark upon my attire. I am beginning to wonder if you have an affinity for women's clothing."

Jonathan laughed with delight, and a glint of mischief lit his eyes. Edward moved to stand beside his brother.

"Cease harassing this poor young woman at once and introduce us, Jonathan," he demanded.

"I don't believe you have met Mother's companion, Miss Evelyn Montgomery," Jonathan responded obediently. "This is my older brother, the Earl of Worthington."

Miss Montgomery shot him a quick look of surprise. "My—my lord," she stammered in greeting. He glimpsed a hint of vulnerability in the dark depths of her eyes before she lowered them and sank into a graceful curtsey. "Forgive me for not properly greeting you."

Edward could only imagine what tales of horror his mother had related about him, for what else could explain the poor girl's sudden strain. Slightly embarrassed by her nervous reaction, Edward sought to put her at ease.

"I am very pleased to discover my mother has the company of such a fine young lady, Miss Montgomery," he said kindly. "I am sure you are of great help to her."

"I try."

"Do not be so modest, Evelyn," the countess said. "Your hands and feet are always kept very busy, but never more so than during a house party. I do not know how I would possibly manage without you."

"'Tis lovely to have the extra company, especially during the holidays," Miss Montgomery said. "Christmas is always such a joyful, magical time of year."

Edward was pleased Miss Montgomery appeared content in her position and pleased also that his mother seemed to appreciate her companion's work. In his experience, all too often a lady's companion was a drab, shapeless creature, an invisible female who lived and worked in the households of wealthy aristocratic families as little more than an underpaid servant. He decided he would consult the account books before he left the estate to ensure that Miss Montgomery was being adequately compensated.

Edward smiled charmingly. "We must make certain not to overwork you, Miss Montgomery, else you will decide to leave us."

Her eyes grew wide. "But I have nowhere else to

go, my lord. My parents died within a few months of each other several years ago. Lacking any suitable relations willing to take me in, I was fortunate indeed to find work as your mother's companion."

Miss Montgomery spoke with a steady voice, but at the mention of her parents' deaths, an unmistakable dark grief flickered across her lovely face. Edward felt a jolt of sympathy for the young woman's predicament. Though technically not an orphan, he knew all too well what it felt like to be deprived of blood relations.

"Considering your circumstances, I hope that you will look upon us as far more than an employer," Edward said, offering the young woman a smile he hoped was encouraging.

A pretty blush of color filled her cheeks and she ducked her head. It wasn't too difficult to follow the progression of her thoughts; clearly, she was embarrassed at having revealed so much about herself.

Jonathan's discreet cough came to the rescue, breaking the mood. Miss Montgomery darted lightly back across the room to leave, but stopped with her hand on the doorknob. "I'm sure it will be a fine holiday celebration now that you are back with your family, my lord."

"I will see you both later," the countess said after her companion had left. "As you might remember, Edward, we dine earlier than is the Town fashion. The houseguests will be gathering in the drawing room no later than six-thirty."

Edward nodded his head politely, wondering why his mother bothered to remind him about the evening meal. She would certainly prefer if he were late, or better still, if he never came at all.

He sighed. This day felt twenty hours long, yet it was far from over. Edward admitted it was partially his fault. He had expected too much. Jonathan's optimism had brushed off on him, making him believe it was possible for the countess to see reason, to forget the past and to move forward and mend the rift between them.

He knew now, it would take far more than an afternoon chatting over tea and trading barbs to alter his mother's opinion of him. It would take far more than patience and a few glasses of whiskey along with some garbled explanations of his actions to reach some kind of peaceful relationship.

It would take nothing short of a miracle.

Charlotte took a late-afternoon lavender-and-rose-water-scented bath, washing her hair and then rinsing it in equal parts lemon juice and hot water. Once it dried and was combed out, she climbed into the comfortable four-poster bed, knowing she would be unable to nap, but deciding a few hours of quiet rest would invigorate her mind and spirits.

Much to her surprise, she slept a dreamless, untroubled sleep for several hours and awoke to find her headache gone. Pleased to be feeling better, she dressed with care for dinner, allowing her maid to lace her tightly into a fashionable dark green silk gown with cream lace trim and a matching green embroidered hem.

Charlotte had always enjoyed wearing fine clothes and tried to look her best at all occasions, but it was now of paramount importance that for the next two weeks she groomed herself with the utmost care. Being in prime looks gave her a boost of confidence and it was essential that she wasn't at any kind of disadvantage whenever she was in the earl's company.

"How should I wear my hair this evening, Jones?" Charlotte asked her maid.

"Not too severe, Miss," the maid replied. With skillful hands, she pinned up a large section of Charlotte's hair and then deftly manipulated sections of the long, shiny tresses into ringlets that clustered around her face. "If you are wearing the emeralds tonight, I can place the matching hair-combs on the top and sides."

"Yes, please. Use the combs."

The maid unlocked the jewel case and retrieved the emerald-and-diamond combs. After pinning them carefully into place, she stepped back to admire her handiwork. "It looks lovely."

"Yes, it does, Jones. You have a deft touch. Thank you."

Charlotte removed the matching necklace and earbobs from the jewel case, then dabbed some lavender-scented perfume onto the inside of her wrists and elbows and behind her ears.

At last she felt ready to do battle. She was going to show the Earl of Worthington that she was a contented, beautiful, sophisticated woman in the very prime of her life who did not waste a minute of her thoughts on him.

She had something to prove. To him, but more importantly to herself. She was, in truth, a contented woman. Life with Grandfather at Quincy Court was good. She had far more freedom than many unmarried women her age, financial security and the opportunity to say and do whatever she wanted, within reason, of course.

If something was missing, well, perhaps that too might come along one day. Being rejected by the earl when she was seventeen years old had been a bitter pill to swallow. For a short time Charlotte had decided she would never marry, but eventually she came to her senses and realized it would be foolish to deny herself a lifelong partner because of one broken relationship.

No, Charlotte had not given up on marriage. She had however adopted a high standard of expectation in a partner. Thanks to her indulgent grandfather, the choice of a husband was hers to make, and even though she was twenty-three, she felt no need to hurry. She had gained maturity and sensibility over the years and felt no competition from the crop of giggling debutantes fresh from the schoolroom who came to London each Season.

Charlotte was courted each year by several gentlemen, though as of yet she had not found the right one. Her goal was to marry someone who was acceptable to her grandfather and appealing to herself.

The trouble was, no man, no matter how handsome, titled, wealthy or powerful, had been truly appealing.

Was that because of Edward Barringer, Earl of Worthington? A little shiver prickled her spine. Charlotte honestly could not say. But now that she had been given a chance to see him again, perhaps she would finally find out.

The guests gathered in the drawing room before dinner, exchanging greetings and renewing acquaintances. Charlotte visited briefly with each of them, then stole away for a moment to a quiet corner, her attention drawn to the outside fading light.

She stood at the long French windows, watching the sun set beneath an orange, gold and pink sky. "Have you ever seen a more glorious sight?" she muttered, her voice filled with soft wonder.

"Yes, it is rather magnificent," came the masculine reply.

Charlotte felt herself flushing. She had not realized the earl was so close. She thought she was alone.

Without being invited, the earl came up beside her and they watched the sun disappear over the edge of the distant forest. As darkness engulfed the view, the twinkling glow of the candle-lit chandelier reflected off the window glass. Charlotte lifted her head and looked directly at him.

He was looking back, his eyes narrowed in puzzlement. She wondered if he was remembering kissing her. She tilted her head a little higher. She felt color flood her cheeks as her mind was swamped with those extraordinary memories.

Many things were different about the earl, but the sheer power and magnetism of the man had not altered. Especially when one was standing so close. Charlotte felt a surge of confused resentment. The last thing she needed was to rekindle her girlhood emotions toward him.

"Was it a sudden, impulsive decision to leave London and come to Farmington Manor?" she asked, desperate to change the strange mood that enveloped them.

The earl's eyes narrowed. "As I have so frequently reminded everyone who has been so shocked to see me today, this is my home."

"Yet you never visit."

He brushed his hand lightly through his hair. "Are you aware of the circumstances of my recently cancelled engagement, Miss Aldridge?"

Charlotte set her lips. Dozens of sarcastic retorts sprung to her lips, but she surprisingly found herself unable to gloat at his misfortune. She looked at him closely, feeling as if she could see through the elegant clothes and sophisticated confidence to the hurt and loneliness beneath. "I read the *Morning Chronicle*, my lord. And the *Morning Post*."

"Not the *Times*?" he asked, his eyes dancing.

"'Tis usually a wasted effort to read that paper. I find their gossip column sadly lacking in sordid details," she replied lightly.

He raised his eyebrow and drawled, "Aye, but what they do not know, they can easily fabricate."

"Was it all a lie?" she could not keep herself from asking. "The newspaper accounts were dramatic and sensationalistic. In these sorts of situations, a gentleman usually allows a lady to cry off, in hopes of saving her reputation."

He gave a short, rather mirthless laugh. "My former fiancée did not cry off in the customary manner. She ran off. With another man."

"It was most unfortunate that she chose such a public—"

He held up an arresting hand. "Please, no offers of sympathy." He gave a slightly self-mocking head shake. "Oddly enough, I find it makes me feel even more morose."

Charlotte crossed her arms, but was saved from making a response by the sound of the dinner bell. The earl bowed and excused himself, then walked over to his mother.

The countess appeared startled to find her son beside her. For a brief moment she looked as if she would refuse the support of his arm, but the earl stood patiently, never moving a muscle, never taking his eyes off his mother.

The guests were all too polite to openly stare, but the countess must have realized they were all very aware of the drama. With a small sigh, the older woman lightly rested her gloved fingertips on the earl's sleeve and allowed him to escort her from the room.

The rest of the guests paired up and followed them into the dining room. Charlotte held on tightly to her grandfather's arm.

"The countess does not seem pleased to see her eldest son," Lord Reginald whispered. "Looks like the holiday fireworks are going to be set off early this year."

"It should be quite a show," Charlotte agreed. "Do not stand too close, Grandpapa, or you might become burned."

Lord Reginald smiled, but his eyes were grave. "Does it distress you greatly to see him again, Charlotte? If you wish to leave, I will make our excuses to the countess and we can depart in the morning."

Charlotte gave the suggestion due consideration, then shook her head. "No," she responded firmly, honestly. "There is no need for us to leave. If it becomes necessary, I can easily avoid the earl. Besides, we have already allowed our staff to join their families for the holiday. It would be unfair to expect them to return to Quincy Court and make Christmas for us on such short notice."

"All right. For now we shall stay. But all you need to do is give the word and we shall depart at once."

Her grandfather led her around the table and a footman pulled out her chair. Charlotte gathered her wide skirt to one side and gracefully sat down. She glanced around the table and realized with some surprise that she was seated on the earl's right hand.

He fittingly occupied the head of the table, but a higher-ranking female should have been afforded the honor of sitting next to him. A second glance about the room confirmed a far more casual arrangement of the twenty dinner guests. Even the countess's companion, Miss Montgomery, was joining them, seated beside Jonathan.

"I came in earlier and switched all the placards," the earl confided. "In my experience, these dinner parties can be far too formal and stuffy."

Charlotte frowned and took a sip of wine. While it was true that a less formal seating arrangement could be more festive, especially given the season, she imagined the earl had pulled such a juvenile prank to give his mother fits. By the look of astonishment on the countess's face, it was working.

Yet Charlotte could not deny the prickle of pleasure she felt, knowing he had chosen to place her at his side as his dinner companion.

There was a flurry of laughter and bright conversation around the table as the first course was served. The leek soup was followed by a roasted partridge, river trout served with mushrooms in wine sauce, chicken in lemon sauce accompanied by peas and venison steaks in cream sauce.

It was clear that Cook was outdoing herself tonight, preparing a feast worthy of a returning monarch. Charlotte lost count of the dishes after the stuffed pheasant was served. She took a small bite of each dish, enjoying the unique flavors and textures, yet tried to pace herself, wondering how many more courses would be served before the cheese, fruit and dessert were finally brought out.

"Would you care for more wine?" the footman inquired politely, tilting the crystal decanter above her glass.

Charlotte set one hand over the rim. "I believe I have drunk more than my share this evening. 'Tis probably best if I switch to something less potent."

The earl looked into her eyes and smiled. "Water is so dull, Miss Aldridge."

"Yes, it is, my lord." She smiled back. And removed her hand.

"Such a fine wine deserves a toast." He turned the stem of his wineglass between two fingers, then raised it to her. "To renewing our friendship."

Charlotte's eyebrows rose and her hand, holding the wineglass, froze halfway to her mouth. "Renewing our friendship? Your words imply we have already established a friendship that now merely requires some reacquaintance. That is not my recollection of our past."

His expression turned to granite. "It was all very muddled and highly emotional that year and yet there is a part of me that feels I owe you an apology, Miss Aldridge."

She gazed at him quizzically, her head slightly to one side, and fervently wished that she had not drunk so much wine. Surely she had misheard him. Or was it truly possible that the earl had said he owed her an apology?

For months after the incident she had dreamed of this moment, for years she had longed to have him acknowledge his behavior. Of course, in her imaginings he was on bent knee, fairly begging for her forgiveness and asking for a chance to make amends.

"For what do you apologize, my lord?"

The earl leaned a little closer to her. "Kissing you in the woods. It was far more than a chaste peck beneath the mistletoe and I fear it was presumptuous and ungallant of me."

Was it truly that simple? The passage of time had helped her forget. Could her remaining pride and pain be soothed by the sincerity of an apology, the acknowledgement that he had been wrong?

"Your guilty conscience marks you as a man of honor, and your offer of an apology shows you are a gentleman, even though it is six years late in coming." Charlotte took a deep breath. Here at long last was her opportunity to retaliate for all the tears she had shed, all the doubt she had carried about her own worth, all the pain she had felt at being rejected.

"But the truth is that your guilt is unnecessary, my lord." Once the words had been spoken, Charlotte felt her body relax. That was the truth. And she could finally see it clearly, could finally acknowledge it.

She shared in the responsibility for what had happened, even though for years she had conveniently blamed it all on the earl. "I kissed you willingly. It was an experience I very much wanted to have and decided to take when the opportunity presented itself."

The earl bowed his head. "You might have been willing, curious even, but that does not excuse my behavior. You were innocent, inexperienced. I should have known better. I *did* know better and I did not control myself. It was most unfair to you."

"Life is not fair, my lord," she said in a steady, firm voice. "Yet who ever said it was supposed to be?"

CHAPTER 7

Edward took a sip of wine and stared at Miss Aldridge over the rim of his crystal glass. She was speaking to Lord Bradford, the gentleman seated on her right, regaling him with a humorous story about her favorite dog. The older gentleman was laughing and shaking his head, clearly encouraging her to tell him more.

Who was this woman? When he had first seen her standing on the front steps of the manor earlier in the day, he thought he had been hallucinating. Charlotte Aldridge was the last person he expected, or wanted, to see. Coming home to Farmington Manor was difficult enough without having to face another one of his mistakes.

"Would you care for more trout, my lord?"

Edward nodded at the footman, then forked up a portion of the delicate fish, barely tasting it. He continued to study Miss Aldridge intently. There was something infectious about her smile. Seeing it made his own face soften in response.

Had he misjudged her? He had placed her next to him at dinner as a form of penance. He had wronged her six years ago, had taken advantage of

her youth and vulnerability and had never acknowledged his responsibility in the matter.

He had pushed her, and that fateful holiday season,
to the back of his mind, yet he admitted now that she
was someone he had never truly forgotten. It was unfortunate that she was so closely intertwined with the
schism between himself and his parents, but he knew
if it had not been Charlotte they so forcefully proposed he marry, it would have been some other
female that he would have rejected on principle
alone.

Edward remembered her as a spoiled young miss,
full of mischief and daring. She was different now,
far more beautiful, still sharp and witty, but not
nearly as obvious and demanding.

It had taken courage for her to acknowledge his
apology and accept a share of the responsibility for
their afternoon's indiscretion all those many years
ago. Courage, honesty and maturity. Excellent qualities for a wife.

*My God, had he just lumped Charlotte Aldridge and
matrimony together in his mind?* Edward shook his
head and stared at the ruby liquid in his goblet, as
if that were the cause of these outlandish thoughts.

He took another bite of food, but his gaze refused
to remain on his dish. Instead it was pulled toward
Charlotte's womanly figure, noting the elegance of
her gown, the sparkle of her jewels, the creamy
slope of her shoulder. She had the most irresistible
touchable skin he had ever seen. He wondered why
she had never married. With her looks, breeding
and wealth, he knew she must have had many offers.

"You are looking far too serious and concerned,
my lord. Pray, do not tell me you have you swallowed a fish bone?"

Bemused, he replied, "If I had, I would be coughing and choking and making a total spectacle of myself."

"Hmm, as I remember, that would be out of character. 'Tis Jonathan who usually draws, encourages and then revels in the spotlight."

"Yes, my brother does have that talent."

They both gazed simultaneously toward the other end of the table where Jonathan was seated. Those beside him, as well as those several chairs away, were all paying rapt attention to his every word.

"He is something of a devil," Charlotte said in an affectionate tone. "If I shut my eyes, I can easily imagine him with a tail and pitchfork."

Edward leaned close, settling a hand on the back of her chair. He realized that he was flirting with her, but he could not seem to help it. "If Jonathan is a devil, then what am I?"

"A dragon," she responded without hesitation, tilting her head as she stared at him. "A tall, brooding, smoldering-eyed dragon, with an excellent Bond Street tailor."

"Do I breathe fire?"

"Absolutely." A teasing smile curved her lips and her eyes sparkled in the glow of the candlelight. "Why, the mere touch of your breath makes one's skin tingle as the warmth moves over the surface."

Edward worked to keep his breath steady as his pulse started racing. "And do you play with fire, Miss Aldridge?"

"Whenever I can, my lord."

A sense of challenge rippled between them. Their eyes met and suddenly it was difficult for Edward to remember that they were not alone.

"I should not have encouraged you," he said,

charmed by the flirtatious glance she sent his way. "'Tis dangerous, considering what I know."

"About me?"

She was a distraction that he did not need at the moment, a distraction with the power to complicate his life, yet Edward could not seem to keep quiet. "It is my firm belief that you have the potential to become a wicked woman."

Her eyebrow arched delicately, raising a corner of her mouth. "Do you really think so? A wicked woman? How perfectly wonderful!"

Charlotte sounded so satisfied with herself that Edward could not hold back his laughter. "You are supposed to be appalled by my suggestion," he said with an easy grin. "Have I been so long without the company of aristocratic young ladies that I no longer remember what is correct and proper?"

"Flirting at the dinner table is always proper, my lord." She lifted her fork to her mouth and took a delicate bite of roasted, stuffed pheasant. "It stimulates the appetite."

Edward groaned faintly. "Oh, it stimulates far more than that, Miss Aldridge."

Her eyes widened, then she swallowed, her throat going taut. "Now who is being wicked? A lesser woman might make a scene over that veiled yet improper statement, but fortunately for you I have never been enslaved by the dictates of convention," she stated, clicking her tongue in a most provocative manner.

"And yet you remain within the bosom of society," he said. "Most impressive."

Charlotte shrugged. "Having wealth and a solid aristocratic heritage is key to my survival. They may not like or approve of my attitudes and actions, but it is difficult for them to openly snub the great-niece of a duke."

Mischief glimmered in her lovely green eyes. "Grimly enduring all those endless lectures from my older, more experienced peers often helps mitigate the damage," she continued. "Yet I have learned that the best way to navigate the waters of society is to possess a hearty sense of humor, a heightened sense of the ridiculous and above all, not take myself or others too seriously."

The glint of humor in her eyes caused him to widen his grin. "You are a marvel, my dear," he said, laying a hand over the one she had set on the table.

She allowed it for a long moment, then he felt her fingers wiggling beneath his palm. Edward reluctantly removed his hand and Charlotte immediately put hers in her lap. Her cheeks were flushed, her green eyes sparkling, but she kept her composure and launched into a spirited conversation with Lord Bradford.

Edward hid a frown, though he was in truth glad for the momentary respite. Touching her hand had stirred up a few sensations he had not felt toward a woman in a very long time. Primal, sensual urges that sent a fire through his veins.

It was so unexpected. He fervently hoped he had been able to hide the fascination he felt from his expression, had somehow concealed the desire that was trying to take control of his body and his common sense.

Fortunately, before he could make an utter fool of himself, his mother grandly rose to her feet, signaling that it was time for the ladies to withdraw and leave the gentlemen to their port. Edward, and the rest of the gentlemen, stood as the ladies departed. Still pensive, he sat down, lit a cigar and wondered how long it would be until they could rejoin the women.

Without so much as a glance back in the earl's direction, Charlotte followed the rest of the women out of the dining room, every nerve in her body tingling.

What had come over her? She had flirted outrageously with him during dinner, but even more distressing, she had enjoyed it immensely! When she had entered the drawing room this evening she had promised herself she would feel nothing toward him—not bitterness or anger or regret.

To that end she had succeeded, but amazingly, the emotions she had experienced were almost worse. Butterflies of anticipation, an odd surge of joy at his marked attention toward her, the warm touch of his strong hand making goose bumps rise on her arms. And when he stared at her, she found herself lost in the deep sensuality of his amber-gold eyes and the playful allure of his smile.

This was not supposed to be happening! Charlotte took a deep breath, startled at the turmoil of her own feelings. It was all so confusing, but she continued to smile, walking blindly through the room until she almost ran into a young woman. Thankfully, it was Lady Haddon, the former Miss Miranda Chambers.

"Charlotte, how lovely to see you," Lady Haddon said jovially. "We were late coming down for dinner and missed the gathering in the drawing room."

"Miranda, you look wonderful," Charlotte replied

truthfully. "The countess mentioned that you and Lord Haddon were planning to come this year."

"I adore the holidays at Farmington Manor," Miranda said. "And this year we have even more to celebrate with the birth of our second child. A boy!"

"Aren't you a clever girl?" Charlotte laughed softly. "Lord Haddon must be over the moon."

Miranda lowered her chin as a faint blush crept into her cheeks. "Charles is rather pleased about having an heir after only four years of marriage. Though he swore to me he would be happy no matter what the infant's sex as long as it was hale and hearty."

Charlotte nodded her head. Though not a view often shared by most of his peers, it sounded exactly like something Lord Haddon would say. He truly was a kind and decent sort. "I assume you brought the children along?"

"We would not dream of having Christmas without them," Miranda insisted. "The doctor assured me that young Robert is a fine healthy babe, more than capable of making the journey. We brought along his nurse, of course, and a nursemaid for our older daughter, Julia. The countess has a beautiful nursery set up for the children, so they are quite comfortable and not underfoot."

"I look forward to meeting them."

Miranda smiled brightly. "I know you are just being polite, but I give you fair warning, I intend to hold you to that request."

They chatted amicably for a few minutes longer and then Miranda left to speak with another group of ladies on the other side of the drawing room. Charlotte gazed pensively at her retreating back.

Marriage and motherhood certainly agreed with Miranda, transforming her from a pale, plain-faced young lady into a handsome woman, with shapely curves, a soft mouth and lovely blond curls. Hearing her speak so loving of her two little ones set Charlotte's thoughts spinning. She had never thought overlong about having children and was surprised at the complicated mix of emotions that engulfed her when she considered the idea seriously.

The gentlemen joined the ladies. Automatically, Charlotte looked for the earl. He was easy to spot, chatting among the gentlemen, then stopping to greet a cluster of ladies who were taking tea.

After speaking with each of them, he lifted his head and glanced over at Charlotte. Their eyes met briefly and she saw a flirtatious spark light their depths. Then the earl smiled and inclined his head. Charlotte struggled to control her suddenly erratic breathing.

At the urging of several of the guests, Miss Montgomery sat at the pianoforte and began an impromptu concert. Smiling with ease, she did her best to play everyone's request, before launching into a round of traditional Christmas carols.

A few of the younger women began singing and the men soon followed. Jonathan sat beside Miss Montgomery, turning her music and singing with great enthusiasm. Even Grandpapa was humming along and tapping his foot.

Charlotte noticed Miranda and her husband sitting very close together on the sofa, discreetly holding hands. Opposite them was the countess, who was silent, yet her expression was pleasant. And the earl—the earl's face was an odd mix of longing and loneliness. She wondered if he was remembering all the happy Christmas celebrations of his past or regretting those many years he stayed away from his home, his family and his friends.

The evening ended when the clock struck midnight. Jonathan reminded everyone of the various activities planned for the following day and the guests gradually departed for their rooms.

After kissing her grandfather's cheek, Charlotte bid the earl a hasty good night. He bowed politely as she took her leave, but his eyes seemed to hold a warmth when he looked at her. She tried not to read too much into it, yet the irony of the situation was not lost on Charlotte.

Even after all these years, and all that had happened, Edward Barringer was still the most fascinating, attractive and appealing man she had ever met.

Edward started his morning with a private breakfast in his bedchamber. He had slept poorly his first night back home and had lain awake until well past three in the morning, his mind crowded with far too many thoughts of the past and the future.

Better, he decided as he watched the dawn slowly bring the light into his bedchamber, to try and cope with the present. To that end he went downstairs and sat in his father's study—his study now—and tried to review a variety of business papers he had brought with him from London.

After nearly an hour of reading through a contract that should have taken only twenty minutes, Edward admitted his concentration was sorely lacking. Leaving the papers scattered on the desk, he stood and walked over to the window.

For a long time he stayed there, staring off into the distance. Beyond the great expanse that was the faded grass of the south lawn were the bare dormant trees of the large woods, and beyond that the gentle sloping hills that defined the southern border of the estate. Though barren and bare, the view had a unique tranquility about it. Still it could not calm his growing agitation.

"Ah, so this is where you are hiding."

Edward's gaze flitted to the door as Jonathan entered the room. "I am not hiding," Edward replied in a tired voice.

"Of course you are," Jonathan responded in a cheery tone. He made himself comfortable in a leather wing chair positioned in front of a roaring fire, propping his feet up on the cushioned ottoman. "Mother and a bevy of the women are trying to recruit helpers for a rather ambitious number of charitable projects they insist must be done before Christmas Day. That means that all the sensible males are in hiding until they have assigned the more difficult tasks to the servants, poor fellows."

"Don't you believe in charity?"

Jonathan raised a hand to dismiss his brother's remarks. "I most certainly do. But Mother's projects are always so over the top, and when you add in all the extra female ideas she is receiving from our houseguests it becomes a colossal undertaking. Better to wait until there are more reasonable tasks to accomplish."

"Planning never was Mother's strong suit," Edward agreed.

"No, when we were younger she usually relied upon you to get everything organized for her."

"Those days are long over." Edward clenched his jaw. "She'd rather the tenants starve than ask for my assistance."

Jonathan gave him a sympathetic smile. "It's not all that bad."

"Isn't it?" Edward opened and closed a fist, striving to keep his emotions under control. He reminded himself that it was going to take time to mend the rift between himself and his mother. Time and an almost inexhaustible amount of patience. "She stared at me as if I were a three-headed monster when I offered to escort her into dinner last evening."

"But she did eventually take your arm," Jonathan pointed out. "And you had your bit of fun and revenge with the placards. Mother was having fits over the seating at the dinner table. I was surprised she managed to eat any of the meal. You know what a stickler she can be for propriety and formality."

Edward looked away, lowering his gaze to the fire. "What makes you think that I am responsible for last night's seating arrangement?"

Jonathan's hearty laugh echoed off the wood-paneled walls. "Aside from me, you are the only one who possesses enough nerve to pull such a stunt." Sobering slightly, he added, "Though I must add it was not the best way to endear yourself to her."

Edward smiled faintly, acknowledging his brother's point. "Did she say anything to you about it?"

"No. Miss Montgomery was in a panic when we all entered the dining room, thinking she had made a grave error in placing the cards, but mother quickly assured her it was not her fault. It was clear she knew exactly who was responsible."

Edward felt a pang of guilt. He had not realized that Miss Montgomery might be held accountable. "You are certain there will be no repercussions toward Miss Montgomery?"

Jonathan shook his head. "Mother knows she is very capable. And there were far too many changes in the entire seating arrangement for it to be a mistake or a case of carelessness."

The door suddenly opened and Charlotte Aldridge entered. She wore a crimson morning gown trimmed with lace flounces on the skirt. Her hair was swept up on top of her head, with a single wavy lock spilling down her left shoulder. She looked perfectly delectable.

For a split second Edward thought her expression brightened when she saw him, but he was not certain.

"Am I interrupting?" she asked with a questioning smile.

"Not at all," Jonathan quickly answered. He got to his feet. "Stay and keep Edward company. I need to confer with the stable master to ensure that all the horses will be ready for our afternoon ride."

Despite his proximity to the fireplace, a chill spread over Edward's body. But there was no gracious way to stop his brother from leaving.

"Is there something specific you needed, Miss Aldridge?" he asked, disliking how ungracious and pompous he sounded.

She apparently decided not to respond to his less-than-friendly greeting, but instead stated the purpose of her interruption.

"We are putting the finishing touches on the gift baskets for your tenants and the countess would like to include a personal gift for the children of each family. I was hoping you might assist me in the selection of the present for Martin Ross, who has just turned fourteen."

"I know the Ross family," Edward replied. "They have farmed our land for generations."

"It seems that young Martin has a scholarly bent and the countess thought a book would make a fine gift. She instructed me to pick one from the library, but I am having difficulty making a choice." Miss Aldridge frowned in concentration. "Something on mathematics, science or history would certainly be appropriate, but rather dull, I think. My tastes run toward poetry, which he might enjoy, but I am uncertain. What would you suggest?"

"It seems as though my mother is overgenerous this season with not only my money, but my possessions," he said, not bothering to keep the rising annoyance from his voice.

Miss Aldridge's nostrils flared slightly and her mouth tightened. "Until that ridiculous tax on paper is repealed, books will remain scarce and expensive, a luxury afforded only by the upper class. A book would be a treasured gift to a young man with a scholarly bent whose family has never owned one," she said pointedly.

Good Lord, she was right. Edward made a disgusted sound, ashamed at how small-minded he was acting. A book would be a special Christmas memory for the Ross lad.

He turned away and walked to the inlaid bookshelf beside the window. "Actually there are several volumes in here that might do," he offered, his fingers running carefully over the leather-bound spines. "*Ivanhoe* is a wonderful tale that will spark any boy's imagination. It was one of my favorites when I was younger."

"It is an excellent book, but I suspect he might have already read it. Any other ideas?"

"How about a biography?" Edward held up two substantial volumes. "Julius Caesar or Alexander the Great?"

Miss Aldridge lifted her right hand to her face and tapped her index finger pensively on her chin as she carefully considered his suggestions. "Alexander," she decided. "He was one of the world's greatest generals, becoming King of the Macedonians at the age of twenty and then conquering the Persian Empire."

"The perfect choice," Edward agreed with a quick smile. He crossed over to his desk and rummaged through the satchel of papers he had brought from London, pulling out a slim leather volume. "And to balance out the lessons, a bit of fun."

"*A Christmas Carol!* What an inspired idea." She took the book and leafed through it. "I do not think anything captures the true spirit of the holiday better than this story. But this is your personal copy. Are you sure you wish to part with it?"

"I can always get another." Hoping to make amends for his earlier rudeness, Edward indicated the chair that Jonathan had vacated and invited Miss Aldridge to sit. Surprisingly, she did so, perching herself graceful on the edge of the chair, the books held firmly in her lap.

"Would you care for coffee? Or tea? I can ring for Harris."

"Refreshments are unnecessary, my lord, but I would enjoy a brief respite. It gets rather chaotic with so many helpers all offering differing opinions on the best way to get things done."

"I can imagine," he muttered.

"No, you really cannot. This is something that must be experienced to be completely understood."

"Or believed?"

Miss Aldridge's mouth twitched. "Pray, do not let me keep you from your work, my lord." She nodded toward the papers strewn across the desk.

Not wanting to lie outright, Edward chose his words carefully. "'Tis nothing of great importance. I was merely reviewing some papers I was unable to read before I left London. Social items mainly."

Her finely arched eyebrows lifted. "They look much more like business reports, with lots of columns and numbers."

He glanced nervously toward his desk, where the papers were openly displayed. "Ahh, yes, it appears as though my secretary included a financial accounting summary of some of the investments he wants me to review."

"They look very detailed for a summary," she commented.

He turned and stared at her in surprise. "Do you have any familiarity with these types of documents?"

"I am learning." She pursed her lips in a determined line. "I am Grandfather's heir, and while I shall always rely upon the advice of others when making any sort of financial decision, I also believe it is very necessary for me to have at least a basic understanding of finances and investments. How else can I properly manage my estate and its holdings?"

"That is a most intriguing concept, teaching a woman the business skills that many men of our class so often lack."

"Do you disapprove?" She caught his gaze and there was a look of challenge in her eyes as if she dared him to say it.

"Apparently, it would be unwise if I did."

"Precisely." She choked back a laugh. "We are sent to school, but once there, women are taught to be ladies, to have perfect posture and to glide gracefully whenever we move. I was a bit of a rebel and took the initiative to read what was inside those books that were perched so precariously upon my head."

He grinned. He liked knowing she had a backbone when it came to things she thought were important. "I realize I am at great risk of igniting your ire, yet I am compelled to say that your posture is excellent, Miss Aldridge."

She accepted the compliment with a serene nod of her head. "I learned the feminine arts first, my lord, but wisely decided as I grew older that I needed to know more in life than how to look fetching."

"You appear to be succeeding in both areas."

Though said in a flirting manner, the compliment was sincerely given. Edward wondered again why she was still single, why no man had the brains, or courage, to take her as his wife.

"I have recently begun to acquire a rudimentary knowledge of business and finances, but there is still so much for me to learn." She took a slow breath. "Perhaps some time you can share some of your own knowledge. I would be most grateful."

"Me?"

"Oh, come now, my lord. There is no need to be modest." She leaned forward. "I know your secret."

The comment hung in the air. Edward wondered if he could simply ignore it, but though he tried, he could not stifle his curiosity. "What secret, Miss Aldridge?"

"Your mother tries to pretend that you occasionally dabble in investments, presumably for fun, and those of us who care about her indulge this whim." She shrugged in an offhanded manner. "But anyone with half a brain knows you run an impressive business empire, with an unprecedented amount of success."

He was too shocked by her frank speech to deny it. "It does not offend you?"

She burst out laughing. "Offend me? Because you have purpose and direction in your life, because you are successful? Quite the contrary. I find it admirable. And fascinating."

"You are very much in the minority," he said.

"Perhaps," she agreed. "I do share your view on the dismal lack of wit among the *ton*, yet you must allow that not all members of the aristocracy display the intelligence of a turnip. There are many of us who can actually engage in sensible conversation for more than five minutes."

"A rare breed," he said with a slight smile.

She sat back in her seat and considered him for a moment. "You, my lord, are a snob," she pronounced.

Edward's expression lightened. "That, I fear, is my true secret, Miss Aldridge." She was probably right. He had dismissed so many individuals of his class, both male and female, as witless, without giving them the opportunity to prove otherwise.

There were men of intelligence within the aristocracy, men who devoted their lives to politics and public services, men who managed large estates and properties with success. Yet sadly they were in the minority.

"Tell me about your work." She must have sensed his hesitation, for she added, "I'm sure a lot of what you must do is tedious and mundane, but surely there is some excitement, some element of risk that makes it a daring venture."

A flippant retort sprang to his lips, but she was so openly sincere he could not make light of her earnest inquiry. Besides, he reasoned, she would be bored to tears within a few minutes, searching for a polite excuse to leave.

So he told her of his first success, the restoration of a run-down cotton mill, how he had naively paid too much for the business, yet by promising the workers a higher wage had managed to turn a profit in less than a year. He spoke of the exotic goods his many ships imported—teas grown in the Far East, silks from China, muslins from India and the many spices from the Spice Islands.

He spoke of the different factories he owned and his concern that the conditions were safe so his workers would remain healthy and produce quality goods at a productive rate. He mentioned his most recent interest in the growing rail lines and his acquisition of a steel mill and a locomotive factory.

She listened intently to all of it, asking pertinent, intelligent questions. It was the first time Edward had ever discussed his empire in its entirety with anyone and it felt good to relate his successes and comment upon his failures.

The clock chimed the hour, startling them both. Miss Aldridge glanced up, her eyes widening. "Gracious, is that the time? I really must go."

Clutching the two books he had given her tightly to her chest, she curtsied, then turned toward the door. Edward hurried forward so he could hold it open.

She gave him a dazzling smile of thanks as she passed through the doorway. He responded with one of his own.

"I look forward to seeing you later this afternoon," he said, startled to realize how much he meant it.

He had no business showing any sort of interest in Charlotte Aldridge. Given their past, given his recently broken engagement, given all the unsettling emotions that were stirring inside him since his return to the manor.

He should have stayed in London. He should have braved the gossips, ignored the pitying whispers and devoted himself to work.

The earl was very aware that many an intelligent, steadfast man was brought to foolishness at the hands of an outspoken, spirited woman like Miss Aldridge. But most dangerous of all was knowing that the prospect did not distress Edward, but rather enlivened and excited him.

CHAPTER 8

Jonathan was feeling weary as he stepped into the outer courtyard at the back of the mansion. The intense animosity between his brother and mother was a physically and emotionally draining situation, especially since he was caught in the middle, trying to act as the peacemaker between two warring parties who were each determined to emerge the victor.

Though he would never admit it to Edward, more than once he had questioned his advice and insistence that his brother return home. Their mother was being far more obstinate than he expected, and Edward's cooperation had been less than complete. The pair had managed to be polite to each other in front of other people, but Jonathan honestly wondered how long that would last.

The only thing he did feel confident about was knowing that it was going to be a very *unusual* Christmas this year.

A gust of wind blew open his unbuttoned coat and Jonathan shivered. The day was bright and sunny, but cold. The air held the distinct smell of approaching snow. Jonathan hoped it would arrive in time for Christmas.

He blew into his fists and rubbed his hands together, wishing he had thought to wear his gloves. He had not realized he would need them for the short walk to the stables.

After ascertaining with the stable master that all was in proper order for the afternoon's riding expedition, Jonathan took the shorter route around the side of the stables on his way back to the manor. As he turned the corner, the flash of a blue cloak caught his attention. It was Miss Montgomery, walking with strident purpose through the terraced garden toward the back veranda.

He was just about to call out a greeting when she lifted her head. Their eyes met. She stopped dead in her tracks and stared at him for a long moment. Jonathan smiled broadly with delight, but Miss Montgomery stared in astonishment.

Clearly, he was the last person she expected to see. She lowered her head hastily and moved even faster, choosing a path that would deliberately take her away from him.

His heart plummeted. "Miss Montgomery, wait!"

At his command she halted, her shoulders stiff with tension. "Is there something you needed?"

"I just wanted to say hello."

Jonathan advanced on her. Trapped, she gazed around nervously almost as though she were considering the odds of him being able to catch her if she ran. Puzzled by this unusual reaction, Jonathan quickened his stride.

"Good morning, sir." She fell into a full curtsey when he reached her side. The gesture embarrassed him, though she clearly made the point that she viewed herself as a subservient, inferior person.

"There's no need for all of that," he chided gently, helping her to rise.

Jonathan liked Miss Montgomery. Very much. She was beautiful, with dark fluttering lashes and a wise smile, but it was not her looks that wholly captivated him. She had a quiet intelligence that soothed him, a gentle manner that charmed him, a musically pitched voice that made him want to listen to her speak all day long. She was the type of woman that men dreamed about, the type of woman one could cherish and love and hold forever in their heart.

He reached down and lifted her hand, then held it between his own. Like him, she wore no gloves. Her skin felt cold, but soon it grew warm. She tried to pull away, but he held on tightly, refusing to let go.

"You should not hold my hand," she said softly.

"Why not? I find I like it very much."

"As do I, which makes it most dangerous."

"Ah, Evelyn."

"You make me feel special, sir, as if someone cares about me. Which is a very foolish notion indeed."

Finally, she glanced up at him, peeking out from under the rim of her bonnet. Her lush, red lips were slightly parted, moist and mere inches away. The temptation to close the gap between them and press his lips to hers was unbearable. Jonathan tried to pull himself away from his unruly hunger, but the power of his craving was far too potent.

"Forgive my boldness," he whispered as he moved his hand to cup her chin, tilting her face upward.

He kissed her full on the mouth. Her lips were warm, her breath sweet and she tasted like heaven.

His tongue played along the line of her lips, back and forth, back and forth and then slipped inside.

He heard her breath catch, felt his own heart pounding in his ears. He tasted her lips over and over until finally he knew he had to stop or else he would disgrace himself.

Their lips separated and he kissed her eyes and nose and cheeks. He moved to her ear and whispered his long-held secret, "I have wanted to do that since the first moment I met you."

Jonathan waited for her maidenly outrage, bracing himself for the possibility of a slap across the face, yet regretted nothing. The kisses they had just shared were worth risking her anger and condemnation.

But to his surprise, she lifted her hand and traced the tip of her finger across her slightly swollen lips. "Two years is a long time to wait for a kiss. I hope you found it as magical as I did."

Jonathan laughed aloud, giving in to an irresistible urge to hug her. She screeched in shock at his sudden move, but allowed it. He then took her hand with a casual intimacy that felt totally natural and began walking away from the manor.

"Why did you try to avoid me?" he asked, still hurt by the gesture.

She blushed prettily. "We have never been alone with each other and I thought it prudent that our interaction remain within the strict bounds of propriety."

"That sounds rather dull," he replied. He lifted a finger and traced the line of her cheek.

Agitated, she stepped back, out of his reach. "My circumstances have forced me to be a practical woman. If we are caught, I could lose my position, be dismissed without so much as a letter of reference."

"I would never allow that to happen."

A rueful smile touched her lips. "I know you would try to prevent it and perhaps you would succeed, but I would still find myself in dire circumstances."

"Even if you were able to stay here?"

"Especially if I stayed here."

Perplexed, Jonathan searched her lovely face, trying to understand what she was so reluctant to say aloud. Gradually, a silence developed; it was the most emotionally charged he had ever endured. Though he had more than his share of experience with the opposite sex, he was not so much of a fool as to believe he could ever fully understand what was going on in a woman's mind without asking her directly.

"What are you trying to tell me, Evelyn?" he asked, enjoying the informality of addressing her by her first name.

"I fear that where you are concerned I have very little willpower."

His heart leapt with delight. "I feel the same about you," Jonathan confessed. "It appears we share an irrevocable, unavoidable attraction for each other."

"I fear that might be true," she whispered, her face the picture of abject misery, her eyes disturbed. "And if it is, I know that my heart needs protection from you."

Something tender welled up inside Jonathan. The need to take her in his arms and console her was almost overwhelming, but he hesitated, worried the gesture would distress her more.

"I would never intentionally cause you harm or bring you hurt," he said. "On the contrary, I would take care of you, Evelyn, if you let me."

Her eyes widened, then she passed a trembling hand over her eyes. "Though I am only a servant now, I was raised in a genteel household, taught to be a lady of grace and virtue. The lessons of a lifetime run deep. It might work at first, when the flush of passion and excitement are all consuming, but I know I could never be happy as your mistress."

For a moment he froze. *His mistress?* "I am not a man who enjoys brief affairs and is then content to find another partner." He set his hand over hers and kissed her palm. "My intentions toward you are honorable. I would have you as my wife and treat you with the proper respect that you deserve."

He had not meant to make such a bold declaration, but once the words had been spoken, he knew they were true. For two years he had admired her, flirted with her and teased her and somehow fallen in love with her. The only possible way for them to be together was through marriage.

She tore her gaze away. "If only life were that simple."

"It can be," he coaxed.

She shook her head. "You need to be practical, Jonathan. You are a second son. You must marry a woman with a sizeable dowry and a yearly income, someone that your mother approves of and deems suitable."

"I never took you for a woman who would scorn a man for his lack of wealth."

"I would never think something so offensive!" Evelyn leveled a look of anger at him. "You may *want* to choose a wife with your heart, but you *need* to choose a wife who is at least equal or better to your station."

"I have an adequate allowance," he huffed.

"For a bachelor. But you will need to supplement it once you have taken a wife and started a family because you do not have a profession or any other means with which to earn a living."

Jonathan hid a wince at the truth of her words. "I suppose I should be the one who works, not my brother," he said glumly.

"You were raised to be a gentleman and are perfect exactly as you are," she said forcefully. Her knuckles brushed his cheek. "Do not ever think less of yourself."

Lord, it was bittersweet to see the admiration in her eyes. "You always say precisely the right things. That is why I *need* you in my life. I only wish—"

"As do I, but wishes are very dangerous things." A deep shuddering sigh wracked her body. "I must go or else I shall be missed."

"We need to talk, Evelyn. Meet me this afternoon. Four o'clock in the library." He smiled slow and sweet. "Nobody ever goes in there."

She looked at him, her eyes wide and helpless. "I dare not," she said, her voice rising with despair. "It would only bring heartbreak to us both."

She turned on her heel and ran from him, the soft soles of her slippers echoing off the brick pavements lining the courtyard. Jonathan allowed her to go because he had no choice, swallowing back all the words that rushed to his mouth. It was one of the hardest things he had ever done, staring at her retreating back and all the while remembering the feel of her mouth beneath his, soft and warm and sweeter than anything he had ever tasted.

Weary in heart and soul, he slowly started walking

toward the house. Fate had dealt him a rotten hand. After blissfully enjoying bachelorhood for all these years, he was finally falling in love. With an unsuitable young woman.

Jonathan gazed up at the sky, marveling at how truly bizarre the world could be. Fortunately, he had always been a man who relished a challenge. He lifted his chin a notch and straightened the collar of his coat.

Convincing Evelyn Montgomery that they could one day be a happily married couple was going to be the greatest challenge he ever undertook—and by far the most rewarding to achieve.

"Charlotte, you must come at once. Everyone is gathering in the kitchen. 'Tis time to stir the Christmas pudding!"

"Grandpapa, you startled me!" Charlotte exclaimed as she hastily shoved the embroidery hoop that held a fine white square of linen into the side cushion of her chair, hoping to hide it from him.

The handkerchief she was so painstakingly embroidering was a Christmas gift for her grandfather. It was foolish to try and hide it since the gift would hardly be a surprise. She always gave him an embroidered handkerchief at Christmas.

Lord Reginald insisted it was the one thing he truly needed from her and she was touched when she discovered it was something he treasured. She had learned, quite by accident, that the handkerchiefs she embroidered were to be laundered by hand, pressed by her grandfather's valet, then stored carefully in a special drawer in his wardrobe.

He had saved them all, including the first one she had crafted with abominable stitches when she was six years old, and the one she made at seven, that was forever spotted because she had pricked her finger so many times and the bloodstains never washed out.

He had saved the impossibly elaborate one she had created when she turned thirteen, far too frilly and gaudy for a refined gentleman. But he had kept each one, and he insisted on carrying them on certain days of the year.

Her birthday, his birthday, the anniversary of her parents' wedding, the day she was presented to the queen. He treated them like family heirlooms, as precious as any painting or property or jewels. Knowing that made the sewing chore a bit less arduous, for Charlotte never really enjoyed embroidery and her skill was average at best.

She shifted in her chair, moving to retrieve the hoop and place it in the sewing basket at her feet, but as she reached down into the cushion she jabbed the needle into her finger, pricking herself. Somehow Charlotte bit back an unladylike oath just in time and stuck her finger in her mouth.

"Is everything all right, dear?" Lord Reginald asked.

"Wonderful," Charlotte forced herself to say. "I'll only be a moment."

Her grandfather pulled out a gold watch fob and consulted the time. "Do hurry, Charlotte. I do not want to be late and upset Cook. She is a genius in the kitchen, but as is true of many artists, she can be a bit sensitive on occasion."

Charlotte let out a good-natured sigh. "Cook's

temperament is the countess's concern, Grandpapa, not ours," she reminded him.

Lord Reginald grimaced. "But if Cook gets upset with me, she might not make the candied ginger cookies I am so fond of having each Christmas. The holiday would just not be the same without them."

"Our own Mrs. Saunders baked several batches of the treats before we left Quincy Court," Charlotte said. "Surely you noticed the large tin I packed?"

Lord Reginald's lips turned downward. "We've been here for two days, Charlotte. The tin is empty."

"Grandfather!"

"They are my favorite Christmas treat," he declared defensively, his cheeks turning pink. "If you wanted to save them for Christmas Day, then you should have hidden them."

"I did hide them!"

"Well, you should have hidden them where they would not have been so easily found." Lord Reginald flexed his shoulders as if to rid them of an ache.

Charlotte rubbed a hand over her mouth to cover a grin. She didn't know how to respond. Lately, she had begun to notice instances where their roles seemed to be reversed, where she was the responsible adult and her grandfather was the carefree child. She supposed she could blame it on the holiday, for it brought out the youngster in everyone.

Yet that did not explain why he on occasion acted like this in the middle of the summer.

"I will speak with Cook this afternoon," Charlotte decided. "I am sure she will be pleased to accommodate my request for the cookies. And since you have already eaten so many of them, I will only need to ask for a small number to be baked."

A look of alarm crossed Lord Reginald's face. "I am not certain that will do the trick. Everyone else is bound to ask Cook for special Christmas treats. The earl requested more mince pies and the countess always likes a walnut tart. And just this morning I saw Haddon give the butler a recipe for trifle that he claimed was Lady Haddon's favorite."

"You like all those foods, especially trifle," Charlotte said in a reasonable voice. "It's a lovely holiday dessert."

"Sponge cake soaked in brandy, custard, blackberry jam, whipped cream—there is not a single thing not to like about trifle," Lord Reginald agreed. He sent her a shrewd look. "But if the family has requests and then all the guests keep asking for special treats, there won't be time to make them all. Something will be left out."

Charlotte snorted. "I promise that your ginger cookies will not be forgotten. Even though you have already eaten enough to last you until next Christmas." She placed her embroidery hoop in her sewing basket and snapped the lid, then she slid her arm through his. "Come, let's hurry down to the kitchen, so we can arrive in time and stay in Cook's good graces."

Lord Reginald's answering hearty smile warmed her heart. It took so very little to please her grandfather. He was an uncomplicated man, good-natured, kind and generous. Though a part of her would always regret not knowing her parents, she was grateful that she had been given the chance to form a unique bond with this very special man.

The smells wafting from the kitchen made Charlotte's mouth water when they entered the room.

Lemon, orange, cinnamon and nutmeg. She wondered if one of the earl's ships had brought the exotic fruits and spices to the shores of England, providing the necessary ingredients for this special pudding.

All the servants were lined up on the far wall, clean and shiny as if ready for inspection. Most of the houseguests were also present, laughing and jostling one another while enjoying generous helpings of the mulled wine that was being served.

Lord and Lady Haddon had even brought their youngsters. Lord Haddon held their daughter, Julia, firmly in the crook of his arm, appearing so comfortable and at ease it was obvious the little girl spent many hours with her father. She was a pretty child, who shared her mother's striking blue eyes and curly blond hair. The baby rested in the cradle of his mother's arms, his eyes wide open and curious, his small hand reaching out occasionally to bat at his mother's cheek.

With Charlotte by his side, Lord Reginald weaved his way through the crowd, winking at her when he miraculously managed to place himself in a prominent position near the wooden worktable.

Charlotte found herself smiling at his antics, glad that he was able to still find joy in life's simple pleasures, happy that he had not adopted the appalling habit that so many others of his age so eagerly embraced, complaining about his health. It seemed to her that a very favorite topic of conversation among older people was a catalogue of their various health complaints, when they usually offered far more detail than anyone cared to know.

"If everyone is here, we can get started," the earl announced, bringing the lull of jovial conversation to an end. "Cook has told me that in order to make a proper pudding it should be stored for several weeks after it is mixed and boiled because the longer the fruit is marinating the better it tastes. But I wanted us all to observe one of my favorite Christmas traditions, and so we have gathered here to each take a turn stirring this magnificent pudding Cook has created."

Cook, a stout woman of middle years, exhibited a modest grin. "As His Lordship has said, two weeks isn't enough time to make a *proper* pudding, but I figure if we put enough brandy sauce on it, it will be passably tasty."

Everyone laughed. "The earl will do the honors of selecting the first person to stir the pudding," Cook continued as she handed him a large wooden spoon.

He cast a thoughtful glance among the eager, smiling faces crowded together in the kitchen. Though she tried to act nonchalant, Charlotte felt a warm blush creep into her cheeks when his eyes came to rest on her. For an instant she thought he was going to extend the spoon in her direction, but instead he moved beyond the houseguests and whisked it toward the youngest housemaid.

"Me?" she squeaked, her face lighting up with delight.

There were cheers and shouts from the staff and approving nods from the guests. Clutching the spoon close to her chest, the maid nervously moved to the worktable and stared down at the large bowl.

"Give it a good turn, girl, and be sure to do it from east to west, in honor of the three kings," Cook instructed. "And don't forget to make a wish when you stir. I'll be dropping three coins into that pudding and whoever finds a coin in their serving will have wealth, health, happiness and their wish come true."

"It smells heavenly," the maid exclaimed with awe.

When she was finished, she nodded toward another of the housemaids, who eagerly came forward. She in turn signaled one of the grooms, a bold fellow who stirred the concoction with a flourish and then bowed to the earl.

He stepped forward and took his turn as if it were the most important task of his day, selecting Lord Reginald to follow him. The older gentleman exhibited nearly as much delight as the young maid in being selected. He stirred the pudding enthusiastically, then called for Lord Haddon.

"Bring your pretty little daughter over here, Haddon," Lord Reginald commanded. "Never too young for a child to learn about having fun at Christmas time."

The viscount placed his hand over his daughter's and they moved the spoon together. Lady Haddon managed to do a plausible job with her one free hand, as she held her son in the opposite arm. She signaled for Charlotte to be next.

Charlotte accepted the spoon with a smile, Cook's words about making a wish reverberating in her mind. It was a silly notion, to be sure, yet there was certainly no harm in allowing for the possibility of a wish coming true. But first she had to make one.

So many thoughts and ideas swirled through her head and she quickly picked the first one. *May I someday find a man who truly loves me, for only then will I marry.*

Charlotte blushed, surprised at her wish, momentarily fearful that others might know what she had been thinking. Sternly telling herself that was impossible, she passed the spoon to Jonathan.

He made a motion as if he were going to lick it and everyone laughed. Then he turned to Cook. "Will you put any gold rings into the mix so the finder will get married in the coming year?"

Cook's expression turned crafty. "I might be throwing one or two in there, sir. But I'll leave out the thimbles and buttons, so no one will be finding themselves forever staying a spinster or a bachelor."

"Good for you," Lord Haddon said. "I always thought that was a depressing tradition, at odds with the spirit of the season."

Jonathan and his brother exchanged a quick look, then Jonathan turned and offered the spoon to their mother. Charlotte noticed the countess had been smiling earlier, but her lips flattened suddenly as if she was worried someone might have seen her joy.

Her expression was focused and solemn as she stirred the fragrant pudding. Charlotte could only imagine what the older woman's wish might have been. The earl and his mother had pointedly kept themselves on opposite sides of the room. Was the countess hoping for a true reconciliation with her son? Or would she prefer that he left at the earliest opportunity?

Charlotte feared it might be the latter, then wondered why she should even care. Yet oddly, she did.

The remaining guests and servants took their turns and then Cook pronounced the pudding was ready to be boiled. Everyone clapped and cheered. Cook turned the mixture onto a cloth, shaped it into a round ball and then slyly pressed several gold coins and two gold rings into the batter.

She pulled the ends of the cloth together and tied the package tightly at the top of the ball before placing the pudding into a boiling pot of water. Once the pudding was cooking, the servants scurried out to attend to their many duties; the houseguests followed at a more leisurely pace.

As she made her way toward the archway, Charlotte felt a hand on her shoulder. She knew, even before turning around, it was the earl.

"I am organizing a party to search for a Christmas tree later in the week. I do hope you will be joining us."

"The weather has turned cold," Charlotte remarked. "Your stable master told me he believed it would snow soon, perhaps as early as tomorrow."

"Then we need to locate the tree as soon as possible, before the forest is covered in snowdrifts," the earl replied. "I shall consult with my mother regarding the other planned activities and set the earliest date and time available. Will you come along?"

There was a pause as Charlotte tried to read his expression. She had the strangest notion that her answer was very important to him. Then the gleam in his eye was gone, replaced by a polite smile.

"I would be delighted to attend the outing," Charlotte replied.

"Excellent." He touched her hand briefly before bowing and taking his leave.

Her skin prickled at the contact of his bare flesh against her own, but Charlotte sternly told herself that sudden shiver of anticipation she felt meant *nothing*.

Nothing at all.

CHAPTER 9

Jonathan sipped on a glass of port, his eyes glued to the doorway of the library, his ears attuned to every sound beyond it. He had been waiting for two hours and his patience was finally rewarded when he heard Evelyn's light, quick step crossing the hall. His mother was out visiting the vicar and his wife with several of the female houseguests, so Evelyn was unencumbered by her duties. Now was the perfect time for a private conversation. If he could get her alone.

She had not met him in the library yesterday as he had requested. The disappointment he had felt when he realized she was not coming was acute. Compounding his hurt was the marked change in her behavior. They had always enjoyed an easy, relaxed relationship, but after their stolen kiss yesterday afternoon, Evelyn had clearly been avoiding him. When they did happen upon each other, she was polite and distant.

He hoped for a chance to speak with her when they all gathered to stir the Christmas pudding, but she never once glanced in his direction. The celebratory spirit of the occasion had been ruined for Jonathan. It all felt dull and flat without Evelyn's warm smile cast upon him.

Jonathan stepped into the hall and approached her. She was moving slowly, her head bent low as she read the contents of the single sheet of paper she held. A list of instructions from his mother, most likely.

"Miss Montgomery, I need to speak with you. Please step into the library."

Her head jerked up, her color instantly deepening. "I am busy, Mr. Barringer. I have numerous items that require my immediate attention."

"No doubt. But this will only take a moment." Still she hesitated, prompting him to add, "I really must insist."

"Very well, sir," she replied, an unusual edge of hostility in her voice.

Jonathan followed her into the library and closed the door.

"The door must remain open," she said primly.

Jonathan exhaled a noisy breath and gently clicked the latch shut. His gaze did not move from her face and she returned his stare with a steady, unfriendly glare of her own. The silence was charged and heavy.

Jonathan drew out the chair on his right, but she shook her head. "I will not be staying that long."

Since she would not sit, he too remained standing, walking toward her until they were toe to toe. "Why do you run from me, Evelyn?"

She stiffened. "I will not answer that," she said sharply. "May I go now?"

Jonathan found himself fighting down a cold

crush of disappointment. He knew it was not going to be easy, but her open hostility was such a strong barrier between them. "I cannot bear to see you so uncomfortable in my presence," he said in a soft tone. "Am I really such an ogre?"

"You know that you are not an ogre. But you must see that I cannot possibly . . . that there is no point . . . we cannot—" Evelyn's words broke off. "I am sensible woman, sir."

"You are far more than that, my dear," he replied in a silky tone. "You are lovely and witty and kind, well, except when you are dealing with me."

He waited for a smile, any crack in the wall she had erected between them. But alas, none was forthcoming.

"What do you want from me?" she asked.

"I want you." Jonathan caught her hands before she could bolt from him and drew them to his lips. He looked down into her face, acutely aware of the tug of desire, the compulsion she so effortlessly evoked just by being so close. "You are everything I have ever wanted, all I ever need. I burn for you, Evelyn."

Her cheeks flamed and she threw a dark glance at him. "You must not say such things. You must not even think them."

"I cannot control my heart, dearest."

Her back visibly flinched. For an agonized moment, they stared at each other, at odds not over their feelings but their differing belief over whether or not there was even a possibility that they could share a future together. Jonathan sighed, knowing that she would not waver in this, fearful that she would not realize that their love could be stronger than any obstacle she thought they faced.

Finally, Evelyn made a little mewing sound and turned away. A strand of her hair tumbled down and Jonathan longed to reach for it.

"We cannot go on like this," he whispered. "At least before we were friends of a sort. And now . . . now you will barely glance at me."

"I am your mother's *paid* companion. I should never glance in your direction."

"My God, Evelyn, you cannot mean that. Surely you think better of yourself."

There was a moment's tense silence. Evelyn looked pained. It tore at Jonathan's heart to see her so distressed, yet he knew not how to fix it.

"Do you not understand what I think of myself is of no importance?" she wailed. "I am fortunate indeed that the countess even considered hiring me. I do not say this to be vain, but young women with decent looks rarely find employment as companions. And I am far younger than most who work in the same capacity."

"And far more beautiful," he supplied.

"Employers do not appreciate beauty. Older women do not want to be reminded that their looks are fading, their beauty is gone." Her eyes flashed with anger. "My role is to be invisible. To dress modestly, to attract no masculine attention, to fetch and carry when asked, to write letters and read the same book aloud over and over, because 'tis my mistress's favorite, and to smile while I am doing it."

She drew a shuddering breath and continued, her voice rising passionately with each sentence. "I am destined to live a solitary life, an outsider looking in on the world. It is not my place to offer opinions or share my feelings, I know all too well that no one is interested in them, no one cares about them."

"I care."

She pressed a hand to her eyes. "I am resigned to my fate, Mr. Barringer. Please accept it, as I have, so that we may both find contentment and peace." Her small smile trembled, then vanished.

Jonathan's heart sank. This was going from bad to worse. She was slipping away from him before he even had a chance to win her heart. The room was cold and silent, the only sound was the howling wind outside as the chill of the winter day seeped in through the window and the sputtering crackles of the fire tried to stave off the inevitable.

Evelyn turned to leave. He hesitated but a moment and then quickly followed, coming to her side as she reached the door. Jonathan stuck out his hand to grasp her arm, intent on stopping her.

Evelyn stiffened. Even that brief contact set off a spark of heat between them. Slowly, Jonathan lowered his face to hers. Her eyes instinctively widened and a sigh shivered through her. Jonathan kissed her hair, her temple, her cheek, then pressed his lips to her ear.

"You have to learn to trust me," he murmured. His hand caressed the back of hers where she gripped the doorknob.

"It will be disastrous if I do." She closed her eyes and swallowed hard. "For both of us."

"I have no adequate words for the sensations rushing through my body, no clear way to convey to you the depth of the emotions I am feeling."

"Then do not speak of it, do not even acknowledge it." Her voice was so calm and steady he would have thought she was unaffected by his declaration, but her breathing was too rapid and shallow, the pulse at her neck visibly beating at too frantic a rhythm to confirm indifference.

Jonathan drew in a deep breath, held it, then let it out slowly. He knew he could physically prevent her from leaving, and was appalled to realize how strong that instinct was inside him. But he had heard the little catch in her voice, had known how hard it was for her to turn away from him. He could not cause her such pain.

And so he once again let her go. For now.

But his frustration mounted. He reached for his wine goblet and finished the contents. He thought about refilling his glass, but decided against it. This sort of situation called for a clear head. He would be no closer to finding a solution by getting drunk.

Ten minutes passed, but his emotions still churned. Jonathan paced the room, his hands clenched into fists at his side.

Damn it! Why was Evelyn so determined to follow the restrictive rules of society? Did she not realize that love was worth the risk of breaking those rules? Or did she deem him unworthy of taking the risk?

Jonathan paced again, then stopped at the window, leaned both hands on the sill and peered out. Charlotte Aldridge was hurrying across the terrace, holding her riding skirt up with both hands as she trod delicately over the stones. Judging by the mud caked on the hem of the skirt, she had finished her ride and been out at the stables for a considerable amount of time.

As he broodingly watched her progress, Jonathan was suddenly struck with an inspiring thought. He needed a go-between, someone who could subtly plead his case to Evelyn.

Someone who could help him convince Evelyn of the real value of love.

Charlotte was the perfect person for the job.

Without stopping to think further, he tore open the door and rushed into the hallway, down the back staircase and through the long gallery. He caught up with her just as she entered the main foyer.

"Ah, Charlotte, just the person I wanted to see. Can you spare me a few moments of your time?" He grasped her elbow firmly, steering her toward the empty breakfast parlor.

She seemed startled at his sudden, slightly overbearing greeting, but offered him a ready smile. "I was going to my bedchamber to change. I'm afraid I am rather muddy and sweaty from my ride."

"I'm hardly offended," Jonathan said with a toothy smile. "Besides, ladies do not sweat, they glow with a radiant sheen."

"This lady enjoys more than a sedate trot around a groomed gravel path," Charlotte retorted with a cheeky grin. "I rode through the meadow and jumped several hedges in the process and that most certainly makes me sweat."

"Nonsense. You look lovely."

"What is so urgent?" Her amused, curious expression suddenly turned alarmed. "Has something happened to my grandfather?"

"No, no. Lord Reginald is as hale and hearty as always. I saw him earlier at breakfast. He and Edward were discussing some complicated financial investment."

Shutting the breakfast parlor door with his hip,

Jonathan released his grip on Charlotte's elbow and favored her with a winsome smile. Her face contorted in puzzlement.

"What is going on, Jonathan?"

He met her eyes and his smile faded. "I need your help, Charlotte."

She nodded. "Selecting Christmas gifts?"

Jonathan inwardly scoffed. Was that how she saw him, a man whose most pressing dilemma was deciding on which presents to buy? Did no one of his acquaintance take him seriously?

He narrowed his eyes, hoping to convey the seriousness of his intent. "I require your assistance in a most delicate matter. One that requires the utmost discretion and secrecy."

Charlotte's left eyebrow rose. "Planning to rob a bank, are you?"

"Charlotte, please." His deliberately disapproving tone told her he did not appreciate her flip attitude. "I find myself deeply enamored with a woman who refuses to acknowledge my feelings."

"And you want my advice?" He could hear the surprise and doubt in her voice.

"Not your advice, your help."

"I cannot imagine there is anything I can do." She frowned. "Your charm with females is legendary. I am certain there is nothing you cannot accomplish if you apply yourself to it."

Jonathan shook his head sadly. "'Tis not so easy this time. I fear that flirting is not in her nature."

"Ahh, so you have at last met a woman who demands more of you than witty banter, a provocative glance and a devastating smile. Good. 'Tis past time that you grow up."

"You malign me unfairly, Charlotte."

"Perhaps." A glint of speculation entered her eyes. "Who is this mysterious woman who has captured your heart?"

"Evelyn Montgomery."

For a moment Charlotte was shocked into silence. Then her lips flattened. "Jonathan, surely you know that nothing of significance can develop between you and Miss Montgomery. She is your mother's companion."

Though the implications of her words did not sit right with him, Jonathan's shoulders rose in a small shrug. "Is she therefore unworthy of some attention and innocent affection just because she must work to keep a roof over her head? Is she truly so socially inferior?"

Charlotte's look sharpened. "That is not what I meant. From what I know of Miss Montgomery, she is every bit as genteel as any current member of society. She is an admirable young woman, who possesses an extraordinary amount of patience and self-discipline. How else would she manage to get on so well with your mother? Not everyone can, you know."

Jonathan wondered briefly if Charlotte was referring to the obvious tension between Edward and the countess, but then realized that there were many individuals who had difficulty coping with his mother.

"We both agree that Miss Montgomery is a very special young woman."

"She is also very pretty."

"Extraordinarily beautiful," Jonathan muttered, then heaved a sigh. Charlotte's eyes lit with suspicion and Jonathan worried that he might have revealed too much. "Her looks are not the reason I hold her in such regard."

Charlotte continued to stare at him, as if she were weighing, measuring the sincerity of his remarks in her mind. "Our circumstances are somewhat similar, those of Miss Montgomery and myself. We are both without parents to protect and nurture us. If not for my grandfather, I too would have been forced to make my own way in the world or had to rely on the generosity of distant relatives."

"Not a very pleasant thought, is it?" Jonathan said softly.

Charlotte's expression darkened. "It's actually rather distressing."

"Then you can understand why Miss Montgomery, above so many others, deserves a bit of harmless devotion in her life."

Charlotte's brow wrinkled. "I understand that a female in her position cannot afford to be linked to an impropriety of any kind."

"She won't be, if you help me." Jonathan leaned forward eagerly, pressing home his point. "All I crave is an innocent flirtation, a courtly exchange of sentiment, like the knights of old held for their ladies."

A muscle twitched in her cheek. "You, Jonathan, are no Sir Galahad."

"Nor do I claim to be." Jonathan rubbed a hand over his face. He must choose his words carefully and convey them with the right amount of sincerity and honesty or else she would not aid him. Charlotte was not a stupid woman; if she suspected his true intentions toward Evelyn, she would in all likelihood refuse to be involved. "I have written several poems and I want very much for Miss Montgomery to have them, but I fear she would simply throw them on the fire without even opening them if I hand them to her."

"Poetry?"

Jonathan nodded, inwardly wincing at the lie. He had in fact written Evelyn several torrid love letters in which he had poured out his heart and soul. "If you deliver my poems and ask Miss Montgomery to read them, then perhaps she will."

"If you are writing poetry then you most certainly are smitten. Only a man with a deep infatuation would behave so ridiculously." Charlotte sighed. "That is all you want of me? To deliver your notes to Miss Montgomery?"

Jonathan could not hold back the grin of triumph that lit his face. "It wouldn't hurt to sing my praises to her every now and again. Let her know what a fine fellow I am, well-liked, charming, much in demand by the ladies."

Exasperation came into Charlotte's face. "I will deliver your poetry. That is all."

"And keep it a secret?"

"Yes, I shall tell no one, not even my maid."

He lifted her hand, kissed it, let it go. "Thank you, Charlotte. I knew I could count on you."

With a slight smile, Charlotte departed. Once alone, Jonathan could not stop grinning. Thanks to Charlotte's romantic nature, he now had a way to communicate with Evelyn.

He would court her. Leave small tokens in unexpected places—a rose on her writing desk, a sweet next to her usual chair in his mother's private parlor, a volume of love sonnets hidden beneath the music sheets on the piano. All items that would barely be noticed by anyone, except her.

He would write her long letters revealing the love in his heart, the needs of his body and his mind. And now with Charlotte's help, those thoughts would remain a secret, an intimacy they could freely share without worry of being caught.

It was a good beginning.

Edward knocked, then opened the door and walked into his mother's private sitting room. Like all other areas of the house, it was a well-appointed chamber. A gilt-framed mirror filled the wall above the marble mantelpiece, antique teardrop-shaped scones hung on the walls. The chaise and chairs were overstuffed and inviting, covered in fine patterned fabrics of complementing shades of gold. Two long windows looked out onto the south gardens, providing much-needed natural light.

Miss Montgomery was seated at the small desk near one of the windows, busily writing as the countess dictated. The pretty companion looked up when he entered, but because of the placement of his mother's large chair, the countess could not see him.

"Good afternoon, ladies. I hope you will forgive my intrusion." Edward walked to the center of the room, so he was in plain view.

The countess pulled a face at the sight of her son. "I am working on my correspondence. I have many friends and distant relations that I write to at this time of year. Evelyn and I are very busy trying to get them finished. It is essential that the letters are completed and posted before Christmas."

Her tone was cold, distant and openly discouraging, but Edward persisted. "I won't keep you long." He regarded his mother steadily. "I'm sure Miss Montgomery is due for a break. No doubt her fingers are beginning to cramp."

"What a ridiculous notion," the countess scoffed. "Evelyn can write for hours at a time and her penmanship remains perfect."

"Nevertheless, I am certain she would appreciate a brief respite from her labors."

Miss Montgomery did not respond right away, waiting no doubt for a signal from the countess. Though Edward did not see it, the command must have been given, because suddenly the younger woman swallowed, then quickly nodded. "I shall return shortly."

For a long moment after she left there was silence in the room. Edward could sense his mother's frustration, but he schooled his features into a pleasant expression and refused to look away. Finally, the countess opened her mouth, grudgingly, as if she realized she had no choice but to speak with him. "You said this would not take long and I intend to hold you to your word. I really must return to my correspondence as soon as possible."

"I understand. Though you might consider sending cards instead of a lengthy letter. They are all the rage in London."

"Cards?"

"Yes, Christmas cards. Several art shops in London have begun selling them during the holidays."

The countess pursed her lips in a grim line. "Lady Thornton sent me one of those cards a few years ago. The picture on the front was pretty, but the inside boasted a rather pedestrian sentiment. I thought it vulgar and impersonal."

"I think the cards are festive and practical." Edward sat in the chair opposite his mother and sucked air into his lungs. "They also save a great deal of time."

"The easy, modern way of doing things will never replace good manners and proper etiquette," the countess declared. "At least for some people."

Edward met his mother's daunting gaze and experienced a momentary pang of sadness. It seemed no matter what the topic, he could not find an agreement of opinion between them. Why did he even bother to try and reason with her when she was so determined to be contrary?

"I enjoy sending and receiving Christmas cards," he said defensively.

"Is that why you are here? To discuss Christmas cards?"

"Of course not." Edward shifted slightly, edging forward in his chair. "I wanted to talk with you about a few ideas I had for making improvements on the estate."

The countess eyed him suspiciously. "As you very well know, you should speak with Willowby, the estate agent. He manages those sorts of things."

"Willowby and I have already discussed various ways to improve the production and profit on the tenant farms. This particular improvement concerns the manor house."

The countess shrugged and continued to stare at him. "I am sure my opinion counts for little. If you have set your mind toward making changes, I am sure I have no choice but to endure them."

"I am trying to discuss the matter and solicit your

opinion, Madame," Edward said, struggling not to lose his temper. "Even though you are acting disinterested and peevish."

The lines in his mother's face grew deep and dark. Edward concentrated on ignoring the ominous cloud of disapproval she was beginning to exude. He tried leveling a look at her that almost dared her to have a tantrum, but that did not work.

His mother was obvious in her disapproval, but never overly emotional. Perhaps that was the problem. Maybe if she started shouting at him and smashing things, she would release some of her anger and frustration.

He wished he could just tell her what he planned to have done to the manor and demand that she accept it, graciously no less. But the need within him to try and establish a bond between them, no matter how fragile, was too strong.

"Well, out with it," the countess demanded. "What are you going to do?"

"I want to put gas lighting in the mansion."

"Why? It is not needed."

"It would be an improvement."

"Candlelight and oil lamps are perfectly adequate for all of our needs. Gas lights are a very unnecessary and costly suggestion."

"I have installed them in my London home and find they are quiet efficient." Edward warmed to the subject, hoping to convey his genuine wish to make life easier for all who lived at Farmington Manor, including his mother. "As for the cost, I have been reviewing the household accounts and have discovered that a great deal of coin is being spent on beeswax candles."

His mother shot him a look. "I had no idea you would object to my having quality candles in my home. I suppose I could economize and put tallow ones in the servants' quarters, though I am told they give off a faint odor that is sheeplike in nature. And the wicks have to be regularly snuffed."

Edward shook his head. "You misunderstand. I do not object to the cost of beeswax candles. I am merely suggesting an alternative that would be an improvement for everyone. Including you."

"I do not believe for a moment that you are interested in improvements. You want to exercise your authority, and make these unnecessary, ridiculous changes just to vex me."

"What purpose would that possible serve?"

"Revenge."

Edward felt a flash of cold travel through him, but it was not the type of chill that could be warmed by a fire. "A harsh condemnation. Do you believe that you have given me a reason to seek revenge?"

The countess eased stiffly up in her chair. "I do not presume to understand anything about you, Edward, but there is no denying that we have had our differences over the years."

Differences! Edward could barely contain his snort of stunned amazement. "I would like all that to end, Mother."

"As if it all never occurred?"

"No, as if it were all part of a forgotten past."

She managed a melancholy smile. "Are you trying to be humorous?"

"My mood is hardly one of amusement."

"Nor is mine."

Edward could see the censure in his mother's expression. For a long moment he stared at her, trying to figure out a way to make her open her mind to accepting the sincerity of his desire to make things better between them.

An uncomfortable silence settled over the room. Edward continued to stare at his mother until a wave of disappointment overcame him. She would not relent.

"What is your opinion of the gas lights for the manor house?" he finally asked, needing to say something.

"They would be an abomination. Please leave your experimenting to your factories and your London home. At Farmington Manor we prefer living with the traditional, time-honored conveniences." A breath puffed out of her chest, an odd sound resembling a brief, bitter laugh. "Though I know all too well that I cannot force you to consider my wishes. That approach will only result in your rebellion."

The countess would not meet his gaze. She was breathing hard, and they both knew her displeasure had nothing to do with the gas lighting.

"You judge me most unfairly, Madame. But alas, that is a long-standing problem between us. There will be no gas lights installed unless you change your opinion on the matter." He turned toward the door. "I will send Miss Montgomery to you straight away so you may finish your letters."

As he walked away, Edward silently fumed and struggled with the pain in his heart that had existed since that fateful day he had defied his parents, all those years ago. He laid his hand on his chest and tried to soothe the aching need he felt for forgiveness, for approval, for affection from his mother.

And he wondered gloomily if that need would ever go away.

CHAPTER 10

The predicted snow had not yet begun to fall several days later, but all the signs were present. The thick cover of grey clouds, the biting cold air, the smell of moisture permeating everything.

A hearty group of the younger houseguests gathered on the south terrace, wisps of breath visible in the air as they chatted with each other. All expressed their desire to complete the chore of finding a suitable Christmas tree before the snow began in earnest, though a few said they hoped it would begin snowing while they were out in the woods.

Charlotte stood among the jovial group, her hands placed firmly inside her new fur muff. Every now and then her fingers would curl around the edges of the heavy envelope that Jonathan had passed to her beneath the breakfast table. The letter was intended for Miss Montgomery, but as she anxiously searched the faces of the crowd, Charlotte decided that since the countess was not in attendance it would be unlikely that her companion would join them.

Charlotte discreetly transferred the precious

letter to the pocket of her cloak, concluding it would be safer stored inside her pocket. Hoping no one noticed, she kept a pleasant smile on her face and watched the earl work his way through the crowd, kissing the gloved feminine hands held out to him and greeting the gentlemen with a hearty slap on the back. He moved with masculine grace and authority, completely at ease among his peers, confident and in control.

It was a marked contrast to his mood last night. During dinner and especially afterward he had been cordial, though distinctly remote, as if he were preoccupied with other, far more important matters. The only time he seemed to exhibit any sort of emotion was when he was near his mother; then his eyes seemed to shoot daggers in the older woman's direction.

Not that Charlotte could blame him. The countess had been in a particularly grating mood, loudly soliciting the earl's opinion and asking for his approval on any number of inconsequential issues. Did he like the wines that had been chosen for the various courses of the meal? Did her choice of musical selections that were played after dinner meet with his approval? Was he pleased with the number of desserts that were served with late-evening tea?

The countess's odd behavior had to be noticed by the guests, but they all took their cue from the earl, who gave no outward indication of his feelings and tried to ignore it. Charlotte decided it must have taken a great deal of self-control on his part. She doubted very much she could have kept her feelings and composure in check under the same circumstances.

Perhaps it was better that the countess did not

accompany them today as they searched for a tree, even though it meant that Miss Montgomery would miss all the fun.

"Are we ready to begin?" the earl asked.

Everyone gathered around him and the men immediately began a discussion about whether or not they should load into carriages that would bring them on a very indirect route to the edge of the woods or if they should simply walk. Lord Haddon cast a dubious eye at Lady Anne and Miss Dunaway, both of whom were wearing dainty slippers, far more suited to a drawing room than the woods, and suggested they use the carriages.

Lady Haddon joined the discussion, suggesting instead that the two women change into boots and once that was accomplished they all set out on foot, with the earl and his brother leading the way.

A few couples paired off, but for the most part the men and women remained grouped within their gender. It was then that Charlotte realized the majority of the group was married or engaged. Jonathan, Miss Dunaway, the earl and herself were the only unattached members of the party.

They entered the woods two abreast and Charlotte was pleased to find herself walking beside Lady Haddon. They chatted amicably, yet Charlotte's gaze kept drifting toward the men in front of them, specifically the earl.

Lady Haddon followed her gaze. "The earl is a remarkable man," Lady Haddon said under her breath. "Everyone is constantly singing his praises. If you will forgive my inquisitiveness, do you think there is any hope that the two of you might make a match?"

Charlotte's mouth fell open with shock and she shut it quickly. "'Tis highly unlikely."

"Pity," Lady Haddon said. "I always thought you would make a good pair."

"Really?" Charlotte felt like sighing. If only it were so simple.

"Oh, yes. You have similar interests and backgrounds, but more importantly, you have excellent balance of temperament between you. Rather like myself and Lord Haddon."

Charlotte's mouth curved into a crooked little smile. "Why is it that all married people wish that others would join them in their matrimonial state?"

"To share the joy?" Lady Haddon grinned. "I've heard it said that there is someone for everyone, and the older I have gotten the more I realized the truth of that statement. I do so hope you will not completely disregard the possibility of a future match between yourself and the earl."

Charlotte merely answered with a vague smile, neatly sidestepping the issue of her feelings on the matter. But Lady Haddon's remarks had brought the possibility out in the open, and once released, it was difficult to ignore.

The desperate anger Charlotte had felt toward him had long disappeared, replaced by a feeling of respect and understanding. And despite all her best efforts to ignore him, she had been unable to sustain a distant indifference. Quite simply, she liked him.

Charlotte's eyes again drifted to the men leading the way. She could see Jonathan waving his arms as he talked, could hear the other male voices chime into the conversation. Then she heard the earl's distinctive laugh and the sound caught at her heart.

Was Lady Haddon right? Did her true fate, the future she was meant to have, lie with the earl? It was an intriguing notion that deserved consideration.

If she dared to think upon it.

"The best fir trees lie off in this direction," the earl announced as he tucked a silver flagon into his inside coat pocket. "Hopefully it won't take too long to find several that we all agree are satisfactory."

"How many trees will we need, my lord?" Miss Dunaway asked.

"There are always two small trees placed on linen-covered tables flanking the entrance to the ballroom," the earl answered. "The children enjoy decorating those with flowers and sweets and garlands of ribbon."

"The adults like doing that too," Lady Haddon added, and everyone laughed.

There was much discussion and good-natured arguing as people began selecting different trees, each person insisting that they had located the *best* choice. The earl began systematically narrowing down the choices until only Lord Haddon's and Miss Dunaway's trees remained.

"Christmas-tree hunting is hard work," Jonathan declared. "I am very hungry. We must return to the house posthaste and feast on the special delicacies that Cook has prepared."

"Wait!" The earl lifted his arm. "We are not yet done with our work for the morning. We still need to find a tree for the drawing room. It will be the centerpiece of our Christmas decorations this year and I have decided we shall try something a little more daring."

"What are you saying, Edward?" Jonathan asked.

The earl had placed himself in front of an aged

evergreen. It stood at least fifteen feet high with full lush deep green branches that cascaded in a symmetrical pyramid. "Now, this is the perfect Christmas tree."

"'Tis far too large," Lady Haddon said. "It will collapse the table."

"Or tip it over," her husband added.

"Or knock into the ceiling and damage the chandelier when it is brought into the house," Lady Haddon said.

The earl shrugged.

"If you place the traditional small candles on the branches and light them on Christmas Eve after services, you will likely set the manor house aflame," Miss Dunaway said with concern.

Jonathan circled the tree slowly, his necked craning skyward, a dubious expression on his face. "It is far too large to be brought indoors, yet 'tis shaped very prettily. Perhaps we can use the top section of it for the drawing room?"

"No," the earl declared, waving his hand impatiently. "We shall use the entire tree. However, Lady Haddon is correct. It is too large to sit atop a table. Instead it shall stand on the floor."

"And promptly topple over," Lord Haddon said with a laugh.

"Not if it is secured properly," the earl said stubbornly.

"The countess will have a fit when she sees it," Lady Tredmont remarked in a loud voice. "I know that I would certainly object to having such a messy, inappropriate item indoors, dropping its needles all over my priceless carpet."

The earl's eyes darkened. "'Tis my house, and if

I choose to have a forest set up in the main ballroom to celebrate the holiday, that is my choice."

There was an edge to his voice that made Charlotte uneasy. Was this large tree a deliberate choice to agitate his mother?

"It will require an entire hothouse of flowers and miles of ribbon to decorate," Jonathan pointed out. "And how will we ever place any ornamentation on the upper branches?"

"We will use a ladder," the earl declared, his voice darkening to a timber that let everyone know he would not be dissuaded. "I have had special glass blown ornaments imported from Germany shipped to the manor house along with a menagerie of wood-carved animals. They will do very nicely as decorations."

There were still grumblings of disagreement, but the earl ignored them all. He signaled for the two burly male servants who had discreetly accompanied them to come forward. After a brief discussion with the servants, the men first cut down the two smaller trees. That chore took less than twenty minutes. When they were finished, they dragged the trees from the woods and loaded them into a waiting cart. Most of the houseguests followed.

The earl elected to stay behind. Charlotte joined him.

"We need to move away so we are not in the sight line of the tree when it is felled," he said.

Charlotte followed his instructions, standing beside him as she stared straight ahead at the enormous tree. It took far longer to cut through this thick trunk. The servants grunted and groaned as they pulled and pushed the heavy saw, the odd combination of sounds echoing through the quiet woods.

Finally the magnificent fir sank to the ground with a graceful *whoosh*. Charlotte felt a pang of sadness to see it lying lifelessly on its side, the branches spread out on the forest floor.

She glanced sideways at the earl, wondering if he was experiencing a similar emotion. But the line of his jaw remained firm and his eyes were shadowed.

The servants secured ropes to various sections of the trunk. Then with a simultaneous effort they began pulling the giant tree through the woods. Charlotte and the earl stood silently until it disappeared from view.

The quiet settled around them. It took a few moments for Charlotte to realize they were alone.

The earl removed his silver flask from his coat pocket and held it out to her.

"Care for a taste?"

She shook her head. He shrugged, lifted the flask to his lips and took a long swallow.

Charlotte's eyes narrowed. Sips of brandy to ward off the chill of the outdoors. Is that not what had started those kisses she had shared with him those many Christmases ago? Clearly, it was time for her to leave.

Yet her feet never took a step. She watched the earl's throat move as he drank. When he finished, he lowered the flask to his side. She could not help but notice how his lips glistened with a drop of the liquid still upon them.

Charlotte's stomach fluttered oddly, her pulse quickened, her heart began to thunder. All thoughts deserted her as she continued to stare at his mouth.

"Don't do that," he said quietly.

She blinked. "What?"

"Bloody hell," he whispered, moving closer.

And before she knew what was happening or could do anything to prevent it, he grasped her by the shoulders and pulled her against him. It was a shock to feel his firmly muscled body against her own, but even more of a surprise was his mouth on hers, warm and firm, his lips slightly parted.

Charlotte instinctively pushed against him, but he refused to release her. His mouth was demanding, insistent, plundering. She fought just a moment longer and then she surrendered, letting herself sink into the moment, letting his lips shape hers, his body heat hers. With a cry of pure passion, Charlotte's lips parted and her tongue met his.

His mouth was warm, soft against hers. She made a tiny sound, the barest whisper, but it was all he needed to take the kiss deeper. Her fur muff dropped to the ground, her hands curled around his shoulders. She could almost taste the desire simmering beneath the kiss, the desire for something more between them.

I should not be kissing him, Charlotte thought, and yet the feel of his tongue and lips was so glorious she could not stop herself. She tilted her head from one side to the other, pushing herself closer, never once breaking the intimate contact of their kiss. Her hands found their way to his chest and she could feel his heart beating under her palm.

A bewildering sweep of heat broke over her body and Charlotte began to feel more than a little dizzy. She clung to the earl and then he pulled back suddenly, wrenching his lips from hers, his breath coming in great gasps, his beautiful eyes a stark reflection of her own need.

"There is something about Christmas and the woods and being alone with you that makes me act like a barbarian," he said hoarsely, his voice as dark as midnight.

She swallowed hard. "Don't forget the brandy, my lord. It seems as though you only want to kiss me once you have partaken of strong spirits."

He gave her a narrow-eyed look, indecision and desire clouding his face. "I kiss you because I cannot seem to stop myself. Perhaps the brandy does give me a sense of false courage, but I can assure you that I am far from drunk."

Charlotte stared at him, moved by the utter conviction in his voice. Yet still so very uncertain of his motives and intentions. She took several steps away from him, feeling an almost physical deprivation without his nearness. "I threw myself at you six years ago and that is something I promise you I shall never do again."

"I know that." His mouth curled into a smile. "Though I cannot promise that I will not throw myself at you."

Charlotte struggled not to smile. There was something so amazingly possessed, so strangely attractive about the earl. She meant every word about not being so easily available to his charms, yet as she stared into his handsome face, it was increasingly difficult not to press her lips to his and run her hands over his chest. Or worst of all, to remain in this secluded spot where she could let him have his way with her.

It was only a lifetime of proper training, coupled

with a fair amount of pride, that held her in check. She turned to leave.

"Miss Aldridge! Charlotte, wait!"

Her mouth wobbled, her chest felt constricted by emotion. Yet somehow she found the courage and dignity to turn around and face him.

"My lord?"

"You forgot your fur muff."

She glanced down at the fashionable bit of fur for a long, puzzled moment. "Thank you."

The earl pressed his lips together, but Charlotte could see a faint glimmer of enjoyment on his face. She tried to fix him with a chilling stare, but it was impossible.

Instead, a smile she could not prevent curved her lips. The man was simply too damn charming for his own good.

Charlotte's thoughts were in turmoil when she returned to the manor house. She wanted nothing more than to spend a few quiet hours in her room, pondering the events of the morning. As she rounded a corner, the flash of a gray dress caught her attention. It was Miss Montgomery, moving swiftly down the hall. Her back was to Charlotte, so she did not see her. After a quick glance in all directions to assure they were alone, Charlotte called out.

"Miss Montgomery."

The companion stopped in her tracks, her ear cocked as if confused by the sound of the female voice. She whirled around, then smiled briefly when she recognized Charlotte.

"Miss Aldridge, good afternoon. Is there some way that I may offer you assistance?"

Charlotte advanced on her. "I have something to give you." She fumbled inside her cloak pocket, pulled out Jonathan's note and extended the envelope.

Miss Montgomery stared down at the note, her expression perplexed. "Do you wish me to have this letter posted for you? Harris, as butler, generally handles that household chore, but I would be happy to give it to him."

Charlotte shook her head from side to side. "The note is meant for you."

"You have written me a letter?"

"No. The letter is not from me." Charlotte leaned forward and whispered, "'Tis from a secret admirer."

Miss Montgomery, who was in the process of taking the envelope from Charlotte, pulled her empty hand away and leapt back as if she had just been scalded with boiling water.

"I have no admirer. Secret or otherwise." She stood at attention, stiff and unmoving. "You must be mistaken."

Charlotte smiled, trying to put her at ease. "There is no mistake. It's from Jonathan."

"Oh, dear." Aghast, Miss Montgomery clutched a fist to her chest as though her heart were aching.

Jonathan had told her that Miss Montgomery was fearful of any attention from him, but Charlotte was unprepared for such a violent reaction. "Do you dislike him?" she questioned.

"My opinion of Mr. Barringer is of no consequence." Miss Montgomery studied her for a long moment, almost as though she was trying to evaluate if Charlotte could be trusted. "Any association between Mr. Barringer and myself is highly improper. I am surprised that you would be a party to encourage him in this matter. He does on occasion need to be reminded that he must not shirk his responsibilities to his family. I would expect as his friend you would remind him of his duty."

A becoming blush colored her cheeks and Charlotte was surprised by how different Miss Montgomery appeared when a spark of passionate life shone in her eyes. She was a young and pretty woman, but clearly also considerate and wise. For just an instant Charlotte caught a glimpse of how lonely and isolated she must feel.

"A few lines of poetry hardly constitute an indiscretion," Charlotte said gently.

"If the countess ever found out . . ." Miss Montgomery began ruefully, her voice trailing off.

"She will not," Charlotte promised. "That is why I agreed to act as Jonathan's courier."

That brought a wan smile. Charlotte could see how tempted the other woman was to reach for the note, yet still she hesitated.

"You do not understand, Miss Aldridge, how much of a risk this is for me. How careful I must be." She wrapped her arms around herself as if trying to contain her emotions. "You do not know what it is like to be grateful and indebted and beholden to others for the roof over your head, every stitch of clothing you wear, every bite of food you put in your mouth."

Charlotte was a bit shocked, but she did not show it. "You are right. I have no notion of what your life is like each day. I imagine it must be awful."

Miss Montgomery shook her head. "I do not want to give the impression that I am not grateful for this job, because I am." Her frustration was visible. "It was difficult at first, but I have learned my place. I do not offer an opinion or participate in an important discussion because it is frowned upon.

"I have managed to survive unscathed because I am invisible, because I have so thoroughly concealed any part of my former self. I have masked my emotions for so long that I truly fear I do not know how to *feel* anymore."

"Then it is past time that you remembered."

Charlotte felt a sudden kinship with this woman who was struggling so mightily with her feelings. She had reluctantly agreed to act as Jonathan's go-between, but now she wanted, in some small way, to alleviate Miss Montgomery's loneliness, her isolation.

Charlotte pressed the envelope into the other woman's hand, wrapping her fingers around it, shielding it from view. Miss Montgomery's skin was icy cold and she was trembling. "Read it, every last word," Charlotte instructed. "Then hide it, guard it carefully."

For a long moment Miss Montgomery silently gaped at the envelope. She looked fragile, delicate and wary, as if the slightest sound might cause her to shatter into a million pieces.

She lifted her head. Her anguished gaze locked with Charlotte's, but then a calm seemed to settle over her entire being. She pulled herself up to her full height. "I will cherish this," she replied, holding the note close to her heart. "And if I should wish to reply?"

A huge wave of relief billowed over Charlotte and she barely managed to stifle a giggle. "I shall be happy to ensure that your letters reach the correct individual," she answered with a broad smile.

Miss Montgomery smiled, too.

Charlotte opened the salon door, anxious to visit her grandfather, pleased that they had decided to arrange some private time together. With so many activities planned throughout the day there had been few chances for them to share an honest conversation, to enjoy each other's company without feeling any restraints.

It was therefore a most unpleasant surprise to discover the countess was in the salon with her grandfather. The older woman was seated in a high-backed, ornately carved chair, which Charlotte immediately decided held an uncanny resemblance to a throne.

"Ah, there she is, Lord Reginald," the countess said, her false smile widening. "I told you she would arrive within the hour."

"Am I late?" Charlotte asked with a worried frown as she curtseyed to the countess. "I do hope you have not been waiting long."

"You are right on time, as always," Lord Reginald declared. Charlotte's heart lightened at her grandfather's sweet smile and she appreciated his little protective lie. Punctuality had never been Charlotte's strength.

"Do sit down," the countess instructed. "Harris will bring tea. And something a bit stronger for Lord Reginald. Then we can all have a cozy chat."

Puzzling over the countess's chummy behavior, Charlotte cautiously took a seat. She caught her grandfather's eye, and Lord Reginald shrugged, indicating he too was in the dark. Charlotte's heart thumped in her chest. Had the countess somehow discovered the note that Jonathan had written to Miss Montgomery?

And if she had, what would be the outcome? Charlotte was not well enough acquainted with the countess to know if there would be accusations or hysterics. Or both.

Harris entered with the requested refreshments and Charlotte quickly rallied. She was being foolish, worrying without good cause. She had been careful, discreet. It was highly unlikely the countess knew anything about the note or Jonathan's infatuation with Miss Montgomery. And if she did, well, Charlotte would deal with it.

She was not so easily intimated or bullied. Especially with Grandpapa by her side.

The countess dismissed her butler and took charge of the refreshments. The large ruby ring she wore on her right hand knocked sharply against the delicate china teacup as she passed it to Charlotte.

The door unexpectedly opened and the earl entered the room. The startled expression on his face told them all he had no idea it was occupied. There was a prolonged, awkward silence as he stood beneath the door frame, neither inside nor outside the salon. The countess refused to look at her son, her face pale but for the two bright spots of color on her cheeks.

Lord Reginald cleared his throat. "The tea is hot, the whiskey warm. Please join us, Worthington."

"I am sure the earl is much too busy," the countess interrupted.

The earl refrained from commenting, but his eyes narrowed and the hesitation he exhibited earlier disappeared. "I should very much enjoy sharing a glass of whiskey with you, Lord Reginald," he declared, though he entered the room with all the enthusiasm of a man being sent to the gallows.

"Oh, goodness, I fear this will make things rather awkward and uncomfortable for poor Miss Aldridge." The countess shook her head sadly and leaned closer to Charlotte. "In fact, this is as good a time as any to apologize to you for the earl's presence at Farmington Manor. I never would have extended the invitation to spend Christmas with us if I knew he was going to be here."

Charlotte raised her eyebrow and took a moment to focus her gaze on the countess. "Where else would the earl be at Christmas time than with his family?" she asked, feeling a great indignity on his behalf at being treated so shabbily by his own mother.

"There is no need for you to be so brave. Really, I cannot understand why you, of all people, would defend him," the countess continued, as if the earl were not in the room, hearing every word. "Not after the disgraceful way he treated you."

Charlotte blinked, then folded her hands together. "I am certain I do not know what you are referring to, my lady."

The countess paused and gave her a sympathetic look. "We all know that you were heartbroken, and rightfully so, when my son failed in his duty to ask you to marry him all those years ago. It was what everyone expected, what everyone wanted."

Horrified by the countess's indelicate comments, Charlotte froze. She lifted her chin and looked toward the earl. He stood still as a statue, his arms folded over his chest, his expression unreadable.

"I do not know what you were told of the events, but the earl did not break any promises to me. He did not deceive me in any way." Charlotte gazed pointedly at the countess.

The countess pressed her lips together and looked to Lord Reginald. He squirmed uncomfortably. "You refused the earl's proposal?" the countess asked.

"As you very well know, I did not make Miss Aldridge an offer of marriage," the earl said. Color had crept into his face, but his tone was remorseless.

Charlotte waited for the sour twinge of bitterness to hit her at his stark truth, but it did not come. She raised her chin. "Exactly. I was never jilted because there was no formal proposal."

"He led you on! He kissed you!" The countess's thin nostrils flared. "It was despicable, dishonorable behavior."

Charlotte felt a flash of sympathy for the earl. How awful that your own mother believed the very worst of you. Was it not a parent's role to defend, not condemn, their children, especially in front of others?

"The earl and I did share a kiss, but he did not lead me on. I can assure you, my lady, that I hardly expect an offer of marriage from every gentleman I kiss."

The countess squinted at her. "Perhaps now that you are older, your views have become more worldly, but those many years ago you did believe a kiss meant a marriage would be forthcoming."

"There is some truth to that way of thinking, but you must understand that any assumptions concerning a marriage between myself and the earl were only that—assumptions. And they were made on my part, due to my naivete." Charlotte's voice was surprisingly calm, considering her inner fury. "It appears you would like very much to hold your son accountable for any misunderstanding between the two of us, but in this case, he is blameless."

"You are so courageous, acting like a true lady even in the face of adversity," the countess said with a petulant twist of her mouth. "I would expect no less from a woman of your breeding."

"And yet sadly I expect far more from a woman of your background, my lady." Charlotte stood, her eyes flaming, and walked to the door. But before she left, she turned around and made her final point. "I only hope your son can find it in his heart to forgive you, but alas if he cannot, I know that no one of good conscience would blame him."

CHAPTER 11

As scenes go, it wasn't one of his mother's better efforts. When Charlotte left the room, the countess remained seated, her back rigid, a cloud of righteous indignation cloaking her anger. But she said nothing.

Edward decided it might be prudent to depart before she once again found her voice. With a nod of sympathy in Lord Reginald's direction and a stiff bow of farewell to the countess, the earl left the salon.

Happily, he spied Charlotte at the end of the corridor. With long, quick strides he was soon beside her, reaching out and grabbing her elbow as she was about to ascend the staircase and disappear to the sanctity of her bedchamber.

"I beg just a moment of your time, Miss Aldridge." She raised an eyebrow. "Has there not been enough drama for one afternoon, my lord?"

Edward ignored her sarcasm, opened the door to his private study and waited for her to join him.

"We need to keep this conversation very brief," she said, walking across the room away from him. "If we are discovered alone I fear your mother might insist that I have been irrevocably compromised and demand that you marry me."

Edward, watching her back, smiled. "I suppose anything is possible, especially when my mother is in such a snit. She did not appear to appreciate your comments."

Charlotte bent her head. "I honestly did not set out to provoke her."

"I believe you. One never intends to do battle, yet it takes little effort for my mother to get under one's skin."

Charlotte grimaced. "She does seem to have a particular talent for it."

Edward could not contain a small smile. "I apologize if she distressed you."

She gave herself a little shake. "No apology is necessary. I was not the one being attacked."

"My mother takes a perverse pleasure in baiting others, especially when she knows they will not fight back." He stared at her for a few brief seconds. "She knew I could offer little in the way of defense, but she never anticipated I would have a champion in you. I thank you for defending me, yet I must ask why. Why did you do it?"

"I was merely stating the truth," Charlotte said with quiet satisfaction. "It seems that the countess had been misinformed about the state of our relationship. I could hardly allow the opportunity to set her to rights slip away without saying anything, could I?"

"We both know 'tis more complicated."

"Perhaps it might have seemed so at the time, but now it is an unfortunate misunderstanding from our past and should be forgotten."

Edward leaned on his desk, cupping the hard

edge with both hands. Charlotte had surprised him greatly with her actions. She had told him last week that she accepted his apology and she had just proven how much she meant it. He was suddenly very interested in learning more about her.

"Forgive me for asking a most impertinent question, but marriage is the preferred state for most females. Why have you never married?"

Her brow furrowed and he was relieved she did not appear shocked or outwardly offended by his question.

"Marriage is a serious consideration. Women of our class marry for social and financial security," she replied, perching on the armrest of a large, overstuffed chair. "I am indeed fortunate to already possess both in abundance."

"And emotions? Are they not a contributing factor?"

"I have observed some marriages that are fraught with emotion. Which, I must say, can ultimately be damaging, especially if the union is not entered into with thoughtful and due consideration by both individuals." She paused and gathered her thoughts. "I am lucky to be afforded the chance to take my time searching for a man who will best please me. A man who has nothing in his past or his personality that would prevent him from giving and accepting love with ease."

Edward could not help but smile. So love was important to her. For some reason, the notion pleased him greatly, even though his own opinion on the subject was not nearly as emphatic.

"I'll own I do not spend as much time among society

as others of my rank, but surely there are some men who are worthy of your love," Edward pressed.

"I certainly hope so." She cleared her throat, but said no more.

"But they have remained unfound?" An odd thought suddenly struck him. "Are you searching hard enough?"

"I am searching very selectively." She glanced at him curiously. "When a woman marries, she gives her body, her independence and her worldly goods to her husband. I find that I treasure the first two far too much to make that decision lightly."

He bit back a smile. "Are you a romantic, Charlotte? Are you waiting for your one true love?"

She raised her eyebrow at his familiar use of her first name, yet considering the intimacy of their conversation he doubted she would insist on formality.

She stood up and paced a meandering course toward the windows at the back of the room. "Some people believe in keeping passion entirely separate from marriage. I suppose I could see the wisdom in that sort of thinking, but it would make for a very dull life."

"Would not a friendship between husband and wife make the love they share more lasting and durable?" he ventured.

"Oh, I want the friendship too, my lord. I want it all." She turned from the window and resumed her pacing. "Some people grow tired of searching for what has been elusive in their life and decide that they can only find happiness if they accept life the way it is, if they let go of their stubborn desire for something more." She took a deep breath. "I am not one of those people."

Their eyes met and he was surprised to see the depth of honesty and emotion reflected back at him. Surprised too to recognize a similar desire within himself. He never compromised when it came to matters of business, yet in his personal life, specifically his romantic life, he had been willing to accept a marriage to the daughter of a business associate because it made financial sense.

For the first time since his former fiancée walked out on him, Edward felt a sense of relief. He had been spared such a marriage without even realizing he would have never been happy, would have eventually come to hate it.

"Do you ever worry that it is an impossible quest?" he asked. "To find and keep this love?"

Charlotte hesitated a moment. "There is a small element of fear that perhaps I am wasting my life grasping at straws, searching for something that does not exist. But then I remember the stories my grandfather told me about my parents and the love that they shared, and I see how content and happy a couple such as Lord and Lady Haddon are with each other, so I know that it is possible." Charlotte blinked back a sudden tear. "In the end, for me, the heart will know what is best."

Her faith had a naive innocence he found charming. Could it really be that simple?

"How will you know when you meet this elusive man?"

"An excellent question." She smiled warmly at him. "I am not exactly certain, yet I continually hope and pray that I shall recognize him when I find him."

Could it be me? His voice caught in his throat. She was smiling at him with the timeless mystery of a desirable female. A flicker of need stole through him. Her lips were luscious, dark red and plump as fresh raspberries, but it was the expression of vulnerability on her lovely face that flew straight to his heart.

A discreet knock sounded at the door and Harris stepped into the study. "Beg pardon, my lord, but there is a problem below stairs that needs attention."

Edward turned absentmindedly toward the butler. "Did you inform my mother?"

"I did. The countess instructed me to speak with you about it," Harris said with a distinct note of disapproval in his voice.

Edward held back a retort of annoyance. It was hardly the butler's fault that his mother had picked a most inconvenient time to be difficult.

Charlotte moved forward, avoiding his eyes. "I shall see you at dinner this evening, my lord."

"I look forward to it, Miss Aldridge."

Though Harris held himself off at a discreet distance, there was no opportunity for further conversation. Edward caught a faint whiff of her delicate perfume as she breezed out of the room. The scent seemed to awaken a primal need within him, and his throat became very tight.

He turned to his butler, yet the earl had great difficulty concentrating on anything the servant said to him.

Miss Dunaway laid a hand lightly on the earl's arm and leaned closer to whisper something in his ear. She was in especially good looks tonight and Charlotte had to concede that most men would find Miss Dunaway's dark, nearly black hair, porcelain skin and clear blue eyes very attractive.

Apparently the earl was one of them. A startled expression crossed his face and he laughed at Miss Dunaway's next whispered comment. She, in turn, favored him with an inviting smile as she noticeably tightened her fingers on his arm.

Charlotte narrowed her gaze. It was ridiculous, of course, to feel such a sharp stab of jealousy. She had no specific claim on him, yet the notion that some other woman might felt very wrong.

As if sensing her regard, the earl halted his conversation with Miss Dunaway and turned and looked Charlotte's way. His gaze gripped her with its usual mesmerizing force and Charlotte's body grew warm. He gave her a slow, lazy smile that shone from his eyes.

For an instant, Charlotte could not catch her breath. She took out her fan and waved it before her face to hide her expression, unsure if she was shielding her reaction from the other guests or specifically from the earl.

She turned back to her grandfather, her cheeks faintly hot, and tried to concentrate on his conversation. But she barely heard a word. She noticed the countess in earnest conversation with Lady Anne, who was an excellent pianist, and wondered if that meant there would be impromptu dancing if Lady Anne could be persuaded to play for them all.

Dinner had concluded a bit earlier this evening and most of the guests seemed to be finished partaking of the coffee and tea that were served after it. But instead of dancing, the women decided on a musical interlude, and began organizing the order in which they would perform.

"Shall I put your name forward?" her grandfather asked.

"Not this evening. I shall sit and be entertained by listening to the other ladies' efforts," Charlotte replied, smiling at his loyalty.

Though he had hired the best music instructors in the land to teach his granddaughter, Charlotte had never been disciplined enough to practice on any of the various instruments Lord Reginald had bought with any regularity. To please him, she eventually mastered three pretty but simple piano pieces, but beyond that, she could barely play a note.

Charlotte settled herself comfortably on one of the green brocade settees located near the windows on the far side of the room, moving to one side to allow her grandfather a seat. He joined her, but she soon noted his attention was on the card table positioned in the corner.

"You should join Lord Haddon's game," Charlotte urged. "There is room for one more."

"Perhaps later," Lord Reginald said, patting her hand affectionately. "I do not wish to leave you on your own."

Charlotte appreciated her grandfather's good manners, but after a few minutes it was clear he was doing a poor job of concealing his interest in the gaming.

"Go," she insisted. "I shall be fine on my own."

She shooed him off with a wave of her hand and after another half-hearted protest, Lord Reginald leaned forward and kissed her on the cheek. "You are a good girl, Charlotte."

"Woman," she corrected in a mock tone of annoyance, rekindling a familiar battle between them.

Lord Reginald gave her a misty-eyed smile. "You will always be my darling girl, no matter how old we both get."

Charlotte grinned with affection and watched Lord Reginald leave. Then she sat back and looked around, wondering when the music would begin. Lady Haddon sat in front of the piano, poised to play, but a group of ladies were gathered around her, all eagerly sorting through sheets of music.

Jonathan was in the middle of the boisterous gang, trying to act as some sort of organizer, but the women were all aflutter, cackling like a flock of country hens. Miss Montgomery was there too, but she held herself apart from the others, both physically and emotionally.

Charlotte felt a twinge of sympathy for the young woman's situation, and wondered if she had read Jonathan's letter of poetry yet, wondered if the sentiments had pleased her. Or if they had made her long for things that would never be.

Charlotte's gaze drifted away from the women and settled on the men. She tried to keep her attention away from the earl, who was clustered in conversation with several other gentleman, but her eyes kept straying in his direction.

He was dressed in formal evening black, accented by a stark white shirt, vest and cravat, as were the other gentlemen, but on the earl the clothes seemed more dignified. He laughed at something Lord Bradford said, then excused himself and began to make his way across the room.

When she realized he was coming toward her, Charlotte sat up straighter and shifted uneasily on the cushions.

"May I join you?" he asked, gesturing to the empty spot on the settee beside her.

"Please do," she replied, sliding over.

He sat down and leaned back, draping his arm across the camelback of the settee. Charlotte tried to smile and make pleasant small talk, but it was difficult to concentrate with his hand so near the nape of her exposed neck.

Fortunately, the room soon filled with the sweet strains of a waltz, making conversation optional. There was polite applause when Lady Haddon finished her piece and Lady Anne took her place. This time it was a lively, baroque tune that echoed through the room, showcasing the older woman's talents and nimble fingers. Even the gentlemen at the card table momentarily halted their play to listen fully.

Inclining his head toward Charlotte, the earl whispered, "At least they are not playing Christmas carols again."

She turned to him in surprise. "Do you dislike carols?"

"Not usually," he answered with a twinkle in his eye. "But you must admit it does get tiresome hearing them several times a day."

Charlotte bit the inside of her cheek to keep from smiling. "You are not showing the proper Christmas spirit, my lord. If you keep this up, in short order you will be grumbling, 'Bah-humbug' like Mr. Dickens's Ebenezer Scrooge."

"There are worse things in the world," he said philosophically. "Besides, Mr. Scrooge was properly redeemed by the end of the story."

"Ahh, so there is hope for you after all," Charlotte said, giving the room a cursory glance. "It appears that Miss Dunaway is going to play the next piece. Perhaps you would like to turn the pages of her music, my lord?"

"There are other gentlemen anxious for the opportunity," he observed. "I shall let them do the honors. And I do wish you would call me Edward. 'My lord' is much too formal, especially given our long acquaintance."

"I suppose I could bring myself to call you Worthington," Charlotte quipped, feeling inordinately pleased that he was so disinterested in Miss Dunaway.

A shadow of distress crossed his face. "'Tis an odd thing to inherit a new name along with a title. In my mind, my father will always be Worthington. There are rare times even now when someone calls the name and I expect to see him standing in the room. Which is why I prefer that my most intimate acquaintances call me Edward."

She felt a flash of sympathy. "What would people say if I acted so improperly and began calling you Edward?" she asked with gentle compassion.

He pulled himself together. "Since when do you care what others think and do only what is proper?"

"You are remembering me as a girl. People do change as they mature."

"Yes, but not always for the better." He gave her a petulant look. "You call my brother Jonathan."

"That is different."

"How?"

"He is my friend."

The earl's eyes widened. "You mortally wound me. Jonathan is your friend, yet I am not. Why?"

Because my stomach does not turn into butterflies at the mere sight of your brother. The words sprang into her mind, but fortunately were left unspoken. "Since it is so important to you, I shall call you Edward whenever there is no one else within hearing distance," she said with a sly grin.

"Excellent. Then we must arrange to spend some time alone together. Are you free tomorrow afternoon?"

At that, Charlotte's mouth fell open. "Time alone? Without a proper chaperone? What a scandalous suggestion, my lord."

"Edward."

"My lord," she intoned forcefully.

"If you are so mortally offended, then why are you smiling?"

Charlotte sent him a quelling look. "I am not smiling. I am in shock."

"You are smiling," he insisted. "I do not understand why you must immediately conclude that I am intent on something improper." He leaned close and whispered in her ear, "I can assure you that I have not had a drop of spirits tonight. I drank only water with dinner and tea afterward."

She tilted her head to one side. "Why would I be concerned about the amount of spirits you have consumed?"

"You accused me the other day of only wanting to kiss you when I have been drinking. Tonight, I have proved that statement false because I have not been drinking and still very much want to kiss you."

She smiled at him, her heart beating fast at the rush of excitement, the allure of the forbidden and improper. He was flirting with her! She waited until the last piano piece had been played. Then concealing her fluttering emotions behind a casual expression of indifference, she leaned forward and whispered, "Good night, Edward."

An answering grin flickered at the corner of his lips. He stood, executed a formal bow and replied, "Dream of me tonight, Charlotte."

Sleep eluded Charlotte that night. Erotic visions of the earl, visions she did not completely understand, filled her mind. After tossing and turning restlessly for over an hour, Charlotte gave up the struggle.

Turning up the lamp she reached for the volume of poetry she kept beside her bed. Love sonnets. Not a good choice, given her current frame of mind. What she really needed was a dull, boring tome to lull her into sleep.

Knowing exactly what she needed could be found in the multi-volumed library on the lower floor, Charlotte climbed down from the four-poster bed, threw on a dressing gown and crept silently from the chamber. The household appeared to be asleep, with no guests or servants in evidence.

The candle she carried offered ample light, but Charlotte was relieved the hallways were lit by the occasional sconce. She turned into the long corridor and began counting the doors, pleased she remembered the overall layout of the house.

A feeling of hushed reverence stole over her as she entered the library. The sight of so many leather-bound volumes brought her an odd sense of comfort. A low fire still burned in the grate, offering some warmth but little additional light. With eager fingers she began scanning the titles on the lower shelf, her eyes alert to anything that might be of interest.

She fully intended to choose something dull tonight, but was also hoping to discover something exciting she would take to read tomorrow. Enjoying her search, Charlotte had no real idea of how much time had passed before she realized she was no longer alone. A sound, a breath, a feeling entered her awareness, causing her heart to skip a beat.

With a start of surprise, Charlotte turned around and saw the earl standing in the library doorway. His long, lean figure filled the space.

"I am sorry I startled you. I saw the light and came to investigate."

He was still dressed in his formal evening attire, but there were signs of uncharacteristic dishevelment that she found remarkably alluring. His coat was missing, his vest was open, the knot of his white silk cravat was untied, the ends hanging on either side of his neck, and the buttons at the top of his shirt were undone. She could see his exposed, naked throat and a few strands of dark hair curling at the top of his chest.

It was by far the most erotic moment of Charlotte's life.

She remained mute, her mind in a jumbled state of turmoil, her body sharp with anticipation. The earl too remained very still, staring intently at her, a strange expression on his face. Charlotte wanted to reach down and make certain her dressing gown was still properly fastened, but she resisted the gesture, knowing that it was indeed closed, and not wanting to draw even greater attention to her state of undress.

It took a few moments to realize it was her hair that intrigued him so much. She had told her maid to leave it unbraided and it was now unbounded and unruly, flowing down her back in honey-gold disarray. The earl seemed incapable of pulling his eyes away from it.

"Your hair is very beautiful," he said huskily.

A frisson of heat ran down her spine at the sound of his voice. Charlotte stood up straighter, her nerves on full alert. "Thank you."

In the sparse light of the lone candle, she studied his face for a long moment. The chiseled features, strong jaw, bold nose, enthralling amber eyes. He was a beautiful man.

"I should leave," he stated simply.

"Yes," she agreed, wetting her dry lips.

Neither moved a muscle.

Whether she was willing to admit it or not, deep down she wanted him, as she had six years ago. Was it passion? Lust? Or love?

Charlotte had no idea.

"We appear to be at a strange impasse, Charlotte. Unable to move forward until we settle our past."

She did not pretend to misunderstand. Though she had privately and publicly forgiven him for the incident all those years ago, part of it remained unresolved. "It hurt when you rejected me," Charlotte admitted a bit unsteadily. "I am not an individual who is used to being denied."

"It did not escape my notice that you seemed to somehow always get what you wanted."

Charlotte narrowed her gaze. "Are you calling me spoiled?"

"I am agreeing with your observation."

Though initially feeling insulted, his smile was so sincere and disarming, it was impossible for her to take offense.

"Well, it therefore stands to reason that the desire for something denied would grow stronger with the passing of time, becoming more and more irresistible," she said calmly. "Hence my continued fascination with you."

His smile widened with amusement. "Ahh, so now I am irresistible?"

Exasperated, Charlotte raised her eyes to the ceiling. "I am trying to be reasonable, logical, in understanding this strange attraction I seem to have for you."

"It is very much a mutual attraction."

Her heart quickened at the tender expression in his eyes. "'Tis not easy for me to acknowledge my emotions," she admitted. "I resented you for a very long time."

"And now?" he asked in a coaxing tone.

Charlotte drew in a deep breath. "I confess to feeling a certain fondness for you that I cannot explain."

"A certain fondness," he repeated dryly. "Words to warm a man's heart."

Charlotte sobered. He exhibited a vulnerability she would never have associated with such a self-assured man.

"What are your feelings toward me?" she asked, fearing the answer, yet unable to resist the opportunity.

He shrugged. "They are all tangled up in the past and the present. But they do exist and though I have tried, I find it difficult to ignore them."

She managed an uneven smile. "Do you wish to ignore them?"

"It would be the most sensible, logical course. I

am well aware of my behavior six years ago. I am certain it sounds odd, but I did not reject *you*, I rejected marriage. I refused to take an heiress as a bride to solve my financial problems, but more importantly I needed to be unencumbered so I could focus all my attention on my business. I know now that I caused you pain and I regret that more than I can say. Above all else, I do not wish to hurt you again." His voice was low, intense. "I am looking to you for guidance."

She sighed. "I have no answers, Edward."

"What do you want, Charlotte?"

"Peace," she admitted.

He stepped forward, reached out and took her hand. "We are not at war."

His words brought a tightness to her chest. For so long she had believed she hated him, and now she knew it was far more complicated. Knowing he had regrets, remorse about how his actions had affected her, soothed her pride, eased any lingering hurt.

His gaze shifted down to her feet, then back up in a slow, deliberate manner, a sensual visual caress, ending with him staring into her eyes.

She could not blink, for it was impossible to tear her eyes away, caught in his stare as though he held her in a spell. Just his nearness made her senses more acute. Charlotte could hear the wind howling outside the window, could feel the warmth from the fire in the grate, could smell the pleasant tang of his cologne.

He looked as uncertain as she felt, as if he too were warring with his conscience and desire. But his eyes were dark with need and filled with something more than uncontained passion.

She raised her hand and rested her splayed fingers on the hard plane of his chest. "What do you want, Edward?" she asked in a husky tone.

"You." His voice sounded strong and confident, yet his eyes betrayed the uncertainty of his emotions.

He leaned forward as he spoke, his face very near, his lips nearly touching her. She remembered the feel of them, the searing heat of his kiss in the woods. Charlotte shivered with indecision. If he kissed her now, she doubted she would resist.

In the hushed silence of the room she could practically hear the beat of her own heart as she struggled for the resolve to do the right thing. Suddenly a noise, sounding like a ball tumbling across the floor, echoed outside in the corridor.

"What was that?" Charlotte asked in alarm, pulling her gaze away.

It was as if a spell had been broken. The earl moved forward and blew out the candle, plunging the room into near darkness. It took a few moments for Charlotte's eyes to adjust.

"Why in the world did you do that?" she hissed. "I can barely see my hand in front of my face. If I take but a few steps I will no doubt trip over something and injure myself."

"Then don't move."

"We can hardly stand here all night."

"Why not? The noise in the hall must have been the servants. We can avoid being discovered if we keep the room in darkness." He smirked with satisfaction.

At least she thought he smirked. It was so dark, it was difficult to fully see the expression on his face. Trapped alone in the dark together and his main thought was that they were avoiding a scandal. How lowering!

"I believe you are possibly the most unromantic man I have ever met," she declared in a huff of annoyance.

"True, I am pragmatic, but that does not mean I do not have other sides to my nature." His hands reached out and grasped her shoulders. "Shall I prove how truly romantic and passionate I can be, Charlotte?" he whispered in her ear.

His hands began moving over her, stroking, teasing, enticing, and her mind was not entirely on the conversation. Fleetingly, she tried to think, tried to decide if she should stop him. The air around them shimmered with sexual awareness. Charlotte watched him, unable to move, wondering if he would let her leave if she turned away from him.

But, oh, how he tempted her to stay! His lips moved lightly across her throat, then he slipped his hand behind her neck and drew her close. Their lips met, melding together in a sensuous, ravenous kiss, echoing the hunger so long denied between them.

Charlotte's knees literally buckled, yet she was in no danger of falling, for Edward held her tightly to him. The scalding pressure of his kiss softened and her body jolted with the erotic touch of his tongue against hers.

She felt bound to him, body to body, heart to heart. A turmoil of emotions and feelings ran through her mind, but she now admitted that her connection to him was more than the irresistible taste of passion he had given her, more than the raging fever he aroused in her so easily.

The vulnerability she felt around him was no

longer frightening; it was liberating. She was facing a crucial decision, an irrevocable step, and for the first time in her life, the answer was clear and simple.

"Lock the door, Edward," Charlotte whispered.

He froze, then closed his eyes and bent his head to her forehead. "Are you sure?"

"Yes, very sure." She turned her head and brushed her lips along the line of his jaw. "And do please, hurry."

CHAPTER 12

There was a part of Edward that knew he should walk away. The staid, somber, considering part of his nature told him to act as an honorable, gallant peer of the realm, to exercise his famous self-restraint and leave. He knew full well if he locked the door he was treading on dangerous ground, he was making an unspoken commitment to be what Charlotte desired in a husband.

She wanted friendship, companionship, but most of all she wanted love—of that she had been very clear.

Was he the man to give it to her?

The lock clicked into place effortlessly. The sound was oddly comforting, strangely reassuring. Edward turned to Charlotte. He, who had always weighed each decision in his life most carefully, and concluded this was the right moment to let his emotions and passion control his destiny.

The gloom of the room disheartened him. The fire, burning very low, offered little light, the candle Charlotte had brought with her was long extinguished. This would not do.

He wanted to see every inch of her, wanted her to see every inch of him. Reaching for a brace of candlesticks, he lit both, then quickly lit a second and third brace. He placed them in different areas of the library and the room soon glowed with a soft, romantic light.

Pleased with the effect, Edward turned again to Charlotte. Her eyes were wide with curiosity and an edge of excitement. He could see no fear or doubt, but that did not mean she was not feeling those emotions.

Edward gentled his expression and approached her, setting a hand on her arm. "It's not too late to change your mind."

"Oh, yes it is, Edward." She stood very still, staring up at him as if he had lost his powers of reasoning.

Her sweet scent rose to encircle his senses, her tempting lips beckoned, her womanly curves teased. She let out a breathy gasp when he traced his thumb slowly over her lower lip. He could feel his blood heating, could feel his control starting to slip.

Stepping closer, Edward gathered Charlotte close, buried his face in her glorious hair, breathed in the scent of her sweetness and was lost. He cradled her face between his hands and kissed her slow and deep, kissed her with all the emotion he had so carefully kept in control.

The next kiss had her leaning against him, softly whispering his name before her tongue began dancing with his. He ran his hands down along her spine, feeling the warmth of her skin through the silk of her dressing gown, passing his hands slowly over the flare of her hips, lingering on the enticing curve of her posterior.

Edward caressed, then cupped her bottom, drawing her fully against his erection, shifting so that she could feel the full, hard length of his desire for her. An urgent shudder racked her spine and sent a wave of heat racing through his body that stiffened his already turgid penis.

His hands found her breasts. He hastily pushed aside her dressing gown, popped open the two top buttons of her nightgown and slid his fingers inside. With his hand still clutching its glorious prize, Edward lowered his head, nuzzling the column of her throat, tasting and nipping at the exposed sections of bare flesh, sliding lower, lower until he was able to drag his tongue across her nipple.

Charlotte's head fell back, giving him wordless encouragement. With a groan of excitement Edward eagerly wrapped his lips around her nipple and suckled her, taking the delicious flesh far inside his mouth. Her breasts were more magnificent than he had imagined, enticingly round and soft, the rose-tipped nipples large and pebble-hard. They strained against his tongue and he felt the ripple of need shudder through her body.

Little mewing sounds came from Charlotte's throat as his tongue flicked to first one and then the other breast. Her honest response spurred Edward's desire, emboldened him to reach down between her legs and caress her womanhood.

Deftly, his fingers parted the swollen lips, gently rubbing until he felt the sweet moisture of her desire. He fondled her with delicate strokes, his long fingers gliding through the silky curls, his fingertip brushing repeatedly over the erect little bud where all her pleasure centered.

"Edward?" she said shakily, her entire body tightening. "Oh, Edward."

His hand stroked her one more time, then stilled.

"Charlotte, are you frightened?"

"No, I am confused. I feel hot, yet I shiver. I feel restless, edgy, yet languid with pleasure when you stroke my body."

"If you want me to stop, you must tell me now," he said hoarsely, knowing he was barely beyond the point where common sense would prevail. "Do you understand?"

She stared at him for a long moment. Then she slowly lifted her hand and stroked his cheek. "I cannot possibly stop," she whispered in a voice so soft he could barely hear the words. "I want this very much." Her breath caught. "I want it to be you, Edward."

A surge of profound emotion shot through him. "I am deeply honored," he whispered.

Edward barely recalled removing his clothing, yet somehow he was naked. His fingers felt too large, too clumsy as he tried to open the remaining tiny buttons on the front of her silk-and-lace nightgown.

"Rip it," she begged, and with a growl Edward hooked his fingers into the neckline and tore the fabric down to her waist. The savage sound sent his blood pounding even harder through his veins.

Heat and possessive ownership surged through Edward as he pressed a nude Charlotte down into the softness of the carpet. Her breasts were gloriously full and ivory soft in the glow of the candlelight. He placed his hand on the delicate curve of her shoulder and dipped his head, capturing a rosy nipple in his mouth.

Charlotte cried out, her body rising to meet his. Her head thrashed against the floor. He used his teeth and tongue with tormenting gentleness, increasing her excitement. Edward lifted his head, keeping his eyes on her face as he cupped her breasts and feathered kisses over the tips. She cried out again and the primitive expression of desire drove Edward's passion higher.

She was beautiful. So undeniably beautiful.

Her skin was the color of rich cream; it glowed irresistibly in the light of the fire. She was perfectly formed, with delicate shoulders, a small waist and curvaceous hips.

Pangs of excited apprehension went through him as he tried to recall all that he knew about bedding a virgin. Almost nothing, actually, since he had never bedded one before. Yet somehow it seemed most fitting that they would both be embarking on a new experience.

He debated how to proceed. He reasoned her knowledge of the act would be limited, since her mother had died when she was so young. Yet discussing the particulars of what they were about to do would certainly destroy the mood. It would be best to simply allow passion to take its natural course, to ensure that her body was teased and pleasured and ready for his possession.

That would be a most enjoyable task.

He kissed her belly, her navel, then slid his hands beneath her buttocks and lifted her to him. The smell of her skin was intoxicating.

"Edward?" Her voice trembled.

"I want to taste you, Charlotte, to worship you with my mouth."

"Do men and women really do such things?"

"Yes, when they trust each other. It brings them both great pleasure." He sensed she might be afraid of what he could make her feel, but he also sensed curiosity mingled with her desire. "Do you trust me, Charlotte?"

"I do, but . . ." She scrutinized him and he could almost see the indecision raging inside her.

"Every part of you is beautiful, Charlotte."

She cried out when he put his mouth on her, shuddered as he stroked the delicate flesh within. He gripped her hips in his hands, not allowing her to hide anything from him as his tongue glided over the swollen bud of her sex in curling strokes.

Her soft eager whimpers turned to sobs as his tongue plunged rhythmically into her, her breath grew rapid and harsh, her hands desperately clutched at his hair. She arched upward, offering more of herself, and he increased the tempo of his strokes until she began to shudder uncontrollably. A second later she cried out in release, her hips jerking hard against his lips and tongue.

He was entranced, feeling her shiver under his on-slaught, knowing he was bringing her pleasure. His breath coming fast and urgent, Edward rose up on his knees. It took everything he had to stay in control.

"Touch me, Charlotte," he groaned. "Feel how much I want you." Almost roughly, he took her hand and guided it toward his erection.

She ran her fingers over it. He jerked at her touch, then pushed against her palm. He taught her the movement that pleased him, then allowed her hand to explore and stroke.

"Tighter," he whispered, moaning at the exquisite sensations her fingers produced. "Harder."

Her hand tightened on his penis and it throbbed in her palm. The pleasure was so intense it was almost painful. Edward rolled himself on top of her, parted her legs and settled himself between them. Still not penetrating her, he slid his throbbing cock back and forth between her upper thighs. With every movement she moaned loudly and rocked against him. She was ready, more than ready, and he knew he had better complete the act or else he would disgrace himself.

Edward shifted himself above her, pushed her legs wider apart with his knee, then carefully guided himself inside the wet heat of her body. She was relaxed from her earlier orgasm, but he soon reached the barrier of her virginity. He had known it was there, of course, but the tightness sent a scorching heat through his blood.

He pushed gently and she moaned softly with pleasure. Encouraged by her response, he thrust a little deeper, bringing himself again against the firm barrier. He knew he had to slow down, had to make this good for her, but it was difficult to think rationally with his emotions and passions riding at such a fevered pitch.

Gripping her hips, Edward held her in place, hoping to allay the initial pain by inching in slowly. Charlotte lifted her head and began showering kisses on his upper arms and his control snapped. Her flesh resisted, but he pushed upward, stretching the soft tissue until it broke, burrowing deeper until he was fully inside.

For a long moment he did not move, reveling instead in the powerful joy of their being one, joined together in the most basic, primal act of man and woman. She looked up at him, dazed. His gaze locked with hers. Her eyes were dark with wonder and passion and an emotion so keen he dared not imagine what it meant.

"Charlotte." He leaned down and brushed his lips against hers. "You are the most perfect woman I have ever known."

"You are the only man I have ever known," she murmured softly. "And that makes me enormously happy."

"Ah, but there is so much more to experience," he replied with a wicked chuckle.

Edward surged forward, propelling himself all the way inside her, then withdrawing to the tip. He repeated the motion over and over until she was panting and straining against him, grabbing his shoulders for leverage, tilting her hips eagerly upward, driving her pelvis hard against his.

Fascinated, he watched her face as he thrust back and forth, driving himself into her heat, marveling not only at the physical sensations of pleasure, but the emotional joy that brought an unexpected and profound dimension to the moment.

Wanting to savor every second, Edward slowed his movements, propped himself up with both hands flat on the carpet, then looked down at where they were joined together.

The sight of his swollen cock impaling her raised his passion to an almost frenzied level. His rhythm became urgent again, his voice cried out in a sound of triumph as he filled her, pleasured her, claimed her.

"Does that feel good?" he asked, changing the way he moved, using the hardness of his body and the strength of his thrusts to stroke her most sensitive area.

"'Tis glorious," she panted. Her eyes squeezed shut, her nostrils flared, her breath came in great, gulping gasps.

"Look at me, Charlotte," he commanded.

Gradually, she opened her eyes. They were glazed, unfocused as they stared into his. She looked utterly abandoned and incredible lovely. Though she was not seeing him, he knew she was aware of every breath he took, every powerful move of his body.

Edward was still watching her when he felt the wild ripple that shook her body as her orgasm began, as she bucked and writhed beneath him, her naked cries of pleasure echoing through the silent room. It made him fight harder to keep his own release in check, even as the urgent hunger inside him threatened to explode.

He held her quaking body tightly and continued his careful thrusts, prolonging the pleasure for her as long as possible. Then her body started spasming wildly, her inner warmth squeezing tightly around his cock, pushing his craving for release over the edge.

Crushing her to his chest, he began to thrust harder and faster, racing toward fulfillment. He focused on the tension, increasing the rhythm that ran through him like wildfire, kissing Charlotte madly, as though he could not get enough of her. His mouth burrowed into her hair, pushing it aside so he could suckle at the delicate pulse at her neck.

She arched her back, shuddered in his arms and tipped her head sideways to allow him whatever he wanted, whatever he craved. Edward's muscles turned to stone, sweat drenched him and then he began to quake and shudder. His entire being was caught in the grip of this blissful, profound union. With a groan of indescribable pleasure, Edward's passion peaked and his seed spewed from his cock in a hot, potent stream.

The raw rush of pleasure exceeded anything he had ever felt before. Collapsing to the side, he buried his face in her shoulder, his fingers clutching her breast possessively, their bodies still joined. Dazed, Edward listened to the sound of their harsh breathing as the pleasure slowly faded.

Fearing he was crushing her, Edward move to withdraw, then felt Charlotte's hands clinging to his shoulders.

"Stay, please. Do not leave me yet."

Filled with languid, blissful pleasure, he acquiesced to her demands. When the heat of their bodies began to cool, he cuddled her against his chest, threading his fingers through the fine locks of her hair. Her breathing became slow and even, and though exhaustion also claimed him, Edward did not succumb.

His mind was too restless to sleep, his emotions too raw to be quiet. Though not a large number, there had been other women in his life, women with whom he had shared a physical relationship for weeks, even months at a time.

Yet never before had he felt this way with any

female. He was unsure if it was because Charlotte had been a virgin or because their mating was a spontaneous moment of unbridled passion, or if the illicit, forbidden aspect of their coupling heightened the level of excitement.

Edward's jaw tensed as he realized it would serve no useful purpose to search for an explanation, because the reason, or reasons, were unimportant. The notion was strangely liberating, as if allowing him for once to just feel and not think. To be honest with himself and acknowledge that this was truly the most extraordinary night of his life.

Charlotte must have dozed for a time, sated and content, for when she opened her eyes the candles were burned low, the fire in the grate all but gone. She lay peacefully within the circle of Edward's arms, listening to his soft, rhythmic breathing, marveling at how comfortable, how natural it all felt.

Edward's lovemaking had been more overwhelming than she had ever imagined and the strength of her longing for him was a mysterious delight, something to be pondered and thought over in the coming days.

There were a great many questions to ask each other, but tomorrow would be time enough for thinking and considering and deciding. Tonight was for reveling in the moment, for rejoicing in the experience.

"We cannot remain here all night," he murmured.

Charlotte nodded her head in agreement, though in truth she felt a stab of disappointment at his pronouncement. It was a bit lowering to acknowledge that the first words he spoke to her after this profound, life-altering event were so impersonal. It seemed that the wild, bold, impulsive lover of her dreams had vanished and the sensible, practical Earl of Worthington had returned.

With rioting emotions Charlotte watched him put on his shirt and trousers, leaving both unfastened. Their clothes were everywhere, strewn on the carpet in a reckless, abandoned manner. He retrieved her dressing gown, then helped her into it, tying the sash securely at her waist. Once they were both wearing something, he gathered up her torn nightgown and the remainder of his clothing and stuffed them into her hands.

"You carry these," he commanded. "And I will carry you."

Before she could even digest his words, Edward scooped her up in his arms and headed for the door. He re-positioned her to one side as he unlocked the chamber with one hand, then using his foot, he kicked open the door and stepped into the hallway.

He glanced both ways before taking another step, she assumed to ensure that there was no one about, even at this very late hour.

"Lurking and prowling about the house is far more difficult with a house full of guests," he whispered, as if reading her thoughts.

"It would be easier if you put me down. I am perfectly capable of walking," she answered.

He shook his head. "I like the way you feel in my arms."

That was certainly welcome news. "You are very

strong," she said, clinging to his neck as he ascended the stairs.

He grinned. "I feel as though I have the strength of ten men tonight."

Her brow lifted indignantly. "Are you implying it takes ten men to lift and carry me, sir?"

"At least. Precisely how many helpings of dessert did you have this evening?"

"Three very large portions," she lied, pressing her full body length wickedly against his.

"Stop wiggling or I shall drop you," he said in a commanding tone, yet his voice was colored with amusement.

"If I hit the floor I shall scream very loudly," she retorted, running her fingers through his hair.

He flexed the muscles of his forearms, but held her rock-steady. Charlotte lifted her chin and stole a quick taste of his lips.

"Stop kissing me or else I really will drop you."

"Well, since it would be my fault for distracting you, I will not scream, though I daresay the noise of me thudding onto the stairs would bring the servants running."

"It is not the servants we need worry about," he replied. "If they saw us, they would say nothing, nor tell anyone else."

"To keep their positions."

"Partially." He reached the top of the stairs, lengthening his stride as he turned down a long hallway. "But they would hold their tongues out of respect and regard for me."

Though a somewhat boastful statement, it was not made in that manner. "'Tis true, I have noticed that the staff admires you greatly," Charlotte agreed.

"Must you sound so shocked? I am a very likable fellow, you know."

Warm in the circle of his arms, Charlotte toyed with his shirt buttons. "I suppose there are certain things about you that can be nearly irresistible."

His heated gaze swept over her. "Only nearly irresistible? Not overwhelming irresistible?"

She made a scoffing sound in the back of her throat, enjoying their teasing banter, yet determined to maintain the upper hand. It would hardly do to let him know how truly irresistible he was to her at this moment, though the fact that she had just surrendered her virginity to him should give him a rather clear indication.

He reached the doorway of her bedchamber, kicked it open, then carried her across the room and set her gently on the bed. He left her to lock the door before going to the washstand. Curious, she watched him pour water from a small jug into a porcelain basin. He dipped a cloth into the water and wrung it out.

Returning to the bed, he sat beside Charlotte. She shifted uneasily, suspecting what he intended. "I can do it myself," she insisted, reaching for the cloth.

"I know," he said, pressing the cloth between her thighs, causing her to jerk in response. "But it is my privilege as your lover to minister to you and I intend to assert my rights."

He sounded so determined, so concerned, that the majority of her embarrassment evaporated. Charlotte nodded her head in silent agreement. She lay back and tried to relax, but it was difficult to feel completely at ease. At least the chamber was bathed in semi-darkness, with only the moonlight from the open drapes and the glow of the low-burning fireplace to illuminate it.

"I am sorry it's so cold," he murmured as he tenderly bathed her flesh and washed away the traces of his seed and her virginal blood. "If it is truly unbearable I can ring for my valet to bring hot water. It won't take long."

"There's no need, since you are nearly done," she replied.

He leaned forward and kissed the tip of her nose, then returned to the washstand. Using the same cloth and the rest of the water, he cleansed himself. "Do you want me to help you change into a clean nightgown?"

"No. I am going to be exceedingly wicked and sleep without one," Charlotte announced. She untied the sash of her wrapper and slid between the sheets of the large bed, shivering at how cold it had become in her absence. "Will you stay with me?"

Surprise flashed across his face. He hesitated, glancing at the clock on her fireplace mantle. "For a few hours. But I must leave before the household awakens."

"Of course."

Charlotte watched him closely as he quickly shed his clothes, then climbed on the bed to lie by her side. She waited breathless for him to turn and take her in his arms, but the minutes slowly ticked by and he never moved.

Perhaps he needed a little encouragement? Charlotte shifted to her side and moved closer to him, hoping he would take the hint. "Are you going to kiss me?" she finally asked.

He leaned over and planted a chaste kiss on her cheek. "Good night, dearest. Sleep well."

That was all? In a huff, Charlotte sat up, leaned back against the headboard and stared straight ahead. "I am not your maiden aunt, Edward, so please refrain from kissing me as though I were some distant relation."

Slowly, he sat up. The sheet slid down to his waist, baring his naked chest. Charlotte's hand itched to reach out and caress it, to feel the warmth, to glide her fingers through the springy hair, to press her palm against the taut muscle.

Edward raised one hand to touch her face, spreading his palm across her cheek, his fingertips reaching into the hair at her temples. "One kiss will lead to two and then three and then I shall have you flat on your back with your legs spread in no time at all."

Charlotte wiggled delightfully, his words sending a warm rush between her upper thighs. "That sounds marvelous," she purred, giving in to temptation and touching his chest.

"'Tis too soon," he snapped.

Her hand stilled, and she felt the hint of a blush fill her cheeks. "I did not realize you would need so much time to recover your strength," she said, lowering her gaze to cover her embarrassment and disappointment.

He made a sound that might have been a laugh. "That is hardly the problem, Charlotte." He picked up her hand, pressed a quick kiss to her wrist, then placed it boldly over his erection. His stiff penis throbbed within the softness of her hand.

"How wonderful," she murmured.

Charlotte pushed herself forward into his embrace, flattening her breasts against his muscular chest. His body was warm and strong, his growing arousal nudging against her stomach. The rhythm of her heart pounded restlessly in her chest as she kissed her way up from his chest to his throat.

"Charlotte." His voice was husky with warning. "You really must listen to me."

"Why?" she asked, reaching his chin and urging his mouth to hers. If she was kissing him, he could hardly argue with her, now could he?

She sought his mouth with another hungry kiss. He resisted for a mere instant, then rolled on top of her. Charlotte's legs opened instinctively. She set her feet flat against the mattress and tilted up her hips. Edward's eyes widened and he clasped her hands in his, pushed them high above her head, then leaned down to kiss her.

She arched her back, weaving her fingers through his. Her breath came in short bursts as his lips traveled from her mouth to her throat. He took a nipple in his mouth, suckling and teasing his tongue over it.

The same amazing sensations she had delighted in a few short hours ago trembled through her entire being and she heard her voice cry out in pleasure in the quiet bedchamber.

Abruptly, Edward pulled himself back, dragging in his breath roughly. "This is madness."

She clutched at his wrists to keep him close. Their eyes met and Charlotte reached for his hands and held them, one in each of her own. He glanced down at her breasts briefly, then returned his gaze to her eyes.

"Being with you like this makes me very happy, Edward. Does it not please you also?"

"It pleases me greatly." His eyes glimmered and she felt their heat. For a time he watched her silently. "'Tis against my better judgement, but I know you like to get your own way too much to be denied. But I want your word that I will hear no complaints from you tomorrow about soreness and aches and pains."

She shivered with delight and wicked anticipation, then shot him a coy look.

"There will be no complaints from me, my lord, as long as you pleasure me utterly," she said saucily.

"I've created a monster," he groaned.

"Aye." A teasing glint flashed in her eye. "And 'tis past time that you did."

CHAPTER 13

"Are you awake, Miss Charlotte?"

Charlotte slowly opened her eyes, expecting to see the first hint of daylight creeping into the room. Instead, the chamber was awash in bright winter sunlight, and her maid was staring down at her with a furrowed, concerned line between her brows.

"Good morning, Jones." Charlotte smiled weakly. "Is it very late?"

"Nearly noon," the maid replied. "You never stay abed so long. Are you feeling poorly?"

"No, I'm fine," Charlotte answered.

To illustrate the point, she moved to sit up. As she did, the sheet and coverlet slipped to her waist, revealing her lack of nightclothes. Jones stared at her in shock, then hastily turned away.

Flaming with mortification, Charlotte snatched up the sheet with a gasp. It had felt so wonderful, so natural to be this way with Edward last night, but the feeling did not linger in the bright reality of daylight.

"Bring me my blue wrapper," Charlotte commanded,

sitting up carefully, making certain to keep the blankets over her breasts and beneath her arms. She slipped on the robe, thankful there were no visible tears in the silk fabric, then went to the wardrobe to select her morning outfit.

"I cannot find your nightgown, Miss Charlotte, and I'd like to clean it. I'm sure I'll be able to make it presentable again. Vinegar and salt can do wonders with a stubborn stain."

Charlotte turned and saw Jones holding the porcelain washstand bowl containing the dirty water from last night. She felt her face flush. Obviously, the maid had seen the bloodstains in the water and assumed her monthlies had come on during the night. She further assumed Charlotte had soiled her nightgown, which would explain why she wasn't wearing it.

Thankfully, Jones did not realize Charlotte was completely naked. She no doubt thought Charlotte was wearing underdrawers.

"Never mind about the nightgown," Charlotte said hastily, deciding it was past time to change the subject. "What I really need is a hot bath. Can you arrange for one, please?"

The maid eyed her oddly, but did as she was asked. Within the hour Charlotte was reclining in a copper slipper tub that had been set near the fire, her head leaning back against the rim, one leg dangling carelessly over the side.

The hot water felt wonderful on her sore muscles and tender flesh. Steam rose like a London fog from the bath water, condensing on her upswept hair, engulfing her body in its luxurious warmth.

"Shall I wash your hair, Miss Charlotte?"

"No, thank you, Jones. I can attend myself. I'll ring when I need you."

The maid sank in a hasty curtsey and left, though her expression remained mystified. But Charlotte had too much on her mind to worry about her maid's reaction to her very strange behavior.

Relishing her time alone, Charlotte lay back and wiggled her toes, spreading little ripples through the water. The door slammed open and Charlotte sighed with annoyance. She turned her head to once again dismiss her maid.

But it was not Jones who had entered her bedchamber.

"My God, Edward, what are you doing in here?" Charlotte levered herself upward, causing water to slosh over the edge. Realizing she was giving the earl an eyeful, she dropped back down into the warm water, crossing her arms across her chest. "This is outrageous."

He gave her a measured stare. "I wanted to see you, Charlotte."

"Well, you cannot! For pity's sake, I am in the bathtub!" she hissed.

"I can see that." He smiled oh, so sweetly. "I do not mind."

"Well, I do." Charlotte could feel the anger growing in her, spurred on no doubt by the nonchalance of his voice.

He came closer to the bath and stood, looking down at her with hungry eyes. "You are so lovely. All dewy and pink, like a delicate rosebud on the verge of blooming." He touched her bare shoulder, then let his fingers slide down until they reached the water.

Charlotte felt herself turn crimson. Drawing her

knees beneath her chin, she tried to shield herself from his hot gaze. "You must leave at once! If anyone caught you in here—" Charlotte shivered violently, unable to voice the rest of that thought.

The earl ignored her near-hysteria, rested his hands on the edge of the tub and leaned down, kissing her on the mouth. "Forgive my bold intrusion. I missed you at breakfast this morning and became worried as the hour grew late and you did not appear."

Charlotte was feeling too mortified to be charmed, even though his kiss had put all her senses on alert. "You could have sent me a note," she chided.

He extracted a soft white handkerchief from his jacket pocket and blotted her damp cheeks. "A note is so impersonal."

Kneeling beside the tub, he moved to dip the linen square in the water. She swatted his hand away reflexively. "Stop it. You are *not* going to bathe me. Now leave immediately!"

His heated gaze studied her face, his expression intent. "It could be a very pleasant experience for both of us. I confess, I have always had a secret desire to be a lady's maid."

Charlotte scowled. "If you leave immediately, I promise to keep your ridiculous secret desire to myself," she said through clenched teeth.

Edward laughed. "Calm down, Charlotte. No one knows I am here."

"My maid will be returning shortly."

"Your maid is being kept busy below stairs by my valet."

He had leaned forward as he spoke and now his handsome face was very near. She blinked as she saw how close he was, his mouth nearly touching hers, making her remember vividly the wonderful excitement of feeling his lips pressed against hers.

Her fingers itched to trace the bold edge of his nose, the strong line of his jaw, the sensual curve of his lips. Charlotte clenched her hands into fists and struggled for the strength to pull herself away and again order him from the chamber.

"Edward?"

Her voice was a plea, a question that she did not even know she was asking. Was she begging for a kiss? Or begging for him to show her mercy and be strong for the both of them?

She felt his hand close over the nape of her exposed neck, massaging the stiff tendons with a firm, yet gentle touch. The motion relaxed her. Charlotte felt her breathing turn deep and even as the tension began to leave her body. She closed her eyes as the gentle kneading continued, his warm fingers stroking her neck and shoulders and upper back.

His hands were gentle, never dipping below the level of her exposed flesh. Yet whenever he would brush his thumbs up her neck to the sensitive spot behind her ears, she would shiver with pure delight.

"Shall I wash your hair?" he whispered.

Charlotte bit back a moan of delight. She wanted to sit there for hours with his hands on her body—her head, her neck, her shoulders, everywhere. But it was too dangerous to allow this to continue. Somehow she had to show him this was madness.

"I already washed my hair," she lied.

"Pity. Then are you finished in the tub? Since you did not allow me to bathe you, may I have the honor of drying you off?"

Charlotte's eyes popped opened. He reached for the towel that Jones had left warming by the fire and held it out to her.

"You have lost your mind," she declared, stunned by his sudden disregard for anything that was proper.

"Have I?" His lips twitched.

"Yes." Charlotte narrowed her eyes, trying to ignore his boyish appeal, telling herself they would both be ruined if she allowed this to continue any longer.

"Hmmm, the set of your jaw tells me that you are not jesting," he remarked. "If I promise not to tease you any longer, can we have a serious conversation?"

Here? Now? He truly had lost his mind. Charlotte gave a scornful huff. "Edward, please, if you have any regard for me at all, you will leave at once. My nerves are overset at the very thought of what would happen if you are discovered in here."

Indignation rang in her voice and it struck Charlotte that she was being somewhat hypocritical, since she had never cared to any great extent what society thought, and even more telling, a part of her very much wanted him to stay. But she was also being realistic, a role that the earl usually undertook, but for some unknown reason had abandoned utterly.

He opened his mouth to say something, seemed to think better of it and shut it without speaking his mind. He took her hands and she looked down at his feet. He was wearing clean boots that were nicely polished, indicating he had not yet taken his morning ride. Proof that he had indeed been waiting for her to make an appearance.

For an instant she felt a pang of regret for shutting down her emotions toward him, for so adamantly trying to eject him from her chamber, but then she reined in her wayward thoughts. This was hardly the time or the place to have a flirtation or a serious conversation.

She waited for his curt bow, his formal departure, but he surprised her once again by bending his head until she felt his breath at her temple. One of his hands came to the exposed top of her shoulder, his fingertips resting lightly on the creamy flesh.

"You are right, of course. I can hardly string three coherent words together when you are in that tub and so delectably close. We will talk later."

He kissed her swiftly on the lips. Charlotte held her breath as she waited for him to leave her chamber, listening for the sound of the door clicking shut. But the rush of relief she felt when she knew he had gone was quickly followed by a sudden, puzzling urge to cry.

Surprisingly, Charlotte sat beside his mother at the midafternoon meal. For a brief instant Edward thought it might have been an intentional decision, a way of avoiding him, since he would never willingly join her and put himself within his mother's range of barbs, but after due consideration he dismissed the notion.

Charlotte was not a cowardly female. If she were trying to distance herself from him, she would hardly need to hide behind his mother's skirts. Still, it was lowering to think she might be trying to steer clear of him, especially after all they had shared last night.

He carried within him a certain measure of guilt over those events, a sense of responsibility that bade him to make amends for his actions and offer to marry her. The notion pleased him on many levels and yet he was honest enough to admit to himself that he could not fully define his feelings toward Charlotte.

He was drawn to her, found himself thinking about her at odd moments during the day and dreaming of her at night.

He could talk to her about his work, a subject he would never consider mentioning in the presence of a lady, yet with Charlotte the words flowed freely and honestly.

He enjoyed sparring with her, became annoyed if she was too willful, yet he admired her spirit and courage, her determination to be herself. She was beautiful and accomplished, though not in the traditionally womanly arts.

She had a quick wit and a sharp tongue and he was probably more than a bit in love with her. He definitely lusted after her, but there was more to his feelings than desire.

Exactly how much more he could not say and Edward strongly suspected that Charlotte would demand that he did say.

He thought she looked particularly beautiful this afternoon. The simplicity of the design of her day gown emphasized her feminine curves and vibrant beauty, while the deep rose hue of the fabric complemented her coloring. Her complexion glowed with health, her hair was sleek and shiny and gorgeous in the afternoon sunlight.

Edward inhaled slowly. The recollection of how her hair had looked spread across her bare shoulders and down her naked back was making his palms sweat and his pulse race. He wished now he had stayed in her bedchamber earlier, had lifted her wet, slick body from the confines of her bathtub, had run his hands over her delicate flesh, had made love to her in the bright sunlight of the day.

He watched her nibble delicately at her meal, inclining her head and smiling, first at his mother, who was seated on her right, and then at Lord Reginald, who was seated on her left. She was flushed and bright-eyed but seemingly in control of her emotions.

He marveled at her composure. Her back was straight, her hair twisted elegantly high to expose the lovely slenderness of her neck, her movements fluid and graceful. It was hard to believe that a few hours ago he had been staring at her gorgeous body in the bathtub, and but a few hours before that they had been making wild, passionate love in her bed.

The memory made him restless, edgy and filled him with an urgency he did not fully understand. He willed her to look in his direction, yet she continued amusing her table companions, never once shifting her attention away from them.

Edward had nearly given up hope when suddenly she turned her head, looking directly into his eyes. The knowing, assessing stare she gave him stripped away all his defenses in a chilling rush. The exclusive connection, the sheer intimacy of the moment shocked him. Edward felt as if the wind had been knocked from his chest.

Charlotte gave no outward indication of a similar reaction and his heart sank. But then he saw the slight trembling of her hand as she reached for her goblet of wine and he knew she too had been affected. A comforting admission.

Edward kept his eyes and his attention on his food and his table companions for the remainder of the meal. The guests lingered over dessert, discussing the Christmas-tree trimming that would take place tomorrow, expressing their interest in seeing the special glass ornaments he had imported from Germany. Even after the dishes had been cleared from the table, the guests milled about, mingling and laughing and wandering off in groups.

The earl thought it the perfect time to steal Charlotte away and have their long overdue private talk, but she surprised him again by announcing she would be joining the older ladies on their afternoon calls to the local gentry. In a flurry of cackling high-pitched conversation, the women departed.

He did not see her again until the evening meal, where she somehow managed to seat herself between Lord and Lady Haddon, while he was again at the opposite side of the table. Bidding his time while the men lingered over port and cigars, Edward plotted his next move.

However, Charlotte somehow outflanked him, joining a lively card game that had no room for additional players. Broodingly, he watched her as she played, trying to devise a way to insinuate himself into the game. She sat beside his brother, her eyes twinkling with amusement and delight, the pile of coins in front of her growing steadily.

After hearing a particularly gleeful laugh, Edward had enough. Deciding he would somehow get his brother to give up his place at the card table so he could take it, the earl moved forward. But he had taken only two steps before he felt a tug on his arm.

"Finally I have you all to myself. Come, sit and talk with an old lady for a few minutes, young man. I need your opinion on a new venture my man of business is recommending."

The earl's initial annoyance at the interruption softened when he saw it was Lady Johnson-Meyer holding his arm. Of all of his mother's friends, he liked the matronly aristocrat the best. She was witty and full of mischief, the only one who had ever acknowledged the true depth of his business empire and did not pretend he merely dabbled in finance for his amusement.

Though she was nearly seventy years of age, Lady Johnson-Meyer had a keen mind and a good business sense and over the years whenever she was in London, she had solicited his advice regarding her own investments. She had placed a sizable portion of her assets in several of Edward's companies and doing so had proven to be a profitable relationship for both of them.

Normally, he enjoyed their conversations, but tonight her presence was keeping him away from Charlotte. Still, he could not be rude.

They found a quiet corner and each accepted a cup of tea from the footman, though Edward left his untouched. He managed to keep up his end of the conversation for several minutes, but the sound of Charlotte's distinct laughter pulled his attention and eyes away.

He saw Jonathan and Charlotte with their heads bent close together, their hands nearly touching as they fingered the pile of coins that was placed between them. Edward felt a jolt of annoyance as something unknown twisted in the pit of his stomach.

"She is high-spirited and more than a bit spoiled, but I always thought she'd make the right man an excellent wife," Lady Johnson-Meyer murmured near his ear.

Edward cleared his throat and turned to the older woman. "Are you speaking of Miss Aldridge?"

"The very same." Her eyes were bright and lively. "She and your brother make a most handsome couple. They are such a striking, attractive pair and seem to get on very well together. Don't you agree?"

"They have known each other for years," he said dismissively.

Lady Johnson-Meyer sipped delicately from her teacup. "I have suggested to your mother on several occasions that it would be an advantageous match for your brother. She has a substantial dowry. And I believe Miss Aldridge should be pleased to have such an attentive, amusing young husband."

Edward thought he surely must have misheard. Jonathan and Charlotte? He peered at the two more closely, taking note of the intimacy of their arrangement, how close together their chairs were positioned, how they whispered and signalled to each other during the game.

Then he noticed Charlotte slip something flat and white into Jonathan's hand beneath the table.

The earl's eyes widened in puzzlement. A card? Were they cheating?

He stood. "Please excuse me, my lady."

The older woman blinked innocently. "Of course. 'Tis necessary to protect one own's interests, is it not?"

Startled, Edward nearly tripped over his feet. "I am sure you are mistaken. Miss Aldridge and I share no more than a brief acquaintance."

"Oh, I am sorry." Lady Johnson-Meyer's eyes seemed to twinkle. "Though I must say that even without my spectacles I can see very clearly."

The earl ignored the older woman's words and headed directly for the card table. The game was just ending, the players leaving the table. Edward tried to corner Charlotte for a private moment. She gave him a dazzling smile of welcome that rendered him nearly speechless, then looped her arms through her grandfather's and held on as though she would topple over without Lord Reginald's support.

Declaring a slight headache, Charlotte next bid everyone good night. His offer of an escort upstairs was firmly denied. On the surface he accepted her decision with good humor, but deep inside he felt an impotent sense of something precious slipping from his grasp, an almost unreasonable fear of losing something he had not known he wanted.

Charlotte was very glad to have her grandfather's escort to her bedchamber. It had been such an unsettling day. She had not set out deliberately to avoid the earl, but soon discovered it had been easier to cope when he was not near her. She knew he was puzzled, perhaps even hurt by her actions, and she regretted it. Yet she also knew it would be pointless to have a conversation with him when she did not know her own mind—or as of yet, trust the feelings in her heart.

She gained the safety of her bedchamber without further incident and silently congratulated herself on her clever manipulations. Jones was nowhere in evidence, so Charlotte moved forward to ring for her servant.

Her heart jumped when a shadow appeared in front of her and her hand went reflexively to her mouth. "Who's there?"

"Don't scream. 'Tis only me," the earl said.

He struck a match. An an oil lamp flared to life and his handsome features became clearly visibly.

"Grandpapa and I left you in the drawing room, surrounded by several other guests. How did you manage to extract yourself from their company and arrive in my bedchamber before me?"

Edward smiled faintly. "I grew up in this house. I also have longer, faster legs."

"And thus the advantage."

"Over you?" He smiled broadly, implying the notion was laughable. "Since there seemed to be no opportunity during the day, we shall have our conversation now. We need to be making plans, decisions about our future."

"What sort of plans?"

"The obvious ones."

"Marriage?" Charlotte smiled weakly. "Is it truly necessary?"

His nostrils flared, with either surprise or annoyance. "In this situation it is the appropriate solution.

There is certainly no pretending it did not happen. Nor pretending it will not happen again."

Charlotte felt her face flush with color. "Are you implying that I am a woman of loose character?"

Edward's visage darkened. "I am telling you that I find you nearly irresistible," he said tartly. "Until last night, I never suspected that I was capable of overcoming a lifetime of strict moral training and behavior to become a seducer of innocents."

His declaration hardly pleased her, especially since he sounded so annoyed. "You did not seduce me. Well, not entirely. I lay with you willingly." Charlotte removed her heavy diamond earrings and placed them on her dressing table. "We cannot marry simply to soothe your guilty conscience. It is ludicrous."

His eyes glinted as he ran his gaze over her from head to toe. "You were innocent and inexperienced. I was not. Therefore, I feel responsible and as such am compelled to do the correct and honorable thing."

"Saints above, Edward, I am not a weak-minded imbecile. I was not unknowingly seduced. Honestly, you give yourself and your charms far too much credit."

He became very quiet and very still. Charlotte had the absurd thought that he was counting to ten. Slowly. "I do not know how I will survive being around you if you continue being so brutally honest, Charlotte. Your opinions most certainly wreak havoc on a man's confidence."

A flush of guilt brightened her cheeks. She had never meant to hurt or insult him. "I will concede that there are sparks between us."

"Sparks? There is fire."

"Sparks fade," she replied flatly, refusing to remember how tender he had been toward her, how
he made her feel special, wonderful, incredible. He
had cared. But was it enough? She remembered
her feelings of jealousy over his attention to Miss
Dunaway last evening.

As a young girl she had always had difficulty sharing
her toys. As an adult, Charlotte now discovered the
sentiment applied even more strongly to her men.

Her men? Was that what Edward was in her life? Her
man? Her current man? But if he were her current
man, that implied there would eventually be other
men in her life. The idea seemed impossible. How
could she ever share the same sort of intimacy with
anyone else?

She and Edward shared an irrevocable, unavoidable attraction. He affected her as no other ever
had; he aroused and thrilled and enchanted her.
She had never felt this way with any other man.

And lately she had been wondering if she even
wanted to, but a part of her held back. "Marriage is
such a final step," she said quietly.

"But necessary. *What's done is done.*"

"Oh, Lord, now you are quoting Shakespeare.
Macbeth, is it not?"

"Yes, *Macbeth* and true nonetheless." He raked his
hand though his hair. "There is something else,
something important we must consider. The possibility that you are breeding."

Charlotte blanched. "From one time?"

"Yes, a man's seed can take hold from only one
coupling. Though as I recall, it was more than one
time," he concluded smugly. "But that is beside the

point. Even if you are not carrying my child, your virginity is gone, and so are your chances of making a good marriage."

Charlotte blinked and rubbed her hand over her brow. "I am sure there is someone who would accept me in spite of my lack of virginity."

The earl smirked. "Someone without honor."

"Would you marry a woman who was not a virgin?"

"Obviously, since I want to marry you."

"You were the man who took that prize, so it hardly counts." She felt impelled to ask again. "Would you consider marrying a woman who was not a virgin?"

Edward let out his breath on a slow sigh. "I suppose it would depend on the circumstances. A young widow, for instance."

Charlotte frowned in perplexity. "Her virginity would have presumably been lost to her deceased husband, a conventional, acceptable situation. What if she had never been married and was not a virgin?"

He paused, giving her a look of bewilderment. "I would not reject a woman simply on that one fact."

"Thank you for your candor. Your answer proves my point. I am not totally ruined for all gentlemen. Therefore, I'd like a bit more time to consider our situation."

"How much time?"

"A few weeks." His face clouded with displeasure and Charlotte hastily continued. "We began this conversation with such civility. Please, let us end it in the same manner. There is no need to carry on as though this is a Shakespeare tragedy, though I'm sure if you think hard enough you can find the appropriate lines and sentiment."

"Now is the winter of our discontent?" He sighed, his expression still conveying befuddlement. "We must be sensible, Charlotte."

"Waiting does make sense. If we married now, we would both be doing so out of a sense of obligation. I only want to marry a man who truly wants me, who desires me above all others. It seems so many of our class spend the majority of their married lives living apart. I do not wish to join their ranks."

"I am not suggesting that kind of marriage." The sound of his steps resounded on the carpet as he moved toward her. "I do not take what happened between us lightly. I have feelings for you, special deep feelings."

"Love?"

His face stiffened. "Falling in love has never been something I have thought about with any serious consideration. Until now." He bent his head, his brow pleating in a thoughtful frown. When he raised his chin and looked again at her, his expression was solemn. "In the spirit of being honest I admit that I have far less of a romantic nature than you do. I have never told any woman that I love her."

"Not even your fiancée?"

"Obviously not." He favored her with a self-deprecating smile. "She left me and followed her own heart, marrying a man who was able to give her what she craved."

"I am sorry."

He looked surprised by her sympathy. "Don't be. Henrietta made the right choice. I am not even positive I know what being in love really means."

"A conveniently obtuse answer."

"But honestly given. Far better than a lie told simply to gain what I want."

Though not surprised by his answer, Charlotte felt the sting of disappointment. She would settle for no less than his love, with the declaration freely given.

"Then our path is very clear. For now we wait and make no decision about marriage."

"But we continue with our courtship," Edward stipulated. "You must not run or hide from me as you did today."

"And you will not enter my bedchamber unless you are invited."

"Agreed." He stepped closer and curled a hand over her bare shoulder. "But as long as I am here . . ." His voice trailed off seductively.

"You are not being fair when you look at me like that," she whispered, as a thrill of sexual awareness shot through her body.

He smiled confidently. "Does that mean you are saying that I can stay?"

CHAPTER 14

All day Charlotte had been dwelling upon the enormity of what she had done last night. How she had changed herself forever. How incredible it had been and how amazing that when she was with Edward, everything else just melted away and it was only the two of them. How she now knew with certainty what she would be missing for the rest of her life if she never married.

The exquisite sensual delights, the intense emotional connection, the sense of something greater than herself. The sheer joy, the sheer *fun* of it all.

Here now was a chance to experience it all again. Did she dare to be so reckless a second time?

Especially when there was something she had not thought about last night, which was very much on her mind right now. Continuing a physical relationship could very well result in her becoming with child. If that occurred, she would no longer have any control over her destiny. Her fate would be decided. She would marry the earl.

Would that be so terrible? Marrying Edward made sense.

But maybe that was the problem. People who were truly in love acted with reckless emotion, not prudent sensibility. Or was it desire that drowned out a sensible response?

Edward said nothing. He simply watched her, gently caressing her shoulder, almost as if he knew she was struggling with her decision, weighing all the arguments in her head. Yet oddly, by doing nothing at all, he was tempting her beyond measure.

They stood in silence for a long moment. "If you insist that I leave, I shall," he said huskily, "yet I harbor a fantasy that a lascivious scheme is lurking in your mind at this exact minute that will soon become a pleasurable reality for us both."

Charlotte found herself smiling. "I fear you spend far too much of your time thinking about sex, my lord."

"Making love, Charlotte," he corrected. "There is a significant difference." His lashes lowered as he looked at her mouth.

Charlotte drew in a sharp breath. She brought her palm up between them and pressed it flat against his chest to prevent him from leaning forward and kissing her, for her mind turned to pure sensation and her wits scattered to the winds whenever that happened.

"I trust that you are telling me the truth about the difference between sex and making love," she said.

"I am." His eyes crinkled with concern. "If I felt it were necessary, warranted, then I might omit the entire truth on occasion. But I will never lie to you, Charlotte."

"The sin of omission is as great a sin as a lie."

His eyebrow arched. "Twisting the truth is a sin.

Withholding information to spare and protect the feelings of someone you care for is the duty of a gentleman. Given the choice, I will always endeavor to protect you."

She believed him. In light of their past, it was a big step, she realized, to take him at his word, to acknowledge that his heart was true. It was also an alarming as well as enthralling occurrence. "I appreciate your honesty, Edward."

"May I stay?"

She could hear the naked longing in his voice, but more important, she saw a reassuring hint of emotion on his face. He did care for her, perhaps with the same level of caution and restraint she cared for him.

Hardly ideal, but far more than she had shared with any other man. Her lips curled into a sultry smile worthy of a courtesan. Blood was pounding hotly through her veins, but her mind was still functioning.

"There is still the risk of creating a child," she said, hardly believing she had the courage to discuss such an incredibly indelicate subject with him.

He nodded. "There are ways to prevent such things from occurring."

"Devices?" she queried, having once overheard bits of a conversation between two married women that had raised far more questions in Charlotte's mind than they had answered.

"Yes." It took him a moment to recover his voice. "However, I do not have any of those with me."

"Can you get them?"

He cleared his throat again. "They are hardly the items one asks for as a Christmas present."

"Edward!"

"I'm sorry. 'Tis just that you look so solemn."

"This is a serious conversation," she insisted.

"It is," he agreed. "'Tis also highly unusual."

Her face flamed, though she agreed with his observation. "Then perhaps it is best if we simply forget the matter entirely." She turned, but he grabbed her hand, stopping her from walking away.

"There are other ways to prevent conception," he said. "I can withdraw. There is still risk, but it is far less if the man pulls out before his seed is released. Do you understand?"

The blush on her face deepened as disjointed thoughts about the mechanics of it all flew through her mind. "I think so, though I am unsure exactly how it would work."

He bent his head and placed his cheek against hers. "Leave that to me, all right?"

Charlotte sighed. The feelings were starting again, where her breath was tight and her heartbeat quickened and her skin tingled all over. She let her eyes flutter shut and bowed her head until it rested against his chest, taking two steps closer when she felt his strong arms embrace her.

She was a fortunate person who had been given many material blessings, had received parental love from a kindly grandfather who adored her. But losing her parents at an early age had taught her a very important lesson.

Life was fleeting, joy could be stripped from you without warning, leaving you to regret those moments when you allowed those opportunities for sheer pleasure to slip away.

"I enjoy making love with you, Edward," Charlotte confessed, just before she wrapped her arms around his neck, lifted her head and gave him a hungry, openmouthed kiss.

He made a sound of surprise against her mouth, but then his arms tightened their embrace and he angled his head and deepened the kiss, his tongue teasing hers. His hands shifted, one splaying over her back below her waist, the other dropping lower to cup her buttocks and pull her closer.

The excitement Charlotte felt increased as her body heated. She lifted herself higher so that his erection rested against the top of her thighs, sliding her body up and down, mimicking the act of love.

She clutched at the lapels of his evening coat, fists clenching tight. Driven by the urge to get closer, she pressed herself against him. It felt so right. Everything else faded to insignificance. Once again, nothing else in the world mattered, except the two of them.

His fingers found the buttons at the back of her gown and with impressive dexterity he unfastened her bodice and pushed the top of her gown from her shoulders. He muttered a few choice words beneath his breath as he struggled with the laces of her corset, but eventually they too were freed and the undergarment thrown carelessly to the floor.

She stood shivering in the cool of the room, covered only by the thin silk of her chemise. He made a sound of appreciation deep in his throat and Charlotte smiled, no longer aware of the cold.

She eased his evening coat from his broad shoulders, attacked the knot of his cravat, gleefully pulling the starched white linen free. She unbuttoned the top of his shirt and saw the pulse beat at the base of his neck moving furiously, a mirror of her own frantically beating heart.

Charlotte bent forward and kissed the spot, then flicked it with the tip of her tongue. Edward responded hotly to her advance, cradling her head with the palm of one hand, holding her steady so he could ravish her with his mouth. He kissed her, fiercely and passionately, thrusting his tongue into her mouth in a pulsating rhythm while his other hand traced the line of her waist, down to her hip and beyond to her upper thigh.

Jolts of sensations coursed through her. Charlotte's body throbbed with a heated urgency that made her eager for his searching hands. His fingertips touched her breasts through the thin fabric of her chemise, brushing back and forth over the hardened nipples. Pleasure flared wherever he stroked, pleasure that made her gasp and shiver with excitement. She caught her lip between her teeth to repress a strangled moan.

"Don't hold back," he gasped. "I want to hear every sound."

He lowered his head and caught her nipple in his mouth and suckled it. Charlotte's hands grasped his hair and pulled him closer. Understanding her need, he tugged harder with his mouth and then his hand came up to embrace her other breast, teasing the rigid tip between his thumb and forefinger.

The sensations were overwhelming. She was throbbing *inside* her body, but he seemed to know exactly what she was feeling, exactly what she needed. His hands moved between her thighs and he lifted her thin silk chemise. He stroked between the folds of her most sensitive flesh, and Charlotte pulled in a deep breath, then pushed against his fingers.

A blush stole through her chest and face, but she

was filled with an agonized need that overcame any residual embarrassment. She trusted him completely, knew he would do whatever was necessary to bring her pleasure, to bring her joy.

He fondled her with delicate expertise, his long fingers gliding through her silky curls to brush repeatedly over the small engorged bud kindling an almost unbearable excitement within her. And as he stroked her, he kissed her, then whispered into her ear sweet bits of nonsense that made her shiver and pant, words of endearment and lust that made her heart sing.

Charlotte thought she must have been possessed by madness last night in the library to allow her passion such unchecked rein, but now she understood there was more than physical desire between them. There was an emotional connection that drove their desire to unimaginable heights, regardless of the past, regardless of the consequences.

Charlotte breathed in sharp pants and put her hands on Edward's broad shoulders to steady her weak knees. Her hands tightened in convulsive squeezes as she felt the tension begin to crest. Then suddenly it peaked and Charlotte arched her back, every muscle in her body straining as she found herself shaking and shattering and coming apart.

All the strength drained out of her and she fell forward, but Edward held her tightly in his embrace. He waited until her breathing was less labored, then guided her backward toward the bed, tumbling them both onto the soft mattress.

Her head still spinning, Charlotte rested against the pillow, gazing inquiringly at Edward, wondering what would happen next. After tossing off his shoes, he climbed on the bed, lay down beside her and waited.

Delighted at the opportunity to take the lead, Charlotte turned to face him. She took a moment to study his face, then impulsively reached out and traced his mouth with the tip of her finger. He smiled.

She put her hand against his cheek and felt the rough dark beard that had already grown since morning. The need to kiss him was so strong her lips began to tremble. Giving in to the temptation, she moved toward him. His lips were welcoming and soft and she gladly opened her mouth as his tongue searched for hers.

They kissed for several long minutes and Charlotte felt the stirring of desire starting to build again. But now it was Edward's turn to experience the bliss. Boldly, she placed her hand over the front of his trousers, feeling his erection through the fine fabric.

"Unbutton it," he coaxed.

Charlotte felt a wicked blush creep into her face. But she followed his command and he groaned appreciatively when she reached inside his open pants and took him in her hand.

She touched him lightly at first. Then with more assurance she began to stroke him, her hand exploring the shape that was starting to become familiar. His hips responded in a slow rhythm as her questing fingers trailed a path from base to tip, then softly circled the head.

Touching his body so intimately gave her an amazing sense of power, of freedom. She felt like a wanton, uninhibited creature who knew no boundaries, no restraints, who existed only to give and receive pleasure.

Caught in the excitement of the moment,

Charlotte tightened her grip, pulling harder and faster on his penis. Edward made a rough sound in his throat and jerked involuntarily. She repeated the motion, this time reaching all the way down to the base where a nest of soft hair surrounded his testicles.

"It's so hard and hot," she murmured.

"For you," he said breathlessly. "Only for you."

He taught her how to make it last, how to use the edge of her finger to spread the moisture that weeped from the tip all around the smooth head, how to vary her grip from soft to hard, slow, then fast, then slow.

She could feel his entire body shaking against hers and her skin longed for the feel of him. She wanted him naked, wanted to feel his hot, smooth skin against her own, wanted her body entwined with his. "Let's finish undressing," she whispered.

Edward needed no encouragement. His eyes never left hers as he wrenched off his open trousers and underclothes, then threw off his shirt. With a wicked gleam, he reached for the bows of her chemise, untied them, then pulled the garment over her head.

His hands roamed her body with soothing strokes from her shoulders to her lower back, her hips to her buttocks and upper thighs. Charlotte shivered and copied his movements, running her fingers over the muscles of his shoulders and back, then pressed herself close until her breasts rubbed against his chest.

His penis grew as if to attract her attention, poking her insistently in her stomach. She rolled her hips teasingly against it, and laughed with delight.

"Wicked wench," he growled.

She teased him further, running her hands all over his naked frame, yet deliberately avoiding the one spot that throbbed so obviously for her caress. Finally, her hand returned to his penis, long and thick and hard. She wrapped her fingers around its turgid length, but he pulled her hand away.

"I need to be inside you," he said with sudden urgency.

"Yes," she whispered eagerly, rolling onto her back.

"Not that way," he said in a raspy tone. "I want you to mount me."

Charlotte narrowed her eyes at him in shock, certain she must have misheard. But he shifted his position, set his hand around her slender waist and lifted her, placing her on the top of his muscular thighs while he lay flat on his back beneath her. She straddled him awkwardly, still uncertain. This could not possibly be right.

"Put me inside you," he said, giving clear voice to his desire.

His words made her light-headed. Tentatively, she shifted her knees, moving forward to slide herself along the rigid length of his penis, gamely following his commands. Edward's hands remained on her hips, his voice a low seductive murmur as he guided her movements.

Their eyes met as her body slowly lowered itself inside his and they were joined. The excitement she felt deepened, yet Charlotte winced when Edward flexed his hips and thrust himself fully inside her. She was wet and aroused, but still a bit sore from yesterday.

"Am I hurting you?"

"A little, but no, Edward, don't stop." She cried out faintly and drew in a ragged breath. She leaned over him, supporting herself on her hands and gazed into his eyes. "Do not stop," she repeated breathlessly.

In response, he thrust upward a second time, filling her with a deep penetration, and she strained with the effort to accommodate him. Her hips began to undulate, but he kept changing the rhythm, the intensity, the depth of each thrust. She hovered on the edge of a second release, but could not find it.

"Stay with me," he urged, moving his hand down to the spot where their bodies were joined.

His searching fingers found the aching center of her desire and she cried out as he circled the sensitive bud. With only a few additional strokes Charlotte reached fulfillment, her inner muscles clamping tightly around him. She could feel his shoulders and arms shaking with the strain of holding back his climax as he waited for hers to end.

Then with a deep groan, Edward put his hands on either side of her hips and lifted her high in the air, abruptly separating their bodies. He quickly brought her down again, pressing himself tightly against the softness of her belly. Charlotte felt his penis spasm and jerk, again and again, until the warm wetness of his seed spilt across her stomach.

The moment was nearly too much for her over-stimulated senses. Dazed, she stayed pressed against him for several minutes until her nose began to twitch. The air was heavy with the tangy scent of their love-making. She slipped from the bed and retrieved a towel and wet cloth. Returning, she carefully scrubbed the sticky mess from his flat stomach and muscled chest, then cleaned herself.

Edward observed her actions with quiet calm, his expression solemn, yet sated. When she finished, Charlotte climbed back into bed and collapsed against him, her hair a cloud of waves around them both. He slipped an arm around her waist, drawing her back against him, cradling her in the curve of his body. She felt warm and safe, protected by his embrace, his physical strength.

"Sleep, sweetheart," he whispered, pressing his lips against her hair.

With a sigh, Charlotte relaxed against him. His tenderness made her feel protected and cherished and that realization made her throat tighten with emotion. Yet, as she drifted off to sleep, she was no closer to making a decision about marrying him, and that confused her even more.

Jonathan lay in the middle of his bed, his eyes closed, his mind racing. From time to time he opened his eyelids and glanced at the mantle clock, pretending the lateness of the hour held no consequence, when it was in fact positive proof that he could not sleep.

The euphoria that had engulfed him when Charlotte had slipped him Evelyn's note earlier in the evening had long faded, leaving him in a melancholy, reflective mood. Evelyn's message had hardly been encouraging.

In a most guarded and cautionary tone she had acknowledged his feelings, reiterated how flattered she was by the attention and closed by stating flatly that they were in no way equals. She could not slip easily into his echelon of society and he should not entertain the ridiculous notion of lowering himself to hers.

His family connections, position in society and wealth were all far above her own, therefore precluding the possibility of a future life together. She urged him to consider forming an alliance with a more suitable young woman, one who would fit with case in his world and bring him the happiness he so richly deserved.

Ironically, it was just this sort of selfless regard for the needs of others, this natural inclination to place his happiness above her own that captured and held Jonathan's heart even stronger. And yet even he must acknowledge that Evelyn had made several valid points.

He should leave her alone. Why couldn't he?

Frustrated, Jonathan left the bed. Slipping into his brocade robe to ward off the chill, he left his chamber in search of a drink. Brandy would be nice, but whiskey would serve too.

He would write Evelyn again, after he had found some rest and his mind was clear. He would tell her that he had indeed made a concerted effort to consider the single women that society deemed suitable, weighing them against her as a potential wife. But even with their advantageous social standing and wealth, all others fell far short, including the lovely Miss Dunaway, who despite her wit and beauty, created no spark of male interest within him.

Though Jonathan thought it obvious to point out that Miss Dunaway preferred his brother, and more importantly Edward's title. Not that he blamed her. It was a mark of her intelligence and good sense that she had set her sights on the man with the greater prospects.

Perhaps he would head to the library for his drink. There was always a decanter of spirits in there, and once he had partaken, he could search the many shelves of books for inspiration that would help him express more clearly the emotions of his heart.

Evelyn enjoyed poetry. His case might be helped by quoting lines from some lesser-known works, lines that would give her pause, would make her think, but more importantly believe, that anything was possible.

Given the very late hour it was no surprise to find the hallway deserted. It was dark, cold and silent, but as he reached the end of the long corridor, Jonathan heard a sound. He stopped, waited, listened and heard it again. Who else could possibly be sneaking around at such an ungodly hour?

He took a few more steps, froze, then peered tentatively around the corner. To his great astonishment, Jonathan saw his brother creeping down the hallway, rumpled and scarcely dressed, holding most of his clothes over one arm and his shoes in the opposite hand.

"Edward?" he rasped in a loud whisper.

The earl whirled around in alarm, dropping a shoe in the process that must have landed on his bare foot because he cursed loudly and began hopping on one leg.

"Bloody, hell, Jonathan, you scared ten years off my life!" the earl scolded in a quiet voice. "What are you doing up at this hour?"

"I could ask you the same question," Jonathan replied, crossing his arms over his chest. "And, while I am at it, inquire also as to why you are skulking around the hallways, carrying, instead of wearing, the majority of your clothing?"

The earl squared his shoulders and straightened his posture. "I am not skulking."

"You most assuredly are," Jonathan retorted. Across the expanse, they studied each other. "Though upon further inspection I can understand why you do not wish to remain visible. You look as if you donned just enough clothes so that you would not completely shock the servants if you were seen."

The hallway was dimly lit, but Jonathan could see his brother's face deepen in color. "This is a private matter."

Jonathan did not bother to hide his astonishment. "A clandestine affair with one of our house-guests? Very out of character, dear brother."

"A private matter that shall remain private," the earl insisted, refusing to address his brother's accusations. "Do I make myself understood?"

His voice was so well modulated, one would have thought he was discussing the weather, but even in the gloomy shadows of the hall, Jonathan could see his brother was far from calm. It must be a very special woman indeed, to affect him so deeply.

Miss Dunaway? She had been openly flirting with him, making no secret of her interest. Yet Jonathan felt she lacked the reckless courage needed to engage in scandalous behavior. Charlotte, perhaps?

Was it possible? Jonathan found he was quite pleased at that notion, never once doubting that his brother's intentions were ultimately honorable, even though he was hardly being circumspect tonight.

Love and passion had the power to do that to a man.

The air was heavy with silence and Jonathan suddenly realized his brother was waiting for his answer. "The incident is forgotten," he proclaimed solemnly.

Edward nodded his thanks and Jonathan assumed their brief encounter had ended. He moved to continue on his way to the library.

"Have you ever been in love, Jonathan?"

The question stopped him dead in his tracks as a bolt of panic shot through him. For a moment he could only stare at his brother, flummoxed. Did Edward somehow know about his feelings toward Evelyn?

"That is a very odd question to discuss at this time of night," Jonathan replied, stalling for time.

"Women seem to place a great deal of stock in it." Edward blew out a loud breath and ran his fingers through his already-disheveled hair. "Love, I mean."

"Perhaps because their capacity to love is greater than ours?" Jonathan suggested.

"Or their need?" Edward sighed. "'Tis a mystery as old as time, I think. Men are more practical and pragmatic in their nature than women, and yet they too have done many illogical and nonsensical acts throughout the ages in the name of love."

Jonathan wondered if his brother was referring to his current state of dishevelment, but since he had promised to forget the incident, he did not ask.

"When the need for love is great, no sacrifice seems too high a price to pay," Jonathan said philosophically. "For man or woman."

Edward did not seem convinced. "Love is a complicated emotion that encompasses so many other feelings. Fear, happiness, confusion, frustration. They all seem to be part of it."

"Yes," Jonathan said quietly. "And when a single smile she bestows upon you can charm you to your toes, and when the sound of her voice erases all the frustrations of the day, and when you are struck by a fear so intense you lose your breath at the very idea of her disappearing from your life—well, that is love."

The earl studied him for a long minute. "Ah, so you have been in love," he commented.

"'Tis a feeling you never forget, brother, even long after it has gone."

For a moment Jonathan was tempted to confide in his brother, to ask him for help in convincing Evelyn to accept his proposal and become his wife. Yet he hesitated.

Despite finding the earl in the hallway in the middle of the night, half-clothed, clearly doing something very inappropriate, Jonathan knew his older brother was at his core a very proper and conservative man. Though they never spoke openly of it, they both knew that when Jonathan took a wife, he would wed for money. Which was the one thing that Evelyn did not possess.

If Edward disapproved of Jonathan's choice of Evelyn, he could easily thwart his plans, making the risk of telling him the truth far outweighing any potential benefit. And thus Jonathan kept silent on the matter.

The earl's mouth twisted slightly. "Well, I might not understand it very well, but I do believe that no matter what the circumstances, love should be given a chance," he concluded.

Jonathan's head jerked up in surprise. His brother was right. True love, real love, the kind of love he felt for Evelyn did deserve a chance. It was such a simple and heartfelt sentiment, one that perfectly conveyed his feelings. The drink and the books of poetry he had thought necessary for inspiration were quickly forgotten.

"Good night, Edward," Jonathan said abruptly.

Grinning with delight, Jonathan eagerly returned to his chamber. He placed a lit lamp on his desk, removed a fresh sheet of his private stationery from the drawer and began carefully composing his next love letter to Evelyn, confident with each stroke of the pen that his words would touch her tender heart.

CHAPTER 15

Though two days ago Edward had claimed it would be easy to erect the giant pine in the corner of the drawing room, it proved to be no small feat. Since the servants' stairs were too narrow to accommodate the large tree, the main staircase was used. It took no less than four of the strongest footmen to carry the majestic pine up the main staircase as many of the guests looked on in awe. A troop of wide-eyed, giggling housemaids followed on the footmen's heels, sweeping, brushing and collecting the fallen needles from the stairs and floors.

Once the pine had been wrestled through the drawing room doors it dwarfed everything around it. Edward soon realized that far too many pieces of furniture would have to be rearranged or even removed for the tree to fit it inside, thus losing much of the seating. A drawing room without seating accommodations was fairly useless. Though hating to admit that he had been wrong, the earl took his brother's suggestion that the tree be erected in the ballroom instead.

Their gloves smudged and sticky with sap, the four footmen hoisted the large pine and obediently trudged through the long hallways. As Edward watched the men struggle with their cumbersome burden, he made a mental note to inform Harris to supply them with fresh gloves, since the ones they now wore were completely ruined.

Jonathan had the inspired idea of standing the tree in the far corner of the room and placing it in a large bucket filled with small stones. It was then secured in an upright position with a wire fastened to the trunk on one end and the wall on the other.

"'Tis amazingly large," Lord Reginald quipped when the tree had at last been successfully secured. "We always have a small, dainty tree at Quincy Court. It sits on a table and still barely reaches the top of my head. Don't think I've ever seen a tree this big outside of a forest."

"I enjoy doing things on a large scale," Edward proclaimed in a tight voice.

"Oh, don't mistake my meaning, Worthington. I think it is grand. Really puts one in the spirit of the season," Lord Reginald said. The older gentleman circled slowly, tilting his head from one side to the other. "A beautiful tree, indeed. But it needs to be adjusted. 'Tis leaning to the right."

"No, it's listing to the left," Lord Haddon interjected, cocking his head. "I noticed it immediately. Call the footmen back so it can be fixed."

"I think it looks fine," Jonathan insisted, adding a third opinion. "Besides, if you move it too much, it might topple over."

They all turned expectantly toward the earl, awaiting his assessment of the problem. Edward stared at all three men and promptly decided he was getting a headache.

"Let us have a drink, gentlemen, and consider our options," the earl declared.

His solution was met with great enthusiasm. After Harris brought the requested items, the earl uncorked a bottle of his finest whiskey and the men indulged themselves. By the second dram, they all agreed the tree was perfectly placed, perfectly positioned, perfectly straight, the perfect size and quite simply, perfect.

"It will look even better once all the decorations are hung," Edward informed them.

"I intend to participate in decorating it, even though that pleasure is usually saved for the young ladies and the servants," Lord Reginald announced. "I'm just surprised that the countess approved, Worthington. Though the queen and her consort have put one up for many years, there are folks who think a Christmas tree is a pagan idol. And having one this big, well, it might be considered sacrilegious by some."

Edward took a slow sip of his whiskey, electing not to tell Lord Reginald that his mother had no idea he had just put an enormous tree in the ballroom. Was not Christmas the best time for surprises?

The clock that stood in the hallway struck the hour. As if on cue, a contingent of female houseguests entered the ballroom. Edward was disappointed to note that Charlotte was not among their numbers.

"We are here to help decorate the tree, my lord," Miss Dunaway said with a shy smile. Her eyes widened with surprise when she got a closer look at the enormous pine, but to her credit she recovered her smile quickly. "It looks even larger in here than it did in the forest! I'm afraid we shall only be able to reach as high as the middle branches."

"Harris and the footmen will bring in a ladder for the top half," Edward explained, deciding he needed to be careful who he allowed to climb it, as several of the other gentlemen had joined them in imbibing in the whiskey. Visions of Jonathan and Lord Haddon clinging to the top branches and swaying merrily filled the earl's head. The last thing he needed was someone falling and breaking their neck on the hard wooden floor.

The ladies had made beautiful paper and lace cornucopias and filled them with sweets, fruit and nuts, and crafted lovely nosegays of dried flowers tied with lace and satin bows. They had also assembled an assortment of dolls and other small toys to tuck among the branches. Miss Dunaway arranged the items carefully on a table Harris had cleared specifically for that purpose.

The butler next brought out boxes of the unusual glassblown ornaments Edward had shipped in from Germany and everyone stopped to admire the magnificent shapes and beautiful colors.

"How kind you are, my lord, to include my children," Lady Haddon said, closing the distance between them. She had her infant son nestled in the crook of one arm while her young daughter clung to her skirts. "I promise I shall remove them at once if they become unruly."

"I cannot imagine either of your children misbehaving, Lady Haddon," Edward said graciously.

Lord Haddon laughed uproariously at that

comment, but grew silent after a stern stare from his wife. The viscount gathered his daughter in his arms and the young family went to greet the other guests. The ballroom quickly became a hive of merry activity as everyone clustered into groups and started in earnest to decorate the tree.

A contingent of older guests reclined in comfortable chairs and offered constant advice on moving the ornaments one branch to the right, then three branches to the left. The Haddon baby, who had caused a minor sensation upon his arrival, went from hand to hand among the older ladies as his very proud grandparents looked on, exclaiming continually over the child's clearly exceptional attributes.

Though Edward had rarely been around young children, he found their presence added another dimension of enjoyment for everyone. That is until the baby began to fuss and cry. Very loudly.

The earl turned and saw a slightly embarrassed Lady Haddon hand off the screaming infant to his nurse, but was further surprised to see that instead of leaving the woman to deal with the situation alone, Lady Haddon followed the pair from the room. Apparently, she took her duties as a mother very seriously.

"'Tis a very good thing that nurse took the baby away." Lord Reginald commented. "He's a charming little chap with the lung capacity of a fishmonger. My ears are still ringing."

"Let's just hope the little girl doesn't start wailing," Jonathan remarked. "'Tis my understanding when one starts, the other usually follows."

Edward turned in astonishment toward his

younger brother. "Precisely, when did you become an expert on young children?"

"They have been in the manor for over a week," Jonathan replied defensively. "It has not been hard to learn a few things."

"Why?"

Jonathan shifted his weight from one foot to the other, looking slightly embarrassed. "I might like to have a few children of my own one day. No harm in finding out a little about them when I had a chance."

Edward nearly swallowed his tongue. Jonathan a father? The idea seemed so preposterous. His brother was such a charming flirt, enjoying a carefree life with almost no responsibilities. Edward could barely imagine him getting married, sacrificing his freedom and shackling himself to one woman for the rest of his life, let alone starting a family.

Lord Haddon walked past them, toward a small love seat, carrying his daughter in his arms. Looking a bit drowsy, the little girl was rubbing her eyes with her fists. "Mummy?"

Lord Haddon patted her back comfortingly. "Mummy will return shortly. Shall we wait for her to come back before we put more pretty things on the big tree?"

The little girl nodded, then climbed into her father's lap. She nestled there, snuggling against him contentedly, chattering away. At one point Lord Haddon bent his head to nibble under her chin, which sent the child into fits of giggles. The sound of uninhibited, joyous laughter made all the adults smile.

"Lord Haddon's oldest child is a darling little

one," Lord Reginald commented. "Reminds me a bit of my own dear Charlotte when she was a tot."

The earl's eyebrow rose. "I have difficulty imagining Charlotte as such a self-contained, obedient little girl."

Lord Reginald laughed heartily. "Oh, not in temperament, but rather in looks. Charlotte had those same golden curls. Looked like a little angel."

"I daresay she never acted like one," the earl replied dryly.

"Oh, never," Lord Reginald said, his eyes merry. "I remember one particular visit when she was barely three years old, she escaped from her nurse, tossed a bowl of porridge all over my best carpet, ripped off her stockings and shoes in a proper fit of temper, tore several pages out of the family bible and then scrubbed chalk all over the newly wallpapered drawing room."

"It must have been a very trying week," the earl sympathized.

"Week? She did all that before luncheon the first day!" Lord Reginald smiled fondly. "She always had great spirit. I'm proud she has retained it as she has grown into womanhood."

"It must have been difficult for you, raising such a child," Edward commented, suddenly wanting to know more.

Lord Reginald chuckled. "She could be willful and stubborn to a fault. But she was never cruel or mean-spirited, so I knew that at her core, Charlotte had a good heart. It gave me hope and the courage to forge ahead during the most trying of times.

"I tolerated a lot of impossible behavior when she first came to live with me, even though I knew it was not good for either of us to always give in to her whims. Yet I found that in my grief over losing my son and daughter-in-law, I could not bear to refuse the pleading in Charlotte's eyes when she wanted something so badly."

"How old was she?"

"Almost five."

Edward tried to imagine what it must have been like for Lord Reginald, to lose both his son and daughter-in-law without warning. It was no wonder that he never wanted Charlotte to be deprived of anything she desired. "It must have been very hard," Edward said sympathetically.

"I cried many a tear and I'm not ashamed to admit it." Lord Reginald gave himself a little shake. "But then there was Charlotte to think of and there was no time to be maudlin. Though I was hardly a disciplinarian, there were things that I would never sanction and Charlotte quickly learned and obeyed those lessons. No bullying or shouting or ordering people about, for me or her.

"Those methods are often used on children, and wayward adults, but that never sat well with my conscience." Lord Reginald smiled slow and sweet, then met the earl's gaze. "The key to controlling Charlotte without breaking her spirit was fairly simple. Bribery."

"You must have very deep pockets, Lord Reginald."

"Bribery comes in many forms, Worthington. 'Tis not always the monetary worth of an item, but rather the value one places upon it. When she was seven, I could almost always get Charlotte to obey me by promising her an extra hour each afternoon on her favorite mount."

"And when she was sixteen?"

Lord Reginald laughed and shook his head. "That is when life *really* became interesting at Quincy Court." The older gentleman held out his empty glass and Edward obligingly filled it with another dram of whiskey. "I admit I have spoiled and indulged Charlotte and I am very aware of the gossip-mongers who have commented that it ruined her. Even though a female sits on the throne, a strong-minded woman is hardly the current fashion."

Edward bit back a grin. "Far better a woman with backbone than a fluff-head full of palpitations, silly airs and inane conversation. I will take spirit and even anger in a woman over passivity any day of the week."

"Well said, Worthington. A very enlightened view. I shall drink to it." Lord Reginald took a hefty sip of his dwindling whiskey. "There are some who say that my Charlotte is a contrary woman and it will take a strong man to master her. But I say she is not a woman to be gained without a struggle, and thus her worth is far above other females."

At that moment the object of their conversation entered the room. Edward tilted his head and watched Charlotte cross the floor to greet some of the houseguests. She wore a lovely gown of deep burgundy silk that flattered her figure and showcased her trim waist.

But it was not only her beauty that intrigued him. Lord Reginald was right. Charlotte filled the room with her presence, exuding a spirit that could not quite be contained. At the first opportunity, Edward excused himself to Lord Reginald and joined her.

"Good afternoon, Miss Aldridge."

"My lord." She dipped a pretty curtsey and selected an ornament to hang on the tree. Edward followed her at a discreet distance, waiting patiently until no one was in earshot before he spoke again.

"I think we might have a problem," he whispered. "Jonathan saw me in the hallway late last night as I was returning to my bedchamber."

The earl was prepared for Charlotte's reaction and caught the delicate glass ornament she dropped before it crashed and shattered on the floor.

It took a moment for her to recover her voice. "Do you think he realized where you had been?"

"As I was carrying, instead of wearing, the majority of my clothing, an imbecile could have effortlessly ascertained that I had recently shared a bed with a female guest. Jonathan is not a fool, though it hardly takes any great intelligence to deduce which female."

Charlotte's mouth twitched. "Why would Jonathan assume that you had been with one of the houseguests? And why me? Did you tell him you had come from my bedchamber?"

"Charlotte!" Edward exclaimed, his eyes filled with turbulence. "I would never compromise your reputation to anyone, even my brother. Fortunately, Jonathan has promised to forget the incident entirely."

"Excellent." Her worried expression shifted to a look of serenity. "If you admitted nothing, then our secret is safe," she asserted. "You could have just as easily been coming from the servants' quarters after pestering one of the maids."

"I think the overpowering scent of pine has addled your brain," Edward said, resisting the urge to grab her shoulders and give her a shake. "I shall let that remark pass because you have been taken by surprise, but just to be clear, I want you to know that I would never do anything so reprehensible as 'pester' one of my housemaids. Or anyone else's housemaid, for that matter."

Charlotte blushed. "Of course not. I am sorry, Edward, for even suggesting such a deplorable thing."

Her voice conveyed her sincere apology, but her expression was so inscrutable he had no clue as to what she was thinking. For one wild instant he wished he had the power to read thoughts. It would make his life so much easier.

Edward struggled to keep his voice low, hoping to avoid drawing any attention to them. Fortunately, everyone else seemed very involved in the tree trimming. "There is an easy way to solve this mess," he said calmly. "I shall speak to your grandfather and we can announce our engagement tonight at dinner."

"No."

He had not really expected her to readily agree, yet it still hurt to hear the rejection. "Why are you being so obstinate?"

"I am not." Charlotte tugged the ornament she had just placed on the tree branch and hastily shoved it onto a higher, thicker one. "You promised me time to consider your proposal and I shall hold you to your word. That is not being obstinate."

Edward rippled with frustration. "Circumstances have changed."

"Nothing dire happened," she said, looking up at him from beneath the thick fringe of her lashes. "And you just told me that Jonathan will not say anything. Our secret is safe."

He assessed her quietly, and realized she was serious. "The next time it could be someone else who sees me," Edward reminded her. "Someone who would not be as circumspect."

"Then we must not take any more risks. You must stay out of my bedchamber." She refused to meet his eyes. "Though perhaps that change in our relationship will also have you reconsidering your offer of marriage to me."

Edward lifted one hand and set his forefinger beneath her chin, leaving her no choice but to look into his eyes. "That comment hardly dignifies a response," he said. "Do you not know me better, Charlotte?"

She pushed his hand away and resumed rearranging the ornaments on the tree. "I hardly know my own feelings, my lord. How can I possibly presume to understand yours?"

His chest constricted. This cat-and-mouse game they were playing was wearing on his nerves. He had told himself he was prepared to wait for Charlotte to make her decision, but he now realized he was not prepared at all. Especially since he realized if she had truly set her mind against him, there was going to be no way of persuading her.

His recent words to Lord Reginald about preferring a woman of backbone and spirit hauntingly echoed in his memory. "I remember someone once telling me that there is no spur to the male heart like rejection. Is that what you are trying to do, Charlotte? Spur my heart?"

Her lovely green eyes turned hard. "What a low opinion you have of me, my lord, to believe that I must trick you into revealing your affections for me."

For a split second he wanted to turn and walk away, to forget all about Charlotte and the confused feelings she stirred within him. To forget her kisses, her sweetness, how wonderful she felt in his arms. Trying to understand her, to placate her, to please her seemed a task beyond his capabilities.

He walked over to the table where the glass ornaments has been carefully laid out, selected one and returned to Charlotte's side. Her head was bent low as she fumbled with a small doll she was trying to set within the tree branches. Heedless of the others in the room, he crouched down beside her. She refused to acknowledge his nearness, but he saw her fingers tremble slightly as she moved them from one branch to the next.

What was it that Lord Reginald has said—*she is not a woman to be gained without a struggle, and thus her worth is far above other females.*

"I am a cad, Charlotte," he said, handing her the ornament.

She sighed. "Do not berate yourself so, my lord. I know that I am not the most even-tempered of women."

"How do we tolerate each other, I wonder?"

"'Tis not easy." A slow smile spread over her beautiful face as she beheld the lovely angel ornament he had given her. "My only hope is that in the end you will prove yourself worthy."

"I shall endeavor to try." Edward braced himself forward on his elbows. After a quick glance to ascertain that no one could see them, he leaned in and kissed her.

Charlotte's mouth met his openly, warm and receptive. She smelled sweetly fragrant and softly feminine. He tasted her like a Christmas treat he meant to savor, with light brushes of his tongue, and she responded in kind, swirling her lips and tongue to meet his and maximize their pleasure.

Knowing they could not continue in so public a venue, Edward broke the kiss, then turned away to collect himself. As he looked past Charlotte, he saw his mother enter the room, her companion, Miss Montgomery, by her side. The lines around the countess's eyes deepened with displeasure as she took in all the activity.

"The countess has arrived," Charlotte whispered. "Do you think she saw us kissing?"

"No, but there is only one way to be certain. I shall go and greet her."

As he walked across the room, the earl fleetingly wondered if it were wise to approach someone who looked as if she had just found a pile of week-old fish in the linen closet and believed you were the one responsible for it, but he did so anyway. Miss Montgomery discreetly, and wisely, drew away the moment he gained the countess's side.

"I am so pleased you could join us, Mother. As you can see, everyone is having a wonderful time."

"The entire north wing of the second floor smells like a pine forest," the countess replied, her face tight. "I came to investigate the unusual odor, and now that I have seen that . . . that . . . *tree*, I finally understand why."

"The smell will be even more prevalent when the rest of the fresh greenery is hung tomorrow," he said in a cheerful tone, forcing himself to smile. "Lord Reginald and Lady Haddon both mentioned how much they are looking forward to it."

The countess paused, narrowing her eyes. "Ah, so you do not hold with the old superstition that it unlucky to bring the evergreens inside the house before Christmas Eve?"

Edward shrugged. "'Tis an old-fashioned notion that you and Father never subscribed to and it pleases me to follow the holiday traditions established at Farmington Manor."

The countess's face went pale. "I am very surprised that you even remembered how your father and I organized the holidays."

"I remember many things from my youth with great fondness, especially the holiday celebrations." Edward cleared his throat gruffly. "I miss Father a great deal, but never more so than during this season he so richly enjoyed."

For the briefest instant his mother looked stricken. She backed into a chair and sat down. Edward braced himself for her onslaught, but her voice was soft when she finally spoke.

"I was deeply grieved when your father died—out of my head, some might even say. It was so sudden, so unexpected." She turned to him and her voice dropped even lower. "I should hope that you will be enough of a gentleman to excuse the rantings of a grief-stricken wife, that you will forget any words that I might have spoken in hasty anger."

It was years late in coming, but Edward felt a great sense of vindication. The very small, illogical part of him that had always feared he had been an unwilling catalyst to his father's death was set free of its burden of guilt.

"'Tis forgotten," he said quietly.

"Good." The countess took a deep breath and gazed about the ballroom. "Though it looks completely ridiculous, I believe your father would have liked your great, oversized tree."

Touching his mother's shoulder, Edward knelt. He knew he probably shouldn't push her, but he could not let the opportunity slip away. "Will you help us decorate it?" he asked, holding out a delicate glass ornament he had pulled from his pocket.

The countess lifted a finely arched eyebrow. "You want me to put that on the tree?"

"Would you prefer another one?"

The countess looked down at the ornament, then back up at his face. Edward waited with his breath held as she hesitated, looking uncertainly into his eyes. "Do not expect too much from me, Edward. Too much has passed between us for it all to be forgotten in an afternoon."

Her words rang in his ears as something tugged painfully inside his heart. "There is fault on both sides, Mother, yet I still hope we will someday move beyond the hurt and accusations. Even during the bleakest of times, I continue to have faith that someday you will no longer gaze at me as if I am a bitter pill you must swallow, that you will tolerate my presences not merely because it is your duty but because it brings you joy. I even dare to hope that eventually we will both strive to do far more than simply learn to rub along tolerably together."

"You hope for a lot."

"I do."

The countess rose and walked slowly toward the large tree. Edward stayed by her side. Raising her arm, she hung the sparkling glass ornament on the highest limb she was able to reach. She turned toward him, her lips trembling. "If given the choice, I would choose not to be a stranger to you."

Edward had to work hard to swallow the lump of emotion in his throat. "I have come to you, Mother. The choice *is* yours."

She glanced at him. "You are very determined. As determined in your way as I am in mine."

The thought brought Edward up short. He shuddered visibly to think that he and his mother were so very much the same.

The countess laughed. "Do not look so stricken, Edward. We share very few other traits." His mother leaned over and took a delicate sniff of the fragrant pine. "You were always the quiet one, thoughtful, well-behaved, yet even as a boy you were never willing to accept limits in your life. Was that why you had to defy us? To leave all this behind and make your own way?"

"I never set out to be deliberately rebellious. I knew pursuing my business interests was the right course for my life to follow and I always hoped that my success would be the path to your forgiveness."

The countess shook her head sadly. "Not every problem can be solved with money."

"I understand that now. Though in my defense, I must point out that money, or rather the lack of it, was our main difficulty."

She pulled a face at him, her eyes narrowing. "Your father had already planned a reasonable solution to that problem, yet you refused to honor that obligation, refused to do your duty."

Edward felt his frustration start to build. "I chose my own path because in my heart I knew I could do nothing less. Would you have preferred that I honor your wishes and been unhappy for the rest of my days?"

"The choice of bride was always yours to make. We would never have forced you to marry someone you disliked." The countess's eyelids drooped low over her eyes. "Though I find it most interesting that you are much in the company of Charlotte Aldridge at this year's house party. And yet you still maintain that you would have been so desperately unhappy with her as your wife."

Edward could barely contain the stain of color that rose to his cheeks. It was ironic how he had indeed come full circle with his relationship and feelings toward Charlotte. What he so desperately wanted to avoid six years ago was all that he seemed to want now—Charlotte as his bride.

What would his mother possibly think if she knew the truth of the matter? He wondered if she would appreciate the irony or bask in her conviction that she had been right all along and he had been wrong. But he was a very different person now. A union with Charlotte six years ago probably would have been miserable for both of them, given his state of mind and the direction of his ambitions.

"I am not the same as I was six years ago. I believe I am a stronger and wiser man for having entered the world beyond the borders of my class."

"You certainly are different." The countess pursed her lips, as if holding back further comment, then surrendered to temptation. "Our children are our most precious gifts, which is why the joy, sorrow and disappointments they bring cannot be fully understood by someone who is not a parent."

"I do not need to wait until I have my own children to understand that you have been disappointed in me, Mother," Edward replied wryly.

"But you will never truly understand how it feels until you have your own children. Though I pray they never bring you the kind of grief that I have suffered."

Edward was unsure how to react to that remark, so he let it pass. "Would you like me to ring for Harris and have the tea brought in now?"

"Yes, Miss Montgomery can serve it. I believe I should assist the others in placing the ornaments on that tree or else we shall be decorating it until midnight." Her lips quirked as she looked straight ahead. "I do hope there are more of those lovely glass ones you ordered. I find that I like them very much, very much indeed."

CHAPTER 16

Jonathan was aware of Evelyn the moment she entered the ballroom. The odd, almost nervous excitement that made his breathing a little deeper and his heart beat a little faster overcame him suddenly and thus he knew she was near. He anxiously scanned the room and spotted her at his mother's side, naturally, but Edward soon approached the pair and Evelyn quietly slipped away.

With effort, Jonathan resisted the urge to immediately rush over and engage her in conversation but instead held back and observed her movements. She sidled close to the grand tree, nodding a greeting to those very few women and gentlemen who acknowledged her arrival, then stood unobtrusively off to the side, her keen eyes taking in all the activity.

She was a woman with the rare gift for stillness. A necessity in her profession perhaps, but a soothing quality he appreciated. She also possessed intelligence and good sense, perhaps a bit too much of that, passion and a warm, tender heart. In a word, she was perfect. For him.

"So, Miss Montgomery, what do you think of our Christmas tree?"

Tiny laugh lines appeared at the corner of her eyes, though she did not smile. "It is quite the most extraordinary thing I have ever seen, Mr. Barringer."

"A very noncommittal, diplomatic response."

The smile still did not appear, though a slight glimmer of amusement flickered in the dark depths of her eyes. "Survival in my position depends on my ability not to offend."

The statement starkly reminded him of how much of her true self she hid, and a part of him felt hurt that she could not trust him enough to speak openly. But he let it pass. Through their letters he had come to know so much more about her and the life she led. He had finally begun to understand the difficulties and challenges she had faced and overcome in her relatively short life and admired her all the more.

Her parents had died suddenly, without having the opportunity to assure her future. There had been very little money and few prospects, leaving Evelyn precariously close to destitution. It had never before occurred to Jonathan what a frighting place the world could be for a woman alone, someone who had no family, no money and no one to whom she could turn for assistance.

Too young, too pretty and without the proper references, a very frightened Evelyn had somehow managed to secure a position as his mother's companion. Jonathan was counting on that courage to tip the balance in his favor and help her take the necessary leap of faith that was required to become his wife.

"Do you enjoy Christmas, Miss Montgomery?" he asked, feeding on his insatiable need to know everything about her.

"I do," she admitted, finally bringing forth a smile. "Though it was a different sort of celebration when I was a child. I grew up in the far north where Christmas was usually white."

"White?"

"Yes, white with snow."

"What else was Christmas?"

Her expression softened. "Family and laughter and warmth. Holly and mistletoe and red satin ribbons with golden bells on evergreen boughs hung over the doorway to the front parlor. Marvelous food, congenial company, joyful songs. And, thanks to the snow, skating and sledding and snowball fights."

"Fond memories?"

"Oh, yes, and ones that I have not dared to dwell upon until now." Her breath escaped on a pleasant sigh. "You have brought it all back for me. Thank you."

On her beautiful face was an expression of deep joy. It made Jonathan's heart sing to see her brief happiness, and the urge to take her into his arms and hold her close was so strong he had to clasp his hands behind his back to resist the temptation.

"I hope that I will also be a fond memory for you one day," he said solemnly.

"I have already tucked the image of you away in my heart." Her jaw quivered slightly. "I know I have been foolish, reckless even, but I am no longer sorry that we have spent this time together, that we have shared our thoughts and feelings and dreams through our conversations and correspondence."

He felt like a young boy who had just been given a wonderful gift. "You like my letters?" he asked eagerly.

She glanced up at him and blushed. "I should not, since some of the phrases border on indecency."

His grin widened. "I meant every word."

"I know." She turned her face away. "That is why I cannot regret this stolen time. The heart is a strong and resilient organ. It survives, it endures, it even grows stronger. I accept that these magical feelings must be paid for with future pain, but, oh, that is far better than never knowing any magic at all."

She acknowledged that what they shared was magical! God help him, he was nearly frantic with excitement. "It does not have to end, my dearest. You know that I will do anything to make you my wife. Think hard upon it before you refuse. Most of us only get one chance for happiness and we must reach out and grab it, lest it vanishes like smoke in our hands."

Jonathan could see her apprehension in the rigid tendons of her neck, could hear it in the shallowness of her breathing. "You are the very devil, sir, to tempt me so."

"I am set on doing far more than tempt you," he admitted, trying very hard not to smile. "Christmas is the season for hope and I find that I live for any scrap of your favor and attention. I beg you to forget the differences you believe separate us and simply enjoy the moments we share together."

"I cannot marry you," she said with great dignity.

"Yes, you have told me that on numerous occasions, both in words and on paper, and yet I continually hope that one day you will take pity on my wretched unhappiness and abject misery and change your mind."

Evelyn opened her mouth, then closed it again without speaking. Her tension slowly disappeared, bringing a smile to Jonathan's face.

"You make it far too easy to forget myself, to forget my proper place," she muttered.

"Your place is by my side," he insisted. "Surely you can see how you have the most extraordinary effect on me."

"'Tis not me but more likely a case of indigestion. I noticed you ate two helpings of pickled onions at luncheon. They are quite sour."

"Ah, so you are watching my every move and even remembering what and how much I eat. It pleases me greatly knowing that I am under your ever-vigilant gaze."

Pressing a hand to her mouth, she turned her back on him. Initially alarmed, Jonathan was relieved to note her shoulders were shaking with laughter.

"You are determined to misinterpret anything I do or say as something romantic and encouraging, are you not?"

"I am." He circled around to the other side so she could not avoid facing him.

Eyes wide and stark, she stared at him. "Really, sir, I must insist that you cease gazing at me like a starving lion."

"But does not my obvious devotion soften your heart, at least a little?"

"The only thing that is softening is your brain.

The lion is gone, but now you have the stupefied look of a gentleman who has just crashed into a wall at a high speed." She tried to speak with a detached inflection, but Jonathan glimpsed the quiet humor in her lovely eyes. "If you do not change your expression at once, people will become suspicious."

He reached for her hand, then took a step to the side so his body was blocking the view of him holding it. He turned it gently so her palm was facing up. Then with the tip of his finger, he slowly traced a line from the center of her palm to her wrist. She tensed, but then he felt her body shudder.

With the fingers of her other hand, she swiftly traced his cheek. The need to take her lips in a scorching kiss was strong, but Jonathan restrained himself. Her hands pulled away. But he noted with masculine delight that her bosom was heaving.

"At least I have managed to refrain from making sheep's eyes at you," he said quietly. "Though I always thought that was a rather unappetizing analogy for a man in love, especially since sheep are hardly the most intelligent of God's creatures."

"But sheep are gentle and lovable," she replied, recovering her voice.

"They smell appalling," Jonathan insisted, wrinkling his nose. "But you need not be so concerned that anyone will suspect my true feelings for you. I assure you, I deserve a medal for discretion."

"Then we had best separate, lest your medal be taken away."

It was the wise, sensible decision, yet Jonathan hated the idea of being denied her company. "At least wait until my mother calls for you."

"'Tis easier if I go before I am summoned. It will attract less notice."

"But I have need of you."

"I know. And I of you." It seemed in that instant that the fragile remnants of Evelyn's resistance shattered. Lips thinning, she lifted her gaze to his face. "You are the first and only man who has ever made me feel this way."

Her cheeks flushed and after an abrupt curtsey, she bowed her head and scurried away, leaving him alone. The enjoyment and delight of the afternoon vanished with her. Miss Dunaway laughed prettily, and Lord Reginald shouted for everyone to come and see the section of tree they had just finished decorating, but Jonathan turned away.

Evelyn was already busy helping Harris set up for tea. Clearly, she would be occupied for the remainder of the afternoon. With a disappointed sigh, he left the ballroom. These brief stolen moments were killing him!

As he climbed the stairs, Jonathan struggled not to concern himself too much over the short time he had with Evelyn. It was better to view this as a momentary stall in his quest to win her acceptance. But it was difficult wooing her when they had so few opportunities to speak directly and privately.

Still, he thought he had made a bit of progress with her today. Despite Evelyn's vocal resolve to be cautious, practical, she had admitted she had feelings for him. The letters and small tokens of affection he had courted her with were clearly having an effect.

Jonathan entered the sitting room of his bedchamber, pleased to see his valet had managed to sneak in the flower he had requested. A single, red, thornless rose. It would be resting on Evelyn's pillow when she went to bed tonight, an unspoken reminder of his constant devotion.

He checked to make sure the small flower vase had sufficient water, then went to his writing desk. Unlocking the center drawer, he retrieved the latest letter he had been working on for Evelyn. However, even with the heavy drapes drawn back, there was insufficient light to read comfortably.

Jonathan reached for several candles and lit them, wishing his brother would consider renovating the manor in the very near future and adding gas lighting, at least in the family quarters. Fumbling with candles all the time was a damn nuisance.

With the area now properly illuminated, Jonathan read the carefully composed letter that had taken him half the night to perfect. As he finished, he heaved a sigh of relief. The note was even better in the light of day, conveying all the sentiments of his heart and the honor of his intentions.

He would pass the note to Charlotte after dinner tonight and request she get it to Evelyn immediately. In three days time it would be Christmas. But for him, the season of hope and miracles was starting early.

Amazingly, the snow that had been threatening for days and days finally arrived. Everyone awoke the following morning to a thick blanket of white covering the lawn, the trees, the bushes, the rooftops. The grounds of the estate, for as far as the eye could see, were transformed into a pristine white fairyland of delicate and ethereal beauty.

There was much joking and boisterous laughter as they all crowded in the breakfast parlor, talking enthusiastically about the change in the weather and the plans to enjoy the snow while it lasted. They were told that several sleds were ready to be put to good use and the carriage sleigh, with its long shiny blades, was equipped with a cheerful driver, sure-footed horses, hot brick foot-warmers and several layers of lap blankets for those who wished to explore the snowy, white wonderland with ease.

Charlotte, feeling as ridiculously excited as a schoolgirl, could not decide what she wanted to do first. Most of the younger houseguests had gathered under the front portico, but a few of the older guests were also among their numbers. Disappointingly, Grandpapa had elected to wait to take a carriage sleigh ride later in the afternoon in hopes the weather would warm.

There was much debate about where they should start and everyone looked to the earl for direction.

"To the sleds!" he announced, and several people applauded.

As she stepped from beneath the shade of the covered portico, the sun was so bright against the snow that Charlotte had to shield her eyes from the glare.

"Take my hand," Edward offered.

Charlotte set her hand in his outstretched one, amazed at the sharp feeling that lanced through her and the way her mind reacted to the contact.

Edward's touch was a bittersweet reminder that

she had been alone last night. He had honored her request and stayed out of her bedchamber, but Charlotte admitted that as glorious as it was, she missed far more than his lovemaking. She missed the physical comfort he gave her, the warmth and the touching, the feel of his strong body cuddled against hers as he lightly stoked her back.

There was that special intimacy of feeling his chest rise and fall against her own that somehow miraculously translated into an emotional closeness as they whispered together in the dark, sharing their thoughts, revealing their dreams, their hopes, even on one occasion, their fears.

"Are you cold?" Edward asked.

"Not really. Just excited to be outside and looking forward to some fun." Charlotte blew out her breath and watched it crystalize in the air, then realized one possible reason for the earl's inquiry. "Is my nose very red?"

"Hardly noticeable," he replied gallantly, and she knew he lied.

Still, Charlotte wondered what that said about their relationship when she felt comfortable enough around him to look so wretched and not overly care.

They fell in step with the others and Charlotte noticed that Lord Haddon had unbuttoned the top two buttons of his coat so his daughter might burrow her head inside and escape the cold. It was precisely the type of gesture she could imagine Edward doing with his own child.

Their child?

Charlotte blanched and tried to shove the thought from her mind. Regardless of the intimacy she had shared with the earl, she was far from ready to start thinking about having his child. Especially since she was still uncertain if she would one day be his wife.

They sank in snow up to their ankles as they walked, but for this outing everyone had wisely donned sturdy boots. The mischievous group somehow managed to hold off the unruly snowball fight until they reached the top of the hill where they would be sledding, but then all broke loose when Miss Dunaway tossed a snowball at Lord Bradford, striking him directly in the center of his back.

The older gentleman turned with an excited roar, bent and scooped up a handful of snow. He quickly shaped it into a ball and hurled back at her, missing by a mile. That move sent everyone scrambling for cover and ammunition. Soon they were all fighting for their lives, laughing and shouting in a wild tussle as the snowballs flew through the air, fast and furious.

A few of the older ladies stepped out of range, but called out enthusiastic instructions to the rest of them. Charlotte was pleased to note that she, Miss Dunaway, Lady Anne and Lady Haddon were holding their own against the men, and by unspoken agreement did not toss any snow at each other but saved the wet missives for their common male enemies.

After a few minutes, Charlotte realized that the earl was a prime target of nearly everyone. She wisely took herself out of his direct line of fire, enjoying the moment immensely when her snowball miraculously landed smack in the center of the back of his head. She could practically feel the icy drops trickling down his neck onto the collar of his shirt.

"Truce! Truce!" Edward shouted. He was mobbed

with a final barrage of snowballs as they all unloaded the last of their ammunition at him.

Amid much laughter, foot stomping and hand clapping to keep warm, they organized into groups for the sledding. The earl had managed to locate four large sleds and it was decided they should go down in pairs.

The servants brought chairs for a few of the older guests who wanted to watch the sledding. They were also provided with blankets for their laps and warmed bricks for their feet. Harris had directed the footmen to clear an area of snow down to the frozen grass, yet Charlotte could not help but wonder what the countess would think about having her beautiful furniture taken out-of-doors in this weather.

Once she started, it seemed that Charlotte would never grow tired of speeding down the hill, then trekking up again and awaiting her turn to go back down on one of the sleds. Her partner for each run was Edward, which only increased her fun.

As she prepared to go down again, Charlotte set herself gingerly in the center of the sled, then wiggled herself backward until her shoulders and back were pressed snuggling against Edward's front. He groaned into her ear as she came in contact with his nether regions and she moved her bottom teasingly until he growled at her to cease at once or suffer the consequences.

When she finally stopped fidgeting, Edward's arms came around either side of her and he held tightly to the steering rope. Looking to her left, Charlotte noticed that Viscount Haddon had just taken command of another sled. Lady Anne was perched in front of him, though they were clearly not in as close physical contact.

"I say, Worthington. Care to wager on who can make it to the bottom first?" the viscount asked with a mischievous grin.

"You're on, Haddon," Edward replied, and before Charlotte could catch her breath, they were off, hurling down the slope at a speed that seemed ten times faster than any other run she had thus far taken.

They seemed to fly through the air, slightly in front of the viscount and Lady Anne and then suddenly they truly were flying as they hit a bump near the bottom of the hill. Charlotte shouted and threw up her hands, knocking into Edward's arms.

He lost control and the sled overturned, dumping Edward and Charlotte into the snow. Shrieking and laughing, Charlotte lay on her back like an upended turtle, waving her arms and struggling for breath. Edward was soon at her side, bringing her to her feet, vigorously brushing the snow from her face and hair.

"Have I mentioned lately that you are an exceptionally clever girl?"

"Clever? Do you not mean clumsy? I knocked into your arms, causing you to lose control of the sled and lose the race. And now I am covered in snow." She laughed. "As are you."

"Clever," he insisted, "for landing us beneath an ancient oak tree, which, if I am not mistaken, is sporting a beautiful cluster of mistletoe in the upper branches."

"Really?"

Tilting her head back, Charlotte caught his eyes

and lifted her lips. Edward kissed her swiftly and warmly and openmouthed. The contrast between chilled flesh and hot mouths was glorious and more than a little arousing. Charlotte teased and licked his mouth open a little wider, then sucked gently on his tongue. To her regret, the kiss ended all too soon.

Edward lifted his head partially and she felt his lips tenderly brush her temples. Charlotte sighed and relaxed against him.

Her gaze drifted lazily to the top of the hill. Someone else had already retrieved their sled and brought it up so the next pair could take a turn. It was then that Charlotte noticed the normally vivacious Miss Dunaway was standing off to the side, a wistful expression on her face.

"You should offer to take Miss Dunaway down on your next ride," Charlotte mentioned. "I do not think she has had a turn yet and I am sure she would like one."

Raising his hand, Edward cradled her cheek. "I want all my rides to be with you."

She smiled. "But you cannot neglect your duties as host."

"Why is it that everyone likes to remind me of my duties and obligations all the time? Am I so negligent a man?" he asked, his mouth thin with distaste.

"No, but you are rather prickly."

"I'm sorry." Edward turned his face to the top of the hill and squinted. "You're right about Miss Dunaway. I'll ask her, and if she has not had a turn, I shall attend to it at once."

With a final hug, Edward left and trudged up the hill. Knowing it was ridiculous to feel any sort of jealousy when she herself had suggested it, Charlotte nevertheless experienced a pang of remorse when she imagined Miss Dunaway taking her place on the sled. Would she snuggle as closely to the earl as Charlotte had dared?

The sound of the hard blades rushing over the icy snow let Charlotte know she would soon find out. She looked up and saw Jonathan steering the sled, while Miss Dunaway clung to his back and shrieked with merriment for the entire ride.

As they reached the bottom, the sled tipped to one side, but Jonathan managed to balance it back on its blades and it slid safely to a halt.

Edward returned to Charlotte's side, looking very pleased with himself. "You were right about Miss Dunaway, but I managed to solve the problem and still keep you as my exclusive partner."

"An excellent solution," Charlotte remarked, giving him one of her very best smiles.

"I actually performed two good deeds and got my brother to have a little fun, too. He seemed unusually glum, standing away from the crowd as if he were frozen to the spot. Has he spoken to you about anything being wrong?"

"Ah, no."

It was then Charlotte realized that Miss Montgomery was not among the party. No doubt her services were required by the countess and she had been unable to escape and participate in the morning's frivolous activities. It was a stark, sharp reminder of her true place in the household.

It was on the tip of Charlotte's tongue to confide to Edward that Jonathan's current infatuation with Miss Montgomery was most likely the source of his down-hearted spirits, but she hesitated. It was not her secret to reveal. She had promised Jonathan to guard his privacy and she would stay true to her commitment.

Still, it felt strangely disloyal to withhold the truth from Edward. She had begun to trust him with her innermost thoughts, had slowly started to reveal a variety of her feelings. Under different circumstances she would have eagerly shared her knowledge, even asked for his opinion and advice on the matter.

"Shall we take on a new challenger and have another race?" Charlotte suggested. "We were clearly winning before we had the misfortune of tipping over. I'm sure if we keep our balance we shall be the victors in the next competition."

Edward gave her a puzzled frown, seeming to sense that she was trying to distract him. But he did not press her further. They continued to enjoy the sledding, making three more runs before everyone agreed they were cold, wet and famished.

They returned to the manor house at a far slower pace, exhaustion from the unfamiliar physical exercise taking its toll. Cheeks and noses red with cold, they had reached the great expanse of the south lawn when the viscount called out.

"Now see what I can do," Lord Haddon yelled. To the utter delight of his daughter and the shock of his wife, he hurled himself backward into a mound of snow, swished his arms and legs from side to side, then carefully got up. "A perfect angel, just like my Julia. And her mother, of course."

"It is inspired," Jonathan said thoughtfully as he examined the viscount's creation. "But I can do better."

Instead of falling on his back, Jonathan threw himself face forward into a fresh patch of snow. Several of the ladies screeched in astonishment, while the gentlemen chuckled and shook their heads. Jonathan imitated Lord Haddon's motions, then lifted himself without marring the pattern.

They all drew closer to examine Jonathan's angel, but no consensus could be reached as to which was the best. That prompted two of the other gentlemen to try, though they followed the viscount's more traditional example and landed on their backs.

Charlotte knew from experience that the earl could rarely resist a dare, yet even she was a bit surprised to see him also dive into the competition. Soon nearly everyone was participating and having a remarkably fun time while doing it.

When they had finished creating their army of angels, they slowly began the long walk back to the manor house, where the earl promised them a simple repast of hot tea, coffee, hot chocolate, hot cider, hot soup, sandwiches, buttered scones and freshly baked muffins awaited.

The food was like ambrosia and everyone agreed such simple fare never tasted so good. It became very quiet around the table after everyone had eaten. Charlotte noticed a few yawns and found herself fighting to keep her eyelids open.

One by one the guests began excusing themselves.

"I think I shall instruct Cook to serve dinner an hour later tonight," Edward said to Charlotte as they sat alone together in the salon. "Though it is barely noon, I have a feeling most of the guests will be sleeping the afternoon away."

"That sounds heavenly," Charlotte replied, resting

her head against his shoulder and closing her eyes. It was highly inappropriate for her to be taking such liberties, but she was simply too tired to care.

"Naps are far more interesting when taken with a partner," Edward whispered wickedly in her ear.

Despite her exhaustion, Charlotte smiled. "You used to be such a proper, restrained, responsible gentleman. When did you turn into such a rogue?"

"After I got a taste of you." He touched her shoulder and let his fingers slide down to her elbows.

Charlotte felt her face heat with a blush. Her pulse began to stir, her stomach quiver. "You would attempt to seduce a woman on the verge of exhaustion? For shame, my lord."

He nuzzled the soft curve of her neck, inhaling her scent greedily. "You need not fear for your virtue, Miss Aldridge. I like my partners with a bit more life, a bit more spirit."

She turned her head and purred against his cheek. "I shall remember that in the future."

"Ah, dearest, I shall never let you forget."

CHAPTER 17

Charlotte awoke two hours later feeling refreshed and revitalized. The afternoon light had diminished, but a good amount of brightness remained, thanks to the reflection off the snow-covered ground. As she came to full wakefulness, she wondered what the rest of the household was doing, especially Edward. Had he also taken to his bed for an afternoon nap?

His indecent suggestion of them spending the afternoon in bed together made her tingle with sensual awareness and she could not help but think what it would be like to make love with him in the middle of the day, with the light of the sun spilling into their chamber.

Nothing would be hidden. It was a titillating, yet slightly wicked thought. She was still not entirely comfortable having her naked body viewed by him, though Edward always lavishly complimented her form, making silly remarks about the beauty of her toes and the delicate curves of her elbows to tease away her embarrassment.

It never failed to fascinate her how nonchalant the earl was about his own nudity, a trait he assured her most men shared. What she did not believe was that most men shared a similarly handsome physique. Edward was long-limbed, lean and toned, his back and shoulders well-developed with sleek, hard muscles, his front even more appealing with a broad chest lightly covered with hair.

It was the hair on his chest, and on the other interesting parts of his anatomy, that fascinated her the most, and she regretted that she had not spent nearly enough time exploring this obvious difference in their bodies.

"I brought hot chocolate, Miss Charlotte, and a few of those lovely cream cakes. Would you like anything else?"

Charlotte's vision blurred as the image of a beautifully naked Edward faded and the sight of her maid came into focus. She cleared her throat. "Some hot chocolate will be fine, Jones."

Accepting a cup of the steaming beverage from her maid, Charlotte relaxed against the pillows and stretched out a few of her sore muscles, deciding she should wait a few days until she tried ice skating or else she'd be walking around bent over like an old woman.

"The earl instructed me not to wake you, Miss Charlotte, but he did want to know once you were awake, if you'd be interested in accompanying him on his visits to a few of the tenant farms this afternoon."

Charlotte grinned. "Please inform the earl that I would be delighted. I shall be down within the hour."

* * *

Edward greeted her with a smile. She wondered again if he too had taken a short nap, for he looked refreshed and well-rested. Jones had said they were going to visit a few of the earl's tenants, but Edward was groomed as if he were ready to meet the queen.

He was immaculately shaven, his hair washed and combed, his body clad in dark trousers and a coat made of fine black cashmere. After confirming that she was wearing her warmest cloak, hat and scarf, Edward escorted her outside.

Charlotte let out a gasp of surprised pleasure when she saw he had instructed the carriage sleigh to be harnessed. Two sturdy black horses were stamping their hooves anxiously on the snow-covered drive, steam coming from their nostrils as they waited to begin the journey.

"We do not have too far to travel. Do you mind the open coach?" Edward asked.

"It's perfect," Charlotte exclaimed, eagerly climbing inside. She waited until the earl was seated beside her before arranging the large woolen lap blanket over their knees.

"I was planning on going alone this afternoon, but it is always nice to have company," he said as he picked up the leather reins.

"The countess was unavailable?" Charlotte asked sweetly.

"What a devilishly wicked girl you are, Miss Aldridge," he said with an affectionate grin. "Though I'll have you know that my mother and I have reached an understanding of sorts. She is trying to be more tolerant of me and I am pretending to be pleased with her efforts."

"Edward, you must try to have more forbearance

or else things between you and your mother will never improve."

The earl sighed. "Forgive my sarcasm. I suppose I am overly cautious and do not wish to build false hopes."

"But you have made progress," Charlotte insisted.

"Yes."

"I'm glad, Edward, for your sake. And hers."

Impulsively, Charlotte pitched forward in her seat to kiss his cheek, which felt cold and smooth against her lips, then put her arm through his and snuggled closer. They traveled in comfortable silence, with only the noise of a lively pair of squirrels chasing each other from tree limb to tree limb to accompany them.

Thanks to the sharp blades of the carriage sleigh they did not have to stay on the roads, but instead glided over the miles of dormant farm land. Charlotte sighed with delight as she took in the pristine view of white-covered ground, the twinkling brilliance of the glistening ice-covered tree branches, the quiet calm of the wintery afternoon.

The wind kicked up, providing an excellent excuse for cuddling closer. Though as Charlotte pressed her legs against Edward's muscular thighs, it was not warmth that invaded her body, but a shivery burst of desire.

When they stopped at the first farm, Charlotte finally noticed the baskets packed into the back of the sleigh, lined up in a neat row, each covered with a bright-colored cloth and tied with a handsome bow. A broad-shouldered young man with a head of shockingly red hair and a cheerful grin came out to greet them.

"Good day to you, my lord. Miss." He tipped his cap and gave a quick bow. "Had a fine bit of snowfall today, didn't we?"

"We did indeed, Jack," the earl replied. "The cold is a bit of a bother, but the snow is good for the soil and makes everything look pretty."

"Aye, that just what the missus says. Will you come inside and have a cup of something warm?"

"We'd be honored," the earl answered. He assisted Charlotte from the sleigh, then reached in and pulled out one of the baskets. He wisely lowered his head before crossing the threshold of the small house.

The cottage consisted of three rooms, the largest being the kitchen where a large oak table stood in the center, several mismatched chairs set around it. The roughly plastered walls reached up to a low ceiling, which was supported by thick age-blackened beams. The earl had to duck his head each time he moved, but he seemed aware of that fact and had no mishaps.

The rest of the cottage was sparsely furnished, yet spotlessly clean, the flagstone floor gleaming. Jack's wife, Glinda, was a tiny girl, half his size in height and width. She smiled shyly when introduced to the earl and Charlotte and insisted that Charlotte sit on her best chair, a sturdy armchair with faded upholstery.

With the pride of a duchess, she served them all mulled cider and freshly baked cookies. The men drifted off to a corner of the kitchen and began talking about the fall harvest and the upcoming spring planting. Charlotte tried to engage Glinda in conversation, but the poor girl was so tongue-tied she had difficulty stringing more than a few words together.

As they said their good-byes, Edward handed Jack the basket. "Happy Christmas to you both," he said. "Let's hope for a healthy year and a fruitful harvest."

"Amen to that, my lord. And a happy and blessed Christmas to you and your family."

With a final wave, Charlotte and the earl departed. They were greeted with similar good cheer and hospitality at the next farm. This time they were served ale and oatcakes drizzled with honey, on blue-and-white dishware bearing the cracks and chips of age.

The old woman at the third farm could not stop grinning and chuckling and exclaiming her delight that the earl was at last home, in his proper place, where he belonged. Edward accepted her endless praise with surprisingly good grace, though it was clear to Charlotte that he felt embarrassed.

Before they left, he brought in an armload of fresh wood from the shed to add to the pile of kindling by the hearth and was thanked repeatedly for his kindness.

Their final stop was at the largest farm, maintained by the Ross family. The sprawling cottage on this picturesque spread of land was made of stone and boasted a second floor. As with all the other places they had visited, Charlotte could see that the property was prosperous and well-maintained.

The woman who had answered their knock wore a lace cap and a white apron smudged with flour. She held a young toddler on her hip who was pulling at her hair and she shushed him nervously when he began to whimper. Her eyes widened when she recognized the earl, and looking slightly flustered, she curtsied, then called for her husband.

Mr. Ross invited them inside and they entered the comfortable house, the earl carrying the large basket, which was covered with a pretty red cloth. A fire blazed in the hearth and the smell of fresh gingerbread waffled through the air.

As he walked past Mrs. Ross, the baby in her arms grabbed for the shiny buttons on the earl's coat, managing to capture one in his chubby fist. His mother gasped in horror and tried to pry the little boy's fingers loose. Assuring her that no harm had been done, the earl reached out slowly, as if the toddler was a wild animal that might easily startle, and patted him gently on the head. "He is a fine boy, with his mother's pretty eyes. You must be very proud."

Mrs. Ross smiled for the first time since they had arrived and bade them to take a seat. They accepted a cup of tea, so as not to be rude, and though they were far from hungry, ate a slice of the freshly baked gingerbread. The earl made a great fuss over Mrs. Ross's baking talents, just as he had made a similar fuss over all the baked goods they had consumed that afternoon.

The children of the household, all five of them, were chased from the room, but Charlotte could see them peeking in, their eyes round with cautious curiosity. Since they were mostly under the age of ten, except for the oldest boy, she realized they had probably never seen Edward until this moment.

"We have brought you a small Christmas offering," the earl announced as the visit came to an end. "A token of good cheer to celebrate the season."

Charlotte was impressed with how Edward handled the exchange, making it seem as if the family were doing him a tremendous favor by accepting the gift.

Mrs. Ross lifted the red cloth and exclaimed with sincere delight over its numerous contents, but it was the gaily wrapped presents that drew the eyes of each child.

"There is one for each of you, but you must promise to wait until Christmas morning to open them," the earl instructed.

They nodded solemnly, each child soon discerning which gift was their own. But it was young Martin's reaction that truly touched Charlotte. Though it was wrapped in fine brown paper and tied with a red satin ribbon, it was easy to tell from the size and shape of the package that Martin's gift was books.

His eyes lit with pure delight as he held the package reverently, obviously thrilled with the selection without even knowing the titles. Charlotte felt pleased to have contributed in some small way to the boy's Christmas delight.

A warm feeling settled over Charlotte on the sleigh ride home. It felt good to do for others, to share the bounty of Christmas, to be with Edward as he gave something of himself to his tenants by showing he held them in respect and with regard. It had been fun to be welcomed with genuine warmth by these good, hardworking families and interesting to see the earl's interaction with them.

Charlotte initially thought that Edward might become bored while at the manor, away from his business office in London, removed from the one thing that seemed to give him purpose and pleasure. But what was bred in the bones could not be easily ignored. He had been pleasant and at ease, even charming during the visits, a man relaxed in

his element. It was that very charm that had first
turned her head and drew her to him.

"You are very quiet," Edward said. "What are you
thinking?"

The drowsy comfort of the warm feelings inside
her allowed Charlotte to loosen her guard and she
smiled. "I am thinking that I am very glad that
Grandpapa and I came to the manor for Christmas
this year."

He met her eyes and his answering smile was
heart-stopping. "So am I."

Charlotte expected that dinner that evening
might be simple fare, since the household was
preparing for the Christmas Eve ball tomorrow
night and Christmas day feast the following day. But
from the moment she took her seat at the long
dining table, with its chairs of burgundy velvet, she
was served as elaborate a meal as any she had eaten
since arriving at the manor.

There was the usual choice of two soups, three selections of fish, four different types of fowl, each
served in its own special wine sauce, along with a
large joint of beef roasted to perfection that the
earl carved himself at the table. Complementing
each course were numerous side dishes of potatoes
prepared several different ways and vegetables
swimming in rich butter and cream sauces.

Everyone ate heartily, their appetites no doubt
stimulated by the vigorous outdoor activity of the
morning and the fresh, cold air. But even the most
ravenous of appetites could barely make a dent in
the overabundance of food. Charlotte suspected

these mountains of leftover food would most likely be enjoyed by the staff later tonight and tomorrow.

The gentlemen elected to forgo their cigars and brandy and joined the ladies as they left the dining room. As the party crossed the hallway, the level of happy chatter increased, blanketing the corridor. Everyone entered the drawing room to discover that two of the larger carpets had been rolled up and carried out while they were eating their meal. The countess then announced there would be dancing for those who wished to participate.

Lady Anne cheerfully took her position at the piano and began playing the first song. Edward appeared at Charlotte's side and claimed her hand. It was at that moment she recognized the familiar strains of the tune and realized she had never danced a waltz before with the earl.

He took her right hand in his left and put his other hand on her waist. His familiar, burning touch had Charlotte tensing immediately. Though she tried to prevent it, desire surged through her, a hot tide that swept her into an ocean of passion and need.

Edward's brow raised. "I think you have missed me in your bed, dear Charlotte."

"Not overly," she lied.

He gave her a skeptical smile. "Your body tells me differently."

Edward rocked forward in a gentle motion before moving his feet and Charlotte had to fight the urge to lean in to him, to press herself wantonly and inappropriately close. He was right—she had missed him in her bed, far more than she was willing to admit.

They had revolved twice around the room before Charlotte could catch her breath, before she could even attempt to master the sensation of being once again held in Edward's arms. Yet when she tried to speak, to carry on a casual conversation, emotions flooded and overpowered her, making words difficult to master and utter, like she was trying to capture fluffy snowflakes on a breeze.

She was too aware of him, too overpowered by him. The subtle brush of his legs against the silk of her gown, the intensity of his gaze as he looked down at her, his attention so absorbed in her every movement. Most unnerving of all, however, was how his eyes remained locked on her face, keen, observant and missing nothing.

"You dance very well," she finally managed to say. "Do you especially enjoy the waltz?"

The faint curve of his lips suggested he was very aware of the agitation of her heightened senses. "I enjoy all things immensely when you are my partner."

She had predicted his answer in her mind, but hearing the words fall from his lips excited her almost unbearably, for they both knew he was not only speaking of the dance.

Against her palm Charlotte could feel the tight muscles of Edward's shoulder. The memory of him without a shirt, without any clothes at all, flashed across her mind. She knew the sleek contours of his beautiful body, the tight muscles on his lean, strong frame. Yet even more irresistible was his handsome face, the bright, teasing eyes, the full, sensual lips, the strong uncompromising jaw.

It beckoned to be kissed, just as his body called out to be touched. She missed a step as the most

insane urge to move her hand up to the back of his
neck and caress his hair in an intimate fashion entered her thoughts.

She missed another step and Edward pulled her
closer, helping her keep her balance so they would
avoid bumping into any of the other couples. Charlotte told herself to relax, to give herself over to
his care, but it was hard to relinquish the very thin
hold she had over her emotions.

She had often thought it would be more enjoyable to be the one who leads in a dance, instead of
the one who was pulled along, but at this moment
she appreciated the skill, strength and control of
her partner. Given the state of her current, heightened emotions, if she were in command she would
most likely lead them into the fireplace.

They reached the end of the makeshift dance
floor and Edward drew her even closer, sweeping her
into the tight turn without missing a step. Charlotte
felt the exhilaration within her flair, felt her skin
flush and prickle. The desire in his eyes let her know
what he was thinking, as they issued forth an invitation, a promise, that he almost dared her to take.

Resolved to finish their dance without totally dis-
gracing herself, Charlotte bit her tongue and
looked over Edward's shoulder. She followed him
effortlessly into another turn, the feel of his broad
shoulder beneath her hand soothing her nerves.

She allowed herself to be drawn a fraction closer
and finally gave herself up to the pleasure of waltz-
ing around the room in his arms. In an odd way
they were in their own private world, alone even in
the middle of a crowd. When she managed to look

beyond the sexual tension, she found it was a comforting, special feeling.

Edward continued to hold her in his arms when the dance ended, releasing his possessive grip on her waist only after she gently reminded him the music had ceased. She curtseyed her farewell, but the earl grasped her hand, then raised it to his lips and brushed a slow kiss over her knuckles.

His eyes, nearly golden in the candlelight, never left hers. Charlotte's breath caught. Edward then turned her hand and pressed a slow, deliberate kiss to the top of her wrist, just above her glove.

It felt like a brand—hot, sensual, possessive. She knew what he was saying, understood his male, predatory need to mark her as his own. The atmosphere between them thickened, growing heavy with unspoken emotion.

"My dance, I believe, Worthington."

Lord Reginald's voice cut through Charlotte's haze, effectively breaking the spell. With a guilty flush she took her grandfather's arm, but when he realized the next set was a lively quadrille, Lord Reginald begged off and asked instead that she sit out the dance with him.

Relieved to be off the dance floor, Charlotte willingly accompanied her grandfather to a quiet corner.

"The countess mentioned that you were out with the earl for the better part of the afternoon. Did you go into town, perchance, to complete any last-minute Christmas shopping?"

"No, Grandpapa, we were visiting some of the tenant farms and delivering the holiday baskets."

"Ah, so your shopping is done? Good, very good. After all, tomorrow is Christmas Eve. It is never wise to wait until the very last minute to attend to these sort of important matters."

Charlotte tried to suppress a snort of laughter. His eagerness reminded her of the Ross children, so visibly excited when they caught a glimpse of their special holiday treats. "I can assure you, there is no need to worry, Grandpapa. Even though we are not at home, you will receive your usual gifts."

"A newly embroidered handkerchief?" Lord Reginald asked good-humoredly.

Charlotte folded her hands primly in front of her and lifted her chin. "I'm not saying. 'Tis to be a surprise."

"Do not be impudent, little miss," he said, dropping his voice so that it would not carry. "It ill becomes you."

Charlotte stared at her grandfather for a moment, then burst into giggles. Lord Reginald soon followed. "Shh, we must not appear to be having too much fun or else the wrong people will join us."

"The wrong people?"

"Like Lady Florence."

Charlotte frowned, but then remembered that her grandfather had been seated next to Lady Florence during dinner and the few times Charlotte had glanced in his direction she had noticed that the older woman had closely attended to Lord Reginald's conversation.

"Have you made a conquest, Grandpapa?"

Lord Reginald's face contorted into a comical look of horror. "I sincerely hope not." He lowered his voice further. "She is fine lady, of course, but my main fear is that she will seat herself with us and we shall be held hostage and forced to listen to the minutest details from her latest bird-watching expedition in Scotland."

"Hmm, that does not sound pleasant."

"Trust me, 'tis torturous."

Lord Bradford interrupted and requested the pleasure of the next dance and Charlotte accepted, deciding it might be wise to separate from her grandfather. She encouraged Lord Reginald to join in one of the card games and he kissed her cheek in gratitude, declaring she was a brilliant girl.

Lady Florence apparently did not enjoy cards.

The dance with Lord Bradford was sedate and fun and she felt her calm returning. She danced next with Lord Haddon and after that with Mr. Dunaway. Out of the corner of her eye Charlotte noticed the earl approaching, but she managed to evade him and he ended up being partnered with Lady Haddon.

It was easier than turning him down, for she had already decided she would refuse if Edward asked her again, knowing she would not be able to keep her composure through another dance.

A sharp pinch at her wrist reminded Charlotte of the note, meant for Jonathan, that Evelyn had slipped to her after dinner. Charlotte had folded it to a very small size and pressed it inside the top of her glove to keep it safe.

Fortunately, the love note was hidden in the opposite hand that Edward had kissed after their dance, for he certainly would have seen it. Scanning the room anxiously, she spied Jonathan at the card table, charming Lady Johnson-Meyer, Grandpapa and Lord Bradford as they played a lively round of piquet.

Charlotte casually sauntered over in their direction

and innocently inquired how the game was progressing. She stood behind Jonathan, gently resting her hand upon his shoulder. He stiffened slightly and she knew he had understood her unspoken message that she had a note for him. He turned his card and made a joke, then leaned back in his chair.

Charlotte, laughing along with everyone else, deliberately dropped her fan by Jonathan's chair. Stooping down to retrieve it, she let the hand that had been on his shoulder travel swiftly down his side. As she pretended to fumble with her fan, she pressed the note into the outside pocket of his evening coat. Straightening, she smiled as if nothing were amiss and made a lighthearted remark about her clumsy fingers.

The note safely delivered, Charlotte nevertheless stayed until the next hand was played, then with the parting advice to all to play fairly, she sauntered away, pleased to have successfully done her part.

However, what she had failed to notice were the earl's eyes, staring hard and curious at her, puzzlingly aware of her every movement.

Charlotte went to her bedchamber later that night in a state of confusion. Dancing with Edward had brought her physical needs to the surface again, and even though it was hours later, her body still tingled from the gentle fire of his touch.

She had deliberately avoided him for the remainder of the night, fearing he would ask if he could come to her bedchamber, or even worse, ask her to meet him somewhere in the house. The library, perhaps, where they had first made love?

Her eyes closed and her body flushed. If he had asked, she probably would not have refused. She had been out-of-sorts for several days now, so desperate to do something foolish and a clandestine meeting in the library would certainly qualify as a rash act.

Her fevered emotions made sleep impossible, and after tossing and turning for several hours Charlotte got out of bed. As she lit the candle by her bedside, she debated donning her robe, slipping from her room and surprising Edward in his bedchamber.

Tempting as it was, Charlotte told herself it was prudent to resist the urge, for indulging in the physical side of their relationship only confused her further. She was still fumbling in her mind with her decision when she noticed something on the floor near her door.

Curious, she moved closer and discovered a piece of parchment. Further investigation revealed it was a sealed note, with her name scrawled elegantly on the front.

Recognizing the penmanship, Charlotte picked up the note and brought it closer to the light. Realizing it had been left beneath her door so she would find it in the morning, Charlotte quickly broke the seal and read the contents:

Dear Charlotte,
  As you read this note I feel certain the household is in an uproar. Evelyn has disappeared, but do not fear for her safety. She is with me and we have left to start our life together. I thank you for all your help; without you our dreams could never have been realized. Do not fear, I shall never tell anyone of the

important role that you played in bringing us to-gether, but I thank you from the bottom of my heart for being such a true and loyal friend.

> *With deepest affection,*
> *Jonathan*

Charlotte finished reading the brief message and closed her eyes in alarm. She could hear Jonathan's cheerful voice in every line, could imagine his excitement and delight at the turn of events. But this was disastrous!

Without a moment's hesitation, she pulled on her dressing gown and ran from the chamber, hoping she would be able to find Edward's bedchamber in the numerous, winding hallways.

CHAPTER 18

It was very late. The fire sputtered weakly, the lamplight barely flickered. Dawn would arrive in a few short hours and Edward had not readied himself for bed, for sleep was an impossibility. His mind refused to rest with his thoughts in such turmoil, with his emotions in such an ice-cold state of confusion.

His eyes had not deceived him earlier this evening. Charlotte had clearly slipped a note into Jonathan's pocket at the card table and had also tried very hard to remain unnoticed as she did it. Edward did not want to be irrational or excessively suspicious; he did not want to believe it meant anything dire, yet the memory of being left a few days before his impending wedding lingered in the earl's mind.

Edward struggled to stay calm, reminding himself repeatedly that things were not always as they appeared, that it was foolhardy to jump to conclusions without knowing all the facts. On the surface it seemed ridiculous, almost melodramatic to believe that Jonathan and Charlotte had formed a romantic *tendre,* and yet the closeness they shared was very evident.

Even Lady Johnson-Meyer had remarked upon it the other evening, suggesting they would make a fine match. And Edward had sensed that Charlotte was being evasive at the sledding party when he asked about his brother's melancholy mood. She seemed to know something, but instead of discussing it, she had tried to deliberately distract him from the issue.

Edward sat down in the chair in front of the dwindling fire, rubbing his chin with his thumb, telling himself this was insanity. He would not believe the worst. Yet it was difficult to tell himself this could be an innocent misunderstanding with circumstances indicating otherwise and the bitter taste of betrayal lingering in his mouth.

Refusing to simply wallow in his misery, Edward crossed his bedchamber, knowing he could not wait any longer to confront Charlotte. Determined, he yanked open the door, but came to a sudden halt. Charlotte stood in the chamber doorway, wringing her hands in agitation, a crumpled piece of parchment sandwiched between her fingers. Jonathan's letter.

"Charlotte!"

"Oh, Edward, thank heavens you are here." Without waiting for an invitation, she barged past him into the room. "Something dreadful has happened. I must speak with you at once. Is your valet about?"

"I dismissed Thompson hours ago."

"Good." She nervously paced in front of the window, then stopped and turned toward him.

"Hurry and shut the door. I do not think anyone saw me, but we must be careful. Now more than ever."

The dread within him began to build. "This could not wait until breakfast?"

"No, by morning it will be too late. To be honest, in all likelihood 'tis already too late." She took an audible breath. "This will not be easy for you to hear, Edward."

"Does it concern my brother?"

Her eyes widened. "How did you know?"

He gave a humorless laugh. "My head is not always consumed with business. I am aware of other things happening around me, though apparently I am powerless to control them."

She shot him a narrowed-eyed gaze. "You knew and yet you never said a word to me about it?"

"I suspected. I also foolishly hoped my suspicions were wrong." Edward struggled to maintain a nonchalant facade.

"I wish you had told me," she said in a forlorn tone. "Perhaps between us, we could have prevented things from getting so out of hand. When Jonathan first approached me—"

"Ah, so he was the instigator of this relationship," Edward said, his voice crackling with the annoyance he could no longer contain. "I had wondered."

"I accept an equal share of the blame." Charlotte pinched the bridge of her nose and shook her head. "I was not coerced. I participated of my own free will. But I never fully realized the depth of Jonathan's passion, the lengths to which he would go to have what he wanted, until it was too late.

"Please believe me when I tell you that I regret my part in all of this, that I never meant for it to happen. I would do anything to prevent you this distress, to spare you this hurt. My only hope is that in time you will be able to forgive me."

Edward's heart chilled. "A pretty speech, Charlotte. I suppose I must feel grateful that at least you have had the courage to tell me in person. Far more civilized than my former fiancée treated me. I wonder, does this mean my taste in women is improving?"

Charlotte frowned. Edward could tell she was trying to gather her thoughts, trying to understand what he was implying. He saw in her eyes the exact moment she caught his meaning.

"You thought that Jonathan and I were . . . that we . . . how could you think . . . after all that you and I have been to each other you believed I would carry on with another man?" She stopped sputtering and gulped in a few controlling breaths. "And not just any man, but your brother?"

Edward had not imagined she would be so upset. "What was I supposed to think? Last night was not the first time I have seen the two of you exchange notes."

"So you thought I came here to tell you that I was jilting you?"

Edward cast her a cool look. "Technically, we would have to be engaged in order for you to throw me over for my brother. I have proposed to you several times over the last few days and still you do not wear my ring upon your finger."

"I have not rejected you," she said half-angrily.

"Nor have you accepted me." His gaze ran over her, taking in her blue silk dressing gown, the curves of her lovely silhouette, her loose flowing hair tied back with a single ribbon. His chest squeezed. "Are you waiting for a better offer?"

"From your brother? Don't be ridiculous. You are the one with the greater income and the aristocratic title." She stared at him with an odd flicker in her eyes. "However, I must concede you have raised an excellent point. You are only an earl. Perhaps it would be prudent for me to set my sights on a duke. Do you know of any under the age of sixty, perchance?"

Edward wanted to shout with frustration. Charlotte's earlier demeanor of distress had vanished, giving him a strong feeling that he had misread something about the situation between her and Jonathan. He turned a fierce gaze upon her. Why did his dealings with her always have to be so damn complicated?

"Why did you come to my chamber, Charlotte? What has upset you so greatly?"

She held on to her indignant anger a moment longer. "I consider Jonathan a dear friend, nothing more." She moved forward and touched Edward briefly on the arm. The small gesture went straight through him, making his heart lurch with longing and desire. "'Tis Jonathan and Evelyn who are involved. I am so upset because they have run off together and I came to you hoping there was something we could do, yet I fear it is too late."

"Evelyn?"

Charlotte rolled her eyes. "Miss Evelyn Montgomery."

"My mother's companion?"

"The very same."

Edward closed his eyes and swallowed against the

tightness of his throat, waiting for the surge of relief
to recede. He could not believe how fast his heart
was beating. Charlotte had not betrayed him with
another man. A thousand endearments crowded
his mind, but he voiced none of them. The opportunity to win her for himself still existed. But first
this new problem must be sorted out.

Jonathan and his mother's companion? Whatever could his brother have been thinking? Or
rather not thinking, just acting, and irresponsibly
to boot.

Edward frowned. "I was unaware Jonathan and
Miss Montgomery had formed an attachment for
each other. How is that possible? Miss Montgomery
is nearly always at my mother's side and I have rarely
observed her in conversation with my brother."

Charlotte turned and walked to the window. "A
marked attention to each other would have been
noticed and most certainly stopped. It could have
even resulted in Miss Montgomery's dismissal, no
doubt without a reference. Instead the pair have
been communicating through the numerous letters I have been delivering for them. If somehow I
were caught, no one would ever question or challenge me, so it was safe. Those were the letters you
saw me exchanging with Jonathan."

"You encouraged this relationship?" Edward
caught her wrist, spinning her back toward him.
"Have you lost your mind!"

"I had no idea their feelings had progressed to this
stage. I thought it a harmless, innocent flirtation."

"Apparently that is not the case." His voice
calmed and the hold on her wrist gentled.

Charlotte held out the crumpled note. "Jonathan

slipped a note under my bedchamber door. I'm sure he intended me to find it in the morning, but I was awake and the moment I saw it, I read it. His message thanked me for all my help and promised faithfully to protect me by keeping my role in his romance with Miss Montgomery a secret.

"As I came here to tell you about it, I passed your mother's bedchamber door and noticed a letter had also been left for her, though it was not placed completely beneath her door. Disregarding any sense of propriety, I opened and read it, and thus confirmed the awful truth of the situation."

Edward took the second letter Charlotte offered, scanned it, then silently cursed. "News of Jonathan's elopement will crush my mother."

Charlotte nodded. "I cannot imagine a worse beginning to their married life. This marriage is doomed before it has even begun. Even with complete family support behind him, it would have been difficult for many to accept such a socially inferior woman as his bride, but eloping will create a scandal from which they will never recover."

"Jonathan has never cared overmuch for the opinion of society," Edward said slowly, hoping the situation was not quite so dire.

"He will care when he and his wife are shunned, when his children are ignored, when his family refuses to give him their blessing and acknowledge this marriage." The lines of worry in Charlotte's face grew deeper. "Will you shun him too?"

Edward glared at her in silent reproach, refusing to dignify her question with any sort of answer. He would never forsake his brother, especially now when he was needed most. Edward knew all too well how it felt to be on the receiving end of their mother's cold barbs of displeasure. It was something he would spare his soft-hearted brother if at all possible.

He picked up his glass and headed for the small table in the sitting area of his bedchamber. "I need a drink."

Edward lifted the stopper off the crystal decanter and poured a generous serving of wine into the glass. "Would you like one?"

Charlotte shook her head. "Too much wine muddles my head when I'm upset. We need to formulate a plan. Quickly."

Edward took a long sip of his wine, then paced the room, thinking. "Is it possible they are still in the house?"

"No. After reading your mother's note I went directly to Evelyn's room. She was not there and all of her personal belongings and clothing are gone. I was afraid to wake any of the other servants and make inquires, fearing it would only alert them that she has gone missing."

"And Jonathan?"

"I leave it to you to search his room, but I am certain you will discover the same."

"You are probably right. But there might be some clues as to their destination. Wait here." Edward downed the remainder of his wine, set the crystal goblet on the table and strode from the room.

Jonathan's valet was nowhere in evidence. The bed was turned down, but the sheets and coverlet were undisturbed. No one had slept there tonight. A quick perusal of the wardrobe confirmed several articles of Jonathan's clothes were missing, as was his leather traveling satchel.

Charlotte was pacing by the window when Edward returned to the bedchamber. "Well?" she asked anxiously. He shook his head and her shoulders sagged. "How long ago do you think they left?"

"An hour, maybe two. They would have had to wait until the house was quiet and the majority of the servants had gone to bed before slipping away."

Charlotte swallowed. "Is there any chance we can overtake them on the road?"

"It's possible, but we have no idea of their direction," Edward replied wearily. "The logical choice is Scotland, but if Jonathan planned this, he might have a special license with him. If so, they can be married anywhere."

"They must have taken a carriage," Charlotte surmised. "One of the stable hands might have seen or heard something. If you know which way they are headed, it shouldn't be too difficult to track them."

"I'll go and see what I can find out." He reached for his black evening coat, thrown carelessly over the back of a chair, and slipped it on. It would offer some protection from the biting cold, since there was no time to hunt down his overcoat. "I won't be long. Try not to worry."

Charlotte bit her lower lip and nodded.

The full moon provided sufficient light for Edward to reach the stables without losing his way or stubbing his toe. Fortunately, the first servant he questioned was the very man who had hitched the horses to the light traveling coach that Jonathan had taken.

It was no small measure of relief to discover that

the servant had no idea Jonathan was not alone when he undertook this journey. At least his brother had been smart enough to protect Miss Montgomery from the staff's curious eyes and wagging tongues.

After assuring the nervous stable hand repeatedly that he had done nothing wrong, and then swearing him to silence, Edward hurried back to the manor, trying to calculate how much of a headstart the pair had really gotten.

The roads were too frozen for any mud to have formed that could mire the carriage wheels and slow their progress, but the wheels could become damaged from a broken road, and if they were trying to avoid detection, it would make sense to travel on as many of the poorly maintained, back roads as possible.

With a little luck, expert driving and a faster set of horses, they could be overtaken. Her eyes huge in her pale face, Charlotte relaxed a little and nodded enthusiastically when he shared the news with her.

"What will happen once you find them?" she asked.

Edward ran his fingers through his disheveled hair. "I'm not sure. I guess I will try to persuade them to return home. If no one has realized they were gone, we can act as if this madness never happened and their lives can return to normal."

"What if you are too late? What if they are already married?"

"That will certainly present an entirely different set of problems. I don't know what I shall do. Truly, I cannot think that far ahead. The first order of business is to find them."

Edward moved to his wardrobe and began changing his clothing, substituting his formal evening wear for riding breeches and boots and a warm wool jacket that could withstand the cold.

"I am coming with you," Charlotte announced. "I can be ready immediately. Where shall I meet you?"

Edward paused in the act of pulling on his left riding boot. "I never said you could come."

"You need me, Edward," Charlotte insisted. "If you find them before they are married, you will have to convince Jonathan to return. He will not be easily persuaded, but it will be harder for him to ignore both of us."

Edward shook his head. "You must stay here and somehow explain my absence. And Jonathan's and Miss Montgomery's. That will be no small task."

"My place is with you," Charlotte said forcefully. "If we cannot convince Jonathan to abandon this elopement, we might succeed in changing Miss Montgomery's mind. Though I do not claim a close friendship with her, she will be more inclined to listen to a woman, and I can offer her a feminine shoulder to lean upon."

Charlotte's reasoning made sense, but Edward was not yet convinced. "It will be difficult enough for me to leave without attracting the attention of half the household. How can we both do it?"

Charlotte sat on the edge of the bed. "'Tis Christmas Eve. Everyone will be busy with the final preparations for tonight's ball and hopefully too busy to notice we are gone."

Edward groaned. He had forgotten about the ball, a complication that would make it nearly impossible to hide what had occurred between his brother and his mother's servant. "Miss Montgomery's absence will be instantly obvious. My mother depends on her exclusively and never more so than when a special event is to take place."

"You are right. What we need is an ally in the household. Someone who can create a plausible excuse that the countess will easily believe as to why the four of us are not available to assist her with the preparations for tonight's festivities." Charlotte impatiently tapped her foot. Then, for the first time since she had entered his bedchamber, Edward saw Charlotte smile. "And I have just thought of the perfect person for the job."

The minutes passed and dawn brought a bright streak of pink and purple to the winter morning sky. With Jones's help, Charlotte dressed warmly in a blue wool gown and donned her sturdiest walking boots. Carrying her cloak, bonnet and gloves, she slipped quietly from her chamber and hurried down the hallway.

She paused outside her grandfather's bedchamber, knocking softly on the door. Lord Reginald had always been an early riser and she hoped today would be no exception. He called for her to enter and she found him out of bed, standing by the window in his purple robe, enjoying the sunrise.

As she approached, Charlotte was struck by a strong chill and wondered at its cause. It was then she noticed that Lord Reginald was not admiring the view but rather puffing on a cigar and blowing smoke out the open window.

"Grandfather! You are not supposed to be smoking those nasty things." Charlotte stalked across the carpet and tried to grab the offensive object, but Lord Reginald twisted and turned, evading her questing hands. "Dr. Harper said they were not good for your lungs, especially in cold weather," Charlotte continued in an angry tone.

"Oh, hang Dr. Harper. The man's an old sourpuss who's never had a bit of joy or excitement in his life." Lord Reginald turned his back and puffed harder on the cigar, the pungent aroma filling the air.

Charlotte's nose wrinkled. "How can you tolerate that odor at this hour of the morning?"

"I like the smell," he exclaimed. "It reminds me of my gentlemen's club."

"It smells like burning rubbish." Charlotte reached a second time, but again failed to capture the cigar. Sensing her growing agitation, Lord Reginald took a final drag. Then with a dramatic sigh he extinguished it and tossed the cigar out the window, staring forlornly down at the pavement below where it landed.

"Happy now?"

"Ecstatic."

They stared each other down for a long moment, each stubborn in their conviction that they were right.

Finally, Lord Reginald broke. "For pity's sake, it's Christmas Eve, Charlotte. Can't a man have a little fun?"

"If you only smoked on Christmas Eve I would not complain. But we both know you indulge yourself whenever the mood strikes, regardless of the fact that you promised me *last* Christmas you would quit."

Lord Reginald lowered his gaze. "I tried. 'Tis not easy."

Charlotte eyed her grandfather uncertainly. "I understand, but you really must make more of an effort."

"Temptations abound, especially in this house. Worthington provides the finest cigarillos for his guests. Imports them from Cuba."

"So do you."

"Yes, but here I can get my hands on a cigar whenever I want one. Back home they are always mysteriously disappearing," Lord Reginald said, sending a sidelong glance at Charlotte. "Though it is hardly difficult to deduce who has been taking them."

"I care about your health," Charlotte admitted. "And I do understand that sometimes the flesh is weak, even for those with a strong will. So I hide your cigars, hoping it will be easier for you to resist temptation if you are not confronting a full cigar box each day."

Lord Reginald let out a grunt. "What can a girl of your tender years know about temptations and weakness of the flesh?"

"You'd be surprised," Charlotte muttered, then blushed, knowing she would be mortified if her grandfather ever learned how weak her flesh had indeed been. With the earl.

Fortunately, Lord Reginald was too busy lamenting the loss of his cigar to take notice of her remark. He cast one final, sad frown at the pavement below, then closed the window. "Though I firmly believe you enjoyed it immensely, I somehow do not think you barged in here solely to lecture me about my smoking."

Belatedly, Charlotte realized it was imprudent of her to have made such a fuss over the cigar when she had such a big favor to ask of him, especially considering that her plan to follow Jonathan and Miss Montgomery had no chance of success without her grandfather's assistance. Quickly, she explained what had occurred, concluding her tale with a heartfelt plea for Lord Reginald's help.

The older man whistled with surprise when she was finished. "Poor Jonathan. He must be besotted indeed to act with such little sense. Running off with his mother's paid companion? Why, 'tis nearly as bad as taking off with the family governess. Darn decent of Worthington to follow after his brother, though, to try and set things to rights. But this is a family matter. I don't know why you should be involved."

"I feel responsible, since I was the one who secretly conveyed their messages. I must now do what I can to rectify the situation."

Lord Reginald walked closer to the fireplace, mumbling and shaking his head. But Charlotte concluded her determination must have shown on her face, for he did not dismiss her outright.

"It will be a very unpleasant shock for the countess," Lord Reginald mused. "And I suppose if I refuse to help, I'll have to live with your sulking behavior for the next three months. Or longer."

Charlotte sniffed. "Grandpapa, I do not sulk."

"Not often, since you always seem to get your own way," he replied almost cheerfully. "But when you are crossed, you are like a bear with a thorn in its paw."

"Then you will help? If only to avoid my appalling behavior?"

He narrowed his gaze and dropped into a chair. Charlotte hesitated, wondering how much she should confide in him. She did feel a great responsibility for this mess, and was compelled to do what she could to fix it, but her need to help Edward came from a place deep in her heart, not her conscience.

"Oh, Grandpapa. The earl cannot do this alone, and I am unable to assist him unless you aid me."

The frown on Lord Reginald's face broke. "I might be able to distract the countess for a few hours, but, Charlotte, you know we will never be able to keep this from the servants. Nothing escapes their notice. They have a network of information that would do the Home Office proud."

Charlotte's pulse leapt. He was going to help her! Thank goodness! "Thus far, none of the servants are aware that anything is amiss. My maid thinks that I have gone out for an early-morning ride. I want you to tell her that I have succumbed to a nasty cough and have taken to my bed.

"Then inform my maid and the countess that at your request, Miss Montgomery is kindly sitting with me. Jones is terrified of catching any sort of illness. She will not enter my bedchamber until she is told that I am recovered enough to no longer be contagious."

Lord Reginald stood and strolled to the corner of the room. He splashed his face with water from the basin on his nightstand, then slowly dried himself with a soft towel. "The countess will not appreciate me spiriting Miss Montgomery away the day of her big party, when her companion is needed most."

Charlotte nodded. "I agree she will be upset, but above all, the countess is a hostess and will go to extreme lengths to accommodate her guests. Especially those she likes. Charm her, Grandpapa. She will not be happy about it, but she will allow it. I am certain if you ask Lady Haddon, she will step in and appease the countess and perform some of the tasks required of Miss Montgomery."

"But what shall I say if Lady Haddon volunteers to take Miss Montgomery's place at your sickbed?"

Charlotte's eyes widened with dismay. It was just the sort of generous offer Lady Haddon would make. How wise of Lord Reginald to realize it. "If Lady Haddon tries to interfere, tell her I am very much afraid she will pass along my illness to her children. That should keep her out of the sick room."

"And the earl and his brother? How is their disappearance to be explained?"

"The earl will pen a note to his mother saying he and his brother have important business to attend to off the estate. That will also account for the missing carriages."

Lord Reginald appeared impressed. "It seems you have thought of everything."

Charlotte grimaced. "Far from it. It's a house of cards, Grandpapa, and I shudder to think how many different things can go wrong. That is why I need you to keep the pretense going as long as possible."

"When will you return?"

"By afternoon, I hope." Charlotte glanced at the window. Sunlight crept through the curtains and brightened the whole room. It was past time they set out on their mission.

"I am not keen at the thought of you and

Worthington alone together in a lumbering carriage for hours."

Charlotte's heart thudded. She had not thought about the time she would spend alone in Edward's company. "The earl is a gentleman. You have nothing to fear."

"The earl is a man and it has not escaped my notice that he finds you very attractive." Lord Reginald cocked his head to one side and looked at her thoughtfully. With effort, Charlotte managed not to squirm.

"There will hardly be time for improprieties, Grandpapa, as we race through the countryside in pursuit of Jonathan and Miss Montgomery."

A faint smile touched Lord Reginald's mouth. "But what of your reputation, Charlotte?"

"My reputation is in your hands, Grandpapa. I know you will faithfully protect it, along with Miss Montgomery's. No one must know what has occurred, especially the countess. The only chance we have of putting this mess to rights depends on complete secrecy."

"I understand." Lord Reginald patted her on the arm. "Try not to despair, my dear. The task ahead of you is daunting, but you must have faith that all will come right in the end. After all, Christmas is the time for miracles."

CHAPTER 19

Twenty minutes later, Charlotte found herself, as planned, standing amid the tall oak trees at the end of the long front drive of the manor house, stamping her feet in the packed snow to ward off the chill. But she was not alone. Unfortunately, she had picked up an unexpected escort when she slipped out the side entrance of the manor house.

One of the household's dogs, a big shaggy retriever with long ears and a panting tongue that hung out the side of his mouth, had followed her down the drive, his tail wagging. She had made the fatal mistake of petting him and rubbing behind his ears, and though she had repeatedly tried to shoo him back to the house or the stables, he showed no inclination of leaving her side.

"Foolish animal," she muttered under her breath. "No doubt you are a male dog."

At the sound of her voice, the large dog thumped his tail with enthusiasm and leaned against her, sitting so close he was practically on her foot. Unable to resist his blatant devotion, and soulful brown eyes, Charlotte stroked his silky head. It had a peculiar, calming effect on her nerves.

The faint sound of carriage wheels made her stiffen and listen hard. Hackles rising, the dog stood and growled. Charlotte stayed hidden among the clump of trees until she heard the earl's familiar voice call out, "Are you there, Charlotte?"

"Yes, but we have a slight problem." Her furry companion bounded toward the coach, barking with excitement.

"Bloody hell, why did you bring one of the dogs with you?"

"He brought himself," Charlotte protested. "And I cannot get him to leave."

"Home, Ranger," the earl commanded. "Home."

The retriever obediently ran a few steps toward the manor house, then stopped and turned, as if waiting for his human companions to join him. She heard the earl swear again beneath his breath. "Home," he repeated, in a deep, commanding tone.

With a loud whine, the dog gazed wistfully toward Charlotte. Then dipping his head low, he turned and started trotting slowly down the drive, toward the house, as commanded.

Emerging from the trees, Charlotte quickly set her right foot on the edge of the carriage wheel and hoisted herself inside. The earl caught her before she pitched herself into his lap, but she waved off his assistance. "Hurry and drive away before your dog decides to turn around and follow us."

The carriage lunged forward. Charlotte shrieked, but held on to her balance, if not her dignity. Once she had righted herself and placed the warm fur lap blanket around her legs, she glanced around.

It was hardly the most elegant coach Charlotte had ever seen. Small, sleek and built for two, the half-open vehicle was painted a glossy black with high yellow wheels, that had an old-fashioned look to them. But the seats were well-padded and upholstered in soft leather and the carriage was drawn by an exquisite set of matched grays who were spirited and primed for the journey.

Obviously the earl had chosen the vehicle for its speed, but also because he could drive it himself, thus keeping their outing a secret from the staff. They took a sharp turn, yet stayed in the center of the road and Charlotte was relieved to note Edward's expert handling of the ribbons.

"I assume that since you are here Lord Reginald has agreed to help us," Edward said, meeting her gaze briefly. "I suspect it was not too difficult for you to convince him."

Charlotte bit her bottom lip, unsure how to interpret that remark. Was the earl implying her powers of persuasion were excellent or did he believe her grandfather was easily susceptible to her wishes? Charlotte decided she would give the earl the benefit of the doubt and believe the former.

"Though he was not completely in favor of me accompanying you, he eventually agreed it was the correct decision," she replied. "Grandpapa admires your dedication to your family, Edward, and was pleased to help in any way possible."

The earl's handsome face looked pensive. "It was good of him, though I admit to feeling more of a twinge of guilt, knowing he will have the harder task, trying to deal with my mother all day."

"It will not be easy, but Grandpapa will do his best."

The earl gave her a lopsided smile and Charlotte was struck with a wave of melancholy, very aware that this journey to find Jonathan and Miss Montgomery was a big gamble that might all be for naught.

"Are you hungry?" Edward's question cut through her gloomy thoughts.

"A little, but there is hardly time to stop for a meal," Charlotte replied, wishing her stomach would not grumble so loudly.

Edward's widening smile let her know he had heard her hunger pangs. "There is a hamper on the floor, wedged on the other side of my boot. Can you reach it?"

"I believe so." Charlotte bent over his lap and grabbed on to the wicker handle. The close bodily contact, even through their layers of clothing, felt unbearably sensuous. Like a fine wine, it was a heady pleasure to be so near Edward.

"Do you need any help?"

At the sound of his voice, a sudden thrill shot through her stomach and Charlotte nearly dropped the basket. "I think I've got it," she mumbled. Tugging hard, she managed to pull it up and place it on the seat between them. "Where did you get it?"

"From Cook."

Charlotte's head snapped around. "What?"

The earl shrugged. "When she noticed there were no dirty breakfast dishes, she insisted on packing the hamper."

"Does she know where we are going?" Charlotte asked in alarm.

"Of course not." Edward shrugged. "She believes

I have gone out with Jonathan on an important errand, remember?"

Relieved their secret was still safe, Charlotte removed her gloves and rummaged through the basket, extracting a muffin that was still warm. Deciding it would be too messy, and too much of a bother, she did not reach for the butter or jam in the small crockery pots and bit into the tasty morsel. After finishing her second muffin, she realized she was being terribly rude, stuffing herself so gluttonously without even offering any food to the earl.

"Shall I take the ribbons while you eat?" she suggested.

His brow raised. "Have you ever driven a carriage?"

"I had a pony cart when I was a little girl," Charlotte replied. "I'm sure once we hit a long stretch of straight road, I can manage the team."

The earl shook his head. "These are not the pair to learn upon. They are far too high-spirited. I am hungry, but I can wait until we stop to water the horses." He stretched his legs forward as far as the coach would allow. "Unless you would like to feed me?"

Charlotte nearly choked on the piece of apple she was contentedly chewing. Feed him! The suggestion brought to mind all sorts of inappropriate sensual images. My gracious, what sort of sexual deviant had she become when the most innocent of remarks set her body humming with awareness?

Resolutely shutting out the pictures, Charlotte broke a fresh muffin in half. "Butter or jam?" she asked tersely.

"Jam, please."

Holding the broken muffin over the basket with one hand, she reached inside with the other, scooped some jam onto a knife, then spread it onto the larger muffin piece. She waited for him to transfer the reins to his left hand, so he could hold the food in his right, but the sly smile she could clearly see on Edward's face let her know she would be waiting a long time indeed.

Calmly, or at least as calmly as she could manage, Charlotte raised her hand to his mouth. Edward leaned his head forward and slowly accepted her offering. His lips closed over her fingertips, deliberately she was certain, and every nerve in her body was set afire.

Forcing herself to ignore the sensations, Charlotte pulled her hand away, slathered the second half of the muffin with jam and waited for the earl to swallow. The moment he had, she unceremoniously shoved the rest of the muffin into his mouth.

For an instant she feared he might gag on it, but somehow the earl managed to chew and swallow the muffin without coughing. She watched him closely, to ensure he was all right, holding the bottle of unopened wine in one hand, in case he needed something to clear his throat.

"Drink?" she asked, raising the bottle.

The earl shook his head roughly, declining the offer. Charlotte continued to watch him. His cheek was clean-shaven. She wondered idly if his valet had been summoned and used the razor or if Edward had done it himself. For all his regal aristocracy, the earl was not an arrogant, or spoiled man. He could and did fend for himself and she admired his self-reliance.

Charlotte's gaze shifted to the corner of his mouth where a stray drop of strawberry jam glistened. Resisting the most absurd urge to lean over and lick away the drop, Charlotte pulled a napkin from the basket and vigorously rubbed the earl's face.

He winced slightly and pulled away. "No need to rub my face raw," he exclaimed. "There must be gentler ways to clean it."

"Then we truly would end up in a ditch," Charlotte remarked dryly. She sighed and looked away.

The earl cleared his throat and muttered under his breath. "That was not what I meant, but it is a delightful image. I'm flattered, Charlotte."

She felt heat flood into her face. Needing to change the subject, she started asking questions about their route and Edward's opinion on where his brother might have stopped to be married.

"Do you think they are heading for Scotland?" Charlotte inquired, having always heard that Gretna Green was the place were most eloping couples traveled.

"It's possible, but Jonathan seems to have planned this for some time. I think he might have bought a special license so as to avoid being married over the anvil." A muscle ticked along the earl's square jaw. "Though it will make but a small difference. A scandal is a scandal. The marriage will still be viewed as an unfortunate mistake, a grave error in judgement by nearly everyone, including my mother."

Charlotte winced. "This is how people in love act, Edward. With passion, with boldness—"

"With idiocy," he muttered.

"Jonathan is a very determined man and he has realized that he cannot live happily without Miss Montgomery."

Edward rubbed the bridge of his nose. "Could he not have fallen in love with a suitable young woman?"

"Now who is acting like an idiot?" Charlotte exclaimed. Her words cut sharply through the air. "We do not choose whom we love."

"I cede the point, but is it so unreasonable to have expected my brother to have approached his marriage in a more practical, sensible manner?"

Charlotte's defiance melted away. "Being in love can cloud your judgement."

"Or fog it completely." Edward shifted the ribbons and slowed the horses as they approached a sharp curve. "It has taken my mother six years to reach an uneasy truce with me and now Jonathan has eloped with her companion. Will my family never be at peace? Must we always be at odds with each other?"

"We still might find them in time," Charlotte said.

Edward merely grunted his reply. Charlotte could not fault his skepticism. They were both well aware the odds were not in their favor.

As they rounded another particularly sharp curve, Charlotte fought to keep herself upright, suddenly feeling all the exhaustion of a sleepless night overtake her weary body. Her head throbbed with a low pain. She moved her fingers to her temples and pressed them firmly in an effort to dull the ache, then rubbed her eyes and tried to ease the tenseness of her muscles, wishing it were possible to sleep, if only for an hour or two.

"Lean against my shoulder," Edward said, obviously guessing how much she needed to rest.

Charlotte was grateful for the offer. Knowing he needed all of his upper-body strength to control the horses, she moved closer and gently lowered her head, trying to put only the lightest pressure on his shoulder. She lay still for a long minute, forcing her body to relax. Her nose was close to his bare neck and she breathed in his clean, comforting scent, a pleasing mixture of tangy soap and salt.

Though hardly a soft cushion, Edward's shoulder provided her room to maneuver into a more comfortable body position. Gradually, Charlotte's eyes drifted closed. Her feet were cold, but the rest of her body was deliciously warm. Cuddled next to Edward she felt safe, relaxed. Her breaths turned even and within minutes she had slipped into the quiet oblivion of sleep.

The section of his upper arm and shoulder where Charlotte's head lolled against his body had lost all feeling, the feather that sat atop her stylish bonnet tickled his nose every time he shifted his head in her direction, and her deep, even breaths reminded him all too vividly of how bone-tired he felt. Yet Edward kept his body locked in the same position.

He could tolerate any discomfort if it brought Charlotte some measure of peace, afforded her even an hour or two of rest. That thought brought a flicker of surprise with it. When had Charlotte's comfort become so important to him, more important than his own? And not only her comfort, but her happiness and well-being?

When had he become the one who wanted to watch out for her, protect her, indulge her? Spoil her. The one to bring a smile to her lips along with a gasp of pleasure, to make her eyes alight with joy and her face glow with contentment. When exactly had that happened?

The earl's throat went dry. The feelings had hit him, fast and hard, and now . . . and now . . .

The sight of an upcoming village broke Edward's train of thought. He slowed the horses to a walk as they entered the picturesque hamlet and looked over the small street lined by shops and houses. He noted two taverns at the middle of the street's length and surmised this was a town of significant population to support two apparently prosperous establishments.

Regrettably, he did not see the one thing he was so desperately seeking—the spires of a church.

The change in carriage speed woke Charlotte and she shifted in her seat. "Where are we?"

"Somerville, according to the sign. I was here once as a boy but barely remember it." Trying not to show the raging frustration he felt, Edward took a deep breath. "The village boosts two taverns, but alas I see no evidence of a church."

"One must suppose the sinners have gained the victory in this small community," Charlotte remarked with a wry grin.

"Apparently." Edward stopped the vehicle in front of the larger inn and jumped out. "Wait here. I'll only be a moment."

He left the reins in Charlotte's capable hands and went into the taproom. A stout man in a clean white apron approached. "Welcome to the Bull and Finch. We have a private parlor sir, for ye and the lady. Won't take but a minute fer my wife to lay out the table and serve ye both a hearty luncheon."

Edward imparted what he hoped was a friendly smile. "I thank you for your offer of hospitality, but we have already partaken of our midday meal. I came to inquire after the nearest church. Is there one located close by?"

The man leaned on the wooden counter and glanced at the earl, his brows knitting. "Strange ye should ask, sir, seeing as ye are the second gentleman today who'd be wantin' a church."

Edward nearly jumped over the counter, but he held back his exuberance. In his experience, locals tended to be closemouthed and suspicious when one exhibited too much interest or made the matter sound too urgent. "The second one to ask you say? Hmmm, how odd." Edward cleared his throat. "So, is there a church in town?"

"There is," the innkeeper said. "And a fine one, too. On the north edge of town. There was a fire in the spring that destroyed the steeple, but the buildin' is open and the vicar should be around at this time of day. Just stay on the main road as ye drive through town. Ye can't miss it."

Edward dug into his pocket, withdrew several coins and hastily pushed them across the counter. "Thank you for your time."

The innkeeper looked confused, but he scooped up the money and it quickly disappeared within the folds of his apron.

Edward returned to the carriage in a much better frame of mind. His initial concerns that they were on a wild-goose chase, traveling on the wrong road, possibly in the wrong direction had been momentarily tempered. He willed the tension away and tried to focus on his driving. Thankfully, Charlotte sensed his mood and asked no questions.

The church was as easy to locate as the innkeeper had told him. As Edward maneuvered his team of horses to the side of the stone building, he recognized the carriage tied to a wrought-iron post as one of his own.

A wave of relief washed down his spine. They had found them! "I know that coach," Edward announced. "It's one of mine. Jonathan and Miss Montgomery must be inside."

Edward sprang from the carriage, then impatiently assisted Charlotte. They entered the church quietly, each shivering in the chilly air. Squinting down the long aisle, Edward could see a couple at the altar, their hands clasped together. The vicar was positioned in front of them, his prayer book open. Three women were standing in a semicircle nearby. The witnesses, in all likelihood.

Without another thought, Edward charged down the aisle, his boot heels echoing loudly on the stone floor. He could hear Charlotte scampering beside him, moving quickly to keep up. The commotion caused the vicar to pause. The church fell silent and Edward's quiet command was clearly audible. "Stop the ceremony at once!"

There was a blur of movement as the couple standing before the vicar turned toward him. Jonathan froze with a gasp when he saw the earl, his face turning pale at first, then becoming rapidly infused with color.

"Oh, dear Lord save us," Miss Montgomery squeaked, turning her face against Jonathan's broad shoulder, as if closing her eyes would somehow make the earl disappear.

The brothers regarded each other with identical blank stares.

The earl opened his mouth to give his brother a sharp set-down, but broke off abruptly when he felt a light touch on his arm. Confused, he looked over at Charlotte, who now stood by his side, her hand clasped on his arm. Her expression was grave, her eyes deeply troubled.

"The vicar was reciting the final prayer and bestowing his blessing on the newly married couple when we so rudely interrupted," she said. Her voice lowered even further. "I fear we are too late."

Edward lifted his head and considered the clergyman for a long, uncomfortable moment. "I am the Earl of Worthington, the groom's brother."

Misunderstanding completely, the vicar smiled. "Ah, so there is family to attend the service. That's wonderful."

"Hardly," Edward said curtly.

There was a gaggle of excited female whispers from the three witnesses.

Jonathan stiffened and leveled a warning look at his brother. "If you are not here to share in our joy, Edward, then I think it best that you leave."

Charlotte reached for the earl's hand and gave it a hard squeeze and Edward managed to swallow his angry retort. She bent her head toward him and spoke in a soft undertone.

"I beg you, Edward. Think carefully before you speak. Words said in anger and haste can be particularly biting and cruel. And once spoken, they can never be retracted."

Edward considered her advice with a scowl, his gaze locked on Jonathan's unrepentant face as his younger brother viewed him with menacing calculation. The earl opened his mouth again, but his brother interrupted.

"You are too late. The vows have been spoken and in the eyes of God and man, we are married. I love Evelyn, and I respect her, and I plan on spending the rest of my life taking care of her and trying to make her happy. There is nothing that you can say or do that will change that, Edward. Nothing."

A nearly blinding anger streaked through the earl. "So, you will selfishly place your own happiness above any responsibility to your family?"

Jonathan's expression was incredulous. "My family should be pleased that I have found such a good, fine, gentle woman to share my life."

"She is unsuitable," the earl stated bluntly. "And clearly you know that or else you would not have snuck off with her like a thief in the middle of the night."

"Edward!" Charlotte cried out.

"No, the earl is right, Jonathan," Miss Montgomery said in a broken voice. "I am hardly anyone's first choice for a wife. My greatest worry was that our union would cause strife in the family and it has started already. Above all, I never wanted that to happen. We have just spoken our vows. Surely the marriage is not legal until we sign the register and the special license you brought? It is not too late to turn back."

"No!" Jonathan's voice came out with resounding force, as explosive as gunshots. "There is nothing anyone can say or do that will alter my feelings. You are my wife, Evelyn, the other half of my soul, and nothing will keep you from me."

Edward stole a look at his brother's bride, certain he would detect something akin to the desperation of a trapped hare. But surprisingly, her countenance was shaken, yet not crushed. She cast an imploring gaze on his brother, clearly seeking his guidance. The former Miss Montgomery apparently had more of a backbone than he had initially surmised.

For a moment Edward felt envious. Not of the beauty of his brother's bride, but of the obvious adoration she had for him. She was clearly ready to sacrifice her own happiness in order to ensure peace and harmony in Jonathan's life.

"Have you considered how our mother will react to this unexpected turn of events?" Edward asked.

Miss Montgomery's face blanched and Jonathan tightened his arm around her, then glared at his brother, for causing his bride distress. "We are prepared for Mother's initial displeasure, but hope her feelings will soften in time."

"And if they do not?"

Jonathan's forehead pleated into a frown. "I respect her and will always love her, but Mother will not dictate how I live my life. You taught me that, Edward."

The earl's lips curled up in an ironic grin. Why did Jonathan have to pick such an inconvenient moment to find his inner strength? He cast a glance at Charlotte, hoping she might have a more convincing argument.

"There will be scandal, disgrace—some might even say ruin," Charlotte said softly. "However, that scandal could be greatly lessened if you had the support of the earl."

"What?" Edward turned his head sharply. Charlotte was supposed to be supporting his position of preventing the marriage, not endorsing it.

"Look at them," she whispered sharply. "Nothing short of death will ever separate these two. We must therefore move on to a new plan. At least it is a marriage by special license and not the scandal of Gretna Green. With you and I to stand as witnesses, the sting lessens even more."

Edward slowly felt his anger wane. Charlotte was right. Jonathan would not forsake Evelyn no matter what they said. His brother was known for having a carefree, genial attitude and that was true, yet he also possessed an excessively strong will. When he decided to do something, he was like a boulder rolling down a steep incline; nothing could stop him.

But even more significant, what Edward saw in his brother's eyes could not be misunderstood. Jonathan was truly smitten. He stood with his arm around Evelyn, protecting her, possessing her, holding her close, treating her as something extremely precious. He was the picture of a man in love.

Edward mulled over his choices and made his decision. "If I could beg your indulgence, Vicar, would you be so kind as to start the ceremony again, so that we may hear it all?"

"With great pleasure, my lord," the vicar said loudly, to be heard above the sighs of relief from the bride and groom and squeals of delight from the three female witnesses, who were his unmarried daughters.

The cleric opened the Bible and began the service,

adding romantic flourishes whenever possible. Edward listened intently to the words he had heard many times, weighing each word and their significance.

"I, Jonathan Anthony Charles Barringer, take thee, Evelyn Margaret Montgomery, to be my wedded wife, to have and to hold from this day forward; for better for worse, for richer for poorer . . ."

Edward suddenly realized that money might be a problem for them. Jonathan had a quarterly allowance, which was generous for a gentleman, but hardly sufficient to support and wife and hopefully someday, children. Edward would need to adjust that as soon as possible, and also look into establishing a separate account for Evelyn. Though it was the usual arrangement, he felt it was not right that a woman should have to rely on her husband for every penny.

"In sickness and in health," Jonathan continued, "to love and to cherish, till death us do part, according to God's holy ordinance; and thereto I plight thee my troth."

A loud sniff distracted him. Edward turned with a slight grin, expected that one, two, or all three of the young female witnesses would be crying but instead discovered Charlotte's eyes were bright with tears.

"'Tis such a moving service," she whispered defensively. "I have never seen a more radiant bride nor a more exuberant groom."

"They do look very pleased with themselves." He cast her a mock frown. "As for the service, the vicar is quite enthusiastic, yet I have always wondered, what exactly is a troth?"

Charlotte smiled through the tears, just as he

intended. The vicar gave the final blessing, again, and they all bowed their heads and prayed. When at last given the signal, Jonathan gathered his bride in his arms and gave her a hard, passionate kiss, pushing aside any lingering doubts Edward might have about his decision to support his brother's choice.

After kissing both of his brand-new sister-in-law's cheeks, Edward pulled his brother into a rough hug. "You have really done it this time."

Jonathan grinned sheepishly. "I have indeed, and I must confess, I have never felt happier!"

The vicar led them to the back of the church where they signed the register and the special marriage license. Edward and Charlotte insisted on signing also, legally recording their participation as witnesses.

With a sincere word of thanks, and a generous contribution toward rebuilding the church steeple that the recent fire had claimed, they took their leave. Once they reached the church courtyard, Edward and Jonathan started discussing the state of the roads for travel and argued good-naturedly over the best route.

"I know we must make haste to return, but can we take a brief rest before we start our journey?" Charlotte asked.

Edward opened his mouth to refuse, but caught the look of longing in Charlotte's eyes. "It would be wise to spare the horses for an hour," he decided. "The Bull and Finch boasts a private parlor. We shall make use of it before we brave the road."

When they arrived, there were a few men in the taproom, but the inn was still uncrowded.

"I see ye found the church, sir," the innkeeper said with a curious look when the four of them entered the tavern together.

"I did indeed," Edward replied. "I also discovered my brother and new sister-in-law inside, just as I had hoped. We do not have much time to spare, but I will take you up on the offer of that private parlor, if it is still available."

"It is, sir."

"Excellent. A bottle of champagne, please. The best the house has to offer."

The private parlor was a pleasant surprise. A square, well-sized room with a timbered ceiling and a large fireplace, in which a cheerful fire crackled. In the center of the room was a comfortable table surrounded by six chairs. Jonathan and Evelyn cozied together on two of them, but Edward followed Charlotte to the fire and held out his hands.

"It is a cold day," he said.

"You did the right thing, Edward," Charlotte remarked without looking at him. "I'm very proud of you."

He smiled into the dancing flames. Her approval meant a great deal. Especially since she might likely be the only one to bestow it upon him. Even the free-thinking Lord Reginald was expecting him to somehow have prevented this marriage.

But gloomy thoughts had no place at this celebration. The champagne was uncorked and Edward poured everyone a glass. He then held his goblet aloft and extended his hand half across the table. "To the beautiful Evelyn and my rascal brother, Jonathan. Long life and great happiness to you both."

They all smiled, touched the rims of their glasses

together and drank. Regrettably, there was no time to savor the sparkling nectar. After a quick second glass each, the bottle was empty and it was time to depart. The women left to take care of their personal needs, leaving the brothers alone.

"I still think it might be better if Evelyn and I continue on our journey north and return to Farmington Manor after Christmas," Jonathan said. "Maybe sometime in the spring?"

"Oh, no," Edward replied, shaking his head adamantly. "You are not going to abandon me to face Mother alone. We stand united."

Finishing the last of his champagne with a long swallow, Jonathan inquired, "Precisely how are we going to break this news to her?"

"Leave that to me." Edward replied with a confidence he was far from feeling. "All you need do is cuddle your new bride and keep your eyes on the road home."

CHAPTER 20

Driving the carriage down the road at such high speed allowed little opportunity to speak with each other, though Charlotte felt too mired in her own thoughts to engage in conversation. She suspected that Edward felt the same.

Who would have ever believed that she, Charlotte Aldridge, would feel such envy toward the former Evelyn Montgomery? Witnessing Evelyn's unselfish devotion to Jonathan and seeing the love he held for his bride had starkly emphasized what was missing from Charlotte's relationship with Edward.

Love. Edward cared for her, desired her, even liked her, but did he love her? Did she love him? She thought she might, but she was reticent, restrained, at times even fearful toward him. She admitted there was a part of herself she held back and she sensed that Edward did the same.

His love, she realized, was what she truly wanted more than anything and she honestly feared she might never get it. Because she did not know how to love him unconditionally in return.

They took a direct route back to the manor, with Edward leading the way. Charlotte could not help but notice the earl turning around continually, checking to make sure Jonathan and Evelyn were indeed behind them.

They made good time on the road and as prearranged, the two carriages met near a cluster of trees before entering the estate's drive. The afternoon hour was late, but they all held on to the hope that Lord Reginald had somehow been successful in keeping the truth of their absence a secret from the houseguests, the staff and most importantly, the countess.

"'Tis better if Evelyn and I walk from here," Charlotte said as she climbed down from the carriage. "If we are seen, we can say that I was feeling better and we decided to take some fresh air."

"A good plan." Edward nodded approvingly.

Charlotte walked to Jonathan's carriage and relayed the message.

"Evelyn will be with you in a moment," Jonathan said.

Though she had not meant to eavesdrop, Charlotte could hear their conversation, with Evelyn trying to disguise the nervousness and apprehension in her voice; Jonathan, calm and in control, assured her that all would be well and that no matter what happened, they would be together as husband and wife for the rest of their lives.

It was eerily quiet after the carriages had driven away. The women exchanged slight smiles and started down the drive. They had walked no more than a few feet when Charlotte heard a familiar bark. She barely had time to brace herself as a scruffy fur ball launched itself toward them. But to her astonishment, the retriever sailed past her and nestled against Evelyn with a doggy sigh of contentment.

"You know Ranger?" Charlotte asked.

"I do indeed," Evelyn answered as she bent her head and nuzzled the dog. "We are old friends."

After receiving his due affection from Evelyn, the dog happily trotted to Charlotte's side, tail wagging enthusiastically. "A bit fickle, isn't he?" she said, scratching behind the retriever's ears.

Evelyn laughed. "Nonsense. He is a superior animal with excellent taste in women. That is why he has decided he likes us both."

After a few more affectionate pats on the head, Charlotte chased the dog off to the stables, fearing his happy barks might draw attention to them. Fortunately, he followed her commands. She and Evelyn took the longer route to the manor house, taking care to keep close to the boxwood hedges that sheltered them from view of the lower level windows.

Thanks to the Christmas Eve ball, the servants were much too busy and harried to be lurking about the hallways. The women were able to gain access through a little-used side entrance and reach Charlotte's room without being seen. Removing the key from her pocket, Charlotte unlocked the door. As she pushed it open, Evelyn grabbed her arm and pointed to the floor.

It was then that Charlotte noticed a covered tray of food had been left outside her chamber. Bless Grandpapa! He had no doubt instructed the servants to leave it there, instead of knocking and entering her chamber, so as not to disturb her rest and recovery. An excellent touch to keep their story believable and a practical way to supply her and Evelyn with some much-needed nourishment.

Snatching up the tray, Charlotte and Evelyn scurried into the chamber, both women nearly bursting with excitement. There was soup, now ice-cold, toast, cheese, fruit, slices of cold meat and mince pie. Forgoing the soup, Charlotte divided the rest of the meal into two equal portions, insisting that a very jittery Evelyn eat her share.

After they finished eating, they tried to rest, but each had too much nervous energy to fall asleep.

"Did Jonathan say anything about how he was going to tell the countess of your marriage?" Charlotte asked.

"No." Evelyn bit her lip. "I only pray I do not disgrace myself utterly. I am unsure how steady I will remain under the censure of her glare. I know for certainty my heart will freeze and the blood will drain from my face the moment she denounces our union.

"My greatest fear is that I shall faint and then everyone will assume I am in an interesting condition and thus our marriage was a necessity to save our unborn child from being labeled a bastard."

"Goodness, I never knew what an active imagination you have, Miss Montgomery. Or rather, Mrs. Barringer."

Evelyn blushed. "It was a long carriage ride. I had too much time to think about my reception."

"The countess has always held you in high regard. She might surprise you and be pleased about the match."

"You are being much too kind. Once she hears

the truth, the countess will most likely want to draw out a pistol and shoot me. Not only in anger, but to save the family the scandal of a divorce."

Charlotte, who was sitting at her dressing table playing with the bottles of fragrant creams and perfumes, nearly dropped the bottle of scent she was holding. "Shoot you?"

Evelyn shrugged, but Charlotte could see her mouth begin to twitch. The image of the countess, so stiff, so proper, so elegant, holding a pistol in the middle of the ballroom was too ludicrous to contemplate. Charlotte began to giggle.

"That is not supposed to be funny," Evelyn said, trying to choke back her own mirth.

Charlotte's giggles turned to gales of laughter. "Well, it is a sure sign we have lost all sense of reason because we both think it is hilarious." She took several rapid breaths and tried to shake off the lingering chuckles. "Come, let's find something spectacular for you to wear tonight."

Charlotte pulled open the door to her wardrobe and began riffling through the many ball gowns. Refusing to listen to any of Evelyn's protests, Charlotte insisted Evelyn try on several before deciding which one she wanted. Fortunately, the gown Evelyn selected needed only minor alterations at the hem and bodice, which Evelyn easily completed.

As the afternoon drew to a close, Charlotte rang for her maid. Jones entered the bedchamber cautiously, almost timidly, making Charlotte wonder how dire Grandpapa had made her fake illness sound.

"I am feeling much better. Thank you, Jones," Charlotte said when the maid had finally stepped completely inside the chamber. "Miss Montgomery has kindly offered to help me dress for tonight's ball, but I should like you to arrange my hair."

"Yes, Miss Charlotte."

"And when you are finished, I want you to fix Miss Montgomery's hair also."

Evelyn's eyes widened in surprise. "Oh, no, that is hardly necessary. Thank you, but—"

"I insist," Charlotte interrupted. "Jones is an artist when it comes to hairstyles and I'm sure she would enjoy the challenge of dressing your beautiful dark locks."

The maid nodded her head eagerly. "I'd be happy to arrange your hair," Jones replied with a friendly smile. "Truly."

After a leisurely wash and several hours of primping, it was time to make an appearance.

"Are you ready?" Charlotte asked.

Evelyn nodded.

"Come, we shall walk down together."

Evelyn reached for something on the dresser that a servant had delivered earlier and Charlotte saw it was a nosegay of beautiful white and red rosebuds mixed with holly sprigs. It was tied with red and gold ribbon, set upon a circle of white Belgian lace.

"A gift from Jonathan?" Charlotte asked.

"Yes. There was no time for a bouquet at the church. How thoughtful of him to get me one now."

"It is lovely."

Evelyn nodded, her eyes shining with tears. "I feel as though I have done him a terrible disservice by agreeing to be his wife. The countess will be furious, and no doubt only the first to disapprove. Jonathan deserves better."

"What could possibly be better than someone who loves him as completely and wholeheartedly as you?" Charlotte asked, amazed at Evelyn's unselfish attitude.

Nervous, scared and dreading this moment, Evelyn's main concern remained her husband and how all of this was going to affect him. Incredible.

"Chin up," Charlotte admonished. She saw that Evelyn was trying to summon a smile, but could barely manage a slight curve of her lips.

She grasped Evelyn's hands and gave them a quick squeeze. Then side by side, they left the bed-chamber. When they reached the entrance to the ballroom, they paused in the doorway. Most of the guests had already arrived and the receiving line had been disbanded. The women could hear the soft murmur of voices as the guests mingled, greeting old friends and making new acquaintances.

More than one brow rose when Charlotte entered the ballroom, with Evelyn by her side. The two women looked stunning, dressed in complementing red and gold silk gowns. Edward, standing near the center of the room, correctly surmised that the beautiful dress Evelyn wore must be borrowed from Charlotte. It was far too stylish and expensive to be part of Evelyn's wardrobe.

The two women passed through a large archway framed with holly, ivy, evergreens and a vast array of fruits and berries all tied with silk and satin ribbons of gold, red and green. The earl noticed their eyes widen when they saw the ethereal glow from the magnificent Christmas tree. The tiny candles positioned on each branch had been lit and an anxious footman strategically positioned to ensure that no guests accidentally came too close and lit themselves afire.

The earl was too far away to easily reach their side and he was pleased to see his brother did not have a similar difficulty. The ballroom was crowded with merry guests, laughing over the sounds of the orchestra. Edward could not help but wonder if this joyful spirit would remain once he had announced Jonathan and Evelyn's sudden marriage. Well, no matter how it all came out in the end, this was certainly going to be the most memorable and talked about Christmas Eve ball ever held at Farmington Manor.

Edward had spent the carriage ride back to the manor contemplating his life and his future. Jonathan and Evelyn's love and selfless devotion to each other had been humbling to see and had forced him to confront some harsh truths about his own relationship with Charlotte.

Above all, it made him envious for the most basic element that was missing from his life—happiness. Despite all the possible difficulties they faced, there was no denying that Jonathan and Evelyn were deliciously happy.

Edward had never thought happiness to be something of great importance, had never expected or craved it for himself. Hell, he had not precisely believed that happiness, like true love, really existed.

But he had felt happiness, albeit briefly and at odd times, when he was with Charlotte these past few weeks. A sense of contentment and joy, but beyond that, a sense of peace with his life and himself, a sense of eagerness when looking toward tomorrow, a belief that tomorrow would somehow be a better day than today simply because she was a part of it.

In many ways, Charlotte was the most exasperating woman he had ever known, and yet with her and only with her, he had found a measure of joy that added meaning to his days. Though he had tried, he could not explain it. He had thought it was like so many of life's great mysteries, something that was simply unexplainable.

But seeing Jonathan and Evelyn together made it all very clear to Edward. Jonathan and Evelyn shared the type of happiness he desired because they had taken their relationship one important step further. They loved each other. Freely, openly, without restraint.

He suddenly understood why Charlotte had refused his earlier proposals of marriage, had been so insistent that they wait. Perversely, he now agreed with that decision. She knew she wanted more, she had told him she would accept no less than unconditional love from her husband. He had not believed that more existed. Until now.

He had cared for her, but he had not declared his love for her. He had shared his body, his thoughts, even some of his feelings, but he had not been willing to share himself completely. He had not committed himself to their relationship with the type of selfless devotion she deserved.

Yes, they had made love and it had been wonderful, magical, but he admitted only to having a deep attraction for Charlotte. He had treated it as a temporary passion, and Charlotte had known that could not result in a lifelong, happy, loving marriage.

Guilt, confusion, perhaps even fear had masked

the true feelings of his heart, but the mask was now gone, ripped away by the truth of his needs. Edward loved Charlotte, needed Charlotte and intended to do whatever was necessary to prove it.

But first he had a commitment to his brother that he needed to complete. Edward signaled to the orchestra to cease playing, then checked to make sure that Evelyn was still standing beside his brother.

"Please gather 'round, everyone. I have a most important and splendid announcement to make."

The earl's booming voice could be clearly heard in the vast room. The chatter of private conversations dwindled as all eyes turned curiously in his direction. Edward was more nervous than he had expected, but Jonathan was depending on him and he would not forsake his brother.

"Earlier this morning my brother, Jonathan, and I, along with Miss Evelyn Montgomery and Miss Charlotte Aldridge, took a carriage ride to Somerville. There, in the lovely village chapel, my brother and Miss Montgomery were married by the town's vicar. It was my great joy and privilege to be a part of such a happy event, and I ask you all to join me, and my mother, in congratulating the newly married couple."

At first they were all unsure how to react. There was an instant of shocked silence and then, as Edward had expected, pandemonium reigned. The guests began talking and shouting at once, exclaiming their astonishment and total surprise.

The surprise soon gave way to alarm and then wariness, as he had feared. A few of the older matrons even glanced away quickly, refusing to catch his gaze. Clearly, they were all waiting for the countess to give them the cue on how they were to respond to this most incredible news.

His mother stood alone, near the orchestra at the far side of the ballroom. Her face was a frozen mask of surprise, her eyes shaded by the candlelight so that he could not see them clearly, but Edward knew they must be blazing with fury.

For an instant he worried that he had made the wrong choice, that he should have told his mother the news in private, instead of announcing it so publicly. Maybe it would have gone better if he had given her a chance to become accustomed to the idea of her younger son marrying her companion, for at this moment she was exhibiting a frosty degree of outrage and offense that spoke volumes of disapproval.

But there was no opportunity to second-guess his decision. *In for a penny, in for a pound.* His course set, Edward forged ahead, determined, for Jonathan and Evelyn's sake, to sway the outcome. Lifting two fluted glasses of chilled champagne from the nearest servant, he crossed the room and presented one to his stunned mother.

"Let us raise our glasses high and drink a toast to the happy couple," Edward shouted, his face wide with an exaggerated smile. Lowering his voice to a mere whisper, he commanded, "Drink, Mother."

The countess regarded him with an unblinking, rebellious stare. "I am not thirsty."

"Drink," he repeated, "or else you will be most displeased by the consequences."

A flicker of wariness crossed the countess's face. Then to his vast relief, she lifted her goblet fractionally and touched her lips to the rim. The crowd broke out in a happy cheer and downed their own drinks. Only Edward saw that the champagne did not reach the countess's mouth.

"He has made a fool of himself over that girl!" the countess hissed. "How could you not only allow this to happen, but to sanction it?"

"Do you really need to ask?" Edward replied. "They are in love."

The countess stared incredulously at him. "Love." She snorted. "What a bunch of rot. Claiming to be in love hardly gives them license to act like fools. An elopement! I shall never recover from the scandal."

Edward's lips thinned out. Though he had known in his heart this would be his mother's response, he had started hoping she might feel differently.

"You may rant and rail and beat your chest all you wish in private, but publicly you will stand beside me and show one and all how accepting and happy you are over this marriage."

The countess gritted her teeth in exasperation. "Never!"

Edward drew in his breath sharply. "I know this is difficult for you, Mother, but you have no choice. 'Tis done. They are married and will remain so until death parts them. Evelyn is of good birth, gently reared and a fine woman who has been an asset to you and this household for several years. Try to remember how much you liked her before you cut her and Jonathan from your heart."

The countess clamped her mouth shut. Edward could see the vivid flush of color climbing her cheeks as she seemed to realize all she could do was fall back on her indignation.

"Evelyn might have held my regard and even my

affection at one time, but all that changed when this odious girl became so openly disloyal." The countess made a look of disgust. "And I most definitely do not appreciate your high-handed attempts to tell me what I should think and how I should feel."

"At last the shoe is on the other foot. Perhaps now you will understand my reaction when you and Father insisted I take Charlotte for my wife all those years ago."

"That was not the same."

"It was very much the same."

The countess lifted her goblet again and this time drank until the glass was empty. She then sniffed. "I did what I thought was best for you, best for the family. Perhaps it was not the right course to consider. Hindsight, while superior when making judgements, is useless in correcting mistakes."

Edward blinked with astonishment. Had he heard correctly? Did his mother just admit she had made a mistake? Extraordinary! It was the nearest thing to an apology he would ever receive and Edward was pleased to realize it was sufficient to erase a large part of his hurt.

"Since you are in such a congenial mood, Mother, I might as well tell you the rest of it. Miss Montgomery is without family, so I am providing her with a modest dowry and will also be increasing Jonathan's allowance."

"You are not only condoning, but now rewarding this disgraceful behavior? Shocking!"

"They are family, Mother, and as such deserve our love and support."

Brighter color infused her cheeks as his mother wrestled with her emotions. Pride could manifest itself in odd ways, but Edward had counted on his mother's pride to carry her through this moment. He held his breath as he waited for her to make her final move. Then, to his great relief, the countess took a deep breath, pasted on a smile and stepped forward to embrace the newlyweds.

The earl was not foolish enough to believe it would be so easy, but the first and most difficult hurdle had been breached. It was a good beginning, the best that could be hoped for given the circumstances.

It was nearly twenty minutes until he was able to have a quick word with his brother. "Thank God that's over with," Jonathan remarked.

Edward shared his brother's feelings utterly. "It actually went better than I expected."

"So, you believe Mother will eventually forgive me?" Jonathan asked with a skeptically raised eyebrow.

"Eventually. We cannot expect too much, too soon. At least she is speaking to both of you."

"So I should be grateful for small mercies?"

"You should be happy you have such a delightful, loving wife," Edward said.

"I am." Jonathan's expression visibly softened. "Evelyn's sweetness overtakes any of the bitterness in my life."

"The power of love." Edward took a deep breath, then thrust back his shoulders. *It was now or never.* "I apologize in advance for upstaging you, but I am about to give everyone something to talk about for years and years to come."

With a cryptic smile, Edward headed in Charlotte's direction. She was speaking with Lord Bradford and Lady Anne, but turned to greet him with a smile. Edward waited until she faced him completely, then reached out to grasp her hands, sandwiching them between his own, and sank to one knee.

"Oh, Edward, do you feel ill? Have you a fever?" Charlotte's face was lined with concern as she bent over him, the back of her bare wrist pressing against his forehead.

The maternal gesture calmed his racing heart. "I like it when you fuss over me."

She jerked her hands from his grasp. "What game are you playing at, my lord?"

"No games." He caught her wrists and pressed them to his chest. "I require your complete attention."

"You have it. Now please, get up. People are beginning to stare."

"Let them. I want everyone to see and hear me. But especially you. Are you listening?"

"Yes."

"Good." He cleared his throat, which had suddenly become dry. "I am a successful man, who has been given much by birth and achieved much through hard work, and yet I have come to discover that for all my worldly possessions and noble title, life without you is flat, uninspired, uninteresting.

"Life without you, Charlotte, is life without meaning, life without happiness. In short, 'tis no sort of life at all." Edward swallowed and took a deep breath, to ensure his voice would remain loud and strong.

"You, and only you, Charlotte Aldridge, are the woman I cherish, the light inside my soul, the love of my heart. It has taken me far too long to realize it and far too long to declare it, but I hope you can

forgive the stubborn pride of a stiff-necked male
and realize I speak the truth.

"You are the most precious, stubborn, intelligent,
amazing woman I have ever known," he continued,
realizing that his future, his happiness, his very life
depended on her reply, and he was not entirely
sure what it would be. "Will you do me the supreme
honor of marrying me?"

Charlotte blinked. It must be the wassail. Or the
scent of too much greenery. Or the exposure to the
cold while taking two long carriage rides today or
the champagne they had drunk at the inn that had
turned Edward's mind to mush, had prompted this
surprisingly public declaration and proposal.

Then again, it was Christmas. A time when everything seemed magical, possible, a truly miraculous
time of year. Did she dare to believe he meant it?

The play of candlelight from the glowing Christmas tree across Edward's handsome face was hyp-
notic. Charlotte's eyes moved over him at leisure.
There was so much to admire, so much to thrill her,
so much to love. She smiled down at him with the
depth of feeling she was finally able to admit and
accept. She loved him.

Not with the naive infatuation of a seventeen-
year-old girl, but with the mature experience of a
twenty-three-year-old woman. She loved him with
all the passion she had held within her heart, with
the devotion of a woman who knew and accepted
his faults as well as his strengths, with the respect he
had earned through his deeds and actions toward
the members of his family and the many people
who depended upon him.

Charlotte saw the tenderness on his face, the love

shining in his eyes. For her. Blinking back tears of happiness, Charlotte knew if she took a lifetime she would never be able to fully or accurately describe how wonderful that made her feel.

One of her hands slipped from his and crept to the base of her neck. She struggled to find her voice through the lump of emotion in her throat. "Yes. Oh, yes, Edward, I will marry you."

He stood, took her hand in his and drew it away from her throat. "Are you certain?"

She smiled widely, her senses flooding with happiness. "Yes, very certain. I love you."

He pulled her into his arms and began kissing her like a man who was starving. Lord Reginald cleared his throat loudly when the kissing seemed unlikely to stop. Laughing, Charlotte wrenched her lips away from Edward's, but could not take her hands from him, needing to feel his muscled arms to assure herself this was truly happening.

Several people crowded in to offer the happy couple congratulations. But before he released her, Edward caught Charlotte around the waist, lifted her off her feet and twirled her around until she felt breathless and dizzy. She was giggling like a schoolgirl when he set her down, and she nearly stumbled into Jonathan's arms.

"Welcome to the family, Charlotte." Jonathan gave her a big hug and kissed her cheek. "I have always wanted a younger sister to boss around and I believe you are the perfect individual for the position."

She laughed louder, pivoted around like a ballet dancer and found herself gazing into her beloved Grandpapa's face.

Words failed her.

"Edward is a fine man," Lord Reginald said.

"He is indeed."

With a wavering smile, Grandpapa patted her hand. "You deserve only the best, Charlotte. That is all I have ever wanted for you, which is why I gave Edward my blessing to propose. But the decision is entirely yours to make."

"I love him, Grandpapa."

"Then you must promise me one thing, dear girl," Lord Reginald said, his eyes suspiciously bright with emotion.

"Anything."

"Promise me that you will be very happy."

"Always."

They hugged and Charlotte held on tightly. Though she was about to start a new life, with a new man, her grandfather would hold a very special and important part of her heart.

The moment they were able, the newly engaged couple broke off from the crowd for a private moment, the earl keeping one arm possessively around her waist. The intimate, loving glance he cast her way warmed her down to her toes. He kissed her lightly, but she sensed the passion smoldering beneath the tenderness.

"My love," she whispered, her voice breaking and her eyes swimming with tears. Her sense of joy was like a tidal wave of happiness, rushing over her with an unstoppable force. "Will it be this way between us forever?"

Edward winked wickedly at her. "Forever is a long time," he said with a smile upon his lips. "But if we work together at it, then yes, dearest, our days shall be like this always."

EPILOGUE

"Oh, my gracious!"

Charlotte's exclamation was less a surprise and more a reaction of astonishment as she beheld the Christmas tree that stood in the corner of her drawing room. Although as she considered the enormous, bedecked, glittering pine she decided that *stood* was probably not the right word. *Dominated* was more appropriate.

"Do you like it, Mama? Do you?" Elizabeth asked, hopping from one foot to the other in excitement. "Tell us, please. We've been working ever so long to make it just right."

Charlotte gazed down at her second child and smiled. The five-year-old's barely contained excitement was contagious, though in truth the tree was far too large for the room and the many branches were groaning under the weight of too many ornaments, ribbons, garlands, toys and as of yet, unlit candles.

"Why, I believe this must be the most magnificent Christmas tree in all of England," Charlotte declared, wrapping the little girl in a tight hug. "Grander than the queen's own, I am certain of it."

"Father told us you would say that," Iris Rose, age three, announced with a superior air.

"Did he now? Ah, your father knows me very well indeed."

"He knows everything!" Iris Rose insisted.

Charlotte bit back a grin. Her third daughter was a solemn, highly intelligent child, wise beyond her years, who adored and worshiped her father. The feeling was mutual, though Edward loved and spoiled all four of his girls equally. Charlotte sincerely hoped Iris Rose would still hold him in the same esteem when she became a young woman and he turned protective and possessive, scowling at her suitors.

"Won't Uncle Jonathan and Aunt Evelyn be astonished when they see our tree?" Elizabeth piped up. "And William, too, though he is still a baby."

"We must make certain to keep him away from the shiny ornaments," Edward said with concern. "Babies tend to put everything in their mouths when they are William's age."

"Did I do that when I was a baby?" Regina wanted to know.

"Once or twice," Charlotte answered, remembering what an active, inquisitive toddler her oldest daughter had been. Unknowingly, she and Edward had chosen the most appropriate child to be Grandpapa's namesake.

What nervous, anxious parents she and Edward had been at first! Constantly fretting over how much Regina ate and slept, wondering if she was too warm or too cold, staying up half the night with worry the first time she came down with the sniffles.

Fortunately, it had gotten easier over the years. By the time Anna was born this past spring, they were old hands at being parents, though the countess on occasion reminded them that they would someday regret indulging their children to such a great extent.

Which was highly ironic, since the countess was often as guilty as the rest of them when it came to spoiling the girls, and they in turn adored spending time with their very elegant grandmama.

Charlotte settled herself on the settee, then reached for her youngest daughter. Holding a baby in her arms had always soothed her, given her great comfort. As she watched Edward lift Iris Rose so that she could closely examine an ornament on the tree, Charlotte's heart filled with love and joy. She was lucky indeed to have so much happiness in her life, to have four beautiful daughters and a husband who loved them all so completely.

It had taken much longer for Jonathan and Evelyn to become parents, but after years of trying, young William was born. At two, he was a contented baby, the pride and joy of his parents' lives. The couple lived a much simpler and more reclusive life than Charlotte and Edward, but thanks to the earl's help and Jonathan's prudence, they suffered no financial hardships.

Charlotte was pleased when, following William's birth, the young family had leased a small property not far from Farmington Manor. It enabled them to visit often and kept the relationship between the brothers solid and strong.

The countess had eventually resigned herself to Jonathan's decision to have Evelyn as his wife, though she was always reserved in her dealings with her former companion. William's birth had done much to endear Evelyn to the countess and there was no denying that she made her husband a very happy man.

"Will Grandpapa be coming down soon?" Elizabeth asked.

"I miss him," Iris Rose injected. "'Tis always more fun when he is here."

"Grandpapa is taking a nap," Edward replied. "But he will join us soon."

Charlotte could barely bring herself to meet her husband's eyes. Such an innocent word, *nap.* Yet for Charlotte a nap was a chance to experience the burning urgency of passion, to renew the emotional commitment, to achieve the bliss and peace of sexual fulfillment with the man she loved.

The earl had once told her it was far more delightful to take a nap with a partner, and during the course of their marriage he had continuously proven that statement correct.

"Grandpapa told me he had something special for each of us to add to the tree," Regina said.

Charlotte, who was cuddling baby Anna on her lap, gazed over the infant's head at Edward. The earl merely shrugged, and she knew that he was aware of whatever extravagant gift her grandfather had decided to give the girls this year. Lord Reginald was shameless in his indulgences and they had long ago given up any attempt to limit his overgenerous tendencies, knowing it was a fruitless endeavor.

As the years passed, Lord Reginald's visits to

Farmington Manor had become longer and longer and he now stayed with them for months at a time. Charlotte sincerely hoped he would consider their offer to move in permanently. Quincy Court was too far away and she wanted him nearer so she could keep an eye on him. His health remained strong for a man in his seventies, but Charlotte worried that he was lonely.

Her grandfather thoroughly enjoyed the commotion the girls brought to the household and seemed to thrive on their antics. There was also an opportunity for Lord Reginald to be among his peers when he came to the manor. Edward had gone to considerable expense to renovate and refurbish the dowager house to his mother's satisfaction. She entertained often, and since it was less than a mile from the main house, Lord Reginald was a frequent guest.

Edward sauntered toward Charlotte, handsome as ever, his grin still seductive even after all these years.

"What are you thinking?" he asked as he leaned over and kissed the baby gently on the head. "Are you concerned that the tree is too large?"

Charlotte smiled. "The tree is always too large, Edward, though in truth I would be highly disappointed if it were not. I have come to expect certain things from you over the years, you know."

"Gracious, I've not become boring and predictable, have I?" he asked in mock horror.

"Hardly." She leaned in and kissed him until her knees felt weak, pulling away only when the sound of the girls' giggles reached her ears. "I truly adore Christmas. "'Tis the perfect time for us to remember and give thanks for the blessings of the season."

Edward put his arms around Charlotte and they snuggled close, the baby between them. "We are lucky that our blessings are not limited to the season, my love, but remain with us throughout the year."

About the Author

Adrienne Basso lives with her family in New Jersey. She is the author of seven Zebra historical romances and is currently working on her next. Adrienne loves to hear from readers and you may write to her c/o Zebra Books. Please include a self-addressed stamped envelope if you wish a response.

<u>BOOK YOUR PLACE ON OUR WEBSITE</u> AND MAKE THE <u>READING CONNECTION!</u>

We've created a customized website just for our very special readers, where you can get the inside scoop on everything that's going on with Zebra, Pinnacle and Kensington books.

When you come online, you'll have the exciting opportunity to:

- View covers of upcoming books
- Read sample chapters
- Learn about our future publishing schedule (listed by publication month *and author*)
- Find out when your favorite authors will be visiting a city near you
- Search for and order backlist books from our online catalog
- Check out author bios and background information
- Send e-mail to your favorite authors
- Meet the Kensington staff online
- Join us in weekly chats with authors, readers and other guests
- Get writing guidelines
- AND MUCH MORE!

**Visit our website at
http://www.kensingtonbooks.com**